W9-ATF-302

Ander

&

Santi

Were

Here

also by jonny garza villa

Fifteen Hundred Miles from the Sun

jonny garza villa

Ander

&

Santi

Were

Here

a novel

WEDNESDAY BOOKS
NEW YORK

This is a work of fiction. All of the characters, organizations, and events portrayed in this novel are either products of the author's imagination or are used fictitiously.

First published in the United States by Wednesday Books, an imprint of St. Martin's Publishing Group

ANDER & SANTI WERE HERE. Copyright © 2023 by Jonny Garza Villa. All rights reserved. Printed in the United States of America. For information, address St. Martin's Publishing Group, 120 Broadway, New York, NY 10271.

www.wednesdaybooks.com

Interior and case stamp designed by Devan Norman
Succulent case illustration © MilaArt/Shutterstock.com

The Library of Congress Cataloging-in-Publication Data is available upon request.

978-1-250-84399-9 (hardcover)
978-1-250-84400-2 (ebook)

Our books may be purchased in bulk for promotional, educational, or business use. Please contact your local bookseller or the Macmillan Corporate and Premium Sales Department at 1-800-221-7945, extension 5442, or by email at MacmillanSpecialMarkets@macmillan.com.

First Edition: 2023

10 9 8 7 6 5 4 3 2 1

For all of us who have ever felt not good enough,

not powerful enough, too melanated,

or unwanted. Take up space. Tell your story.

author's note

As a person who was born in and lived my entire life in Texas and the United States, I want to be clear in that this book isn't meant to speak for undocumented people. It isn't meant to be a voice *for* them. It isn't meant to define their experiences or their journeys. I cannot and will not write that story.

At this book's center is a nonbinary Chicano teenager. A person who falls in love so quickly and fiercely and wonderfully with a boy who's trying his best to exist within the limitations that are created to make it impossible for him to live and thrive and find happiness. A person who is incredibly imperfect at times in their allyship. Because this, I could speak on. The ways in which I might passionately overstep, I can speak on. The ways that the country I was born in, and raised not to question, demonizes and fetishizes my neighbors, I can speak on.

And I think it's important. I think it's vital that we realize how even those in power who claim to be allies of immigrants, working on their behalf, only ever want to talk about a specific person: the valedictorian, future first-generation college student who came here as a baby. It's never about the boy who wasn't brought to the United States as a child; who, instead, came here as a young adult. A boy who wasn't top of his class. Who didn't even graduate high school. The latter isn't as easy to hold up as an example, a political tool to show promise and capability. He's not as easy to fight for, so we forget about him.

We need to recognize the ways even *allies* objectify people with "the potential of migrants." How easily we erase their humanity and only see capital. How anyone we don't see as *profitable* is thrown out. Is not even allowed inside. Is invisible but also criminal.

And while this story has a happy ending *of sorts*, before we begin, I want to recognize all the stories and lives and people who don't get that. And I hope that, together, those of us who can will stand side by side with *all* our undocumented hermanes. Even those who aren't DACA kids, who aren't refugees with a morning-show-worthy backstory, who aren't STEM geniuses. I hope that, together, we can uplift these voices and the voices of all undocumented people to make this world a more just, loving, and moral place.

x Jonny

Ander

&

Santi

Were

Here

"*C hingada madre.*"

The words come out as a rough whisper through exhausted breath. I plop into a chair, lean toward the outdoor space heater for warmth, and crane my neck to the left and then the right, loud cracks relieving the stiffness in my muscles. Or whatever it is that happens when I pop body parts. I don't know. I'm not a fucking scientist.

I *am* tired, though. Taquería Guadalupe, my family's restaurant and a Santos Vista favorite here on the Westside of San Antonio, isn't usually so busy on a Thursday, but today's lunch rush had us seating people even out on the patio. After putting on a smile, taking orders, carrying food and drinks for hours, and giving all the tables a good wipe-down once everything finally stopped being so wild, I'm surprised my legs work at all right now. No lie, I could fall asleep here and be perfectly content.

The only thing that'd make it better is if it wasn't so cold outside. I've been craving springtime for about two and a half months now. Those March and April days that have me begging Tita—the Lupe of Taquería Guadalupe—to let me work outside. Crop-top-and-shorts-with-a-negative-inseam weather. When there's a cool breeze, the sun's out but not frying me, and it's not raining all the time yet (plus it doesn't get humid like the coast or dry as shit like West Texas). Those days where I'm tempted to blow off work and spend sunup to sundown shirtless at some river instead.

That's Heaven.

Way more preferable to these January days when I feel like I'm trapped in one of those grocery store freezer-aisle coolers. I'm not made for weather below seventy degrees. But some days, I just need to not be stuck inside. I need that sudden gust of wind that flows through the patio, biting my face to keep me awake, carrying with it the smell of mesquite wood, masa, meat, and purple Fabuloso and a chill that would sting if it wasn't for the warmth coming from the heaters.

And it's been a pretty good day. Can't complain after getting a fifty-dollar tip from some Beckys and Karens—the kind who think Google Maps is taking them to a fancy River Walk or Pearl restaurant and accidentally end up on the "bad side of town." The type of white women who only like their margaritas with sugar on the rim and think they can empathize with brown people because they read *American Dirt*.

Ignoring passive racism for forty-five minutes and acting like my only goal in life is to be every girl's gay best friend is something I can grin and bear when their money is paying for my next pair of swim shorts. I should put that on my resumé. And at least they were quick to catch on to me casually pointing out the THEY/THEM/ELLE and PLEASE DON'T CALL ME SIR buttons pinned onto my sweater.

I stretch my arms and tilt my head back. A yawn comes out that becomes more of a tired moan and then turns into humming along to norteños playing over the patio speakers. My hands go up, adjusting the white bandana tied across the top of my head. Then I check my fingers, making sure the burgundy of my nails is still intact. I look down to inspect my TAQUERÍA

GUADALUPE sweater, a color somewhere between baby and Argentinian blue, and khaki chinos rolled up, exposing the skin of my ankles. Sometimes I don't catch a salsa or grease stain until way after the fact, and then I'm rushing to the kitchen, scrubbing it with dish soap.

Nope. Nothing. We're good.

"AJ!" Ronnie shouts from the half-open door leading from the restaurant out onto the patio. Or leading from the patio into the restaurant? *Both?*

I'm not sure how long he's been watching me. Hoping not long enough to know I've been sitting down on the job for the last ten minutes, even though I know he'd never say anything to my parents or Tita. But how'd I not hear or see him until he said my name? Sneaking up on me like a friendlier cucuy in a bright green taquería tee under an unzipped black hoodie. "What're you doing sitting out here? Está pinche frío."

"The heaters make it better," I tell him, watching as he takes a seat next to me.

I've known Ronnie since he started working at Lupe's as a busser when he was sixteen and I was six. He was the first trans person I'd ever met, and even when I was that young, I could tell there was something about him and his energy I was drawn to. That felt familiar. Growing up, as someone who sometimes feels more boy and other times more girl but 99 percent of the time somewhere in between or not existing on the graph at all, having someone like him around made the process of figuring out who I am a lot less lonely.

Twelve years later he's still here, running the patio bar and being the guy in charge of the place when Tita and my parents aren't around. Like right now.

"You can head home if you want," Ronnie tells me. "I think we've tired you out enough for today."

"I'm gonna sit here for a couple more minutes. That cool?"

My head's tilted up and my eyes are closed, so I only hear him tell me, "Yeah, that's fine." But I also don't hear him leave. Must not be eager to get up and do anything either.

"El mural de pan dulce es muy popular," he finally says. I open an eye and see his finger pointing across the street to the painting I did for Rosalinda's Panadería. Large pink, yellow, even light blue and green conchas cover the entirety of one of the walls outside. I also added some golden sparkles to give it the perfect amount of aggressive cuteness without being too busy.

"Every day—it could be forty degrees outside—there's always three or four muchachas taking pictures for the Gram."

"Hm." It comes out like a small laugh. Today the regular muchachas dressed to match the aesthetic of the mural and do their one-leg-up-and-peace-sign poses aren't there. Instead, it's two much less assuming people: one that's probably about my age, standing up against the wall, and another who could be a tíe or maybe an older cousin, standing toward the street, busy talking on their phone. The one near the wall takes their own phone out and—*oh my fucking god*—starts taking selfies.

The loud, abrasive squeak of my chair as I jump to my feet makes Ronnie cringe. "*Why are they taking a selfie like that?!*" I turn to Ronnie, my eyes wide in frustration and mouth open, and my arm is held out to the mural. "That's not how you capture the moment correctly."

"Cálmate, kid," he replies, waving a hand up and down, motioning for me to put my butt back in my chair. "You can't control what people do with your art."

"*I can try.* There's a tripod in the office. I'll go give it to them if it means I don't have to see this happening right now."

He only scoffs and rolls his eyes at me while crossing his

arms over his chest. "Oye, how many more are you doing before you leave for Chicago?"

Way to obviously brush off my very valid concern over *my* work.

"At least eight more with Beautify," I answer with just enough bite in my voice to tell him I'm not over this while continuing to glance over at the mural, eyeing both people now sitting on the sidewalk, backs against the wall. The one who doesn't know how to properly photograph art sits next to the dark smudge that is my signature. "Could be a few others depending on how much time I have on my hands and if I can get some commissions."

It's been a little over half a year now since I sat Mami, Pa, and Tita down—at this exact table, actually—and told them I had emailed the School of the Art Institute of Chicago (which has to be, for absolutely no reason, the longest name ever for a college) with a plan to defer my acceptance for a year. And then I slid my iPad over to them so they could read an offer I'd already accepted from this local nonprofit, Beautify Not Gentrify. It was a chance to take part in their first Youth Community Residency Program.

What I remember most, though, is how the excitement in my voice decreased with each word I spoke because of the way their faces went from interest to disappointment and anger.

"You're staying another year?"

"You aren't going to college?"

"Why didn't you talk to us about this first, Ander?"

It wasn't a great moment for us.

"Yes."

"I still am."

"Because I didn't want y'all trying to convince me this was a bad idea."

The memories of Pa's frustration and Mami trying to hold in her screams are so vivid I could paint in detail the creases on his forehead, her eyes wide with rage, and how she sucked in her cheeks to keep herself from saying anything she might regret. As much as I tried to explain how amazing of an opportunity this was—*is*—they still think that since I didn't go straight to SAIC, I'm going to end up as a taquería waiter for the rest of my life. Which is a thought no one put in their heads except for themselves. They accused me of throwing away my talent and have spent the months since asking me what is here that I couldn't do in Chicago.

I can point them to the "Como la Flor"–inspired mural that covers the side of the H-E-B a few blocks down, where everyone in the neighborhood gets their groceries, and the *No Human is Illegal* piece I did for the RAICES offices in graffiti font and Sylvia Rivera on Club Sixty-Nine at the Main Avenue Strip and the *Last Supper* I did on the Iglesia Santos Pedro y Andres CCD Building that took three weeks to finish as things I wouldn't have been able to do in Chicago. As proof that the past half a year hasn't been a waste of my talent.

Even though there's this voice in the back of my head that constantly tells me I made the wrong choice. That I fucked up my entire future by staying here because now I'll be stuck painting pan dulce and Selena for the rest of my life. And, yeah, that's not terrible. I wouldn't be mad about that future. Everything about the art I get to do feels like me: Mexican, queer, and done in a way that's loudly and proudly both.

But then I think about that meeting with the Seattle School of Art and Design and how they, to my face, rejected me *because* all they saw was a person who paints pan dulce and Selena, and how, for the very first time, I felt a shame about it. And, because of that, there are times where I don't know whether I love or hate where I am right now.

I was hoping doing this—staying here a little while longer—would help me figure out who I am and what I want as a muralist; as an artist. That doing all this cool shit with this residency would've made the thoughts go away. That I'd either figure out a way to change my entire aesthetic or start embracing it so that a few old people in oversized cardigans won't get to me.

Rich white kids get to spend their gap year backpacking through Europe and collecting STIs in hostels like Pokémon cards. Not that getting paint all over my hometown isn't the most incredible opportunity I've ever been given, but I doubt Kayleigh Lynn and Chad are having identity crises in Paris right now.

"Ey, your fans are coming," Ronnie says, pulling me out of my thoughts.

"What? Who're—Oh. *Ughh*."

I don't know if I'm more annoyed about those two walking up to us or that the one who was taking selfies is actually kind of cute. Looking cozy in a faded navy hoodie under a denim jacket, and gray sweatpants that are taking all of my strength to not stare at.

"Ronnie?" Sweatpants asks.

Ronnie's got a blank look for a second before the light bulb in his brain comes on. "Oh, Santiago, right? You're . . . the interview." He smiles as he stands and holds a hand out. "Nice to meet you, man."

They shake hands and then Sweatpants Santiago looks over at me definitely not staring at his face, but I catch myself and look into his eyes quickly enough to maybe not have been caught. The person with him starts talking to Ronnie in Spanish, but it all goes mute when Santiago gives me a smile. Not a huge one, but it's soft. Cozy like his hoodie probably is. And I smile back at him. Taking in those tired, dark brown eyes and pretty, full eyebrows. His nearly buzzed hair and skin that's a little darker than mine. His hands holding on to the railing between us.

Okay, maybe he's a little more than *kind of cute*.

"I gotta take this," Ronnie tells me as he gets up, and I pop my neck again turning my head from Santiago to him.

"Oh. Yeah. That's fine. I should probably get home anyways. I'll see you later?"

"You know where to find me."

I watch as Santiago and his friend person head toward the front door of the taquería and, just before going inside, catch him looking at me one more time, giving me one last smile. And this time a little wave. I hold my hand up too, and smile back, until it's been actual minutes since he's gone inside and I'm sitting out here alone, realizing that it is actually fucking cold out here, and thinking about how comfortable it might be if I had a very specific guy's denim jacket right now.

2

*C*hachi!" Mami yells into the backyard at my sister Carla and her friends. "What are you doing? What— *Where did you get a piñata?* Actually, no quiero saber. ¡Ven pa'ca! Time to eat, pendejitos."

Sometimes it's better not to ask questions. Like when I come home with my best friend (and coworker the past three years) Zeke to find Chachi and her friends Raúl, Benny, Sammy, and Frankie throwing piñata limbs at each other. All of them screaming as bright, multicolored burro parts fly through the yard. Honestly, this is average for a Friday night at the Martínezes: my parents, Tita if there's a Spurs game on she can watch with Pa or if she just feels like adding to the chaos, and anywhere between six and eight teenagers—only two of which Mami gave birth to—all talking at a solid "Mexican nine."

Chachi's friends follow her into the house, everyone with a donkey leg or head in hand. She's always been the type to surround herself with guys, do *guy* things. (Mami's words; none of me believes we should be gendering *things*.) She keeps her hair pulled back into a messy bun, never any makeup, and out of my parents' two kids, she's definitely got the more masc style. It's hard not to think of her as anything besides *boyish*. Definitely more boy than me.

We all line up in the kitchen, where Pa and Tita are finishing the pile of homemade corn tortillas. Zeke is at my side, paper plate in one hand and phone in the other. Texting either his Human Evolution class group chat or his hole-of-the-week while we wait for chicken colorado, rice, pinto beans, roasted jalapeños, and cooked spinach and calabaza. In his usual only-ever-half-here mental headspace.

Mami calls him, me, and our other friend Mo *los trillizos*, which I've always thought was a stretch. In no way do we look like triplets. I'm shorter than both; Zeke and I are browner than Mo, and Zeke's always had these wild curls compared to my middle-part hairstyle that Mami says reminds her of Shawn Hunter from *Boy Meets World*, even after I've told her a million times I don't know references from the boomer generation (and get a chancla to the head every single time I've said it). And I've stayed twink while Zeke's started embracing the freshman fifteen and his little pancita and the cub lifestyle.

Also, we used to date. Zeke and me. Mo liked to keep things strictly platonic, besides that one week our sophomore year. So, in addition to best friend and coworker, Zeke's also my ex-boyfriend. And referring to them as my triplets weirds me out. I'm not some white from Alabama or English royalty.

But I can kind of get where Mami sees it, especially when we're standing next to each other, wearing our glasses and over-sized, nearly-the-same-color-pink long-sleeve tees, navy cotton shorts, and calf-high socks. It's just what happens when we spend way too much time around each other. There's a difference.

Tita follows us back to the dining table, her gold JEFA hoops shaking as she walks over makes them look like they're dancing along with whatever music's playing inside her head. She sets down a glass filled with a soft pink liquid and plenty of ice by my plate before her hand goes through my dark hair.

"What is this?"

"A paloma," she answers. "But if your mami asks, it's jugo de pomelo y e'Sprite."

I smile, grabbing the cup and taking a slow sip, tasting her heavy hand and the 1800 tequila mixed into it. (Not that I've drank enough tequila in eighteen and three-quarters years to know the difference in flavors between brands; that would be *illegal*; I'm not twenty-one; I could *never*.) Then I slide it to Zeke sitting beside me so he can get a quick drink before Mami catches on.

My attention goes back to the iPad I'd left at the table to get food and a half-finished design of a La Chalupa concept that popped into my mind a couple days ago displayed on the screen. The Lotería card—not that weird thing Taco Bell does. Soon it will be my latest mural, now that I've got approval from Beautify on a place at Juan Diego Creek Park. Zeke is all eyes on his homework, Chachi and her friends are circled up on the living room floor even though we have more than enough couch space and chairs for them, and Mami, Pa, and Tita sit with us at the table.

"You have another project coming up, mi'je?" Mami asks from the opposite side of the table. Her head is tilted up, trying to be metiche and see what I'm doing.

"Yeah, on Monday."

"Qué bueno. Make sure you take some pictures for your portfolio to show the university. You've been keeping them up to date on what you're doing with your year off?"

"It's not a year off, I—" I take a deep breath. *Don't let them get to you, Ander.* "*Yo sé*, Mami. I've been sending things to my advisor and keeping him updated."

"Juni and Beautify seems to be keeping you busy."

"Busy enough."

"Maybe you should think about doing less of other things so you have more time for that. For your art."

I look up at her, my eyes squint as I try to read her mind. *What is she talking about?* "Art *is* my only thing."

"I mean . . . never mind. Eat your food. We'll talk later?"

"What is there to talk—"

"Your semester going all right, Ezekiel? Still enjoying school?" Pa asks, fully ending our whatever that attempt at "talking" was. His eyes quickly going over to Mami, doing their telepathic parent talking.

They love getting in my head about stuff like this and being super passive-aggressive with their constant questions about how well Zeke is doing at Incarnate Word while I'm still here. They can call me a disappointment to my face next time. It's cool.

Not as if their child has used their time before college getting real world experience SAIC freshmen can only dream of and creating art that has been in the *Express-News* and travel blogs. That's all over the motherfucking neighborhood. *And Instagram.*

Like, yeah. Doing nothing with my life. Sitting at home and going through crayons.

And, sure, I realize this is some weird, unhealthy way of showing that they love me. That they're—whether they're saying it out loud right now or not—proud of me and my talent. They've always said that. They tell me all the time.

They've just never been in love with me sitting here at this dining table with them instead of in Chicago. As proud as they are, there's always some disappointment there because of that.

"It's all right. Getting the rest of my basics out the way, you know? School is school."

Around the tenth or eleventh time they asked, we came to an agreement that he'd stop overselling the college experience in front of Pa and Mami. Keep it as dull as possible. Even though I know my brilliant whore of a best friend is thriving and living his best life at UIW, and he has no regrets about going right into it after graduation.

I tune them out. This mural idea needs my attention more than they do. Specifically the girl's dress that's got to be the right color at the bottom. This, like, navy that turns indigo that turns violet that turns white. Only dropping my concentration to switch the Pencil for a fork and pick at my dinner.

Zeke's toes slam into my shin. Not hard enough to hurt, but enough to snap my head up to him. He gives an overly enthusiastic smile, but one of those where his mouth stays closed and doesn't show any teeth.

You good? he mouths while Mami, Pa, and Tita are talking between themselves, moving on from harassing me and, indirectly, my friends. Mami listens to Pa talk about some raid that happened at La Carnicería on Abigail and Ruidoso. Tita's voice is stern but quiet as she cusses ICE out, but also sad as she lets out her worries for the families that went home today to find out their spouses and parents are gone.

I nod, giving him a small smile back. *I'm fine.*

"Did you hear about Josué's family?" Mami asks Pa.

"No. ¿Qué pasó?"

"Denied asylum. ¿Tú crees? And now they're stuck in Matamoros, his wife and four kids."

Pa whispers his own string of cusswords in Spanish about this country's entire immigration system. Quiet enough for him to believe we can't hear him, but loud enough for us to definitely hear every word. "What are they supposed to do?"

"I don't know, mi amor. Josué is thinking about leaving. He can't stand them living in tents there on the streets. You know how bad it is for hondureños in México."

"I don't blame him. I'd do the same if it was you and les niñes in that situation."

"And Estevan. Over at Juanito's garage. They stopped him on his way home a couple nights ago."

"*He has kids here,*" Pa answers. In a way that I can tell, like every time they talk about this, is chipping away at his heart. "Is he going to try to come back?"

"He'd rather wait the ten years than get caught again and be permanently thrown out."

"Chingada madre. Those girls will graduate high school before they see their dad again."

These conversations have been the norm for what seems like most of my life. Pa sitting me down when I was five and explaining why everything in the restaurant always got so chaotic just before people in black jackets with ICE on the back showed up. Seeing more than a couple cooks rushed out the kitchen when we've been able to get a tip and a head start. Hearing how one or two wouldn't be coming in for shifts anymore and knowing exactly what that meant. Or my old high school classmates talking about a mom or dad being deported, or the handful of undocumented students always on edge about whether DACA will stop existing and they'll get sent to a country they have no memory of.

I had parents and Tita making sure I didn't grow up like those Mexican Americans who try to forget they're tied to that first word. Who talk shit about immigrants and stay ignorant about it all. Who think they're better because we don't stumble as badly through the English language as our parents or grandparents do. That we're somehow immune to racism if we buy into it. My friends, like Mo, made sure of that too. He'd take me to LULAC Youth meetings (before they got all defensive and transphobic about the *x* in Latinx and we peaced out), where we'd usually spend at least a few minutes hearing something about immigration policy and the government and how to call our congressperson or senator.

I'm not desensitized. This stuff is fucking angering. And Santos Vista always seems to be the place where random stops happen. The school walk-throughs Chachi and I grew up with. The way security guards at Santos Vista High School think they're also ICE agents and how some governors or presidents really try to make that a thing. Actual born-here citizens feel scared about walking around at night not because of gangs or criminals but because they might end up *accidentally* in a cage when these pinche terrorists want to act first and give us their half-assed apologies later.

But . . . maybe I *am* desensitized. Or maybe because I know that there's some degree of separation from it, I've let myself not think about it. The stories of my bisabueles coming here from Mexico isn't personal for me. I was never super close to undocumented classmates or anyone who had family aside from a few people at Lupe's. I know that as long as I have my license on me, I'm good. I'm away from it all. I have nothing to be afraid of.

Even the way my heart hurts doesn't compare to maybe the way Pa's does, having seen his own friends and employees taken into custody. I've never ached. I've never felt broken like so many people from around here have.

I understand. I've been to the rallies. But to say that it moves me in the same way as my family or Mo or the people at RAICES would be a lie. Maybe it's because I've never had a reason or trauma to give me that sense of empathy about it.

And maybe I'm extremely grateful for that.

3

A J, this is so fucking cool." Zeke's been looking at some new drawings on my iPad, showing me his favorites every so often. We're sitting out on the roof of the garage, huddled together with colchas to keep warm. After Tita left and my parents went to bed, we were both still wide awake, and, like usual, no matter how cold it is, this is where we end up.

I figured out how to take the mesh screen off my window about five years ago. Got some duct tape and stuck it to the bottom of my wooden bedframe so Mami and Pa wouldn't find it or suspect anything, in what can only be called a stroke of genius (at least, until they caught me out here and I had to tell them how I got through the window). It's not as if those things have any actual purpose. No one misses it.

And with it gone, I found my perfect chill spot. On the roof, above the garage. Late at night when the streets aren't yet asleep but are quieter than usual.

When the sun stays up late in the summer evenings, I like to come out here and paint. Whether using Procreate or actual brushes and poster board. Or even taping down huge rows of butcher paper and going at it with spray paint, trying my best not to stain the roof. Racing the sun and getting as much creativity out as possible before the visibility goes to shit.

A few months after Zeke, Mo, and I started hanging out, I

shared this spot with them for the first time. And since then, it's become *our* chill spot. The place where I told them I'm gay and nonbinary. Where Zeke came out as "something not straight" and then bisexual. And then Mo came out as gay too and gray ace. Where we snuck off to after stealing some of Pa's beers and tried alcohol for the first time. Smoked weed for the first time. Had all those conversations about life and fear and uncertainty and the future.

"That one's for Mo," I say when I see Zeke laughing at one of the paintings. Giraffes on a red desert landscape that I imagine is how Jupiter looks and an added road sign, with SATURN—400 MILLION MI., and then EARTH—ALSO FAR AWAY written below that.

"Damn, that was the funniest shit. He was high out of his mind that night. Kept going on about 'Y'all realize giraffes are aliens, right?'"

So, yeah. Some of our conversations weren't super philosophical. We aren't usually figuring out how to create a new socialist government and shit like that. Except for Mo. That and giraffes is about all his mind runs on. But after a night of fucking around and getting into our usual pendejadas like running through every aisle at H-E-B or partying and then coming back here and hanging out for hours, by the time three or four in the morning hits, intellectualness is no longer a thing.

And to be fair, giraffes are weird as fuck.

I laugh with Zeke, remembering our friend who left us for Denton. The same friend who wants to be a senator one day and has a picture of him and Bernie Sanders as his lock screen and brags about Alexandria Ocasio-Cortez following him on Twitter but also truly and actually believes that giraffes are not from this planet.

"Remember how he was, like, 'Have you ever *really seen one*? Stared at a giraffe right in the eyes as it chews on grass or whatever the hell they eat?' Talking about how their nubs at the top of their heads are there to receive telepathic signals from other giraffes on their home planet."

"Pinche cabrón, I swear to God, dude. I miss that mother-fucker."

"Me too."

"I'm gonna—" Zeke starts. "Never mind." He drinks the rest of his Coca-Cola to shut himself up and then when it's empty carefully walks over to my bedroom window, trying his best to keep his balance so he doesn't fall off the roof (again). He sets the bottle inside on my desk, and then comes back over to me.

Neither of us talks for a while. I know that he was about to say something like he's going to miss me too when I leave. He'll miss what the three of us used to be.

But I made him promise not to bring it up once we got into the new year. It's not something I want to think about or ac-knowledge. Mo—as much as he'll be our friend as long as he'll let us call him that—has got his new friends and new life and that's just what happens when people move away. I'm not ready to think about how I'm up next.

In our silence I can hear Ambar Lucid coming from my lap-top, sitting on my desk next to the open window. The back-fire of a car close by. Chachi and her friends still up, playing video games and yelling in her bedroom. If I turn my head, I'd see the glow of her television from her window. I can smell the burning wood coming from some mexicano's pit, preparing to spend all night and into the morning smoking a brisket and going through cases of Bud Light. Feel Zeke's shoulder and arm and leg against my own, trying to stay warm.

"By the way, my Co-Star told me to check in on my low-maintenance friends today," Zeke says, turning his head toward me. "Not that you're in any way low maintenance, but—you know. In case it's one of those days where your mental headspace and ego and way-too-healthy self-esteem aren't at a hundred, I want you to know that I'm here for you. I believe in you, and you're, like, the most talented person in the world who's gonna fucking make life your bitch."

"Wow," I reply, trying to keep a straight face as I meet his eyes and sound as touched and overcome with emotion as I can force myself to be. Feeling the smallest twitch at the corner of my mouth. "Next time you can just tell me you're in love with me, Zeke. Let me find out you're trying to words-of-affirmation yourself back into my pants."

He pushes himself into my shoulder as he lets out a *perra*. "This is why you only have two friends."

"I have *lots* of friends."

"*Okay.* Even then, sorry to break it to you, but you and me are never revisiting the romantic and/or sexual thing."

"Don't tell my mom that. You know she's been hoping for us to get back together even more now that Mo's gone and no longer an option."

"Well, if she can't have a smart child, she can hope for a smart son-in-law."

Now it's my turn to push him. "That's hurtful. You're supposed to be checking in on my mental health right now, not dragging me. Bitch."

"Whatever." Zeke's glare at me turns into a smile and quiet laugh.

"Thanks," I tell him. Almost in a mutter. My eyes go from him to our feet, so I don't have to look him in the eyes when I tell him, "I, uh—I was having some thoughts today, though."

"The usual?"

"Yeah."

Zeke's the only person I talk to about this. Although, I never told him about SSAD rejecting me and why they did. I already had to hold back Pa from punching everyone involved. I'm not interested in getting my best friend mad about it, especially now when there's nothing anyone can do to change the past.

It's not that he completely understands where I'm coming from or why I feel the way I do. Sometimes it can be really obvious that he's having trouble finding the right words to say. Maybe because Zeke's so far into using the STEM side of his brain and I do my best to only use the artsy side of mine, it just doesn't click. But it's better than figuring out how to explain to my parents that sometimes I'm so confident in what I'm doing here but other times I just hear the SSAD people calling me a "Mexican tagger" and telling me that what I do is too niche to ever be impactful outside of where I live. Imaginary voices telling me that SAIC and RISD only let me in because they needed some culture in their student body and I was the name they pulled out of a bowl.

I know it doesn't make sense, but under that confidence and being very open about knowing that I'm talented, I'm scared. It's a weird space to be in mentally, aware that I'm really good at something but still so afraid of the future. Afraid of this feeling that I have to decide between creating things that I love and things that even white people will appreciate. And how me not going to SAIC and instead painting mostly really Mexican murals in a really Mexican city plays into all that.

What if this is the decision that boxes me in? Digs me into a hole too deep to ever get out of? What if I'm only ever seen as the "Mexican tagger"? Just a queer, brown commodity who only gets to make art about a specific thing?

"Remember the night before you took that residency?" Zeke starts. "We sat on the roof and you let out all your worries about how 'What if me taking a year off puts me behind everyone?

What if I'm setting myself up to never be as good as I could've been because I didn't take that one course this one specific semester? What if going with Beautify only makes me look more like the diversity pick when I eventually get to SAIC?'"

"*Yeah*," I groan, knowing he's about to make a point.

"In the end, you went with your gut. Because you know that life isn't about letting opportunities pass you by. Every big leap, every cliff you've dived off of has had a cloud to catch you, because, ultimately, you know what you're doing, whether we see it or believe it or not. And I know that there's a lot of thoughts and opinions about the type of artist you are or you can be, but I also know you, AJ. I know that if you really regretted this choice, if you actually wanted to go and do white people art instead of the really awesome shit you're doing right now, you'd do something about it."

"What if it's too late? What if I made the wrong choice?"

"Then it happened," Zeke answers, like it's the easiest thing in the world. "But you gotta know that you have so much more freedom to do whatever it is that's living in your head than anyone at SAIC does right now. And you have the time and resources. Beautify is like a seed, right? And these projects are like every rainstorm that waters you and makes you into the flower you're supposed to be."

"How am I the flower if Beautify is the seed? Wouldn't that make Beautify the flower too?"

"*Pinche*—whatever. You get it. I'm just trying to say stop worrying and do the damn thing."

If only it was that simple. "I just—what if by the time I figure it out, there's no more room left for me at the table because we already have Keith Haring, Banksy, and Takashi Murakami?"

"You're gonna have to remind me who all of those people

are, but even without knowing, I can confidently say *fuck that*. Once the world sees Ander Martínez, they'll make room. Trust me on that one."

I don't know. White artists can make outline people and soup cans or appropriate Indigenous cultures because *vibes* and end up in museums and as household names. They can do what they want. They can make art about anything.

I can try. Most days I believe I can do just as good of a job as any of them. But will I ever belong in that space the same way I feel like I've made my own space here?

I wish this didn't have to be so complicated. But I guess an easy life would be boring, right? If I was so scared of failing, there'd be so many things I would've never tried. I have to remember that and keep going. To try my best to not think about what happens if I fail. To instead think about what happens if I succeed. What happens if I'm great.

It's a work in progress. And, honestly, sometimes I worry I'll never get there.

4

Ronnie slumps into a chair across from Zeke and me after setting down red oval baskets filled with tacos de pastor, barbacoa, and chicken tinga. I was supposed to meet with Tita for something important after I got done with my pre-mural painting meeting at Beautify, only for her to leave right when I show up. Must not have been that important.

But I'm already here, might as well have lunch and give Zeke a ride home.

"Get this," Ronnie starts. "Not much happening out at the bar today, so la jefa has me help out with a couple tables. Guess no one's trying to get day drunk during lunch for some reason. Anyways, this group of kids, white, probably from Trinity, comes in asking for—and I shit you not—Texas Pete for their tacos."

"*Texas Pete?*" Zeke asks, sounding like he's never been more grossed out in his life. "That's some Bill Miller's shit."

"What kind of tacos did they get?" I add. As if there's maybe one option on our whole menu that could make me side with them. I don't know what that option is, but I'll hear it out. I'm feeling forgiving today.

"Carnitas."

"*¡A la verga!* No mames."

"¡Sí, AJ! I told them we don't carry that shit. Which was a

lie. We do, from when your pa wanted to try that spicy chicken strip taco—"

"This is why we don't let him watch *Chopped* anymore."

"But more important, why would anyone want that trash when salsa verde is *right here*!" Zeke says while chewing on a taco de pastor.

"I think you mean salsa roja," Ronnie replies.

"*Ronnie*," I gasp. "You're like my big brother, but you keep being all about salsa roja like this, and I'm gonna refuse to be seen with you."

"It's a hill worth dying on, kid."

I roll my eyes at Ronnie and then take the exact chicken tinga taco he was reaching for. Making sure to put way too much salsa verde on it just to be petty. Even if I'm about to unalive myself eating it. Like he said, hill worth dying on.

He rubs a hand across his freshly buzzed scalp while letting out a hot, heavy breath after taking a bite of his own taco loaded with *even more* salsa roja than I had salsa verde. Both of us are biting our bottom lips hard, trying not to cough or be the first to grab our water. But then the aftershock of whatever secret, illegal peppers Tita puts in the salsa verde sets fire to my entire body, and as much as I try to close-mouth scream through the pain, it's no use.

I throw myself toward my cup and chug the whole glass in seconds.

"That's not even fair," I say while catching my breath. "Verde is hotter than roja."

"Not true. Have you tasted Jefa's salsa roja? She doesn't play around."

Zeke watches Ronnie and me struggle to eat the rest of our tacos, laughter coming out of him every few seconds, muffled by his fist or straw while taking sips of lemonade. We have no other choice. Mami, Pa, and Tita would disown me if they found out I wasted food goofing off.

"Okay, so does *any* bottled hot sauce belong on tacos?" Zeke asks.

"Tabasco is the only one that I won't judge you for," I answer. "Or, I'll only judge you a little bit."

"Tabasco's for bitches that eat Chipotle," Ronnie says. "Then you got Louisiana, which is ideal for pizza. Pinche Pete goes on fried chicken and burgers. Valentina and Cholula are both for snack foods: popcorn, chips, chicharrones, pinwheels. The only difference is that if you grew up poor, you stick with Valentina because you can get basically a jug for two bucks. Cholula, though, three dollars only gets you one of those five-ounce bottles. Cholula's for rich folk. Oh, I will accept Valentina on tripas tacos."

"What about Tapatío?"

"Gonna be brave but honest here, Tapatío is Cholula's ugly brother that's also cheap but not as voluptuous as Valentina."

Zeke slaps his palms against the table as he lets out a loud, "*Shiiiiit!* Someone give this guy a PhD in Sauce Studies."

While Zeke heads outside to go warm up my car, I follow Ronnie to the front counter, handing Maritza the now empty food baskets and thirty dollars for a tip because anyone who has to wait on the three of us probably spends most of their time thinking about if this job is worth it. As she fills up a to-go cup for me of horchata, I spot the blur of a person from the corner of my eye heading behind the counter and past the kitchen, toward the office.

"We're doing more interviews today?" I ask Ronnie, getting ready to head out onto the patio, hoping happy hour and a dinner rush will bring people to the bar.

"Mm, I don't know, kid. Could be."

"Tita isn't back from the bank yet." I take out my phone to check the time. It's only a five-minute trip. She should've been back half an hour ago. Probably saw someone she knows from church. "I'm gonna go make sure that's what they're here for. Kind of looks like someone who might be here to fix that one wonky heater outside."

I head toward the hall, texting Tita, asking while it's on my mind if she wants me to come back later or if we should just forget about whatever it was she wanted to tell me, and, at the same time, start speaking at the person in our hallway.

"¿Estás aquí para arreglar el . . . uh—" *Fuck, what's the word for heater in Spanish?* "—o sea, *la máquina de calor*?" I ask the person. When I pick my head up from my phone, their back is turned to me and they're talking on their phone to someone. They hang up, turn around, and—

Santiago.

Same hoodie, but not wearing the sweatpants today. Instead, a pair of faded gray jeans and worn-looking work boots. And, after he seems to get over a familiar shock at seeing someone he probably wasn't expecting to see, there's that smile again.

"I'm supposed to do, uh . . . paperwork," he tells me. His accent's different. I didn't catch that last time. Maybe he's from the Valley or Laredo. It sounds really nice with his voice. Warm.

"Oh. Cool. I, uh, yeah. The bosses aren't here yet, but if you just wanna wait out here, I'll text them and let them know you're waiting for them."

I reach for my phone again, opening up our family group text but stop typing midway. When I pick my head up from the screen, I catch him watching me, his hands in his pocket, back against the wall.

His eyes are so pretty. That's all I can think for a minute, forgetting what I'm supposed to be doing. Lost in eyes and then the glint from what looks like a gold Virgen de Guadalupe pendant hanging on a chain around his neck.

"I—Sorry," I finally say before tapping my pocket and feeling keys, including the one for the office. "Actually, if you promise not to steal anything, I can open the office for you, so you don't have to wait out here. The bosses aren't known for being on time to anything. I usually tell them things start an hour before they actually do, and even then, they show up ten minutes late."

He glances down at the floor while letting out a small laugh and then comes back up to me. "I won't steal anything. I promise."

He stands close behind me as I unlock the door. When I first saw him, I thought he was taller than me, but now those few inches are obvious. I can smell the scent of the Dove bar soap he uses. I only know it because Mo used to use the same one and I always thought it smelled really good. That charcoal soap with the gray stripe. Smells better on Santiago, to be honest.

And when I turn around, there he is, our chests nearly touching. We give each other awkward smiles as I hold the door and he scoots past me.

"Thanks," he tells me while falling into a chair.

"Claro. Make yourself comfortable."

If I hadn't offered Zeke a ride home, I could make up an excuse to stay with him. Get comfortable with him. Everything about the way he looked at me that day out on the patio and then the way he's looking at me right now tells me he'd be into that. Something like *They might not love the idea of finding you here by yourself, so I'll stick around* or *It could get boring waiting alone.* But now Zeke's texting me four, five messages asking where I am and what's keeping me. This is what I get for being nice.

Especially when Santiago asks, "You staying with me until they get here?"

I really want to. And I know I'm not imagining the hopeful look on his face that I might say yes. But instead, with so much regret and reluctance in my voice, I tell him, "I—I should go. Have fun, or—yeah. Maybe I'll see you around."

"Ojalá."

I smile at that. "Same here."

Ugh. Fuck Zeke. I should make him walk home. That's what he'd deserve for getting in a wreck and putting me in this situation.

"*What took you so long?*" he groans when I finally make it to my car, finishing up a message letting Tita know to expect a person in the office when she gets back.

"Someone's here for an interview, but Tita and Mami aren't back yet. Made sure he was okay waiting there."

"Cute or nah?"

Of course that's the only thing Zeke needs to know about this whole situation. But also, "Yeah, actually. He is." And if I didn't have to drive my best friend's pinche pendejo-ass home, I could be listening to how hot he sounds saying *ojalá* and making out with him on the office couch. Or something. "You owe me. You owe me big."

5

B ebite, siéntate, por favor. Go find a table. I'll be there in a minute."

Tita ended up asking me to come back about an hour after I dropped Zeke off. Everyone's got me driving all over the neighborhood today. This better be *actually* important.

Wait. Am I in trouble? Like, work trouble? Something she couldn't just tell me at home? Is she about to get on me about those few days I was late a couple weeks ago? Or maybe someone complained about me? *¿Las Beckys?*

I grab a table at the corner of the restaurant. My hands clasped, eyes taking in the white walls lined with a chipped crimson-red border at the top. It's been like this ever since I can remember. Longer than I've been alive. Maybe even longer than Pa's been alive. Outside is the opposite. Red that was probably pretty bold fifty years ago with a white border, now just plain and faded, nothing showy. The opposite of Tita, in my opinion.

Tita power walks over to me a minute later, handing me a cup of lemonade and taking the seat across from me. She looks at me with loving eyes behind large circular framed glasses. Her hands together, resting against her lips like she's praying.

"You're so pretty, Ander Justino."

"Did you take shots in the kitchen again?"

"*No.* Not yet. I—Dio' mío. I'm going to come right out with it, mi bebite. I don't need you as a waiter here anymore."

"What the—" I start to say before forcing the rest of what was about to come out to a screeching halt so I don't cuss in front of Tita. "Why? Are we going out of business?"

"*What?* No."

"Then what did I do?"

"Oh—nada. Verdad. It's not—I'm not firing you. I'm—I'm letting you go."

"That's the same thing, Tita."

"Okay, *but* it's only because we want to give you as much free time as possible to do your painting right now. It's important for us to make sure you remember you're not here to be a waiter. You're here to make the best impression you can for the *Sack* people."

"SAIC." That's all I say. I don't want to get into it with her about how they're all assuming I'm seconds from giving up on my dreams to become a taquero when they literally have no evidence to back that up.

"That's what I said."

"I—" I was about to correct her, but then it hits me. This doesn't sound like Tita. This sounds like—

"Mami is making you do this, isn't she? This is all her idea; I know it. A couple days ago she was all, 'Maybe you're doing too much.' This is what she was talking about, right?"

"All of us agree on this, bebite."

"Is she forcing you? What is she offering? I'll double it."

Tita has this sympathetic pout going on. Like she feels sorry for me and knew this is how I'd react. Maybe she realized she had to be the person to break the news—I would've gotten into an argument with Mami, and Pa probably would've ended up letting me stay. Her hands go over mine, squeezing them.

"So you're just gonna get rid of me?" The words come out softer. Way more hurt than the reaction I'd been having. It's not that working here is so important. I like working here. I love it, honestly. But it's more than that. I love it because this place has been a big part of my life for forever. And this feels like they're pushing me out. Like they're cutting the cord a whole eight months before I leave.

"*Ander*, mi alma. No, of course not. No digas eso. We'll still need you. *I* am going to be needing you. There's something else; a special project. If you'd be interested."

I almost jump over the table, my hands slamming down to keep me grounded. "*Why didn't you start with that?*"

"Porque you have to start at point A to get to point B, bebite. Otherwise, you're walking backwards."

"I—What?" Still unconvinced that she hasn't been taking shots with the cooks.

"We're planning for an entire restaurant makeover this summer. Your Pa and I decided that it was about time we moved on from what we have now. We're thinking of some pastels inside, bien Puebla."

"And you want me to help paint?"

"This part is up to you. If you'd like to do the inside, pos sí, I would love it. But we can also contract some guys to get that done. Hire other local artists who've been good to us."

"*No*," I almost yell. "I'll do it. I can do it."

"Qué 'ueno," she says, and pats my hands a couple times before clasping them in hers. Giving a good squeeze and shake. "We'll talk more on the inside later. What I'm really needing from you is, well, actually, me sigues."

Tita abruptly stands up and starts heading for the front door. I grab my cup and follow her outside. She stops and stands a few yards away from the front-facing wall of Lupe's. TAQUERÍA

GUADALUPE in a basic block script, painted in gold, goes across it, from the front door to where the wall ends on the other side. My first big project after I got really good at sign painting. I usually touch it up once a year so at least there's a little pop of something on the building.

"If you're up for it, bebite, I'd like to—¿cuál es la palabra?—commissary you."

"Commission."

"Sí. That's what I said."

"You—Yeah. Wait. You want to *pay me* to paint something on the restaurant?"

"Two somethings, actually," she corrects. "Well, three if you're doing the inside too. Anyways, the wall facing out onto the patio también."

"No way!?"

"Sí, güey."

I walk up to the wall, reaching out to touch it. Feeling a part of Santos Vista that my family has spent half a century making a name for ourselves from. Imagining Abuelo Willie putting on the first coat of paint. Dedicating it to the same woman who's letting me add something unique to this place decades later.

"I'm thinking of doing white. I don't want to do some weird color and limit what you could do. Unless you think of something else, and we can work with that. *However*, this wall is going to come with one, eh, specification. Okay? *Lupe's Tacos* needs to be on here. Big."

"Not Taquería Guadalupe?"

She looks at me with a smile as her arm reaches out to touch the wall too. "No. Rebranding. Everyone already calls this place Lupe's anyways. We're getting new shirts too."

"I like it."

"Me too. And something—¿cómo se dice?—*aesthetic*." Her

hand leaves the wall and swipes through the air as she says the word, as if she's going to make glitter and cilantro appear out of thin air. "But I need to see a sample first, okay? Do it on your little painting program and show me so I can approve. Same with the patio wall, pero there you can go wild. I won't give you any requirements as long as it's nothing, you know, sucio."

"I—Gracias, Tita. This—this is huge."

Shit, this is so exciting. And nerve-racking. And my mind is already going at a million miles an hour, thinking about every potential idea I could bring to life on this building.

"So, this is something you'd like to do?"

"Of course. I'd love to."

"Good. We'll talk pay later. Don't spend too much time on this right now. Oye, we want you to go focus on doing *your* art, okay? We'll come back to this in a couple months. I just couldn't keep it in and wanted you to know. Think it'd be a nice way for you to still be around while doing something more fun than bringing people tacos. And I can show off mi bebite preciose muy linda even when you're away in Michigan."

"Chicago."

"Qué la—*That's what I said*."

"No—whatever. And don't think I'm still not mad that y'all are kicking me out. You could've at least waited until I scheduled some projects. Why now? Why this sudden decision?"

"Because, well—because I already hired your replacement."

Why did I think you were joking about this?" It's still early and cold enough for my words to come out in a fog.

"Why would I let you believe something like that for this long?"

"I don't know. I—Shut up."

Juni Pérez, one of the guys in charge of Beautify Not Gentrify and the one who first offered me the residency last year, stands next to me. Both of us look across the water of Juan Diego Creek Park at a giant blank concrete wall that slowly slopes up like a narrow hill. Because it is. The wall is actually a man-made cutoff of what used to be dirt and land the city put up to create this lakelike waterway that connects to the San Antonio River.

The wall is about eighteen feet up at its highest point and comes down to about twelve feet high before it stops and becomes a staircase on either side leading to small piers and then sidewalks that lead away. It runs nearly the length of half a football field (a fact Juni has on good authority from one of his straight coworkers, but that means little to the two of us).

"How do you expect me to do this? It runs up against the water."

"Found a ten-foot longboard and had a guy attach some hooks," Juni answers. "I'm going to tie rope to the hooks, then the other end to some stakes that I'll have with me up at the top. Stick those in, and you're steady. I'll carefully maneuver you in whatever direction you need me to go. Might have to hold your feet while you paint upside down or something for the higher parts."

"I can tell you're being half-serious about the feet thing."

"You don't trust me?"

"Not *that much*."

"Yeah, I wouldn't either," he says with a smirk. "Concentrate on the water-level stuff right now, if that's fine with your process. We'll have some scaffolding tomorrow for you, so today focus on not falling in the creek and catching multiple diseases from the cold and whatever's in that water. That work?"

"Not loving the longboard idea, but sure. That'll work."

"Then you ready to get started?"

I stare at the wall and the water. I get let go from Lupe's, and the next morning I die from hypothermia and being eaten by some river monster. This is what my life has come to, I guess. At least I'll be way too scared about every single part of this to be thinking about how my family betrayed me but also are letting me do something so wild, and I haven't figured out how I'm supposed to feel when I put both of those together.

"Ready as I'll ever be."

Street art is never just show up, paint, and leave. There are steps, and most of the time there are aspects of the surface and the environment that make this process incredibly clunky. Like trying to chalk-outline segments of a wall, which would be tiring enough already—but doing small parts at a time because I have to get Juni to run back and forth between two stakes and adjust rope, carrying me from one side of the wall to the other, all in sixty-degree weather? Clunky as fuck. I could usually do this part in a couple hours, but in these conditions? Hell no.

This is not something sane people do.

Which says a lot about me.

It takes me a minute to stabilize myself on the board. Lots of screams and, more than a few times, a *qué la verga* and *pinche pendejo güey* come out while I try to stay balanced and keep from crying when I almost fall in. Taking deep breaths helps keep my shaking hands calm, at least from the fear. Can't help the cold. But I need some control—otherwise, the outlines are going to look like crap.

"Are you still alive?" Juni yells from above after getting the rope tied down. Seeing me on my hands and knees as I cling to the side of the board like a scared cat.

"Barely." My forehead touches the board as I let out a closed-mouth scream. "You're enjoying this, aren't you?"

"With such an incredible intensity, yes. You aren't?"

I'll think back on this one day and laugh about it. But today is not that day.

"I'm regretting every decision I've ever made in my entire life that's led me to this point."

"Cool, well, while you're doing that, might want to remember we're on a time line."

I let one hand off the board for all of five seconds, only to show Juni how pretty my middle finger looks.

"Also, you could be in Chicago right now, where it's, hold on . . . negative eight degrees outside. I think, even in your current predicament, being here might be the least amount better."

"I wouldn't be so sure."

The vision I had for *La Chalupa* in my head and on my iPad finally starts looking like something close to a mural. I draw out the boat along the length of the bottom of the wall. That will give the illusion that a giant woman is rowing up the creek with all the grace of someone who was born for this. I'm able to get that much done and most of the lower greenery in the background before lunch, coming back at the lines with black paint for the rest of the day.

It's a tiring process. And something that always takes days, especially when working with a canvas this large. The amount of mental concentration, my hand and arm going nonstop, the cold wind sharp against my face—this is something that, if I didn't absolutely love it and couldn't see myself doing anything else in the world, I would hate. It's most of a week of pushing myself and sleep deprivation, getting my second wind about the time the color starts happening and then a third wind when I see the final results before sleeping all of the next three days. Usually on a couch because I don't have the energy to make it upstairs to my bed.

On the last day, Juni does his daily check-in on my progress and on the scaffolding and its metal beams, set up along the length of the wall with wood running across, to see they're at least stable *enough* before running off to do the millions of things he's always busy with. Meeting with city councilmembers, drafting grant proposals, and all that other nonprofit stuff he's complained about in passing since I've known him only because he knows I'm too busy painting to actually be listening. But he's nice enough to leave a Bluetooth speaker and a Tupperware container full of cantaloupe with me. Also, sometimes it's cool to be able to do this by myself and blast La Doña as loudly as the speaker will let me.

"*AYYY-JAYYY!*"

So much for the solitude.

Chachi is waving at me from the pier at my left, screaming my name in quick repetition.

"*¿Qué quieres, pendeja?*"

"Pa wanted me to make sure La Llorona didn't get you, since we haven't seen you for days," she replies. "I told him you probably were overcome with the shame you brought on this family because you got fired, so you ran away from home and were looking for a way to avenge your honor."

"*I wasn't fi—*"

"And I heard that there'd be things to climb. *Why didn't you tell me about this?* Can I hang out with you? Please, please, please, please, plea—"

I let out a loud, annoyed huff and hit my head against a dry part of the wall. "*Yes. Santa mierda.* Fine. But no diving."

"Counterproposal, one dive."

"No. Diving."

"What if I, like, happen to fall in a cannonball-like fashion into the creek?"

"Then you better hope La Llorona takes you with her."

"Ugh," she groans. "Fine."

Chachi disappears as she runs up the stairs, and a minute later, the sound of footsteps comes from one of the large planks of wood above me, shaking the scaffolding. She jogs to the far end of it and then climbs down to my level, running back over to me.

"I saw this from the other side of the creek. It's looking really good. Frankie said the lady's chichis are too small, though."

"Frankie thinks *all* chichis are too small."

"True enough, sibling." She picks up the container of what's left of melon, opening it and making throw-up sounds when she sees what's inside before closing it shut and dropping the Tupperware back on the plank. "You need help?"

"Uh, sure. Get a picture up of La Chalupa. Can you paint the fruit and stuff she has in her boat? Grab some brushes, a palette, and the red, yellow, and green paints."

Chachi gives me an eager thumbs-up. "Aye, aye, Capitán."

Every once in a while, especially when it starts feeling too quiet, I'll cling on to the sides of the board and look down to see what my sister's doing, fighting how scared I am because I need to check on Chachi and make sure she's not ruining my mural.

"Don't get wild with the strokes," I tell her while watching as she goes back and forth with the brush.

"Is that what your last boyfriend told you?" she replies with a grin, her fist making fast up-and-down motions in the air.

"Necia."

"I know what I'm doing, AJ."

"I know. Still. I have high expectations."

Days like this, when I'm rushing to finish projects and trying to not let myself get even minimally sloppy, are when I'm glad I taught Chachi at least the basics of painting. She's come to my rescue more than a handful of times the past couple of years, helping me on the last bits of whatever I'm doing. Making sure I hit that deadline right at the last minute.

"Thanks for helping," I tell her while we sit next to each other on the grass on the opposite side of the creek. Boxes of Dairy Queen chicken strips sit in our laps while we gaze at my finished mural of this larger-than-life woman eternally rowing through the creek, completely visible now after whatever company Juni hired took down the scaffolding.

"No problem. One thousand dollars, please."

"Shut the fuck up."

Chachi pinches me and then goes back to her food. "I like her. She's my new god."

"Don't tell Tita that. She'll choke you with a rosary."

"My new god, La Chalupa Grande, will protect me. Oh, can you take me to Taco Bell? We can buy chalupas and offer them to her."

"You—You're weird. ¿Tú sabes?"

7

Okay, but making her get rid of me? You gotta realize how shady that is. *And* to hire someone else before you've kicked me out. *Your own child*. That's low. Cruel. Just tell me you hate me."

"Ander, my love," Mami starts, sitting on the other end of our L-shaped sectional. Ever since I got home from my last day at the mural and saw her here too, I went from too exhausted to feel anything to remembering how *actually*, my own family betrayed me and I've been too busy to yell at them about it. I've been tense, trying not to say anything. Trying to think, *Maybe this will end up being better for me, so I shouldn't complain.*

Nah. That ain't happening. I'm her child. Complaining is in my DNA.

"We're giving you three whole projects," she continues. "Isn't that better than being a waiter?"

In theory, yeah. Sure. And I won't lie—since then, if I wasn't thinking about the *La Chalupa* mural, I was thinking about what the Lupe's murals were going to look like and all the things I could do to the inside of the restaurant. Chachi said I should re-create *Los dos Fridas* but with Tita: "The one where she has the monkey, and switch its face with mine."

That's going to give me nightmares for a while.

"I can do both."

"No. We were relying on you too much. Giving you full-time hours. And it's important that not only you but me and your pa and tita realize that your job isn't to work at the taquería. You want to be an artist, go do that. Get Juni to give you more things to paint."

"Juni can't make projects and commissions appear out of nowhere. And definitely not enough to fill seven entire months of work. So it's *my* fault you and Tita and Pa were scheduling me five days a week? I was *too good* of a worker?"

"I didn't say that." Her voice is so sarcastic, and she *never* tries to hide it.

"*I am, though.*" I throw myself forward, my butt barely on the sofa. "I never call out. *Okay*, I don't call out that much. I always let y'all know weeks in advance when I have projects. I don't get complaints. And I don't complain about being there *and* painting. I can do both."

"Just because you can doesn't mean I want you to."

"Why not schedule me less? At least give me part-time hours."

"We don't need you, mi'je. I promise, the restaurant will be okay without you. *We* will be okay without you. Think of all the extra time you'll have to do what you want to be doing instead of wiping tables."

"But I *want* to work," I whine. My hands move in the air with the words like they'll help give more *oomph* to my argument. "It's not like I spend forty hours a week painting. It's gonna be boring around here with nothing to do and Zeke busy with school or at Lupe's."

"Well, cabrone, if you were at school right now too, you wouldn't be so bored, ¿verdad?"

I let out a long groan while throwing myself against the back cushion of the couch. "This is your way of punishing me because I didn't do what you wanted *half a year ago*? You're still gonna be bitter about this? Enough to say that forcing me to mope around the house is better than doing something productive?"

"It won't be my fault if you're lazy the next eight months. Find opportunities. All the ones you were so convinced were here and not at college. ¿A dónde? Dime."

There's never any reasoning with her. Never any convincing her that my life doesn't have to be this clean, straight-lined journey. *Things come up.* And nothing about me is straight.

"*You're so annoying,*" I mutter as I get up and start for the stairs.

"*What'd you say?*" Mami snaps.

"I—Dije que . . . yo soy amicable."

"Uh-huh. Sure. I'm gonna *ami*-kick your ass." She tries to keep her little chuckle from coming out. "Go find something to do, *punk.*"

I wake up in the middle of the night craving water. Maybe the dream I was having starring Lunay got me needing to rehydrate. Who knows.

I quietly walk toward the stairs and realize the lights in the living and dining rooms are still on. And I can hear Mami and Tita's voices. Swear, working at a restaurant that stays open almost twenty hours a day ruins this entire family's sleep schedules.

I sit down at the topmost step, listening to them talk.

"You realize the risk and you did it anyways," Mami says.

"I did. Sí. And I'd do it again too, Thalía. If we can help, we should."

"He's not our problem to be helping, Guadalupe. We have the rest of the staff to worry about. And the way we're already worrying about half of them. There's no room to be adding to that."

"So you want we should get rid of him?"

"No, I—I just wish you would be smarter about this. Talk to us before making decisions like that. When it comes to situations like this."

"If it was Chachi or bebite, you'd want someone to show them the same basic kindness, no?"

"*That's not the point*. This is the reality of the situation. There's no what-ifs."

"Well, if anything happens, it's on me. ¿Bueno?"

"Yeah. *When* it happens, it will be."

The next morning—with last night like a vague dreamlike memory I don't put even a second of thought into—I drive to the Beautify offices, mentally manifesting a reality where Juni has shelves of lists of places needing art. But from the little half frown and tilt of his head with crossed arms, I'm getting the impression that he won't have anything helpful to say. Maybe if I make up something. I could tell him my parents won't let me come back home unless I find projects. Nah, he'd read right through that.

I could count on one hand the number of times I've been in his Beautify office. He keeps it pretty plain. Some photos of him visiting family in Puerto Rico hang on one wall, another with different flyers of all the events Beautify puts on. His desk always meticulously clean in a way that Marie Kondo herself would be, like, "Okay, but we can have *one* thing." A box of pink conchas and two iced coffees sit between us.

"AJ, according to our contract, we only do one commission a month. I say this with all the love in my tiny little heart, but it's not policy nor, if I'm being completely honest, is it our job to get you more than that."

Yeah. Nothing helpful at all.

I let out a groan as I throw my head back against my chair. The bright light in the middle of his office ceiling stings my eyes and I immediately regret coming here.

"But," he continues, "I do have some friends around the city who might know someone. It wouldn't be anything Beautify-backed, and these might be gigs in the whiter—don't want to say *gentrified*, because of my job, but gentrified-as-fuck—parts of San Antonio."

"I'll take it. Whatever they want. I'm open to anything."

"Be open to stop acting desperate," Juni says with a face like he just ate a sour piece of mango. He takes out his phone and is tapping on the screen faster than I've seen any human's fingers move. "Let me text a couple of the girls and see what I can get you. Something to think about too is investing in a website. Yes, I can talk you up real big to people and tell them what you're doing and where to find it, but if I could send them to, I don't know, Ander the Art Ho dot com instead of 'Visit the Beautify website, go to Community Engagement, and then click on Youth Residency,' that'd be a lot more convenient with this sort of stuff."

"Website. Yeah. Okay."

"Or even an Instagram would work. You don't have an account for your works?"

"I post art on my personal IG, but it's nothing like a website would do. The image ratio is wonky, especially when I have projects that are superlong because they're going on walls."

"Space it out into three," he tells me, as if this is the easiest solution in the world. "Use an entire row to focus on one project or do multiple shots in one post and have us swipe through them to get the whole gig. Honestly, it's not—Oh, I have something for you."

"Already?"

"Are you not prepared?" he asks with an annoyed face while a finger hovers over his phone screen. Like he was about to get this whole thing set but now has to wait on me. "Did you come in here looking for work and expect nothing?"

"*I'm prepared*. But I did expect nothing out of this, that part's right. What is it?"

"A couple friends are opening up a boba shop over at the Medical Center, and they want some anime characters on the walls."

"I didn't take you for the type of person who has friends who watch anime."

"My friend group is quite eclectic, thank you. So, what should I tell them?"

"Tell them I'll take it!" I yell, nearly falling over my words they come out so fast. Worried that if I don't answer quick enough, Juni is going to change his mind. Also, maybe free boba will be involved. I hope free boba will be involved.

"Okay. Good. They're gonna tell me what characters, and I'll work off the assumption you know what any of those names mean."

"I—My sister will."

"Well, thank God for her."

8

Mami! *Mami!*"

"*Pinche chamaque,*" she groans back, walking out of the kitchen, a small towel over her shoulder and her hands caressing her favorite wooden spoon, looking at me coming into the living room like I'm a moving target. "¿Mande? What are you yelling about?"

"I need money."

She lets out a few of those low, from-the-gut laughs. Qué fea. "Don't you have money?"

"Well, now that I don't have a job anymore, I have to make sure I save what I got for Chicago. You know, *for school.*"

I can tell she hates me right now. The way her face is all tense. I've seen more relaxed rocks. This is so satisfying.

"What do you need money for?"

"Juni says if I wanna get more commissions, I need a website."

"*Okay.* Free websites exist. Go do one of those."

"They're the worst! Gonna make me have *Ander Martinez dot this is a free website they didn't pay for it dot com slash reminder that they're poor.* How am I supposed to easily share that with people? Weren't you all 'Go get all the work, Ander; go paint the whole city because you're overqualified to work at our taquería'?"

Her glare is so intense. Should've been ready to put your money where your mouth is, Mami. A couple of shifts could've paid for this, but look where we are now.

"Well, websites are expensive. So you'll just have to use your brain and figure something out."

"Or I could use my body and make some money that way."

"I didn't realize Mami could run that fast," I tell Chachi while rubbing the back of my right shoulder, bruised from the multiple hits by her wooden spoon. A bowl of chile and lime chicharrones dressed with shredded cabbage, jalapeños, and half a bottle of Valentina sits in between us, and the first episode of *Demon Slayer* is playing on our TV. I haven't really been paying attention to it, but the second I asked her who Kamado Tanjiro and Kamado Nezuko were, she started screaming, "*I must show you!*" and now we're here.

"That's why she always gets picked first during football games at Tita's," Chachi says, and then stuffs two chicharrones in her mouth. "Besides Pa, she's the best receiver in the family, but she's got him on speed. No one can catch her."

"You act like I pay attention to family football games."

"*Just like you're paying attention to the show,*" she snaps. "Keep up."

I look at the TV for the first time probably since the episode started and—"Wait, why is there a bunch of blood? Chachi, *why is there blood*? And—*Oh my fuck, watch out! What are we watching?*"

"*I told you,*" Chachi huffs. "Tanjiro—"

"The one with the cute earrings?"

"Yes. Him. His whole family, except for his sister, is killed by demons."

"That's gross. What happened to his sister, then? She's fine?"

"Oh, AJ, you simple creature. Of course she's not okay. Nezuko's alive, but she was turned into a demon. And then a demon slayer was, like, Kill her she's not your sister anymore she's a demon. She'll kill you and not think anything of it. It's the moral thing to do. But Tanjiro's a stubborn little bitch and was all, No, I can cure her, I'll find a way."

"Does he?"

"You gotta watch the show to find out."

"I'm not doing that. The only reason I'm here right now is because I need to know what they look like, and honestly, Google would've been faster. Where's the blond kid? There's a blond kid they're asking for. And someone wearing a pig head."

"*Oh*, Inosuke. I like him."

"That doesn't surprise me. Someone wearing a pig head seems your type."

My SAIC advisor—or, the guy who was going to be my advisor and most likely will be come August—likes for me to keep in touch with him about my residency and everything I'm doing. He suggested it when I told him I'd be taking a gap year but still working on art, and as much as I think it's kind of a waste of time, it makes Mami and Pa feel like I'm actually doing something college-ish. Usually it's just through email, but this time he wanted an actual Zoom call, so for the past five minutes, he's been looking at another screen nearby with some of the things I've been working on displayed for him.

He finally looks at me and he's giving me that look—the one that says, *I don't have anything nice to say.*

"What inspired this?" he asks.

The *this* he's asking about is a portrait I did of a little kid eating a hamburger. "There really wasn't any inspiration behind it. I wanted to take a minute to work on people and faces."

Although there are times when I like doing pan dulce and giraffes and graffiti words, I see most of my work, and what I really want to do, as this sort of realism meets street art and the twenty-first century. Like a Shepard Fairey except less political and less afraid of using actual skin tones, as much as I appreciate the pop art reds and blues. So, I make sure to keep practicing that whenever I have time and no other ideas.

"This just seems so . . . generic."

I don't know. I could put an Astros hat on the kid and make the background match whatever their colors are, and I bet Houston would be paying some big bills for this near their baseball park. He calls it generic. I think of it as having mass appeal.

"Why isn't this boy Mexican?"

"Who says he's not?"

"He looks pretty white to me."

"There are white Mexicans, Professor."

He gives me that *I'm over your bullshit* face Mami does a lot. "This doesn't *feel* like an *Ander* Martínez work."

I cringe when he says the *An* part of my name like *ant*.

"It's pronounced like *On-der*." I've had to tell him this I don't know how many times already.

He just ignores me and goes on. "I think it's important to recognize your strengths and think about the opportunities that could be most beneficial for you. Did you consider at all my suggestion of studying and reinterpreting classical Mexican muralism?"

"I don't have an interest in Mexican muralism."

"But you're a Mexican muralist. Look, all I'm saying is that I'm here to help you be the best you. A white child eating a hamburger isn't you. You're more . . . a Mexican child eating a tamale."

If my camera and microphone weren't both on right now, I'd

scream and flick him off. And the only reason I'm not calling him every cussword I know in both languages is because I still care a little bit about our relationship and care even more about not fucking up my college career before it actually starts. Like, it is physically hurting my chest holding in the yell. I think my eyes might be watering from restraining myself so hard.

"Anyways, I have to get to class. Think about this conversation, and I look forward to seeing what you bring me in a few weeks."

He doesn't wait for me to say bye. Not that I want to, but in those first few months, I thought it was weird he doesn't even do a sign-off on his emails before realizing it was just his thing.

I get up from my desk, throw myself onto my bed, and finally let out that scream into my pillows. As mad as I am at him, I'm madder at me and knowing that I'm about to think way too much about everything he said and how that's tied to what's expected of me. How I can't just practice; even the stuff that's meant to stay in my iPad and is only for me gets critiqued, and not even for something actually technical. How one school didn't even want me because I'm a "Mexican muralist" but then this school is tying me down, and not even to a specific style of art but to a topic and subject. When he says he wants to bring up my strengths, it's a lie. I mean, *he* probably believes it. Thinks he's doing something great by telling me to focus on Mexican artists and modernize what they did. Nah. He wants to make sure I know my limitations and where my lane is. I can't please anyone.

I need some air.

I change into a pair of chinos, grab a jacket, and head downstairs. My mind is a million places at once as I drive to Lupe's, but instead of going inside, I park and start walking down San Martín Street. I see a mural I did and then another. I see the other shops along the road, naming the owner of each one in my head and thinking about how I've grown up with them coming into my family's taquería, some afternoons buying tacos for their staff or some late mornings sitting with Tita and having coffee.

As I look around and take it all in, I know for certain that I don't hate the art I do. I like it a lot. And I don't hate Mexican muralism, I just wish that people thought I could be interested in anything else. I can be a Mexican muralist and not be obsessed with Diego Rivera. And I wish that my art could be something I do without having to worry about what people think, or because *I* think it's cool and great instead of because this is the box I'm being put in.

But also, if I wanted to do something else, why does the first reaction have to be *Why?*

Maybe I want to do something wildly colorful like geometric art or pop art. Maybe I want to do things with a message like Banksy. Maybe I want to stick with what I'm doing. Either way, I should be allowed to do any of those.

And I should be allowed to do what I want any way I want. I hate that sometimes Mexican artists can be problematic with their queerphobia, like some of the hate I got about doing the Sylvia Rivera mural or just about a church hiring a queer person like me to paint on their building. I hate that queer artists can be high-key racist and there are a lot of spaces for us I'd never feel welcome and it'd basically be me trying to conform to what the white gays want or get pushed out, like when my gay college advisor tells me to paint more tamales but has never had one discussion with me about the gay artists who've inspired me. I hate that this thing that I do for anyone and everyone to see sometimes feels incredibly lonely. And I hate this feeling that stays in my mind and my stomach that if I don't go into SAIC with the most amount of confidence in what my art is and what I'm doing, I'm not going to last. They'll find some other brown kid who fits the mold better.

I hate that sometimes liking the art I do seems like I'm settling for what people expect me to be doing. That they get in my head and make me overanalyze every idea I have and make me ask myself, *Is it because I want to paint this, or is it because I'm supposed to only want to paint this?*

You're being hard on yourself, I can imagine Zeke telling me right now.

Well, life is hard.

9

Hey I'm dragging you outta your house be there in ten.

I send Zeke one of those upside-down emoji faces and a brown thumbs-up before slowly starting to lean to the side of my desk chair. Feeling my ass gradually having a harder time keeping my body seated. Until finally—*thump*.

I'm lying on the laminate wood flooring of my bedroom. The skin of my back cold against it. My hands cover my face as I let out a subdued yell.

Zeke's pretty used to this by now. Knows that, if he hasn't heard from me in more than forty-eight hours, it's rescue-AJ-from-themself hours. Force me to do *anything* that gets me away from my thoughts about my upcoming projects and the talk with my advisor that keeps playing in my head while I think of comebacks way after the fact and things I wish I'd said. That gets me away from my sketchbook, Copic markers cluttering my desk space, and tablet that's being used for porn more than Procreate, now that I have little to no work and too much free time. Finally, a reason to get out of my house for the first time in—actually, I'm not even sure how long I've been hermitting here.

Yeah, I need to leave. Now.

Luckily I don't have to dig too deep into a laundry basket full of clean clothes I haven't put away yet before finding a pair of shorts and a long-sleeve shirt I thrifted and turned into a crop top. A faded purple with COLORADO ROCKIES in bold white on the front. It's one of those weird February days where springtime puts *just the tip* in Texas before pulling out and letting winter keep rearranging our guts for a few more weeks.

I'll take it. I'm not complaining. Spring Slut is my ideal style aesthetic. And 'tis the season. Even if temporarily.

I wipe off the **202** written on my mirror under **days left until saic** in chalk marker and replace it with a **201** before getting a couple selfies for Twitter.

"I'll be with Zeke if y'all need me," I holler out to Pa as I rush downstairs and out the front door. Chachi throws up a piece sign from the couch without looking back. Way into whatever episode of whatever anime she's currently bingeing.

"Gets fired once and goes into hiding," Zeke says immediately after I get into the car. Not even letting me get my seat belt on before dragging me.

"I fucking hate you. You know I wasn't fired."

"Same thing. How many days has it been since you left your room, *Miguel Ángel*?"

"Don't worry about it," I reply while adjusting the seat so it reclines a little. "You know how sometimes I get into a mode. It's my methodology."

"Yeah, and then you turn into motherfucking Gollum," Zeke adds. "Calling your Copics 'my precious' and shit."

"Shut up," I groan as I push his shoulder. "The artistic process isn't always glamorous. Even if the artist is."

"And how much time has actually been spent working?"

"*What?* All—well, a lot of it. Most of it. I'm not really used to doing anime-style art, so learning how to do that's been a whole moment. And when I'm not working on that, I'm trying to figure out this tile idea I have for the inside of Lupe's."

"Would've thought you'd take the first couple of days having the house basically to yourself to turn it into a revolving door of guys."

"*Not even, pendejo.* You know that's not me."

"True, true. You're more puta in theory than puta in practice."

I give him a glare but can't hide the little smile forming at the corner of my mouth. As much as my style might say otherwise (and my family has a *lot* to say about how I dress), Zeke's right. If anyone's the puta in this car, it's him. A tease? Sure. I'll claim that. ¿Puta? Not really.

At least, like he said, not so much in practice. Especially when I've only ever had two guys in my bed and one of them is sitting next to me. Even the other one wasn't some fling. We'd talked for a few weeks, were dating, and he was someone I really liked. Other than that, sure, making out and a little under the shirt or over the pants with a guy I met an hour ago at some house party, but that's not the same. And I'm cool with that for now.

"Being puta en mí corazón is a very valid form of putería," I tell him. "At least, until I meet a guy who I can be a puta for."

"You should make a mural that says *Soy puta en mi corazón*."

"*Te odio.*" I don't need him knowing I think that's actually a really good idea.

I only half listen to Zeke talk about everything that's happened at Lupe's, and how different it is without me. He's too focused on the road to notice me on the phone for most of the ride. Giving more attention to guys flirting in the comments on my selfies post. However, when "Como un Bebé" comes on, I ignore them so Zeke and I can get our lives to some Bad Bunny and J Balvin.

He parks in front of the restaurant, waiting for "La Canción" to finish before turning his car off. "Food first, and then we're gonna get into this blessed-ass weather and go over to my aunt's. She cleaned out her pool, so we'll get some sun, and then by the time it gets dark, it'll be cool enough to hang out in the hot tub."

"As interested as I am in seeing you shirtless with this cute little pancita, I didn't bring trunks. You should've told me before I left the house."

"First, you're gonna have to get in line, amigue. Second, you had, like, at least three pairs of shorts at my place. I brought them with me. You're good, AJ. And you need some sun. Staying inside and getting all vitamin D deficient isn't a good look on you."

"I feel like you're fishing for some sort of dick joke with that, and I'm *not* gonna give you that satisfaction."

I follow Zeke into Lupe's. Mami waves from the counter, breaking her conversation with a customer for only a second and then going right back to it. I point to the side of the door going out onto the patio, so she knows where to find us.

It's a busy afternoon. All the families in Santos Vista must've come straight to Lupe's for lunch after Mass. Even outside, most of the tables are taken up with people who also wanted to enjoy our first not-cold day in months, filling the patio with the noise of all their conversations and kids running around, nearly drowning out the music.

"Any ideas what you're gonna do with that space?" Zeke asks, pointing with his head to one of my walls.

"Not a fucking clue," I tell him, attention back to my phone screen. "I did this Jarritos-bottles-in-Pride-flag-colors thing a while back but never ended up using it. If no other ideas come to me, I'll stick that on there."

"Mexicans do love our Jarritos."

"Hey," I start, picking my head up. "Back to the topic of the pool. Does your cousin still live with your aunt? Because, swear, last time we were all hanging out, he was giving me major undressing-me-with-his-eyes eyes. And I'm not above walking around wet, shirtless, and in two-inch swim shorts for attention."

"He moved to Houston last month."

"*Ay, la verga.* I can never have any—"

"Buenos días." The voice comes out of nowhere. Like this guy Nightcrawler'd his way from the kitchen to our table outside. Pretty sure I jumped.

Even more sure I jumped when he starts apologizing and Zeke is hiding his mouth behind his hands but unable to also hide his shoulders spasming from laughter.

"It's okay, I—" I start to say as I look up at his face and both of us make the connection at the same time.

Santiago.

Oh my god. *He's* my replacement.

Not that he wasn't cute before, but he's a lot cuter without the plain oversized hoodie. Instead he's got on the familiar TAQUERÍA GUADALUPE tee, gray with navy lettering, under a navy corduroy long-sleeve shirt. Faded army-green-colored denims. The strong eyebrows and an adorable, nervous smile I'm now seeing for the third time. Also, yeah, now that I'm hearing it again, the accent definitely gives me more paisano than Westside. And he seems a little beat up by the crowd, exhaustion showing on his face. But also, his eyes are not being stealthy about how they're going from the exposed part of my stomach to my legs. I might not be a puta in practice, but I'd let him hit it. Respectfully.

Why does Tita have him here on a weekend? Sunday is our—*their*—busiest day by far. Usually it's a few weeks before she has someone come in for the after-church crowd. Did someone not show up for their shift?

Bet they regret firing me now.

Both of us jump this time when Zeke does this ugly cough to get our attention.

"I, uh—¿Para tomar?" he asks.

"I—Sweet tea, porfa."

"Big Red for me," Zeke adds with an even bigger smile, taking the menus. "Thanks." He sucks in his laugh as this new waiter leaves.

"I swear to God, if you say anything—"

"*Ba-bo-se*," Zeke interrupts, drawing the word out slowly in a tease. "Both of y'all."

"That's not even true."

"You're fucking hilarious, AJ."

"*Stop.*"

"Couldn't stop staring at the guy for a minute. When he asked what you wanted to drink, bet you were about to say—"

"*Stop.* It's only because I realized he's the same guy that was waiting for Tita and Mami that one day."

"Oh, no way? Still, you were thirsting. *Hard.* Should I ask if he's single? I'm sure we'll work a shift together at some point. Figure out his type. Although, the way he was looking at you too—"

"I'm going to break this chair over your head if you—"

"Sorry," Santiago says, placing the drinks down along with chips and salsa. "Ready to order?"

"¿Listos, Ander?" Zeke asks, and then turns his head to Santiago, giving us a smirk. Barely holding it all together. "I'm pretty sure they've got a good idea of what they want."

"I want you to go to hell."

"Don't know if they—uh, I'm not seeing it on the menu, AJ. Not sure if they serve that here," he answers playfully.

Santiago's lips twitch like he almost let out a laugh, and *José Clemente fucking Orozco*, he's got a dimple. I didn't notice that before. Why the fuck is that even something people find attractive? Why am *I* people?

"Two chicken fajita tacos," I tell him. "On corn tortillas."

"And I'll have the gorditas de pastor."

"Bueno. I'll be back in a few minutes." He puts his pen and server pad into his waist apron and takes the tray he used to bring our drinks and chips, carrying it under an arm.

And then, in what had to only last a second or maybe three, he takes one more glance at me. His eyes take in all the skin that my clothes aren't covering. Long enough for me to notice, but this time not enough for Zeke, busy chugging his Big Red, to think anything of it.

And right before he walks away, he smiles. It's not, like, covering half his face or anything, but it's more than what he's given me before. One of those real, authentic smiles that radiate curiosity, and with the dimple added, I'm about to—

"Okay, but besides that time you let him into la jefa's office by himself, we don't know him, right?" Zeke asks once Santiago is out of earshot. He reaches for a chip and dunks it into the salsa. "Like, he didn't go to Santos Vista and we just never acknowledged him?"

"No. No way." I would've definitely remembered him. Acknowledged him. Did many, many consensually unspeakable things to him. "I mean, I saw him when he came by for his interview too, but he's not from the neighborhood. He might've gone to Jefferson or Lanier? Or could be from out of town and is a freshman at Our Lady of the Lake or something. Did you hear the accent? Could be from somewhere near the border."

Now that it seems like he's going to be around, I'll be needing *all* the details. And, thankfully, I'm related to the two women who'd be able to give me all the chisme about this guy.

saw my replacement today."

"You see her every day, mi'je. She's right there," Mami replies with an evil-ass grin across her face while she points to Chachi coming out of the kitchen.

"When I never come back home, I want you to remember this moment."

"Cállate. ¿A quién viste?" Her face is blank, mouthing words I can't understand or follow. "*Oh*. You're talking about Santiago. El chulito."

"*Yes!*" The word comes out with way too much excitement.

Mami eyes me. One half of her face showing concern, the other, judgment. "*Okay,*" she says in a way that acknowledges she isn't seeing any importance to this conversation. It's not like we ever spend time talking about specific people on staff unless it's her complaining about someone. And even then, she usually keeps it between herself, Pa, and Tita. "He do okay?"

"Mm-hm. He's fine. Not, like, *in that way*, but—you know what I mean. I could kind of tell he was new. Still getting used to it all."

"Well, *he is* still getting used to it. I'd be more concerned if he was comfortable out there on a first day. On a *Sunday*. A little nervousness is good. Means he wants to do good."

"Yeah. True," I tell her, rocking myself back and forth on the balls of my feet.

She takes a drink of tea, staring at me while the cup goes to her mouth and then back to the table. "Is that all?"

"I—No. Uh, I know that you are, for reasons I don't understand at all, very against me working at the taquería. *But* I was actually thinking that, like, if *you* think it might be a good idea for him to, I don't know, get shown the ropes on a weekday when it's not as busy, I wouldn't mind. To help out."

She keeps her eyes on me. Her face becoming more and more curious. Which is never something I want when it comes to Mami. "What? Why? You've never in your life volunteered to do *more* work at the restaurant."

"Yeah, but I never complained about getting more hours. *You said that*. I'm trying to be a good child."

"*Hah*," she scoffs. "Okay." Her head goes down to her dinner and then right back up in a hasty motion. "Wait. Don't—*Ander Justino Martínez*."

"*What?!*"

"Estás diciendo que solamente quieres ser un hi'je más bien. But something tells me different. Intentas ser una boca."

"Are you actually slut-shaming me?"

Mami side-eyes me so hard, I'm pretty sure they actually went all 360 degrees around. "Don't say that word. I know how this works. You're your mami's child. When I first saw your papito, I—"

"I'm throwing myself out a window if you don't stop talking."

"Cállate. I'm being serious. You're not subtle. I see in your eyes the interest. How you get when you've got your coño locked on someone. *Not him*. Okay?"

"Why not? Not that I've 'got my coño locked on him' or I'm

trying to do anything with him at all or whatever it is you're accusing me of. I—Why?"

"He's an employee."

"So was Zeke. And Sergio."

"I'd already known Zeke for years. And Sergio was only there for two weeks."

"It was a good two weeks."

"*Cochine.*" She takes a liga from her wrist and busies herself with her hair, pulling it back and tying it into a chongo. "He—No. *No.* I don't want to get into this with you."

"Fine. All right. I was only wanting to help you out. I promise."

"Pues, thank you for your concern, but we got it. *I* promise. If you want to help me out, go find more places to paint. Go do things that make you happy and will look good for the career that you want."

"Uh—" I start before stopping myself. Don't want to push it. "Yeah. You're right. I'm going to bed."

Mami's not giving me anything on Santiago, I text Zeke while running up the stairs to my room, nearly tripping on a few. Ignoring Mami's "¡Cuídate, pendejite!"

You find his Instagram yet?

Haven't started stalking but thanks for the reminder.

When I get to my room, I close my door with a little more force than I meant to. I hop onto my bed, tap the Instagram icon on the top row of my phone, and then—lie here. Mind blank. Unsure of what to do next.

It's not like I'm going to type *Santiago* into the search bar, and he'll be the first person to come up. Am I really the kind of person who'd type a first name that, while not incredibly common, isn't super rare either and start clicking on profiles one at a time until I *maybe* find his? Is that what I've become?

Yes and yes.

Surprise. Nothing. No *this specific Santiago*.

I should've figured out a way to get Mami to say his last name. I can't go back now and ask. That's only going to validate her (accurate) assumption about me—and maybe also my coño—when it comes to Santiago.

I can ask Tita. Should've started with her. Abuelas always give their grandkids what we want.

Wait, no. It's ten o'clock. She's been asleep for three hours now.

Santiago's face comes to mind. His arms that were covered by the sleeves of his shirt, and his hands and fingers. His eyes that were still, obviously, tired, but had this gleam that went with his smile. How good he managed to look in something so basic. The styled rips in his pants that showed skin through the frays that I kept going back to when he would talk to Zeke and I had a couple seconds to let my eyes wander where they wanted.

I roll over to the corner of my bed and grab my iPad and Pencil from the floor. And then back onto my stomach, making myself comfortable. I open Procreate and let my hand take control.

Thinking about him as I draw every feature that, after seeing him now three times, I've got pretty committed to memory. The smile. The dimple. The slight roundness of his chin but sharpness of his jawline. Fill in the eyebrows. Get the exact brown of his body.

And then he's here. In front of me. Just as I remember him.

My eyes glue themselves to the portrait until they're too heavy to keep open. Tapping and re-tapping until my eyes are straining and my fingers are too tired to keep the screen from going black.

––––––––––––

"What? How did you––" I start while frantically grabbing for Zeke's phone. "I spent like, a serial-killer-level amount of time digging through all the apps last night. *Even Facebook.* And I found *nothing.*"

"Then I guess you'd make a shitty serial killer," he replies, letting his phone fall into my hand. "Also, I have that cousin, you know the one, she's about to go to UT and who's, like, a professional IG lurker. I think she was the one who found out Lorde had that page where she ranks onion rings."

I'm ignoring any other words coming out of his mouth. Because there it is. There *he* is.

"You only tried *Santiago*, though, right?"

"Three extra letters make that much of a difference?"

"Obviously."

So he goes by Santi. Or, at least, on Instagram he does. His handle is @santi_ve, and Santi is also his display name, in a font that you'd have to generate off a website. I like that. Santiago sounds kind of old. Santi, though, that suits him.

There aren't a lot of pictures. It looks like he only started this profile about a year ago. Or maybe he had one of those self-reinventions and deleted everything before then. If so, I'm not crazy about the new aesthetic of selfies with only half of his face and in the weirdest angles.

Okay, I'm kind of lying. I can see the artistic value in it. And a part of me might think it's actually maybe incredibly cute. Sue me. I'm an art student. I'm supposed to be able to find appreciation for that sort of stuff. It––

I let out a long, annoyed groan and show Zeke the screen with a picture of the right half of Santi's face in front of something bright pink and light brown. "Remember how I told you I saw him when he came by for his interview? Right before that, he was taking this selfie at my concha mural. The guy who had no idea how to properly take pictures with art."

"Does that kill his chances?"

"I never said anything about him having a chance."

"He does, though. You obviously like him, AJ."

"He—shut up. It's annoying, but not the biggest red flag. I can teach him how to not take such fucked-up pictures of art."

"So, I should definitely ask him if he's interested in you when we're working the same shift tomorrow night, right?"

"*No!* Zeke, you better not fucking embarrass me. I swear to God, I will get Tita to fire you so quick."

"I'd bet a week's worth of tips he's into you."

"How are you getting that?! We spoke to him for all of five minutes if you take all the interactions and put them together. And most of those were him asking if we needed a refill."

"Which means he'd be an attentive lover. Also because I have eyes. It's so obvious, AJ."

"That is a *huge* reach. He probably doesn't want to get involved with the boss's grandkid."

"You don't know that. You wanna be puta for him, and you can't say that's not true."

"*Can you stop?*"

I want him to quit talking. Let me process this for a second. Obsess over his pictures in peace. The one of him on a swing at what looks like Castro Park. And another of him in a backyard, maybe? Or the woods. Not entirely sure. And then—

"He's been to my *Como la Flor* wall too."

"What?"

"Another mural. Keep up, Zeke."

"Oh, then see? I can be like, Hey? You like art? You like

Selena and pan dulce? Oh yeah, that art, I know it. I actually know the artist. You kinda do too, but lemme introduce you. And then, boom. You're lying on the center console of your car while he—"

"'While he' nothing. I was only trying to point this out. Not have you go into whatever that was."

"You said I owed you after coming in between y'all last time. Just showing you how I can bring my wingman charm to this whole situation."

"You don't have any 'wingman charm.' So, no. Please don't."

11

H m?" I mumble sleepily, holding my phone to my ear, my face still buried into my pillow.

"Bebite," Tita's voice calls. "You're not up yet? It's eight thirty."

"Then I've got an hour and a half before my alarm goes off."

"Ay, qué huevón. Escúchame, your mami said you wanted to help out Santiago?"

"Wha—" I almost throw my entire body off my bed trying to sit up so quickly. I knew that mexicana Aquarius wouldn't be able to go more than a few days without telling fellow mexicana Aquarius and Queen of the Metiches that is my tita about our Santi conversation. Bet she was actually talking shit about me and wasn't in any way seriously suggesting letting me work after they decided to let me go.

God, I love Tita.

"I, uh—I mean, if you think it'd help. It didn't seem like Mami was into the idea."

"Yo sé. Well, Ander, she's not the boss right now and Ezekiel called me a few minutes ago, saying he's caught a bug, pobrecito."

"He *what*?"

I don't believe that. We hung out all day yesterday. I go to his Instagram; he's got a video on his Stories from not even an hour ago at his university's cafeteria eating waffles. Zeke isn't sick. He's fine. He—

Oh. *Oh*. He's good. Fuck him.

"Can you come in around seven tonight? I'll have you and Santi outside for the evening shift."

"Yeah, I can do that, Tita."

"Bueno. I'll see you—Well, no. *I* won't see you. Your mami will see you later, then."

"Does she know you're calling me right now?"

"No."

If only Tita could see me wiping my hand over my face. She definitely hears the big groan-sigh I let out. "She's going to love seeing me there."

"Not as much as *I* love *you*, bebite."

"You're not gonna say anything about how I'll be the one handling however she takes this?"

"That was the plan," Tita responds without any regret in her voice. "Seven o'clock."

"Seven o'clock," I say back through a tired yawn. "Love you, Tita. Bye."

I get to Zeke's and my text thread, ready to type something like **you whore** or **I hate you more than anyone else who has ever existed**, but nothing comes out. Not even a less betrayed **what were you thinking?** or **why didn't you tell me you had this plan in your head?** or even a **thank you, you fucking devil**.

Whatever. I still have an hour and nineteen minutes before my alarm goes off. I can bury myself under my blanket and—

Wait. My eyes go to my carefully coordinated closet, staring at the line of shirts hanging and arranged by color, then sleeve length, and then whether it's a crop, tee, button-up, or hoodie.

What do I wear?

Actually, hold up. It's work. There's only one option. But also, no there isn't. We'll be outside. I can choose between a TAQUERÍA

GUADALUPE sweater or a long-sleeve or even a short-sleeve layered look like Santi did. And then do I wear my blue one? Pink? Yellow? Green? That weird sand-eggshell color Tita must have found on page eighty-seven of the Google Shopping results? And what pants do I wear with it? Fuck this weather for it being too cold at night to wear thotty shorts.

Wait. Again.

Why am I thinking about this now when I have one, two— like, ten hours until I need to be at work? I'm really putting all my mental energy into this when I could be back to dreaming about my future exhibit at the Met.

Is it because some part of me thinks it's either I will go to Lupe's as the *catchiest* of catches in work attire—so much so that Santi will immediately desire me like Tita desires Kawhi Leonard—or I don't bother showing up at all?

Yes. That's exactly my thought process.

Pink long sleeve won.

It's, like, a pastel-y pink, so definitely not overly aggressive. And with my black skinny jeans, torn at the knees, it's a complete vibe. Paired with white sneakers and a white bandana, and my hair looking like it's waiting for someone's son to come mess it up. A perfect in-between of well thought out and *Oh, this? I just threw it on*. A triple threat: something that will get a boy's attention, get me a compliment, and a DM later tonight asking "You up?"

I could literally drive to work with my eyes closed. This same route that has become part of my almost daily life since I was born. Even before then as little embryo Ander or whatever other names went through Mami's head before she let Pa go with a name inspired by the main character of his favorite movies, The Matrix Trilogy.

So glad she didn't let him go with Neo. I do *not* look like a Neo. Ander, I can live with. Neo? I would've had to change that.

I could let my subconscious tell my hands where to turn left or right and my feet when to break and hit the gas. I've memorized the bus schedules well enough to know that if I'm running a few minutes behind, I'll be even more stressed because the 113 going into Downtown from the Southwest side will *always* end up in front of me when I'm not perfectly timely. When the train usually comes through the neighborhood. And what time the main roads are most likely to be busy. It's predictable. Regular. Never takes any thought.

Except for tonight. The one time I should've been thinking.

Because when I'm supposed to take a left and turn onto Casiano from Apache like I do every single day, I instead do the quickest of a glance to my right toward a familiar, work-uniform-looking, light-blue long sleeve and see Santi standing at the corner, waiting to cross. Why that surprises me so much that he takes all my attention away from the road, I don't know, but my hands try to turn anyways while my eyes are still on him, which is definitely something I was explicitly told not to do in my driver's permit course. My head snaps back forward when I hear honking from an oncoming car and my reflexes and will to live take over, swerving back to the right and out of its way just before barely missing it, my tires making that *skrrrt* sound as I try to keep some control on the wheel, and miss my turn. Screaming the entire time.

My car screeches when I turn into the lot of an abandoned warehouse at the intersection, braking and letting my brain process. *Am I adrenaline crying?* No. Okay. Good. I *am* breathing like I've been sprinting through the neighborhood, and my hands are glued to the wheel, unable to move at all even though I need to turn off my car or, like, I don't know, *something. Anything.*

Make a fucking decision, Ander.

But, hey. At least I'm not crying.

I notice someone waving at me. No, not someone. Santi. It's one of those slow, awkward, *How many fingers am I holding up, sir?* kind of waves. Not a thrilled-to-see-me, *what a coincidence* wave.

I force a smile and enough strength to pull a hand away from the wheel while he comes over and press down on the small button that slowly lowers the passenger-side window.

"Hey. ¿Estás bien?" Santi asks, lowering himself a little to look into my car. "Do you wanna step out for a second? Standing might help get the—¿cómo se dice?—jitters out."

This is so embarrassing. What did I do to deserve this? Why couldn't it have been anyone else besides him?

"I, yeah. Sure," I manage. Hoping that he doesn't notice my hands shaking a little while I turn off the car, unbuckle myself, and open the door.

Standing next to him, I can't help but stare for what is definitely a way-too-long amount of time. Seeing him this close, just the two of us, I get to take in the details. The faint shadows of hair on his upper lip and chin. The few fading scars going up the outside of his left arm that are only visible because his sleeves are pushed up to his elbows. His eyes that seem more awake than the previous two times I saw him. (Maybe he got a nap in. Or could be because he almost saw me die.) And the way his eyes are glued to me, and his mouth keeps trying to say something that's not quite ready to come out.

"You sure you're okay?" he finally asks.

"I—Yes. Sorry." Each word is like a golf ball that requires the most amount of force to say. I lean back against my car, my hands gripping on to the bottom part of where the window would be if it was up, and take a deep breath. "Just had a . . . thing."

"Casi chocas," he replies matter-of-factly. Like, we both know it wasn't *just a thing*.

"But I *didn't* crash. Only almost."

Now he stares at me. Like he's trying to decide whether he should listen to the majority of his brain that's telling him I'm a danger to society. That's what his eyes are telling me.

I need to de-clusterfuck this situation.

I swallow the bile and whatever remaining shock is left, putting on the most encouraging *please believe me* smile I can manage.

"I'm good, I promise. You—Were you walking?" I ask. I can turn this scenario on him and force us past the last few minutes. Pretend they never happened. "Do you need a ride? We're going to the same place, and, I mean, it'd be kind of shitty for me to let you walk when you're right here."

Santi's eyes stay staring. More, calculating. Asking himself if he wants to get into the car with someone who almost got into a wreck.

"I swear I'm a better driver than this," I add in this tempered yell. "I've never gotten into a wreck. Drive like an abuelo. Seriously. And you can pick the music if you want. We're both here, might as well, right?"

His stoic face turns into a smile. A familiar one. A mixture of the smile he had from Zeke teasing me and when we had our little shared-glimpse moment. And I know that this situation has been de-clusterfucked.

And I realize again how close we are. Even closer now. One of us or both of us have slowly scooted more and more toward the other until we're only maybe two inches apart. How I'm so close to texting Mami that I won't be making it to work and I heard from *someone* that Santi won't either, and then pull him those last two inches and all of a sudden we're making out against my car in this abandoned parking lot.

"Promise you won't hit anything?"

"Do what?"

He laughs as his head turns toward the street. "I said, promise you won't hit anything?"

"Oh. Yeah. Promise."

That smirk comes back, and he shakes his head a little bit. As if half of him can't believe he's about to get in the car with me. "I'll take your word for it," he says before starting for the other side of the car. "Santiago, by the way. In case you forgot. Or Santi."

"I didn't." Is it weird that I didn't? The way he's sort of beaming right now is saying that he's happy about it. As long as I don't tell him about the Instagram stalking, we've got nothing to worry about.

"I'm Ander. Or AJ."

"I remember."

"Oh. Cool."

Santi remembers me. No big deal. Not at all feeling like the most important person in the world right now for the least important reason ever. And now we're both beaming.

"I'd only seen you in small moments. Thought I might've been imagining you."

Wait. Has he been thinking about me? Has he been wondering where I've been and whether he'd see me every day for the past couple of weeks since we first saw each other at Lupe's?

"Working there a lot less now. Like, usually-zero-hours-a-week less."

"Oh." The word drops in tone. The way people say things that disappoint them. Right? He's sad about this?

"Not because I got fired, though." *Smooth way to continue this conversation, Ander.*

"I wasn't thinking that."

"Oh. Right. Yeah."

When we get settled inside, Santi's hand, for whatever reason, from actually deciding with his whole chest this is what he's going to do or out of habit, falls onto the center console, right next to mine. Just enough for our pinkies to be touching. And the feeling of it is like an electric spark shooting through my entire body.

Some force out in the universe is shitting on my life. I had all the ingredients to go into work acting like, *Oh—hey, Santi. Yeah, I work here, remember? Wow, it's slow tonight, maybe I could, like—totally throwing out ideas right now—show you what the back of the building looks like and you could press me up against the wall and we could make out until we pass out from oxygen deprivation.* And instead, I make a fool out of myself while also being a general danger to society in front of the person I wanted to not seem like either in front of, and now he's in my car.

And his pinkie is touching my pinkie. Which, much like the fucking dimple, I didn't ever think I was a person who got moist for this sort of thing, but, well—

I'm going to crash.

12

I't's uncomfortably quiet in my car.

I forgot that I told Santi he could pick the music. He must have too because he hasn't said anything. And now that I'm driving with one hand on the wheel and the other in the middle of this moment of minimal contact happening between us, I'm not about to reach in my pocket for my phone. God herself would have to come down and rip our pinkies apart.

But without the music to distract me, I can hear even the smallest movement from Santi in his seat. I can feel his eyes when he looks at me and even more so that emptiness when he turns away, to his phone or toward the window. It's like my mind is going through some sort of mental overstimulation right now.

"¿Qué pasó?" Santi asks, ripping through the silence. His face turned back toward me after sending a text. "What had you distracted?"

You. You distracted me.

"I don't know. My mind must have gone somewhere else for a second."

"It's here now, though?"

"Mostly. But that's the usual."

"Hm." The sound comes out like a laugh. And then he maneuvers himself in his seat, his limbs all adjusting into a more comfortable position for talking. His hand moves too. Pushing even further into mine. His pinkie *and* ring finger now on top of mine.

What is he doing? This has to be some sort of flirting situation, right? He's flirting with me. He has to realize that we're basically holding hands. Okay, we're not, but *what is happening?*

"I—Never mind," he starts, and then cuts himself off.

"What?"

"I, uh . . . I was wondering if you had an extra bandana. I forgot to bring one with me."

That's not what you were about to say. I hold in a groan and those words, burying both with a sigh. Being a metiche isn't going to get me anywhere. Never mind? Okay, never mind.

"There's a bunch in the glove compartment," I tell him, tipping my head in the direction of his knees and the dashboard. He moves and *boom*, I'm immediately grieving for the fingers that were once making themselves comfortable on top of mine. Thankfully he's busy digging through the organized chaos that is more bandanas than anyone could ever need on top of papers, a couple pairs of sunglasses, and probably an expired condom at the bottom—otherwise, he would've seen how I stared at my hand, thinking back to happier times three seconds ago.

"You mind tying it back for me?" Santi asks when we get to the last stoplight, only a block away from Lupe's. The building visible from my car.

"Do you not know how to tie a knot?" I tease.

"Would you feel bad if I said I didn't?"

"I—Less than I probably should, but whatever. Sure. Turn a little bit."

"Here," he calls, holding on to both ends of a pink bandana that matches my shirt. Trying not to read into that decision.

"Tell me if it's too tight," I say while pulling and then beginning to knot the ends together.

"Nope. It's good." Santi turns back to me and adjusts the bandana, raising it up a little higher. Then he clasps his hands behind his head, face up and to the side, posing for me. "What do you think?"

"You look like you're ready for Fiesta," I say through a laugh. Glad that he somehow managed to turn what could've been a super-cringey car ride into, well, *this*. And even more glad that I didn't say what I was actually thinking.

You'd look better wearing only *the bandana*.

"I'll take it."

When we finally make it to Lupe's, I pull out my phone, and my heart legitimately stops beating seeing the five missed calls and two texts from Mami. Shit, what time is—*Oh my fuck*. Twenty minutes late. With Tita or Pa, this would be a stern glare and then a *Get to work, pendejite*. But with Mami, I—

"You coming?" Santi asks. I didn't even realize he'd already unbuckled himself, opened the door, and got out while I was sitting here wondering if there's a future where I'm not murdered by my own mother in the middle of a restaurant.

"Yeah, uh—" I rush out, slamming the door behind me. Although a lot of me says to get back in. That it's probably the safest place for me to be. Mami won't smash my car window to get to me. Probably.

We walk in together, and Mami's head goes back, as if this was the last thing she expected to see right now.

"I was about to tell your tita that you were gonna be a no-call no-show tonight."

"Sorry, I—"

"Tita?" Santi asks, going back and forth between Mami and

me. Very slowly connecting what I thought were extremely obvious dots.

"Abuelita. That's my mom," I tell him, nudging my chin forward. "The big boss is my abuela."

"*Oh*. That—that makes sense. With the key and everything."
I can see a spark in his eye igniting as his mouth twitches. "So,
wait. You're the artist."

"Yep. That's me." Praying that he found that information out
from someone in my family and not Zeke trying to play matchmaker.

"*Cool*. So then you—"

Mami clears her throat to get our attention back, her face
tilted, mentally asking both of us what we're doing wasting
her time like this. And then her pointer finger does this left-to-
right between Santi and me. "What is this? What's happening?
What's going on? Why are you two exactly the same amount of
late to work?"

"I rode him." The words come out without thought but
sounding like I deliberately chose them. And seeing Santi and
Mami look at me with two drastically different faces but both
exuding so much surprise makes me want to fly to Chicago right
now and never come back.

"I gave him a ride," I rush to correct. "I gave him a ride.
With my car." The words coming out purposefully stressed.

"He gave me a ride," Santi repeats.

"*I get that*," Mami replies in a quick, cut-y'all's-shit tone of
voice. "Good. Or—I mean. Dio' mío. Santa María ruega por mí.
Okay. We've got a party in the patio tonight. Some author who
had a book come out today, I don't know. He writes about basketball or movies or music or something. No importa. Santi, I
have you covering about two-thirds of the crowd. Ander will

take the other third and help out Ronnie when he needs it, and all of us will be around if you need help, okay?"

"Sí."

"Perfecto. Pues, ándale. We've got about ten minutes before they start showing up. It's gonna be a long night."

If I'm being honest, Santi doesn't need the help. Sure, it's probably nice to have extra sets of hands to bring plates filled with tacos, bowls of chopped onion and cilantro, baskets on baskets of chips, queso and guacamole, y todo. But he's actually quick as fuck on his feet, attentive as hell, and so sociable. I think the writer throwing this thing might've invited him to his after-party.

But that doesn't mean I'm mad at Tita for asking me to come in. For the opportunity to share glances, pretending we aren't looking at each other when one of us catches the other but unable to hide that guilty smile. Or whenever he stands right behind me without any sense of personal space, to ask a question when he has one. Like, *shit. I'd pay her.*

At around nine thirty, most of the party has stopped ordering food, good with the chips and salsas that we've been bringing by the bucket or leftover tacos on someone else's plate. Prime break-taking time. I sit on a barstool, leaning onto the counter, and first watch a couple guys ordering drinks from Ronnie, who hands me a Coke in between getting them their Bud Lights, then let my eyes go to Santi, who got dragged onto the dance floor by three little kids. He mimics their jumping and arm flails to the music of the band on the small stage we have set up. They're surrounded by men holding their wife's or girlfriend's side with one hand and their beer in the other as they move right foot, left foot, right foot on the open floor.

"AJ," Ronnie calls as he sets his arms down on the counter and leans in closer to me. "You've been staring all night."

I glare at Ronnie from the other side of the bar counter. "I'm not *staring*, pendejo." Although the way my heart rate immediately goes up when he says something might say different. "I'm making sure he's doing all right. You know, supervising."

"No. See, what you *think* you're doing is that. Observing. But there's a difference between being an observer and being a babose. You're doing the second one."

"No, I'm not."

"Kid, I know what I'm seeing. Don't worry, though, he's into you too."

I nearly choke on the Coke in my throat. The glass bottle makes a loud *thump* sound as it hits the bar counter.

"I didn't say I was into him."

"Zeke told me."

Reminder to self to end his life.

"Anyways, crush incoming."

"What—"

"Hey," Santi shouts as he throws himself up against the bar next to me. A smile beams across his face while he speaks. "This is a lot of fun."

"Yeah. I liked your little dance," I tease. Unable to concentrate on much else besides how if he took a step forward, he'd be standing in between my legs and how much I want that.

"I'll teach you if you want." He's obviously checking me out as he smiles and his eyes go from my torso to my face, complete with a quick moment of barely sucking his bottom lip in before gently biting it and then turning to Ronnie, asking for a Topo Chico.

That just happened. He did the smile and then turn. That move where a guy gives a second of attention and then dares

you to do something about it. *And* he added the lip bite. *The* lip
bite. Not that exaggerated version guys do to joke around. The
real one. The lemme-rail-you lip bite. It was so obvious. Does he
even know he did that? He had to. That shit takes practice to get
right—otherwise, you look like you're trying to get out a fart.

What the fuck?

"I, uh—" Any ability to form words after that are gone. My
brain's spending more energy trying to get back whatever cool
I can because the minute a guy gives me *that look*, I swear my
knees involuntarily buckle and I get the immediate urge to ask
him to spit in my mouth, please.

"You should take him up on that," Ronnie interrupts. "AJ
can't dance for shit."

"I can dance, ass."

"You should show me next time," Santi says. "And your
paintings too, artista."

"Actually, you've already seen a couple of them."

"¿Qué? ¿A dónde? ¿Están aquí?"

Shit. He doesn't know I've been on his Instagram. He doesn't
even know I know he has an Instagram. But, I mean, who *doesn't*
have an Instagram?

That's not important. I need to get myself out of this hole
I've dug. I—

"Ander! Santi!" Mami yells from the door into the restaurant. "Come get the dessert. It's almost ten."

Thank God for her.

"¡Ya voy!" I call back. Spinning myself around on the stool,
thinking, I've done this a million times since I've been alive. I'm
the Simone Biles of jumping from barstools. Of course I won't
make a fool out of myself even more tonight.

Wrong.

My life flashes before my eyes for a second time today as my body leaves the stool but my foot gets stuck on one of the little bars connecting the legs and I start falling to the concrete floor. Time seems to slow down so I get to take in every second of this horrible decision as the ground gets closer and closer.

But then I stop, midair. Limbs wrap around my stomach, catching me in time. Santi's limbs.

I almost take both of us down, but he's able to stabilize himself and then me. I'm sure that he can feel my heartbeat and the heavy rise of my lungs against his arms. Just like how I can feel how tightly he's got me. How closely he's pulled me to him. How I can feel his breath on the back of my neck.

This thing I'm doing, putting myself in danger to get him closer to me has got some *major* flaws, but there's an effectiveness to it that I'm really appreciating right now.

"Ey, cut him off!" some *actually drunk* man teases.

"I've asked you this a lot today, but, *again*, are you okay?" Santi's left a hand on the middle of my back, even after I've steadied myself.

So, no. My brain is about to turn into a mushroom cloud any second now.

But I need to brush that off. "Yeah, I'm good. And I swear I'm able to, like, human."

"If I tell you I believe you, promise not to run me over?"

I laugh and swat at his chest. We're flirting. Shit. Yeah, why did I never try this human-disaster method for getting either of my other boyfriends?

"No promises, but I'll try my best."

He smiles, dimples in full effect. And I'm realizing that I drew it a little off. I'll have to do it over. Or not. Probably a little weird to draw him *again*.

"Okay. ¿El pastel?"

"Yeah. Yes. Let's go."

13

A nder!"

"¿Qué, Mami?" I yell. The click-clacking of her heels gets louder as she walks through the main dining room over to the front where I'm at.

"Don't *qué* me like I'm one of your friends," she snaps from the counter. "I need to run. Pa is with Chachi at the emergency room."

"*What?*"

"They're fine. She tried to jump from the top of his truck and do a slam dunk into the basketball hoop. Didn't work. Doctors are saying she's a little concussed, maybe. We don't know. Might just be how she is, tú sabes. She has a thick head. She'll survive."

"That's *your* daughter."

"No te creo. But I need to go. Can you put the money up in the back? Don't worry about counting it, I'll have your pa do it when he opens in the morning. Get it all in the safe, put out the paperwork for him, all the regular stuff, and lock up. Por favor. But you need to have someone here with you, all right? It can be Ronnie, I don't care. No one is allowed to close the store by themselves. Especially you. And I already don't like leaving you here so late, pero tu hermana pendejita—"

"I don't mind staying," Santi says, holding onto a broom and on his way to the patio.

Mami stares at me and then starts muttering something I can't hear under her breath as she swipes at her phone. "Fine. Whatever. Text me when you get home if we're not back yet." She comes around to hug me goodbye and leans in close to my ear. "And when I say *you*, I mean, when we get home, there better be no other person in that house other than the one that came out of me."

"That is disgusting."

"Imagine being there. You weren't all lindite like you are now. Like a little slug monster."

I turn when I hear what sounds like someone holding in a cough, seeing Santi trying not to laugh from overhearing Mami call me a little slug monster. Which is great. Terrific. Exactly the image I want Santi to leave with tonight.

"Shouldn't you be checking on your daughter?"

"Probably," Mami says through a laugh, seeing the chaos she's created. She kisses my cheek on her way toward the door, power walking to her car. "Bye, love you, all that. See you later."

The whole process of closing the restaurant down is pretty simple. Help the kitchen clean and wash everything. Make sure all the food that needs to be ready for the breakfast crew in a few hours is organized as neatly as possible. Mop, sweep, lock up the outside bar, wipe down tables, stack chairs. Oh, and clean the bathrooms, which is always the manager's job. Mami, Pa, and Tita made sure I knew that just because they own the place doesn't mean any part of keeping it looking decent is beneath us. That being the boss doesn't mean we're exempt from cleaning toilets. It means we should be the *most invested* in making sure they stay clean. Doesn't make it less gross, but I guess they have a point.

"You sure you're fine staying?" I ask Santi while the rest

of the staff leaves. "I can get Ronnie to stick around if you're tired."

"I don't mind," he replies, leaning over the counter, half observing me start the process of closing the register.

"Okay. It won't take long. Promise."

"Is there anything else I should be doing?"

"No, don't think so. Everyone was pretty on it tonight. So, sorry if it's boring."

"I don't mind," he repeats as he hops onto the counter. "Doing nothing can be nice sometimes."

My eyes go from the register to Santi, sitting on the counter, half a foot from me. His back is facing me, and his eyes are concentrating on his phone. He's reading something. Didn't clock him for the reading type.

"Be right back," I tell him while taking out the till. "Don't go anywhere."

"Not without you."

"What?"

"I don't have the keys," he answers. As if my confusion is a little judgment worthy. "And la jefa said you can't be here alone. Why would I go?"

"Oh. Yeah. It was supposed to be—Never mind."

I know he was trying something. It wasn't some innocent, non-double-entendre-having "Not without you." It was like, *"Not without you."*

Or maybe I'm reading too much into it. Maybe that smile he gave me the first time we met was only a smile. And that our fingers touching was nothing more than fingers touching. And the way his eyes and lips were asking for it earlier were, I don't know, him checking how chapped his lips were.

Maybe Ronnie and Zeke are wrong about him liking me and

I believed them and tried to convince myself I see it too, because I'm estúpide. No, no *maybe*. I'm estúpide.

"Here," I tell Santi, handing him my unlocked phone, opened to Apple Music. "Put on some going-home tunes. And put your address into Google Maps."

"Oh." His hand is uneasy as it slowly starts reaching out for my phone. "You don't have to take me."

"I'm not gonna let you walk."

"I don't mind."

"It—I'm not comfortable with that. At all. I can call a Lyft if you're tired of me or something. Which is fine. But it's super late, and . . . I'm not about to defend this decision. So let me know what I'm doing."

Santi huffs out a loud sigh. The rise of his shoulders and his less-than-eager eyes half-visible in the yellow lights outside Lupe's. "CLUBZ okay?"

"You know CLUBZ?"

"Of course I do."

"CLUBZ is *always* okay."

Santi's body language is different on the drive to his house. Arms crossed. Head toward the side window. More tense than relaxed. *I get it, you don't like people doing you favors.*

He's going to have to get over that if he wants to work for my family.

But I can also tell that he's more tired than tense. His head falling a little and then back up, like he's fighting sleep.

"Do you drive?"

"I *can* drive. But I don't have a license."

"Oh," I reply softly. "Like, suspended?"

"What?" Santi looks at me with this curious almost glare. "No. Nothing like that."

"Sorry." The word comes out quickly and with a lot of em-barrassment. "I didn't mean to assume anything."

"It's okay. Don't worry about it."

We get stuck on Fernando Norte Road. If I had nudged the gas just a little more, I could've beaten the arms of the railroad crossing gate coming down. Maybe I'm still trying to be extra cautious with Santi in the car.

Or my subconscious knew I could get an extra five minutes with him.

"Better believe I'm taking you up on that invite to show you up in dancing," I tease, trying my best to keep up a conversation. My fingers nervously tapping on the steering wheel to the beat of "Ciclos."

"Hm," he laughs. "Estoy ansioso."

"I have a group that goes to the Main Strip sometimes. There's a club that does Latinx Night every Thursday. It's eighteen and up. And my friend Mo's uncle is the owner, so sometimes he's able to get us drinks."

"I, uh—" Santi starts. He clears his throat and shuffles in the seat. That tenseness in his body becoming even more obvious. "I don't have an ID."

"Oh. Okay." I want to get some clarification on that. Like, he doesn't have a license *or* an ID? He lost it? It expired? Actually, you know what? Not the night to press any more into questions that are crossing a line he's not ready for me to step over. "Well, my tita puts on some pretty cool kickbacks for the staff. Second Friday of every month. Gets a DJ, sometimes a band. How about then?"

Santi turns his head to me. His eyes neither here nor there. But the line of his mouth begins to form that slanted smile. "Yeah. Sounds fun."

"Cool. It's a date." My fingers go from tapping to clenching on the wheel when I realize what came out of my mouth, and I almost give myself whiplash twisting my face from him to the train slowly passing us by. "I mean, you know. It's a, like—"

"It's a date," he repeats.

I turn back to Santi, who's still looking at me. All of those features I drew only a foot away from me. And I smile back at his smile. Perfectly fine using up all the time in the world memorizing the exact brown of his skin and near black of his eyes that glow from the orange tint of the streetlights. The uneasiness in his face that's so different from earlier. That has my curiosity piqued, but again, line. Don't cross it. So I'll just keep shamelessly eyeing him as he does me.

Until a car starts honking and I realize the train has been long gone now.

"Shit. Sorry," I say as I press on the gas. "Let's, uh—let's get you home. Yeah?"

"Yeah," he tells me with a laugh. "Sure."

I end up on the southern corner of Santos Vista. Closer to Highway 90 than Downtown at this point. Pulling into the driveway of a house that's not too different from any other in the neighborhood. Wooden. Weathered blue paint. White rusted bars over the windows. Next door to a pink house that leaves its Christmas lights up all year and one of those Santa María shrines with the statue standing inside half a bathtub sticking up from the ground.

"I guess I'll see you around?"

"Yeah," Santi answers. "Thank you, again, for the ride. Not the one your mom thinks happened, but—"

"*Oh my god*, can we please forget that? I'm *begging*."

He lets out a cackle and reaches for the door handle. "We'll see. Maybe your family will give you more than zero hours again," Santi adds. "I liked working with you."

Can my heart stop but also be going a million beats a minute at the same time? Because that's what it feels like. "I—Yeah. I had a lot of fun tonight. But I'll be a pretty familiar face regardless."

"Sí. Porque tu familia."

"Yeah. Heir to a taquería dynasty."

He chuckles as he opens the door and sticks a leg out. "Cool. Buenas noches, Ander."

"Buenas noches, Santi."

At 4:37 a.m., I'm lying in bed. Freshly showered. Might've been in there twelve minutes longer than usual. Not important.

What *is* important is the notification waiting for me on my phone. @santi_ve is now following @ANDERpinta. Guess I'm not the only Instagram stalker now. There's another one a minute later, when Santi heart-reacted to the IG Story of us eating leftover cake behind the patio bar after the party ended.

Still uncertain about where I am in his head, but I can dream.

14

So, I need a favor.

I can't help but let out a long string of Spanish cusswords under my breath seeing Zeke's text.

Tita already told me. I got you. But this is what you get for trying to play mf matchmaker. And now I have to work twice as fast on this anime mural.

OKAY BUT IT WORKED AND YOU'RE GLAD YOU GOT TO WORK WITH HIM. DON'T LIE. Anyways, how's the painting going?

First, you're still a bitch, no matter how good last night was. And two, it's fine. This Japanese script they have me doing is a little tricky. Hoping I don't fuck up and make it an entirely different word.

Do you know what it means? Like, what the words translate to?

Not a clue. But the owners are Japanese, so I trust them. Anyways, I gotta go so I can make sure to finish it all by the end of today now that I'm covering for you.

Alright. Catch me up when I'm not a plague.

I won't say Zeke was asking for it, but the next morning, he has a 101 fever and is hugging his toilet like me the first night I found out what happens when I drink too much (or any) moonshine. All the signs of a flu. And needing to take a full week and a half off from school and work. Nine days of him quarantined to his room, chugging hot tea and caldo.

And six of those nine days, I'll be back at Lupe's, covering his shifts. Every single one of them with Santi. Breakfast shift on Thursday and Friday, closing on Sunday, lunch on Monday, opening on Tuesday, and closing it out with a final Wednesday breakfast shift.

So much for them letting me go.

Hey, I'm picking up a shift tomorrow so if you happen to also be working tomorrow morning and don't want to ride the bus or walk, lmk, I message to Santi over Instagram. Acting like Tita didn't text me his schedule because she can't say no to anything her grandchild wants.

You don't have to.

I realize that. I'm a nice person.

OK.

OK you want a ride or OK you agree I'm nice?

Both. See you at 5:45.

Fuck that's early.

When I pull up to his driveway in the morning, Santi's rushing out of his house with five other guys behind him, all heading to a truck waiting on the curb.

"Morning," he mutters sleepily while putting on his seat belt. Giving me a tired smile before leaning back against the headrest. Not even glancing at the men packing into what has to be an already full vehicle.

If it wasn't so early and if I had a mental headspace that isn't solely focused on getting coffee into my body, I'd probably ask about it. Because, at any other time of day, I'd have lots of questions. But now isn't the time. Especially because I was painting until 1:00 a.m. So, I'm going to assume he's staying with some cousins and tíos. That's not at all out of the ordinary here. And it would explain him randomly showing up into my life and the not-from-around-here accent.

Perfect. No more questions. Answered them all on my own.

During the morning, both of us are inside waiting tables. More not-so-secret glances. Hitting an arm with an elbow as we pass each other. Struggling to hold in a laugh when one of Santi's stares while walking to a table almost makes him trip over a chair.

Guess I'm not the only one who has trouble "human-ing."

"*Why do you put that much salsa on your taco?*" I ask Santi while we sit for our break. Watching him pour more salsa roja than even Ronnie could handle. A container of barbacoa, a small stack of warm corn tortillas, and two large lemonades all sit in between us.

"I like the feeling of it burning my mouth."

"That sounds like something I should be concerned about."

"People like spicy things."

"Yeah, but you're drowning the barbacoa in this, like, ocean of red. And it's salsa roja! I—" Maybe I'm not attracted to him. This might be a bigger red flag than him taking pictures the way he does in front of murals.

Wait. Nope. Seeing him laugh, trying to keep his mouth closed while it's full of taco, and the smile that comes with it when he bites into the greasy meat. Never mind. I'm attracted to him. I can forgive him for this.

"Ronnie me dijo que odias la salsa roja," Santi says after he swallows his bite. "So then what makes a good barbacoa taco to you?"

"Some onion, cilantro, and avocado slices. Salsa *verde*, if you want. But only a little."

"Wait. *Wait*. Aguacate with barbacoa?"

"*Yes*. It's a thing."

He takes a long sip of his drink, staring at a far corner of the restaurant. "I don't like aguacate."

"*What?!*" An old couple eating at the opposite end of the dining room stops with their tacos midair, looking over at us when I yell, and I set my eyes to the table, hand over my face as Santi stifles a chuckle.

"It's nasty," he says.

"*You're* nasty."

Santi lets himself laugh at that, taking another bite of his salsa taco with a little bit of carne and shaking his head.

And that's how most of the week goes by. Becoming his regular transportation to and from work, as reluctant as he is to let me. Taking our breaks together and talking about the scary movie he saw recently that I have not and will not watch *ever* because I hate scary movies and the music we're listening to and the books he's reading that I'm not because literature was never my thing (in addition to every other class in school that didn't involve painting or drawing), but now he's convinced he can change that.

Sometimes he'll try to give me some of his tips for gas money, which I make him keep and tell him to stop or else I'll break his hand.

"Consider it my family's contribution to your well-being." Yeah. Definitely that. Not at all as something that is hugely beneficial for me and the growing need to spend time with him.

Santi has this really infectious, easygoing air about him when he's comfortable. And the touchiness comes back in force in those times. When he presses his entire side against me as we man the register and to-go order counter. Or this one time he leans his head on my shoulder while we sit at the bar and he listens to my favorite Girl Ultra songs on what would've been an unbearably slow Thursday morning, had it not been for him. How cute it was when he asked if it was okay that his head was fully in my personal space, and I had to figure out how to just say yes with how loudly I was thinking, *This is the best thing that's happened to me in a very long time, so please don't move.* And when his fingers gradually go from resting on mine to inconspicuously trying to invade the space in between my own.

But then Friday, from the second he sat in my car, it's felt like a wall's been put up between us, in the middle of these really cute moments. A 180 into a Santi that all of a sudden has boundaries that he's just now remembering. Becoming quiet and trying to keep his eyes at anything else except for me. Spending half a shift rolling silverware into napkins and disinfecting taco trays if it puts a little distance between us.

"You okay?" I ask Santi halfway through our break. I've tried starting up five different conversations and all I'm getting back is grunts and *mm-hm*s and lots of silence. He doesn't even look at me; just keeps his eyes to his tacos and agua de Jamaica.

And when he gives me another *mm-hm* as an answer, I have to ball a bunch of napkins in my fist under the table to hold the yells in my head wondering what the fuck's got him acting this way. But before I can figure out how to ask that without seeming as frustrated as I am, he hops out of his chair.

"I'm gonna hang out outside for a while."

I hear exactly how he meant it. *Just me. Don't ask if you can come too. You aren't invited. I don't want you around.*

On Sunday night, Santi falls asleep in my car on the way home. We get stuck waiting on the *longest* train in the history of trains. He'd been all over the place since I picked him up, but ever since he got in my car after work, his emotions all seemed so heavy and walled up. More than tired. *I'm* tired too; he's guarded and uncomfortably quiet, even more so than he'd been during yet another entire shift of trying his best to avoid me.

I haven't bothered turning to him during the drive; seeing the light of his phone in his lap was enough for me to know that we were going to do the silent thing tonight. Until I hear a small snore and glance over at him. The side of his face is planted into the headrest, facing me. Swear, I spend what feels like entire hours in a trance. Consumed by how at peace he looks.

When we get to his house, I fight myself for a good three minutes, debating whether I should wake him up or let him sleep for a while longer. Some part of me is very into the idea of us falling asleep in his driveway and waking up to the sun rising and filling my car with the glow of the morning.

But I do. I wake him up. We say our sleepy goodbyes and good nights.

Monday and Tuesday play out the same. This Santi who seems cautious about being friendly or whatever we are with me.

And then on Wednesday we hit our final day of working together. I'm definitely reading into the situation, but something inside me says that Santi is sad about it too. He's been friendlier today. A little more eager to let me into his space or stepping into mine. Almost as eager as I am for him to take *all* my space. And I know Mami hates that I'm here after she tried to get rid of me, but if there was a way I could give Zeke another flu, I would. Even if that meant another week of going between being convinced there's something between Santi and me and feeling incredibly unwanted.

"Hey," I start while he steps out of my car. "I don't know when I'll be working again, but I'll be at Lupe's a lot. So don't be shy about asking for a ride, okay? You can message me on IG if you want. If anything, it'll help me get out of the house."

"I don't want you to have to do that."

"We're gonna go through this weekly, huh? I thought we were past this."

He shakes his head as he chuckles, a hand holding on to the open door and the other to the roof of my car. "I don't *need* you to do this for me."

"I know. It's not like this is an actual hassle. It's a few minutes out of my day. Just don't leave the neighborhood, yeah?"

"Why are you so persistent?"

"Because I already decided I'm doing this. Me letting you know you can ask is my way of giving you the impression of control. I'm decisive."

"You're a lot."

"You like it."

Santi rolls his eyes and pats his hand on the roof of my car. "I'll see you later, Ander."

"Don't be lying. I'll crash next time I see you trying to walk, if I need to prove my point."

"Then we'd both be stuck walking."

"Well, if you don't want that, then I'll be expecting a DM from you telling me to put some pants on and get in my car."

"You don't have to put pants on."

"What?"

"I'll see you later," he replies with a proud grin, knowing we both heard what he said. "I promise."

15

P romise breaker.

Santi spends the next few days forgetting I exist. Morning after morning spent waiting for him to text me, ask for a ride, or even just say hi. Looking like some Grindr bottom expecting the top they've been messaging for two hours to give them the **OMW** message, only to end up ghosted. Or something to that effect. Maybe not quite as sad.

And then Mami calling me a stalker because I asked when Santi works next when I'm just trying to be a good person.

"If he hasn't asked you for a ride to Lupe's, it's because he doesn't need it, mi'je. He's shown up to all his shifts. *Early.* Don't worry about people who don't need you spending time on them."

"*Whatever.*"

"What?!"

"I love you."

It's all chance that I'm even at Lupe's at the same time as Santi. Sitting inside the restaurant at a two-seat table against the wall, having a late lunch and getting lost in Procreate for a while after a trip to get more Copics and paints and checking in on a couple of my older murals. I honestly didn't come by looking for him.

When Santi turns the corner into the main dining room from

the front counter, we're both equally caught off our guard. His face a mixture of *shit* and a smile that says he's obviously not hating me being here right now as he walks over with a water and a Coca-Cola.

I mean, he works at my family's restaurant. If he actually thought he'd never see me here again, that'd be very incorrect.

"Hey there, stranger."

"Hi," he says as he sets the drinks down. It's a soft hi, like a child who thinks they're about to get in trouble. But his mouth stays open and his eyes take in today's long-sleeve crop top and short shorts and I doubt he even realizes he said anything until he's clearing his throat and remembering I can see him seeing me. "Haven't seen you around here lately."

Well, if I hadn't been so busy waiting for you to give me a reason to come around—

"Stuff came up. Not, like, huge stuff. I was still very much available. You know, in case you'd wanted a ride or something."

"I didn't," he answers. "I mean, I didn't need one."

"That's fine." I try not to sound like I'm taking any of this to heart. I just want him to tell me where he's at with me so I can get a better handle of his constant up and down.

"Do you know what you want?"

"Two tacos de carnitas. With cotija cheese."

"You put cheese on carnitas?"

"*Yes.* And stop with that 'huelo mierda' face."

"Cotija *does* smell like shit, though."

"Yeah, well, it also adds a sharpness to that super-fatty pork. Plus, all the other stuff that goes in it. Try it. Promise your life will be forever changed."

"Don't get them started, Santi," Mami tells him while walking with used plates and cups toward the kitchen. "Ander thinks they're pinche Guy Fieri. ¿Vamos a Ciudad Sabor, mi'je?"

"Shouldn't you go wash those?"

Mami's eyes go wide in a glare, and her head tilts a little to the right. "You get *one*. Go back to coloring."

"It's not—*Ugh*. Okay."

"So," Santi starts as Mami walks away, "the tacos con queso de mierda?"

"Yes. Please. *Burro*. Thank you."

Mami comes back after a couple minutes to check on me and ask what I'm working on. I let out a "Don't touch me with your dirty dishes hands" when she scratches my head, which gets me a slap to the back of it and a middle finger as she returns to the front. I can hear her tell Santi to clock out and eat something before he leaves.

In the middle of me getting back into my productive zone, concentration solely on the iPad in front of me, the distant sound of a phone ringing slowly brings me back. Juni's name is on the screen, waiting for me to answer.

"You busy right now?" his voice asks.

"Oh, *so* busy. Meet and greets. My exhibit at the MASS MoCA opens next week. You know. The usual."

"Well, in between all that, I got a really boring job for you. The building next to Lupe's—that three-story brick apartment building from the, like, 1930s. You know that building?"

"If you say *building* one more time, I'm hanging up."

"And miss out on a conversation with me? Doubt it. Anyways, I'm sure you know the buil—*it*. The back is covered in, like, some sort of plywood or something over the brick."

"Yeah. I know it."

"I'm going to help power wash the wall, and I need you to paint it. Plain white for right now."

"'For right now,' meaning that in the future you'll let me cover it?"

"For right now, meaning that's all we're being asked to do. *But*, yes, I am in conversation with some people currently and we'll see if we can't get that wall for you by August. Are you free day after tomorrow? Do what you can with that, and we'll work on whatever you don't finish."

"Yeah, that's fine with me."

"Perfect. Thanks, AJ. And I promise a more creative project for you very soon, all right? Everyone loved *La Chalupa*, and my friends can't stop telling me how much they love what you did at their boba shop. Literally begging me to come by and see. You have a lot of people talking."

"Thanks."

"No, thank *you*, joven. I'm sure I don't tell you that enough. But you really came through and turned out to be the best inaugural resident Beautify could've asked for. And I'm not saying that *only* because I had two bottles' worth of mimosas for brunch."

"Well, you give me food and free art supplies and spaces I would've never dreamt of, so we'll call it even."

"*Dream bigger, AJ*. This is only the start. Only a matter of time before Netflix is begging for a documentary and you've got work in all the biggest cities in the world, and I get to tell everyone, 'I knew them way back when.' Anyways, enough gassing you up. My avocado toast has arrived. I will see you in two days."

"Two days."

Santi walks back over with a large tray of food as I'm hanging up, Juni asking someone for red pepper flakes the last thing I hear. A little bit of his stomach is peeping from the way his shirt comes up with an arm holding the food steady and I'm acting like some kid in the 1600s getting wet over a girl showing her ankles.

"Want some company?" he asks. And then it clicks. That's his food too.

"I *guess*. I mean, I was really busy doing lots of important things, but—"

"Lo siento, Diego Rivera," Santi jokes as he sets the plates onto the table and then takes the seat across from me. "Can I see?"

"I guess," I say again, this time with the slightest bit of actual reluctance while handing him the iPad, and look at him taking it all in. "It's honestly just fan art. Nothing that'll go up anywhere."

"This is the coolest thing I've ever seen in my life."

"No mames. It's—I mean, again, not my original idea."

"I love this book. Didn't think you read."

"What made you think I don't read?" I ask, trying to sound defensive. "I mean, *I don't*. But Chachi lent that one to me. Said I'd like it."

"Did you?" Santi doesn't look at me when he asks. Too busy zooming in to see the skull I drew and gave this airbrushed effect on the corners of purple, pink, and blue. He smiles at its mouth without any teeth except for a few gold caps. And then gives an even bigger smile reading the words that circle the skull.

"For something I had to actually sit down and read? Yeah. I did."

I let him see a few more projects, each one followed by a "This is my favorite" and then "No, wait, this one is my favorite" and an "Okay, no, *this one* is my favorite; yeah, definitely."

"Hey," Santi starts. Breaking into a softer, more serious tone. "Can, uh—so, like, if you were already planning on leaving after you ate and didn't have anywhere else to be and wouldn't mind, I—um, would you be okay taking me home?"

I hide the little bit of a laugh that wants to come out behind a smile. Knowing that there had to be some big discussion going on in his head for a while for it to come out that way. Not wanting to sound dependent but trying to let himself be something close to that without hating himself for it. Also, I'd like to think that maybe he wants to spend a few more minutes with me.

Or maybe he just doesn't want to take the bus.

"Yeah. Claro que sí. I don't mind. ¿Listo?"

"Sí. Oh, actually, be right back. I have to go pee."

I roll my eyes. "Fine. I'm refilling your cup of tea and stealing it. *Ya*, go pee."

"Yeah. Okay. Ahorita vengo."

I turn my head, watching Santi as he runs the twenty or so steps to the bathroom, laughing under my breath, and shaking my head as I grab his cup, taking the rest of his drink before getting that refill. And then it all comes to a screeching halt when I walk to the front and see Zeke with that goofy smile that takes up half his face every time me and Santi come up.

"Don't say *anything*," I tell him as I lean on the counter. "And more tea, porfa."

He makes this weird, excited, suppressed squeal noise as he fills the cup. Taunting me with "Qué preciosos" and "Can y'all adopt me?"

"I hate you so much."

"That's inaccurate. But text me later. I need the details."

"There are no details."

"I refuse to believe that. Ronnie told me about y'a—*Hey, Santi!* What's up? Are you working with me today?"

I feel Santi's hand at the small of my back again and my entire body goes full goose bumps mode. Craving for it to go to my side and pull me in or accidentally end up inside my shorts or graze my hand, teasing my palm and fingers like he does whenever he gets touchy.

"I was here this morning," he answers. "Ander's giving me a ride."

"They're pretty good at that."

"What?!"

"You're a good driver, AJ," Zeke clarifies with a wink.

"I don't know about that," Santi says. "The first time they almost cr—"

"We're done here." I grab my tea from Zeke and start for the door. "I'll text you later."

"You better! Bye, Santi!"

I hate both of them.

16

You awake?

T he second I see the blinking . . . I suck in my breath
and bite down on my lip to fight a smile. I was crossing all
my fingers for this ever since I woke up half an hour ago to a
text from Zeke about staying up all night with a study group and
having to bail on hanging out with me while I paint.

**Sí. Hard to sleep in when the whole house is up at five in the
morning.**

**Thoughts and prayers. But if you aren't planning on going
back to bed as soon as everything quiets down do you wanna
hang out?**

Right now?

I'll give you some time. Around 7:30?

What do you want to do at 7:30 in the morning?

**I have a project today. Nothing exciting. Actually it's the op-
posite of exciting. But I could use a hand if you're available for**

free labor. I can pay you in food. Like food that I would have to spend money on and not get for free because my family owns a restaurant.

This time the ellipsis seems to taunt me. Fading in and out, making me question if he'll actually reply, if that reply will even be yes, or if he'll end up ignoring me and text me something hours later about how he fell back asleep.

Yeah that's fine. I'll see you at 7:30.

I let out this gay-as-shit closed-mouth scream. Santi said yes. He wants to hang out with me in an environment that isn't work. Or at the very least is too nice to tell me no. Either way, victory is mine.

Can we get pizza? he adds.

Pizza is MY FAVORITE.

"We're just painting it white?" Santi asks, staring at the length of the building from my parked car. His eyes squinting from the sun that's giving us a comfortable amount of warmth.

"Yeah."

"Is this what you usually do?"

"Don't think I'm not hearing the sarcasm in your voice." I grab Santi's hand and nearly choke on my own breath when he maneuvers to get his fingers between mine and then squeezes. Every millimeter of his palm and long fingers sending electric tingles up my arm and through my body.

I hope he didn't catch that.

I lead him up to the wall, where ladders, paint rollers on

extendable sticks, and buckets on buckets of paint wait for us. "But, no. Sometimes the work is basic, and that's fine. I can think about all the things I could paint on here when Juni gets permission."

I give him one of the rollers and a stick, thankful he knows what to do with it. As smart as Zeke is, when it comes to anything that's not related to science or whatever else he's brilliant in, there's zero thought behind those eyes. I always have to prepare myself to spend at least a half hour trying to help him figure out how painting works.

"Feel free to take off your shirt," I tell Santi, winking at him as the words leave my mouth. "You know, if you don't want to get it dirty."

"I'll show you mine if you show me yours."

"Fair. Okay. Fine." I pull at the bottom of my shirt, tugging it up and off and doing a half-ass folding job, mostly because I'm more busy looking at him looking at me as if he hasn't seen my stomach multiple times now. "Your turn."

I watch as he grabs near the neck of his own shirt, pulling it forward from behind and over his head. How the muscles of his arm move as he yanks it off. The way the waistline of his shorts is low enough to make me lose the ability to breathe for a second. His body's a little more toned than mine, but since doing tennis in high school, the most active I've been is when I'm painting or the times Zeke's snuck me into the UIW gym, so that's not surprising. Although I will defend the argument that painting murals is pretty labor intensive and muscle building too.

Now I'm imagining him doing some manual labor at his house. Like, watching him dig up a tree or something as I sip on sweet tea from the porch.

"Eyes are up here," he teases.

"Shut up. And give me your shirt. I'll put it in my car."

I can feel Santi's eyes on me while I walk to the other side of the parking lot. Then when I'm walking back over to him, I almost trip seeing his tongue glide across his lips as he looks at me and does that lip-bite thing again before looking away.

I really asked for this like some puta más estúpida.

I can do this. Focus on the almost *too simple* task of painting a wall. Not on the faint trace of V-lines at Santi's hips and the happy trail going from his belly button to his shorts and the faintest patch of hair in the middle of his chest and his Virgen de Guadalupe pendant just above it shining in the sun or the way he is obviously checking me out even after he called me out for doing it to him. I can do this.

"How long have you been into painting?" Santi asks as we start rolling paint onto the wall. Either suppressing his own hormones right now or maybe it's only *my* current level of horniness that's making small talk seem impossible.

"All my life. I was one of those kids who was into drawing on walls, so my pa decided to cover them in butcher paper instead of telling me not to. He likes to take credit for me being a muralist. He even keeps a box filled with paper that I painted on when I was, like, three. Secretly believes they're going to be worth a lot one day."

"They will be," he affirms. "You did the Selena mural and the conchas, didn't you?"

"Yeah."

"They're really good."

"Thanks."

"I—I'm kind of surprised you're here instead of New York or California trying to make it big."

"I'm actually going to Chicago at the end of August."

Santi stares at me for a second, his smile from our casual

conversation fading before he finally replies with an "oh." As if his offhand comment that I could end up somewhere else was supposed to *only* be offhand. A hypothetical; not something with an actual answer to it.

"But that's still half a year away. And if Juni figures out how to get me this wall, you'll have to help me with it."

His smile comes back as he puts some weight on the stick like it's a cane. "I can do that. You have an idea of what you'd want to do?"

"Nope. So, if you have any, let me know. I've always wanted to do a Pancho Villa mural. Or something from *Avatar: The Last Airbender* but make the characters Mexican."

"What would that even look like?"

"I'd need a long wall. Maybe a warehouse space or something. Other than that, I haven't figured out the details yet. It's still only something that hangs around in my head but with no real, clear vision."

"Which element would you bend?"

"Earth. Then I could create giant rock walls and paint them."

"I kind of assumed you'd say water, but that makes sense."

"I mean, I'd be age-appropriate Sokka's moon princess any day, but nah." I dunk the roller into the bucket of paint, letting the excess drip back down. "Which one would you be?"

"I think I'd be an Air Nomad. But one who doesn't shave his head bald."

"Yeah, the short hair works for you. I don't see you bald."

"So you like my hair?" Santi asks, rubbing a hand across his head.

"I didn't say that," I say back, trying to be as convincing as possible. "*Anyways*, if you keep the hair, where would the arrow go?"

"Maybe they'll let me have one that gets covered in hair, like Aang when he was in the Fire Nation. Or I can have a small one on my forehead or something."

"Or, and this is just an idea, but right—" I jab my roller stick toward Santi, hitting him on the stomach and going up before he has a chance to react, making a vertical rectangle on his torso. "There."

"*Ay, la verga.* Okay, all right," he says with an evil smirk across his face as he dunks his roller into paint. "That's how it's gonna be."

Santi flings his roller at me. Slow enough for me to dodge, but the excess still flies at me, covering the entire front of my body in specks and globs of white.

"Yeah," I reply. "That's how it's gonna be."

I'm not sure how I'm going to explain to Juni how the majority of two buckets of white paint ended up not on the wall, but that's a problem for tomorrow Ander. My only concern is trying to cover Santi in as much paint as possible. Both of us dunk our hands into the gallon cans and start attacking the other. Screaming so loud and laughing so hard I'm surprised no one comes running back here to see what was happening.

Or they did and saw two kids doing some sort of weird gay mating ritual and thought, *Yeah, I'mma head out.*

Tita is definitely judgy when she comes from next door to bring us aguas frescas and instead of seeing us do actual work, she sees Santi running after me, catching me, and—while hugging me—smearing white paint from his hands and wrists onto my stomach, chest, neck, and cheek as I scream-laugh. Both of us looking like we just got caught jacking off when we catch her face. Santi keeps ahold of me, more unable to react from surprise than anything else. At least, *probably.*

"I'll leave these on your car, bebite," she says calmly. Not making any comment about us. Turning around and walking away as soon as the drinks are out of her hands.

And the second she's gone, we both let out those ugly cackles. The ones that start with a sound like an old sprinkler turning on and then could get confused for gritos.

Through tears in my eyes I turn my head to Santi. His arms seeming to have decided to make themselves comfortable around me, if only because my hands are resting on them, gripping on to the skin of his wrists. My entire back against his front.

And when I turn my head, his eyes are on me. Thinking thoughts that are loud even when unspoken. Thoughts that I know are the exact same as the ones going through my own head.

"We, uh—break time?" Santi asks. "Before the ice melts."

"Yeah," I reply. A small break in my voice catches with the words and I try to clear my throat to make it seem like a casual thing and not because I was busy in my own head. "That's a good idea."

Neither of us calls it out, but Santi quickly—and almost so slightly I don't feel it—tightens his grip on me before letting me go. Leaving white handprints on my skin and the want for his hands to be there as long as they can.

17

Santi walks behind me into my house carrying a large box of pepperoni-and-mushroom pizza.

"Where is everyone?" he asks.

"Mami's closing tonight. Pa and Tita are at a Spurs game and then they'll be drinking all night at her house afterwards. Like, most days when she doesn't have to be up, Tita's asleep by the time the sun's down, but on Spurs nights she turns into a whole-ass frat boy. And Chachi's staying with one of her friends, I think. Or she's gone full Ninja Turtle and living in the sewers. Either is equally as likely. You wanna eat down here or in my room?"

"Uh, I'll let you choose," he answers while looking around the living room, taking in the sectional, television, the dining table at the far end of the open space, the kitchen at the far right of our house, and finally at the staircase that I'm sure he's assuming leads to my room.

I glance over at the table covered in papers and whatever else Pa was working on earlier. Not anything I want to put any effort into cleaning up for him.

"If we go to my room, you can't wear those shorts."

"Is that what you tell all the guys you bring over?"

"No, pendejo." I glare at him and start walking to the kitchen. "They're still a little wet from washing off, and there's paint on them. Up the stairs, first door on the right. Dresser by my desk, second drawer from the top has a few pairs that belong to Zeke. Pick one while I get us drinks."

"You got it, jefe."

"Don't call me that. And do you want a beer? We have Dos Equis."

"Do you have limes?"

"Yeah."

"Then sí, por favor."

Santi's already changed by the time I get to my room with plates and beers and bottles of water. In shorts that are a couple inches shorter than the ones he wore that came up just above his knee and are hugging *everything* so well. Feeling very thankful to whoever's looking out for me up there in Heaven. Jenni Rivera, maybe.

He stands in the center, gazing at all the art on my walls, some framed and some taped. Leaning closer to a couple, oblivious to me a few feet away.

"See any you like?"

"These are cool," he says, pointing to a poster near the foot of my bed. At the top is FRIDAY THE 13TH SPECIAL and then under that, BASIC CHIPSTER AESTHETIC TATTOOS $13 with a bunch of appropriately styled pieces like a menu below that: a cactus, taco, the Mexican flag, a chola, and a bunch of others.

"In high school, a lot of kids would tell me I should be a tattoo artist. And, nothing against that, but it was never something I wanted. But in honor of hearing that at least a thousand times in four years, I came up with this."

"I've always wanted a tattoo, but I'm scared of needles."

"They aren't that bad. I have a small one on the inside of my left thigh. One of those strawberry candies every abuela keeps in her purse."

"I know."

"*What?*"

"I saw it that time I was your waiter. The red and green caught my attention. And then lots of times today, in your car and when we were sitting down drinking our aguas frescas. Every time you squatted down to pour more paint into the trays. When we were using the water hose to wash the paint off each other." He rolls his eyes at my interested smirk. "You knew exactly what you were doing when you got that tattoo."

"*Okay.*" I laugh and hand him the drinks and plates. Shaking away the memories of spraying him down with the hose. "Whatever. I need to change out of my shorts real quick, so hopefully it won't be too much of a distraction for you."

"No te miro," he says, turning his back to me as I walk over to my dresser, pulling down my shorts and digging for a clean pair. "Those are one of my favorite candies."

"Mine too," I reply, taking a quick glance behind me; seeing him walk toward some more art.

"Tell me about these," Santi requests. He's near a thin poster with rows of photographs taped to it. "Are you a photographer too?"

"Not in any serious way," I say while pulling up a new pair of shorts. I walk over and stand close to him, looking at all the pictures of different places and people around Santos Vista. "Sometimes, especially with my Beautify projects, people want some sort of neighborhood inspiration, so I'll take pictures and then, when the opportunity comes, use them as a reference for murals."

"Ay, qué wow. I really am standing next to our generation's Diego Rivera. Como qué Frida."

"Cálmate, cabrón. Shut up and eat some pizza before it gets cold."

We sit side by side on my bed, backs against the wall. Not

saying much. The exhaustion from being in the sun, even in the comfortable late winter, and painting all day finally catching up to us.

"Thanks for inviting me today."

"Thanks for saying yes. Would've sucked to have to do all that by myself."

"I guess I should also thank Zeke for being too tired from studying."

"I would bet he's expecting it."

Santi lets out a little chuckle and scoots himself slightly closer to me before taking another bite. "And you two used to date?"

"Who told you that?"

"He did."

"Of course he did."

"I started it, though. I brought you up. He mentioned how you two are exes but also best friends."

I want to get deeper into the topic of him actively wanting to talk about me with my friend, but for now, I'll let it slide. "Did he mention anything else?"

"Not technically. But he's not good at being, I don't know the word . . . tact? Those couple of days we worked together after he got over his flu, he'd always mention you and make little hints," Santi answers before squeezing a lime wedge into his bottle of Dos Equis. Taking a slow few swigs. "Your amá was more obvious."

"*What?!*"

"I—don't get mad at her, but she told me that she has a feeling you like me. Or, that she knows you like me. It—she's worried. And it's not her fault. I'm worried too. Because I like you too."

I nearly drop my bottle of water all over my lap and bed. "Wait. You do?"

"Wasn't I obvious about it?"

"Like, ninety percent obvious and ten percent super confusing."

"Yeah. I was trying my best to not be un baboso, pero es muy difícil. Especially because I felt so comfortable around you. And more especially because the minute it's not cold outside, you're always wearing the cropped shirts and the shorts with the tattoo—"

"I get it," I say, trying to sound more annoyed than flattered, but I know that's not working. "But you didn't want me to know you like me?"

Santi tilts his head back and lets out a loud sigh. "Short answer, yes. But it's actually more complicated than one word. I don't know if I'm ready for that yet. To explain to you why or to ignore what makes it so complicated. What I do know, though, is that every time I saw you, I was worried I'd never see you again. I *prayed* that I'd get to see you again. And then I did, when you let me into the office and then again when you showed up that Sunday. And now we're here. Which makes it all even more difficult."

"Why?" I ask before realizing that I let myself speak without thinking first. "I mean, you don't have to tell me. You said you aren't ready to get into it, so—"

"It . . . *things*. Lots of things. Things that have been so easy to forget about when I get to work with you and spend time going there and back to my house. I was forgetting about what makes my life so complicated. Which is nice, but it's not something I want to forget. And—and it's tough when someone else is brought into the mix. Even tougher when I'm reminded why my life is complicated."

I'm getting the sense that whatever it is, this is the same reason Mami was being all *Don't date him, ughh* with me. But

I wish someone would fucking tell me. Is he still in the closet with his family? Did he try to single-handedly take down capitalism and is now in a witness protection program hiding from Jeff Bezos?

And I'm remembering that middle-of-the-night conversation between her and Tita. How I've known what they were arguing about had to do with Santi, but I never actually thought about how big of a deal it is until now. Until *he's* telling me.

Another sigh comes out of him. This one more of a groan, and I'm hoping that Santi doesn't think I'm annoyed at him. Not that this whole situation isn't some level of annoying, but *he* specifically is not. Which makes sense in my mind.

"I'm sorry for all the times I seemed standoffish because I've been dealing with this," Santi continues. "You didn't deserve that. And I—I don't want to stop seeing you. I don't want to avoid you. But I get it if this, if us hanging out but knowing where I'm at with us, doesn't work for you."

I slowly put down my plate and place a hand, palm up, on his leg. "C'mon. Follow me."

I help him out onto the roof of the garage, my hand that's not still holding his ready to stabilize him if he gets shaky. We walk to the middle of the roof and make sure we're both steady as we sit down.

"This is where I come when I need a moment. Quiet. A space to think or to work. Where my best friends and I hang out late at night. Multipurpose. But especially for those times when my brain needs to stop thinking for a while."

"I like it," Santi says, his eyes toward the street and all of Santos Vista visible from up here. He closes them and picks his head up slightly, feeling the light breeze against his face. "This is a good spot. I can tell."

"It's seen me through a lot. Good and bad."

His hand squeezes mine and then his thumb starts softly going back and forth, up and then down to the middle of the space between my own and my pointer finger. "I'm sorry."

"It's whatever."

Santi's chest rises as he inhales and then goes back down with a strong exhale. He turns his head, his face visible at the edge of my vision.

"What?" I ask, my eyes meeting his.

"I—I want to kiss you."

"Then do it."

"I can't."

I know, I almost tell him. *Please*, I almost tell him. Both fighting to but neither of them making it out of my mouth.

"You deserve to be kissed," he continues. His free hand rubs from the side to the back of his neck and, God, how I wish his hand was my lips instead. "You make me feel happy. Being around you makes me feel happy. But I know that giving us a name and—I have to go against my own happiness a lot. Doing that helps me stay on the path of least destruction. And sometimes I think I've gotten used to that, but you—it hasn't been easy since I met you."

"Do you need to see me less?"

"*No*," he gasps. "I—I don't know what I need. Not yet. Or I think I actually do, and I'm not ready to listen yet. But it's not less of you. I'm sure of that."

"You know, you can tell me. Not that you *have* to tell me. I don't want you to feel forced about anything, but this whatever-it-is that's obviously got you clenched pretty tightly in its fist—you don't have to hold on to it alone. Okay? So, whether you tell me now or tomorrow or next week or never, I just want you to know that you *can*."

"Thank you." He takes a deep sigh as we both stare into each other's eyes. Me looking for clues and Santi looking for comfort. "Can I hold you?"

"Yeah," I reply, letting go of his hand so it can reach around my waist and pull me to him. My head rests on his shoulder and my hand squeezes his leg, bent up at the knee. And we sit in silence, hearing the locusts in the field behind our row of houses. I concentrate on and try to match the pattern of his breathing.

And consider everything that we could be.

18

I can feel Ronnie's eyes on Santi and me as he puts up strings of papeles picados along the patio roof and we fill plastic Easter eggs with candy and then hide them under tables, in bushes lining the patio fence, and anywhere else we can fit them. He's been like that the past few weeks, whenever he sees me come inside Lupe's to wait for Santi to clock out or especially when I visit him during his lunch break. We'll be minding our own business, and there's Ronnie, watching, usually with Zeke right beside him, giving me a wink.

They know that Santi and I decided to be just friends. We might be doing a horrible job at it, more like friends who flirt with each other all the time and hold hands and get caught looking at each other constantly with big babose smiles. But this is the line Santi drew. I'm fine with that. Mostly. And I need them to stop inserting themselves into it.

Since Easter is only two Sundays away, instead of a regular Lupe's second-Friday staff kickback for March, Tita is replacing it with an egg hunt for everyone's families and a huge dinner and Lotería afterwards, closing down the restaurant for the entire day. Which I'm a little pressed about because February's was also canceled since it fell on Valentine's Day, so this was supposed to be Santi's and my sort-of-official first date. Sure, it wouldn't be going anywhere anymore, but it's the thought that counts.

"Stop eating all the candy," I yell at Santi, shoving his arm, fully bare from the tank he's wearing. Swear he's been picking out all the Snickers bars from every single bag and thinks he's being sneaky, putting them in his mouth two at a time.

"Nadie los echará en falta," he whines back. His mouth half-full.

"That's not the point."

"¿Los estoy interrumpiendo?" Tita asks as she approaches the circular table we're sitting at, a bunch of plastic, dollar store Easter baskets in her hand.

"No, Tita," I say with the slightest bit of annoyance in my voice. Ronnie's been a lot, and so has Zeke, but her? Astronomical levels of too much ever since that day we painted the wall. As if she's waiting for us to confirm an assumption that *isn't true.* There's nothing to tell. And literally everyone here thinking different is making the fact that there's nothing to tell harder because I *wish* there was something to tell.

Just *stop*.

"Can I bring the plastic grass for these and have you two make them all lindos for me?"

"Claro que sí, jefa," Santi answers. And then minutes later, he's up to help take bags of fake green, pink, and yellow grass from Tita's arms.

"Does your family do the whole Christianity thing too?" I ask Santi, taking handfuls of yellow grass and filling a white basket.

"Mi apá. He was super into Jesús. We used to spend all of Holy Week going to Mass. From Palm Sunday to Easter Sunday. And we didn't grow up with the *bunny*."

"What? Really?"

"Uh—" Santi fumbles with grass in between his fingers, staring at them moving. As if this was something he isn't supposed to say. "We were bigger on the religious stuff. Doing the Cruci-fixion walk, things like that."

"Wow." I'm kind of lost for words, realizing there were kids who didn't grow up throwing hands over plastic eggs and shit-ting themselves the first time they saw an adult-human-sized rabbit smiling at them. I grab the bag of chocolate candy closest to me and toss it in front of him. "Then, fuck, eat as much candy as you want. Catch up on what you missed out on."

"*Well, now that I have your permission,*" Santi says with so much sarcasm in his voice I could push him off his chair and not regret it one bit.

Cabrón.

<hr>

"*Mm.*" The literally full-on moan that comes out of Santi's voice only a second after he bites into his gordita, filled with so much carnitas, cilantro, radishes, salsa, and cheese, is both weird and also kind of hot? I'm surprised and impressed at how he man-ages to fit it all into his mouth. He lets out another *mm* while chewing, his eyes closed as he happily nods and the food sends him to some other plane of existence. "Why didn't you tell me how good the gorditas are here?"

"They're just gorditas," I tell him with a smirk.

"Gorditas are my *favorite*. And these are better than any I've ever had."

"Well, tell Tita. She'll be happy to hear that."

The two of us sit on stools lined behind the bar, with Ronnie next to me and Chachi on his other side and Zeke at the end. They spent the entire Easter egg hunt pretending they were Mexican fútbol announcers or something, making comments in that Univision *goool* voice. Santi and I both couldn't stop staring at them. Me because I thought they were being annoying. Santi, though, I don't think I've ever seen him more entertained.

I laugh when he takes his first bite into his second gordita and a little bit of cheese sticks to his cheek, next to his lip. "You got a little—" I start while making short swipes at my own cheek with my thumb.

Santi's tongue goes out and angles to the side, and he lets out barely understandable ¿Y ahora?'s until he's able to just graze the cheese enough to taste that he's hit it, and then gives up, using his finger to swipe himself clean and putting it in his mouth.

And I wish my first thought wasn't *Put that finger in* my *mouth*, but it was and—actually, yeah, no part of me is ashamed of that.

When we start playing Lotería, Santi scoots his stool close enough to me that he can rest an arm across the back of mine. I very purposefully avoid Mami's watchful glares at us, her eyes big and pointed the moment his hand went behind my back. I wonder if Tita told her about what she saw at the building next door. Either way, both Mami and I are aware that I took her *not him* instructions, and while we haven't thrown them in the garbage, I definitely have that trash bag in hand and the dumpster is in sight.

Both of us get close to winning every game, with one or two lines of three beans, anxiously waiting for that last rectangle to be called. And, while I'm calm about it because this is a child's game that means nothing, Santi will sit there tensely, his face only inches from his card, muttering "pinche cazo, pinche cazo, pinche cazo" and then letting out a loud groan when la araña is called instead and some waiter's four-year-old daughter ends up winning.

Nearly an hour into it, Santi's card is covered in beans, with what has to be four or five different *almost complete* lines. He's been screaming through his teeth for the last few minutes. His hands grip on to his head like he wants to crush his own skull before the one closest to me goes to the inside of my leg, holding on to my skin.

He must've felt me do the smallest of flinches because he quickly turns to me with cautious eyes, like he's scared he hurt me. "Sorry. Is this okay?"

"Yeah, no. Claro." I answer as I spend a minute rubbing my hand up and down his arm, noticing how bright the light Easter-y lavender of my nails looks against the browns of our skin. He smiles and then lets himself go a little higher, right up to where my shorts that are barely covering any of me start, and it takes me a second to remember how to breathe and to keep holding in the sound that's trying to come out at feeling his fingers there. He looks at his hand with a small but proud smirk, and then his eyes go to the visible strawberry candy on my other thigh, lingering at the tattoo.

"Shouldn't you be paying attention to the game, cabrón?"

"I—*Ya, fuck*. What was the last card they called? ¡Ronnie, ayudame!"

While he gets back into the game, my concentration is only on his hand on me. On the way that he probably doesn't even know he's making small back-and-forths and squeezes when he gets excited about adding a bean to his card. On how these little crumbs of a pseudo-relationship are sustaining me like a gay seagull.

So what if we can't be together. We're together right now. I can literally feel him here with me. And this is good. I'm good, he's good, we're good.

19

I got a call from Juni, the day after the Lupe's Easter kickback, about some more of his friends asking if I'm free for a mural commission. These cousins opening a nursery at the St. Mary's Strip who want their street-facing wall to be covered in cacti. Easier than anime; at least I already know what cacti look like.

"Are all of your friends business owners?"

"Basically. I really should be in the market for lazy friends. Someone who I can sit on a couch all day with. These putas always doing something. Like, *Calm down, Marta*. Binge a thing on Netflix for an afternoon. The world will be here tomorrow. Society will not have grown past its need for overpriced plants."

It was an easy enough piece to put together. They loved the concept I sent and wanted it up as soon as possible *and* were willing to pay me more to get it up as soon as possible. So, yeah, I came running first thing Monday morning.

Days one and two I worked on my own. Came over here right after dropping off Santi at Lupe's in the mornings. Spent the entire time getting distracted thinking about him. Caught myself standing here, facing a wall, arm raised with a paintbrush in my hand, doing absolutely nothing, lost in the thoughts.

Thankfully, only lost enough that I was still able to get a lot done. Because I can be daydreamy *and* productive. I'm a professional.

Hey, Santi texts just after I hit snooze on my phone's alarm. Not yet ready to get day three started. **Would you want some company at your mural today?**

He's asking me if I want to hang out with him? If I want to spend time with him? Inviting himself into my space? That's different. Not the spending-time-together part, but him being the one who brings up the idea. Usually it's me asking if he wants to get a paleta on the way back to his house after his shift or if he wants to come over and watch Netflix (and *only* watch Netflix, as much as it pains me and as much as I do like the cuddling that always happens).

Are you sure? You don't wanna spend your day off doing nothing?

I'd rather be doing nothing with you, he replies, and the Pisces moon part of me is about to have me crying. It's too early for him to be this cute. **Or something. Help paint. Whatever you want.**

What I want, when it comes to him, wouldn't be appropriate for outdoors.

Yeah, I'd love some company. Can you be ready in thirty minutes?

Thirty minutes, Santi texts back with a brown hand emoji giving me a thumbs-up.

Okay. Guess I'm getting started on time today after all.

I don't know who's staring harder: Santi at what I have of the mural so far, with this big smile like he's never seen a bunch of cacti before, or me at Santi, standing there, shirtless, the sunlight on his skin and reflecting on his gold chain necklace.

Probably me.

"I—So you wanna help me?" My throat catches on the *I*, but I get there.

"Sure," he says with this childlike eagerness. "Tell me what to do."

I show him how to paint over the slap-brush knockdown texture of the wall. Maybe even hold his hand while he holds a brush and guide him through a few strokes. And then I watch him as he starts filling in one of the cacti with green paint. How concentrated he looks. How I can tell he really wants to do this right.

"Don't break it," I tell him when we get into the lift basket and Santi is begging to be the one that makes it go up.

"No te preocupes," he says back before pushing on a lever, making the machine jump slightly, then slowly rise. His hand goes to my side, like he's making sure I stay steady. I am. I've done this before. It's nothing new. But I still fully lean into him.

Santi watches as I add a little light blue or green here and some navy there on one of the larger cacti, adding highlight or shadow where I need it. He'll ask questions about how color works and "Are you seeing this in your head before it's even on the wall?" and pass me whatever color I need or take a spray paint can from my hand and switch it for a brush. And at times when I stand quiet and still, thinking about what I need to do next or what this little part of this plant is missing, he'll stand behind me, his front against my back, arms wrapped around me, and his head on my shoulder, and think with me.

About the painting? Probably not. And if my own questions

weren't right at the tip of my tongue, needing every bit of my attention to keep in, I'd ask him what's going on up there. What sort of not-painting-related thoughts he's thinking.

A whole twelve hours later, we're finally done. Our arms sore and our skin a little browner than it was this morning. Santi stands next to me, again, staring at the now complete field of cacti covering the whole side of this nursery. Green with yellow and orange and pink blossoms and bright prickly pears.

"This is my favorite mural ever," he says while grabbing my hand.

"I—It's nothing. It's just plants."

"*No.*" The way it comes out feels almost like he's insulted at that. "It's more than that."

"If you say so." I turn around and take a seat on the curb of the sidewalk, watching people slowly start going into Paper Tiger across the street for whatever musician is performing there tonight. Santi sits down next to me, grabbing my hand again and holding it close to him.

"I do. I like what you paint."

"I do too. I just—" Am I really about to have this conversation with him? Bring Santi into a room in my head that only Zeke's ever known before?

Looks like it. If he was able to be vulnerable with me, I can with him. I trust him.

"Remember when you asked how long I've been into art? And I said pretty much my whole life? That's true, it has been. But I also basically taught myself. I didn't have access to an art class until high school. Stuff like that isn't just available anywhere here, especially in communities like Santos Vista. I started by trying to copy the pages of coloring books or things I'd see around the neighborhood. I looked up YouTube videos about shading and color theory until I was fourteen and finally had an actual teacher. Which I think is why so much of what I do ends up being cacti and, I don't know, Mexican in aesthetic."

"Is that a bad thing?"

"Honestly, I'd never thought of it as good or bad until I was applying for colleges. I'm happy with that being what I do. It feels like me. Until RISD—this school up in New England—asked if that was all they should expect in my portfolio. And then this school in Seattle rejected me, to my face, because of it. Because it's not *serious* art. I'd never felt so . . . ashamed. I actually felt ashamed of what I do."

Santi's grip on my hand tightens, and I stare at them. If I look anywhere else, especially at his face, I'm going to start crying saying this.

"And then with the school I'm going to in Chicago, they're cringe in a totally different way. A while back, my advisor basically told me to stick to this sort of stuff. The 'brown girl eating a tamal' sort of art. And it really hit a nerve because it makes me almost, I don't know, embarrassed about liking the art that I do. White guys doing street and urban art can do whatever they want, but me? I've gotta stick to cactus walls. A part of me thinks about what if I found a way to fight myself into those spaces? They'd probably still be dicks and racists, but at least I'd get more attention. I wouldn't be the Mexican who only does Mexican art."

"But there'd be less heart," Santi says back. My eyes follow as he opens and starts massaging into my palm and tracing the lines and letting his fingers glide up and down and then lock with mine. "I got to see this hand create something beautiful today. I got to see the love you put into it. I see it now when I turn my head and look at it. And not just this one but all of them. The *Como la Flor* and *La Chalupa*. When I see those—when I see this one—it feels like . . . it feels like home. And that means a lot to me. More than I can explain."

His head turns to me and I can see how much he wants me to hear every word he's saying. "You're good enough to paint whatever you want. So you should paint whatever you want. But I hope you don't let *them* take away the love I see you put in these."

Fuck, my eyes are getting watery and, yeah, there goes a tear. I let out a laugh as I wipe my cheek with my free hand.

"Stop getting me emotional. But I won't. I promise." We stare at each other for a few more seconds before I let myself get closer, and as much as I'd love to kiss his cheek right now, I stop myself, resting my head on his shoulder. "Thank you for today."

"Any day."

After picking up chicken sandwiches at this spot up the street from the nursery and eating them in my car, then coming back to my house and taking showers and putting on clean clothes, Santi stays for a while. We hang out in the living room, I introduce him to *Vida*, he can't stand Melissa Barrera's character ("You're supposed to think she's annoying"), and we lie on the sofa together. Well, I lie on the sofa, and he lies on top of me. His head rests on my chest, and I can't keep my hand and fingers from rubbing and scratching his head, enjoying how I can physically feel him relaxing from it.

"Ander," he starts in this soft, breathy voice like he's seconds from falling asleep. "I . . ."

"You what?"

"I . . . I had a lot of fun today. Estoy feliz de haber pasado hoy contigo."

I really wish I didn't feel like he wanted to say something else. I wish whatever he was about to say didn't get caught in his throat. That he didn't have to keep himself from saying what he really feels. But I get it. I know.

"I am too."

20

Take my shift tonight! I have a test tomorrow and I'm freaking out about it.

What time do you clock in?

Six.

THAT'S IN AN HOUR ZEKE.

Tf were you doing right now that you can't be over there in an hour?

hate him. And anything within the past nineteen years of my life I may have said that might dispute the fact that I hate him was said when I was not in the right headspace and should not be taken as truth.

And weren't you already gonna drop Santi off at Lupe's anyways? he adds.

Yes but now I have to change out of the clothes I've been wearing since last night and put pomade in my hair and wear shoes and ugh.

Sorry I'm making you come out of your cave, Gollum.

That gets him a row of brown middle finger emojis.

So that's a yes?

You owe me.

Thanks I love you!

———————

"Why are you wearing real clothes?" Santi asks as he slides into the passenger seat.

"What's that supposed to mean? I always wear real clothes."

"I guess I've gotten used to you always wearing shirts that lost their bottom half and the short shorts the last two weeks. I'm not used to you in . . . wait. ¿Estás trabajando esta noche?"

He looks actually caught off guard, now that he's connected the dots and realized what me wearing a work shirt must mean. Which, to his credit, I haven't in a few weeks since Zeke came back from faking and then actually getting sick.

"Sí," I tell him while tying a bandana around my head, watching as he gets comfortable and puts on his seat belt. "I'm taking Zeke's shift tonight. Is that okay?"

He stares blankly for a couple of seconds before shaking off whatever was in his head and giving me a smirk. "*Qué la*, and I was looking forward to hanging out with Zeke today."

"Were you also looking forward to walking to work today?"

Santi laughs, his attention going from me to my stash of bandanas. "I'm sorry, I'm sorry. But I see you working more than I see him at all."

"I don't think that's true. But I'm definitely working more than I thought I'd be. So much for Tita firing me."

"I'm not complaining," he says with that incredibly infectious smile.

"What?" I ask Santi after catching him staring at me for at least the tenth time tonight.

"I—nothing. Was thinking about something."

"Wanna tell me what you were thinking?"

He's quiet for what seems like whole minutes before letting out a big sigh. "Ye—maybe later."

Tonight's slow as shit. Zeke literally could've studied at the front counter for five hours and no one would've said anything. Honestly, he probably would've been sent home. Tita's already let half the kitchen and waitstaff take off early because we've only had maybe seven customers since Santi and I got here three hours ago, and all but two of them were to-go orders.

The entire neighborhood must have gotten together and agreed that this specific Thursday, everyone's cooking their own meals and eating at home. It is a cute early April evening. If they have a grill, they should feel obligated to be using it tonight before we skip the rest of spring and get straight to summer.

By nine o'clock, Tita's calling it. No use in staying any longer.

"Bebite," she calls out, walking towards the table Santi and I are sitting at, sharing a quesadilla. The three of us are the only ones still here. "Go home if you want. I'll keep Santi with me and take him home."

"I—Why don't you go, Tita?" I glance over at Santi—mouth open, about to take a huge bite of quesadilla—for only a second before going back to her. "Go catch the rest of the Spurs game. I can close up."

I don't love the idea of someone else getting time that's

become mine and Santi's. A weird jealousy even when I know that the last person I need to feel that way about is my abuela. But those ten, twelve minutes aren't something I'm interested in sharing if I don't have to.

She gives me a look that knows exactly what I'm thinking. She, *especially*, caught on a long time ago. We both know how this is going to end. That she's going to fold. I'm sure Tita's seen this exact situation play out with her son and my tías and tíos and is now seeing it be re-created a generation later.

"That's a good idea," Tita replies, her voice almost theatrical. Like she's fully convinced herself she's in her own little telenovela. "Your papi hates watching by himself."

She takes her keys out of her pocket and sets them down on the table since Mami took mine a few weeks ago. "There are containers that the boys didn't get a chance to wash before I let them leave. Get through those and that's about it. Everything else is already done, yeah?"

"I think so."

"Good. Te quiero." Tita bends down to kiss my cheek and then goes to Santi and does the same to him. "I'll see you two later. Be safe. *Be good*. And make good choices."

I watch Tita leave, waiting for the door to close behind her before turning to Santi. "Ready to get to work?"

"Claro, jefe," he teases.

"Okay, now you're trying to make me mad."

He takes our empty plate to the kitchen while I close the register, both of us used to this process. It only takes me a few minutes to get everything into the office, lock it up, and then get over to Santi, grabbing a sponge and a clear container full of what used to be . . . beans, probably? I don't know. I'm not about to smell brown goopy liquid for the sake of clarification.

We stand side by side, quietly washing each container and

then setting them up on the wire racks above the sinks. Every now and again, Santi will lightly hit my arm with his elbow like we do so often now, or I'll press my side onto him for a second. One of us will let out a chuckle or dare to look at the other for as long as possible before it's obvious that we're staring instead of doing our job.

And then he decides to retaliate for an elbow hit by flicking his wet fingers at me, getting droplets of water on my shirt and face.

"We're really gonna do this *again*?"

"I don't know what you mean," Santi answers before flicking his hand one more time and getting even more water on me.

"*¡Maldito pendejo!*" I yell, getting my hand wet and making a throwing motion at him, watching water fly and land on his shirt and how he closes his eyes when he feels drops hit his face, laughing through a yell.

Both of us start acting without thinking. Using the containers as buckets to fill up with water and douse on each other. Sponges are being thrown. The entire kitchen is getting soaked. The restaurant is filled with the sound of old-school Juanes mixed with Santi's and my laughter and screaming.

Santi is about to throw more water at me when his face goes from wide smile to fear as he loses his footing, one leg up in the air and the other trying its best to stay stable but unable to keep from slipping. He drops the container full of water and reaches both hands out. My body reacts without even needing me to think about it. I grab him, throw my weight back onto the sink, and pull Santi with me. Our hands let go and wrap around each other to make sure he doesn't fall.

And if he does, I'm going with him.

I can feel his adrenaline-rushed heartbeat as his body presses into me, sandwiching me between him and an uncomfortable giant metal sink. His forehead rests against mine, each inhale and exhale audible with his mouth so close to my own. Both of us are trying to calm down. We silently call a truce and return to earth and this room, where the air smells like soap mixed with the always-present aroma of tortillas and pastor and onions.

And nothing is more grounding than opening my eyes and seeing Santi's right here in front of me. My mind goes from *Don't let Santi fall* to fully processing how close we are and how comforting his thumbs rubbing circles on the small of my back is and then going back to how close our mouths are and how much I want to make that last bit of space not exist anymore.

But I want to give him that power. To know that whenever he's ready, if he's ever ready, all he has to do is let me know, and I'm game. Sending all those signals with my eyes straight into his.

And then I'm not looking into Santi's eyes. Because they close the second before he erases any space left between us and his lips hit mine. I forget about where I am, how late it is, how messy the kitchen is now, how wet our clothes are, all of it. He and this moment we've been back and forth about for so long are the entirety of what I know and what matters right now. My only focus is on his mouth and how mine wastes no time with surprise before being just as certain as his is of this.

Until he rushes to pull back and his face seems so worried and afraid. "I'm sorry. I—I didn't mean to do that." Oh shit. He thinks he crossed a line. *No. No.* "I mean, I did. But I shouldn't have without asking you. I—"

"Do it again," I tell him. "Keep kissing me. Please just keep fucking kissing me."

He lets me pull him forward and we go in for another kiss. Our tongues gliding against each other's. Heavy breaths and soft moans fill our mouths. He helps me hop onto the sink's ledge and stands in between my legs and through it all doesn't stop kissing me. And when we tire ourselves out, Santi leaves his lips close enough to graze mine—but careful not to go any further.

Neither of us says anything. Not with words, at least. But so much is said in the way we look at each other while his hands go from my legs to my hips and under the bottom of my shirt and mine go up his arms and shoulders and neck.

Finally. And, *This is better than I could've ever imagined.*

<hr>

"Is this what's been on your mind all night?" I ask Santi while tossing him a clean work shirt from one of the boxes in the office, after we've cleaned up the mess we made in the kitchen. Watching him as he sits on the couch and puts it on. Kind of wishing he'd just stay shirtless.

"For a lot of nights," he says. "And I was going to tell you when you took me home tonight, but I couldn't help it."

"So . . . is this you deciding we're putting a name to us now?"

Santi grabs my hand and pulls me onto his lap. "Is that okay with you?" he asks.

"Is that okay with *you*?"

"I want to do both. I can live a life that's both complicated and happy. Even if it's just for a little while. And especially if it means I get to have you. I need that."

"What—why now?"

He grins and lets out a chuckle. "There were a lot of *almost* times. Painting the white wall. The entire day of the Easter thing. Hanging out with you the day I helped with the cactus mural. Those times that my brain said I had to be smarter. Think clearly and responsibly. But can't I have one chance to do something not because I have to but because I want to? So now, because . . . because maybe this is the first time my heart's been louder than my brain, I want to listen to it."

One of my hands rests on his shoulder and the other is right over his heart. The same one that said *fuck responsibilities*. I want to make sure he never regrets that decision.

"You deserve that. *The happiness*. And all the things you want, without the complicated parts. And you have me for as long as you want."

He laughs and lets his hands roam to my lower back again. "So, you'll be part of that life?"

"Te dije. Mientras me quieras. And only if you don't stop kissing me."

"Claro que sí."

One of my hands rests on his shoulder and the other is right

"Your amá's not going to be happy about this, is she?" Santi asks when I park into his driveway.

"*Yeaaah*, I'm gonna be spending the rest of the night figuring out how to tell her. But I will. Sometime tomorrow I'll let her know."

"Well, if she asks, tell her I'm going to tell you."

"What does that mean?"

"That—Let's hang out tomorrow, okay? After you tell her. And assuming she doesn't kill you. I only have a short lunch shift. You don't have to worry about taking me, but I'll see you at Lupe's around three?"

"Yeah. Okay."

"Okay." Santi pulls me to him, letting us have a few more minutes of making out. His breathing getting heavier as one of my hands goes further up his thigh is making me dizzy. Finally, we pull away, knowing that this has to end at some point, for right now. "Buenas noches, mi cielo. Te veo pronto."

"Buenas noches, querido."

21

Pa has one hand to his face, covering his mouth and nostrils. His other hand is resting on the dining table, fingers tapping and tapping and tapping in a mindless rhythm. This is how I found him, after coming downstairs when he yelled my name the second I opened my bedroom door this morning. Letting me sit here wondering if I forgot to lock up the taquería on the way out of the Lupe's last night, even though I distinctly remember locking it. Right before Santi pressed me against it and I learned that he can pick me up, which has been on my "Qualities I'd like in a boyfriend" list for a while now.

"I know you know the answer to this question, but . . . AJ. Mi'je. My child. You know we have cameras in the restaurant, right? *Including* the kitchen."

"What? Okay. Oh. *Oh.*" Shit. He saw everything. Santi and I going from washing dishes to goofing around and making a mess and playing grab-ass to us trying to swallow each other's tongues and Santi *literally* playing grab-ass. So much of me is glad that I didn't let myself suggest the other ideas that were going around in my head last night. "Pa, I—"

"Ander," he says over me, holding out a hand. His voice is stoic. Less angry and more . . . hell, I don't know. Somewhere in the middle of a Venn diagram where the circles are annoyed, concerned, and disappointed. "Next time you want to pull that kind of fun, don't—make sure you clean up *everything*. Okay? You left a puddle under the sink. And when your mami went to see who missed that last night, well, she isn't the happiest right now. She says she talked to you about Santi? About not doing exactly what you did."

"I mean, it was mostly her calling me a puta. But, sure."

"Pues, not about the puta part, but the important stuff. You're going to do the exact opposite of what she asked you not to do?"

"I—Do you know? About Santi?"

"Yes."

"Then . . . is it something that I need to worry about? For him? Don't tell me what it is. He's going to later today. But how prepared do I need to make myself for this?"

"It's something that shouldn't be a big deal," Pa answers. He pats my hands clasped together on the table. "But that doesn't mean that it isn't. Or that there wasn't a reason why you were told to not get into something with him. And I want you to think, really put some thought into it, mi'je. About *everything*. What's worth fighting for. What's worth losing?"

"What do you think the answer to that is?"

"I think that the worst sight in the world is seeing you hurt. But one of the best sights I've seen in a long time is you and Santi working together at Lupe's and hanging out. And the happiness he puts on your face." Pa stands up and walks around to give me a hug. His hand doing four, then five of those strong hand pats that dads love to do.

"Te adoro, Ander. Okay? In case your mami kills you for not listening to her, I want those to be my last words to you."

I let out a laugh and tighten my hold on him for a minute. "También te adoro, Pa."

"Y ten cuidado."

"I will."

I get to Lupe's about fifteen minutes until three. Enough time to get a lemonade for the road and, hopefully, too little time for Mami to go She-Hulk on me in front of God and some poor viejitas trying to have a concha with their afternoon cup of coffee. But who knows, she might be in the mood for a quick ass kicking.

Santi's the first person I see when I walk in. Going from slouching on the counter, bored out of his mind to smiling and standing up straight, waving at me.

"Estás temprano," he says when he comes around to hug me and peck at my cheek.

"Wanted a lemonade. Might make a few scribbles on here while I wait on you to get out," I say, holding up my iPad. "Mami hasn't said anything to you today?"

"She did give me an unusually long glare when I got here," he says while rushing back behind the counter, grabbing a Styrofoam cup and filling it with ice and then highlighter-yellow lemonade, capping it with a lid, and handing that and a straw to me. "But that's it. Why?"

"No reason."

"*Okay.*" His voice tells me he clearly knows there's obviously a reason. "You aren't hungry?"

"We can go eat somewhere else."

"Okay. Oh—I gotta go pee."

"Why do you always tell me?"

"Conversation," Santi replies with a playful smile. He gives my cheek one more quick kiss before walking toward the bathrooms. "If anyone asks for me, tell them I'll be right back."

"Yeah. I'll be here."

I take a seat at the small table at the entrance of Lupe's. It—like most of the tables in here—has been around since I can remember. I used to spend most days growing up doing homework right here while Pa, Mami, and Tita worked. Or with the coloring books they used to buy me that I'd end up not coloring, using computer paper to practice drawing the pictures instead. It still feels the same. Work in front of me. Cup that would be usually filled with fruit punch fourteen years ago. Hours of observing the handful of groups hanging out inside and—

And I almost choke on my drink. All the air in my body is taken from me. My mind starts going a million miles an hour.

Because two men with the unmistakable ICE jackets are walking out of Rosie's. Their eyes and fingers pointed toward Lupe's.

I can hear Tita from the kitchen accounting for everyone. She must've gotten a call from the panadería. It's a process I know as well as painting: What to do when we see them approaching. How to get any undocumented workers out as calmly and quietly as possible with whatever amount of time we have. And, if we can, drive them home while attracting the least amount of attention.

I mentally list the guys I saw through the pass working in the kitchen right now. The couple of waiters here. We're fine. Everyone on the clock is a citizen.

"Where's Santi?" Mami asks, nearly throwing herself toward me. Her eyes frantic.

"He's in the bathroom. Why?"

"Because—*fuck*. I—"

"*Oh my god.*"

This is what he was going to tell me. It's all clicking. Why Mami has been against me and specifically Santi together. Where he lives and all the other guys that stay there. His accent. That he doesn't have a license or even an ID.

"Hold on. I got this." I jump out of my chair and sprint to the bathroom, leaving my drink and iPad at the table. My knuckles furiously tap against the door as I repeat Santi's name over and over again.

"¿*Qué?*" he asks when he starts stepping out, only for me to push myself in there with him and shut ourselves in.

"Change shirts with me."

"¿Perdón?"

"ICE is coming. Change shirts with me. Sit at my chair. Pretend you're a customer. Ándale, *please.*"

"I—yeah, yeah," he rushes to say through a breathy voice. I hate seeing how fear sinks immediately into every part of his body. How it's a physical thing that comes out of him like a gust of wind hitting my body.

I want to tell him not to worry. I want to tell him it'll be fine. And don't worry about me knowing. I don't care. I just care about him and knowing that he's going to be good.

But these things are never certain.

They usually don't go questioning patrons, but I've heard stories of agents thinking they're big shit and answer to no one. So this is the best idea I've got.

"Act like you're a customer, all right?" I tell him as we rush back, before handing him my iPad. "Sit down with my drink and stay as calm as you can. Look through this if you want. It'll make you seem more unassuming. Zero-nine-two-five is my password."

Santi slides into my chair and stares at the iPad, grabbing it with just enough time to settle in before the agents walk through the front door. Standing only a foot away from him. His eyes stay focused on the screen, swiping through my Procreate designs, trying his hardest not to pay attention to what's happening behind him. I don't want to leave him, but I can't seem out of the ordinary either.

"You keep working," Tita told me when I first started waiting here. "There's nothing they can do to you, and we need you to take up as much space as possible so we can get people out the back. Recuerda, we belong here. Show them that you can't be bothered and be a shield."

I grab the plates of another table Santi was waiting on and a plastic container of pink cake. Acting like it's any normal day and Tita and Mami aren't trying to keep their calm while talking to domestic terrorists. These two aren't familiar. Probably new, at least around Santos Vista. I see Mami's eyes as Tita speaks to one of the agents. Looking like it's taking all the strength she has not to punch them.

I'd pay her every dollar I ever make to see that just once.

I set down plates for the couple of tías sitting in the main dining room, making sure they're all right and thrilled they seem to catch on to what's going on. One of them even winks at me. "Qué lindo joven."

"Refill on the lemonade?" I ask Santi when I get to him, dropping the cake and a fork in front of him. Immediately noticing that he gulped down my entire cup when the sounds of ice and air come from the straw.

He continues to stare somewhere between the screen of my iPad and the tabletop as he speaks. "Uh, yeah. Sorry."

I want to crouch down and tell him it's okay. That if he can get through the next couple of minutes, it'll all go back to normal. That—Shit, I don't know what to tell him. My mind is almost as blank of thoughts as his is full of them.

"Don't apologize," is all that comes out. I push the cake closer to him. "Buen provecho."

I walk over to the canisters of lemonade, punch, and horchata, setting the cup under a nozzle and ignoring the ICE agents walking through the kitchen as I watch liquid fall into the cup.

"ID," is all one of them tells me. Coming up close enough

to where he's not touching me, but very much in my personal space. A hand held out, waiting.

"*That's my child*," Mami tells him, walking up to us like a lioness about to trample a hyena.

"It's okay," I say back as calmly as possible, reaching into my back pocket and taking out my wallet. "Here."

He scans my license with one of those things that I see bouncers use at clubs to make sure it's a real card. My entire body feels heavy waiting for him. Even though I know I'm a US citizen. That I was born here. That Mami keeps a copy of my birth certificate in the office only twenty feet away, in case something happens.

Because something could always happen.

So I hold my breath until he, with the least amount of care in the world, hands my license back to me.

"Are you done?" Mami asks him.

"Is that everyone who's on the clock right now?"

"Yes."

"Then, yeah. That's it for today." Both agents smirk as they leave, jotting down scribbles in their notebooks. They give us a small wave that they and we know is more of a signal of *Can't wait for you to fuck up next time* rather than goodbye.

I follow Tita to my table. Santi's attention immediately locks on to us.

"Are you okay, mi'jo?" she asks.

"Sí, doña." He's lying. I can hear it in his voice. See it in his eyes. In how his hands shake and haven't let go of my iPad. I know what *okay* Santi looks like.

Tita sighs and takes the unused fork from the table. "Bebite, you're taking him?"

"Yeah, I got it."

"Bueno. As long as he's not walking around while those demonios are out there. Vete. We got it from here."

22

Tell me what you need me to do. If there's someone you need me to call or a place you need to go."

"No," Santi spits out while struggling to buckle his seat belt. "I—I don't know." Now that it's only the two of us, I can feel how that heavy fear hasn't gone away. It's different, though. Not as heart-thumping, body being thrown into the lions' pit. It's more like my car is slowly filling with dread and anxiety until it swallows him whole. He's crossed his arms tightly over his chest, like he's trapping himself to the seat, making himself immobile.

"I don't want—I can't be alone right now."

"You won't be," I tell him, putting a hand on the back of his head and softly scratching, then down his neck and to the upper part of his back. I want him to know that I'm here. That he's here. Neither of us is going anywhere without the other. "I can take you to my house. You can stay with me as long as you want."

Santi looks at me. His eyes void of any emotion even close to comfort. But I can see the want in there. His need to find it. "Can I?"

"Yes. Of course."

I glance over at him when I can as I drive. During stop signs and at red lights. Knowing I can see and feel Santi right now helps ground me, but at the same time, I can't push away the worry of how far away he seems mentally. Like he's escaped to some safe corner of his mind where no one can reach him.

"Hey, uh, do you need anything? Like, food or something."

That gets his attention.

"Yeah," he mumbles.

"We can stop at a drive-through. Just tell me what you want."

"Don't judge me, okay?"

"*Yeah*," I reply. A little scared now.

"A couple Hot 'n Spicys and a large fry from McDonald's sounds real comforting right now."

I can't help it. I let out exactly one cackle, which gets Santi laughing too. Shit, I'd buy every spicy chicken sandwich every single McDonald's in San Antonio has to keep Santi laughing. To keep that empty look of hopelessness off his face.

"You got it, querido. McDiarrhea's coming right up."

Santi and I sit cross-legged on the couch, facing each other. I fold a big paper McDonald's bag and place it down between us with a stash of fries, sandwiches, chicken nuggets, and barbecue sauce packets. Our Cokes and bottles of ketchup and sriracha mayo sit on the floor by us.

"I realized something," Santi starts in between bites.

"What?"

"We're still wearing each other's shirts."

"We—Oh yeah." It didn't even occur to me that the old Santos Vista tennis tee I put on this morning is still on Santi. It's a little tight on him and if it had been any other time, I wouldn't be able to get over the *very good thoughts* I have about that. "You're right."

"I should get that back from you at some point," he says. "I need my work shirts."

"Are you asking me to undress right now?"

He laughs, covering his mouth full of french fries. "*No*. At least, not right now."

I throw a fry at him. "Come, puto."

He seems to be more present than earlier, but still deep in his own head. Which is both valid and depressing. I'm not going to sit here pretending I can relate to all the fears that entered his space, but how do I help him at least feel better? Because food only seems to ever go so far. I want to know that he's as content and unworried as I can help him be in this moment.

He looks up at me, taking a few seconds before asking, "Has all that been—la migra walking into your family's restaurant. That's not anything new, is it?"

My hand, holding a chicken nugget, stops midair as I think about it. How I was born about the same time ICE and Homeland Security became a thing. Only a year or two before walls on the border started getting put up. None of it is new. "The first time I remember them at Lupe's is . . . I was maybe four. The viejita who would babysit a few of us in the neighborhood had to go to a funeral or something, so Mami and Pa had to watch me at the restaurant that day. They gave me some coloring books and chocolate milk, sat me at the front of the store, and I was good. I was a pretty quiet kid."

"*Qué la*. No te creas."

"Okay, I was a kind of quiet kid," I say, glaring at him. "As long as I wasn't bored."

Santi gives me a look like he still doesn't fully believe me, but I ignore it and keep going.

"But then ICE and Customs agents walked in and immediately started acting up. The way Mami tells it, she's sure there was this white family there who saw a little kid by themself and assumed. Those agents did too. Thinking I was the kid of an undocumented waitress or a cook, even when my family was telling them I was theirs." I raise my free hand, my thumb and pointer finger almost touching. "I was *this* close to being taken because they didn't want to believe my parents. Ever since then, we've kept copies of my and Chachi's birth certificates at the taquería, photocopies of our Social Security cards, licenses. Everything. And it's usually the same few guys, so I don't get bothered. But when it's some new fuckers, there's always a little bit of fear there. Like going through a checkpoint and worrying that Border Patrol is gonna think I'm lying when they ask if I'm American. It's weird how, because we're brown, we start doubting everything."

"Your amá seems the type to not put up with their shit."

"That's definitely her," I reply, a quiet laugh leaving with the words.

"And I guess now what I needed to tell you is out in the open."

"I'm sorry that had to be the way I found out."

"I—I wanted to give you a chance to back out. I *want* to give you that chance. And now I kind of wish I'd told you last night. I got caught up in how good it felt to call you mine and I needed to hold that close to me, just for a while, but that was selfish of me."

"Hey—" My free hand reaches over and squeezes his. "Don't be sorry for that. Okay?"

"Well . . . either way, if I'm not the type of person you want to get involved with—"

"That's not happening," I tell him, squeezing his hand even tighter. "Some shitty line on a map isn't gonna decide who I—I told you. You've got me. All of me."

"Okay," Santi whispers. I can hear the unmistakable relief in his voice under the uncertainty. "And did you really not have any idea? About me?"

"*No*. Not until everyone was trying to find you at the restaurant and it all light-bulbed in my brain."

"¿Verdad?" he asks. His head tilts like he's having a lot of disbelief about this. "You saw a bunch of guys packing into a truck and thought, what?"

"That everyone around here has a ton of tíos and primos."

Santi laughs, and that turns into him choking on a bite of spicy chicken and then frantically reaching for his drink. "I don't know whether that's nice of you to not think about it or, like—"

"Ignorant?"

"I wasn't gonna say that."

"I wouldn't disagree. It's okay. I mean, no, it's not okay. But—and maybe it's from seeing things like what happened today happen on any given day on the news or in real life or hearing about it from my family or people in the neighborhood—I was raised to know this reality and want better than this, but to also keep my distance from it. In every way we're taught to not get too close. Whether it's because we don't want to be mistaken for someone who isn't a citizen, or for some because they think they're better because they did it *the right way*. Who even go put on a Border Patrol or ICE jacket, trying their best to be gringo. To be the least amount *us*. All they are is pinche porquería. I've always thought they were porquería and awful people. Like, the worst of us. But now . . . now it's more than that. I hate it. Even though I didn't realize I hated it until right now, sitting with you, thinking of how if we'd acted three seconds slower, things might've turned out a lot worse. Which makes me kind of hate myself. Because I needed that degree of separation to be a lot smaller before I had a reason to hate it."

"No creo que seas ignorante. Y no te odio," Santi tells me. "I opposite of hate you."

"I opposite of hate you too."

Santi eats enough McDonald's to last the rest of his life and I go through a few chicken nuggets, knowing I should eat something but too stressed about everything that's happened today. I come back from throwing away our trash to Santi having made himself comfortable on the couch, lying down. I take my seat back, sitting sideways so he can use my lap as his pillow. Both of us spend what feels like entire days looking at each other. I watch him play with my hand that was resting on his chest, gently massaging it with his fingers, observing the new mint-colored polish on my nails, and bringing my palm to his lips. And then as he lies completely still, never falling asleep, never making any noise, I wonder if he still feels trapped and lost or if he's managed to find some comfort with me.

"This place reminds me of home," Santi says quietly. "I know I said that to you before already, but even more than just you. This whole neighborhood. But you're my favorite part."

You're quickly becoming my favorite part too.

"When I was little, and on those days my amá wouldn't let me go play with my cousins, I liked to people watch. Spend all day memorizing the schedules of all the grown-ups who'd walk past me. Make up stories about how they lived their lives. I knew exactly what time the stray dog on our block would go by the carnecería near my house and wait for the butcher to come out with scraps."

"Sounds nice."

"It was. Probably still is in a lot of ways. That's the thing about home, right? When it's good, it's really good, mostly. I know I was happy there. But sometimes we happen to fall into the itty-bitty part of it that's bad. And then once you're in it, that itty-bitty part becomes much larger. It takes over your whole existence."

My free hand goes to Santi's head, feeling the short hairs tickle my skin, as I wait for him to continue. I want him to have control over how much he shares, and to know that whatever amount of his world he lets me into, I'll carry it carefully.

"My apá got our family into a lot of shit. Shit that got him and my older brother killed and my 'manita, amá, and me almost abducted. We were forced to leave in the middle of the night and travel up the entire country only for us to get stuck in Nuevo Laredo trying to earn enough money to pay for someone to get us across. But I guess we got lucky, right? I didn't end up in a cell with fifty men sharing one toilet. 'Manita didn't get taken from her mother. Living in a tent on the other side of the river instead is a blessing, right?"

"Are they still there?" I'm committed to not asking any other questions. I just—I really need to know that they're okay. That Santi isn't the end of these lives turned upside-down.

"Yeah. They are." He sniffles and wipes the corner of an eye. "I couldn't stay in Nuevo Laredo. I wanted to, but it wasn't an option. A teenage boy struggling, there were a lot of eyes on me. I knew I'd end up in something I wouldn't be able to get out of. But I send them money when I can. Have a phone call with at least one of them every other week, and I try to text and call my older sister too."

"You have an older sister?" Okay, so that commitment to one question went out the window faster than I expected. But Santi having another sibling came out of nowhere.

"Mhm. She's a lot older than I am and been up here for most of my life. Came with a tía. She's the reason I like to read. Would send me books when she could and buy herself a copy too. Then during phone calls we'd practice learning English with them. She'd read it first and then make me read it the next time."

"That—that's really cool."

"My original plan was to get to Arizona, where she is. But that didn't work out. Getting to San Antonio was hard enough, and moving too much or too far, that's how you attract attention. Especially because it's my second time here now."

"What?" I swear, I'm not *trying* to keep asking questions.

"My apá took me with him when I was little. So now that I have a record of that here, I'd be permanently banned from coming back if they catch me again."

"We won't let that happen," I nearly shout. "*I* won't let that happen."

Santi sits and turns his head, bringing mine closer with a couple fingers for a kiss. Greasy fry lips y todo.

"Yo sé."

"I'm with you. Through happiness and destruction."

"Through happiness and destruction," he repeats before bringing his mouth back to mine.

"Hey," I whisper into Santi's ear. At some point between movies we fell asleep, and suddenly the day went from four o'clock to ten and I'm spooning him. "Querido. Santi."

"Hm," he mumbles while stretching his legs and then grabbing my hand, pulling it to his chest.

"How're you feeling?"

"Better."

"You staying here tonight?"

His head turns up to the wall before his body follows, turning until he's facing me. "Is that okay?"

"Yeah. I told you, you can stay as long as you want."

"But what about your parents?"

"They won't care. And everyone's in Austin tonight. Chachi had a roller derby tournament today. They almost didn't go, but I told them we were okay and you're safe. It doesn't end until around ten, and then they usually end up visiting some of Mami's side of the family up there for a while after. They're never back until one or two in the morning, at the earliest."

"Is that you telling me if I stay the night, we can . . ."

I realize he's waiting on me to finish that sentence. "We could. If you want to."

His eyes stare into mine as his hand glides over my hip and my waist and arm and then finally to my own hand. "I want to."

In an instant, we're running upstairs, the worries of earlier today at the back of our minds. There's only us, here together in a moment that is both beautiful and frightening, for however long the world wants to give us. And we're going to make the most of it.

23

I wake up clinging to a pillow, the morning sunlight creeping into my room and straight toward my face. A long, deeply satisfying yawn so big my eyes close escapes me. I reach over to the other side of the bed, feeling—nothing.

"What the—" I whisper while swinging my body around to the empty space where Santi slept. And then back around, looking down, over the side of my bed, seeing his phone next to mine on the floor.

A light tapping jolts my head to the door. "It's me," Santi's voice says from behind it before twisting the knob. Walking in wearing nothing but a pair of my shorts and carrying two iced coffees and two bowls of arroz con leche.

"Who got Starbucks?"

"I went with Chachi," he answers while handing me breakfast.

"Dressed like that?"

"*Sí, amá.*" If he keeps up with that sass, I'm about to show him how amá I am and throw one of my slides at him. "We didn't get down."

"So, keeping the amount of people who get a view of your bulge first thing in the morning to a minimum. Cool."

Santi carefully gets on the bed, bowl and drink in each hand, making himself comfortable next to me, sitting cross-legged so he can put his drink in the hole created by his legs. "Next time

I'm here, I'll have to make sure to bring a pair of my own shorts, so I won't be worrying about a ball popping out."

I watch him take his first couple of spoons of arroz con leche. Making sure I see that peacefulness he was able to find last night still here today.

"I'm good," he tells me, his eyes to his food, feeling my stare. Knowing that's exactly where my head is.

My face falls to his shoulder, and my mouth feels the hard bone underneath his skin as I kiss him. "Do you need to talk about what happened or life in general some more?"

"Yes. No. I—I'm okay. No, I don't need to talk about it anymore. Not right now. I don't want to think about what happened yesterday. Except for last night. That I'll be thinking about for a while. What's that thing Americans say? Out of body out of heart?"

"I literally have no idea what you're trying to say."

"Whatever." He hits my arm with his elbow. "I want to do anything else except for think about the bad things that have happened recently."

"Okay. I can do that." I take a long sip of my drink, my body starting to feel functional as soon as the caffeine hits my tongue. "My family's having dinner tonight. You wanna hang around for that? If you're not feeling it, I get it, but still. Zeke and Ronnie are coming, so it won't be super intense."

"Why's everyone coming over?"

"I—it's my birthday today."

"¿Qué?" Santi almost chokes on his spoon in his surprise. "Why didn't I know this? Why didn't you tell me about it sooner?"

"I was gonna mention it yesterday, but then everything happened and I honestly forgot. And I had thought about telling you before, when we were just hanging out, but I also didn't want you to feel like you *had* to come since we weren't technically anything other than friends."

"No. I want to come. I—"

"What?" I ask when he looks like he's starting to dissociate.

"It's—your family. This'll be the first time I'll be around all of them as your boyfriend."

"Are you scared of them?" I ask, trying to keep the laugh buried deep inside my chest.

"I respect your family a lot, but your parents and la doña are terrifying. En serio."

"'Te'l hocico. These are the same people who *love* Zeke, so trust me when I say you have nothing to worry about. And if they act up, I'll protect you."

"Okay." Santi moves his head and puckers his lips, asking for a kiss.

"Do you need to do anything before then?"

"Nope. Nothing."

"Then . . . wanna go on a date with me?"

He chokes again when the question comes out, this time on his coffee. Like this was, somehow, the last string of words he expected me to say. "Right now?"

"Yeah. Is that a problem?"

"No, I just wasn't expecting that. I can think of something. Dame un momento. To treat you for your birthday."

"No. *Please.*" I squeeze his leg after patting it a few times. "For my birthday, you can let *me* take *you* on a date."

"I don't think that's how it usually works."

"I don't care."

Santi raises an eyebrow before breathing out all his annoyance, remembering that he's dating someone who likes getting their way. "Can we go by my place so I can change real quick, though?"

"Sure."

"Where are we going?"

"It's a surprise," I tell him with a lot of excitement in my voice. Smiling while putting all the details together in my head. "Like, legit, when we're done eating, go downstairs so I can get some stuff together."

"What does that mean?"

"Don't worry about it. Nothing freaky, I promise."

"I wouldn't say no to *some* freaky."

"Maybe practice not choking on your breakfast and then we'll come back to that suggestion."

"*Shut up*, that's different. But—" Santi takes one more big spoonful of arroz con leche before setting the bowl aside. And then his hands go to the back of his neck, unfastening his necklace with the Virgen de Guadalupe pendant and then holding it out to me. "Here. I want you to have this."

"I—no. Santi, that's yours and it's obviously special and—"

"It is special. But so are you. And it would mean a lot to me."

I let out a quiet sigh before nodding. "Okay. As long as you're sure."

"Claro, cielo," he replies while putting it on me. "Feliz cumple."

"Gracias, querido." My fingers glide over the chain down to the pendant.

After it's clasped on, he comes to my cheek, slowly kissing his way down to my neck, the feeling of his lips on me and where his hand's going already making me light-headed and thinking about the things that happened on this bed last night. "Also, before we do anything else, and you get too into your breakfast, I wanna give you one more birthday present."

———————

"Why don't you let me carry the duffel bag?"

"*Because I can do it myself*," I snap. "And you're going to look inside and ruin the surprise."

Although, I've been regretting how much I packed ever since

I put the strap over my shoulder and realized how heavy it is. Once we get to Elmendorf Lake—sitting in the middle of a park only a couple minutes outside of Santos Vista on the Our Lady of the Lake University campus—I can throw this shit down.

"Okay," I say when we reach a grassy area just before the water. "This is a good spot." I couldn't have asked for a better park day. Sunny, nice breeze, perfect temperature.

"For what?"

"Cálmate, querido. *Damn.*"

I open the duffel bag and start taking out pencils, paint markers, regular paints and brushes, two palettes and four canvases. Santi watches me with intense curiosity as I sort everything and lay it all out on the grass and then set the bag behind me when it's emptied.

"Ready?"

"We're painting?"

"Yeah."

"But I—Yours is going to be a lot better than mine."

"Better is relative. And it's not a competition. We're relaxing, spending time with each other, and I wanted a chance to show you something I like to do on a day I'm not getting paid for it. But in case you mess up beyond the point of no return and are *sure* you can't rescue it, I brought extra canvases."

He takes one of them and starts inspecting all the paints, taking a marker in his hand, then placing it back down. "What should I do?"

"Whatever you want."

I help Santi fill the palette with the different paints he wants to use and show him how to mix them because "What if I want to do a teal; you didn't bring teal." But after that he refuses to let me see, making me sit facing him so it'll be harder to get a peek as he uses his bent knees as an easel. Which sucks because

I'm trying to be nosy and see what he's doing. But like this, with him in front of me, I could try a canvas version of a Santi portrait.

The front of his right foot taps up and down on top of mine as he gets to work. His tongue sticks out the slightest bit too and his eyes squint in concentration. And so much of me wants to watch him and think about how fucking perfect my boyfriend is and how I get to call him boyfriend now instead of actually do anything, but I need to get to work.

I start with a pencil, sketching markings that will be covered up by the end to help get the lines more exact. And then he glances out to the lake for a minute and, perfect. That's the pose. Going from navel up, only worrying about his body. I can think about background later when I'm not trying to get this done within a few hours.

Sketch complete, and now markers. I get some good shading practice coloring in the black of Santi's hair. Fill in the brown of his skin. The gray of his tank and maroon of the loose open shirt over it, giving myself a second-long break to admire the black denim shorts and gray tennis shoes and how good he looks today. *Okay, I told myself I wasn't getting distracted. Admire my boyfriend later.*

About an hour in, as I'm daydreaming and unconsciously fiddling with the Virgen pendant hanging off my neck, Santi's head perks up and then suddenly he's jumping up and running off, past kids playing soccer, a group of people doing yoga, and another group practicing ballet folklórico. Ignoring my shouts of "*Where are you going?!*" and sprinting away with his canvas held carefully under his arm so I can't peek while he's gone. I don't know if he has the ears of a barrio German shepherd, but somehow he hears a lady selling bags of mango further down the park path, coming back with two bags of fruit covered in red.

"I forgot to ask if you like Tajín, chamoy, and lime with your mango."

"I do."

"Okay, good, because I don't think we could date if you didn't. Pretend this is your birthday cake. From me. Feliz cumpleaños, cielo."

"Gracias, querido," I tell him, letting him kiss me while I take the bag from him.

I could watch Santi try to eat mango with one hand while painting with the other and attempting to keep his canvas upright with his lap and feet all day. Laugh at the struggle and groans whenever he starts having a hard time. And how he'll switch between hands, figuring out how to best paint and eat at the same time.

"Almost done?" I ask when it starts getting close to six.

"Yep," Santi answers. "You?"

"Yeah. Who shows who first?"

"This was your idea. You should have to go first."

"Mm, I think that since this was my idea, *you* should actually go first."

"How does that even make sense?"

"Because. My date, *my birthday*, my rules."

"Vete a la verga. No mames con la pinche 'my date, my birthday, my rules.' Whatever. Hold on." He takes the last couple slices of mango from his bag and bites into them, wiping his fingers into the grass. "Okay. ¿Listo?"

"*Ya. ¡A ver!*"

"*Bam!*" Santi yells as he turns his canvas around. There's a scoop of what looks like pink raspa in an outline of a white Styrofoam cup on the left side, with a few fingers holding on to the cup. The background is that damn teal he was so invested in.

"Querido, this is really, *really* good."

"*Cállate. ¿Sí?* Does it get artist approval?"

"Full approval. I like how the pink is stronger in some parts like actual raspa syrup on ice. Fingers are difficult for a lot of people and these aren't half bad. And the colors work really great together. The vibes are radiating off it. I'm gonna need you to not come for my gig."

"Pues, I already took one of your jobs. Might as well make it a habit."

"I'll fight you in front of everyone at this park right now, Santiago. Don't think I won't."

"Bet," he replies jokingly. "Bueno. Your turn, cielo. ¿Qué pintaste?"

I slowly turn my canvas around, showing him the portrait. I'm incredibly happy with how it turned out. Even happier that I managed to do a cloudy sunset moment behind him. But it's always intimidating showing someone a portrait of themselves for the first time.

"That—You painted me?"

"Do you like it?"

"It . . . it's incredible. Can I hold it? I don't wanna give it ojo."

"You can have it."

"What? ¿Verdad?"

"Yeah. It's for you."

Santi takes it from me, holding it cautiously in his hands, making sure not to touch any parts that might still be drying. "Qué hermoso."

"Are you gassing yourself up or are you complimenting my work?"

"Two things can be true at the same time. But—thank you for this." He stares some more at the painting, letting his fingers hover-glide over the canvas. "I'm gonna be in awe of this for a while. Of you."

"I have a good subject," I tell him while getting up and putting everything back in the bag.

"I want to give you my painting," Santi says, holding his canvas to me. "If you want it."

"Claro. We still have a little time before we gotta be at my tita's, and the house should be empty. Wanna help me find the perfect place for it in my room?"

"Yeah. I think I can do that."

24

Santi and I *do* find the perfect spot on the wall near my desk for the painting. And, if my family asks why we're late to Tita's, that's the excuse we'll give. Not because making out in my car when we got to my house led to my head ending up in his lap while parked in the driveway. And definitely not because he wanted to reciprocate while playing "hide the fingers" when we got to my bedroom.

Santi lets out a small *whoa* when we walk into her backyard. Tita's turned on the green, white, and red lights hanging from her pecan trees that she only uses for special occasions. At least thirty Chicanes are scream-talking and *eyy*-ing at me when they see us come in. There are ice chests with bottles of liquor and sodas and kegs at the heads of foldable white, rectangular tables. Pa and a couple of his siblings are grilling fajitas, and the smell goes from my nose down to my soul.

I pause when I see my family. Well, my *immediate* family. I get the feeling Mami knows exactly why we were late. Tita knows. I can see in her smirk when she sees Santi and me walking in puro puppy word-I'm-absolutely-not-using-yet. I'll take that compared to the serious line Mami's mouth makes when she remembers that she's still holding in the rage she meant to yell out at me yesterday but didn't get a chance to because of everything that happened with Santi.

I'll ignore her all night if she's going to be petty about me making my own choices that always manage to both be the exact opposite of what she wants me to do, and *always* end up working out. That's my entire thing. She should be used to this by now. *And learn to trust her now fucking nineteen-year-old child.*

Not like I'd be able to hear her nagging over all the voices and the Selena coming from the speakers anyways.

I say hi to her first and Santi moves for Pa, giving him a respectful handshake. Pa starts talking about who knows what; I'm praying it's not some sort of weird "Now that you're dating one of my children . . ." talks like he did with Zeke. They'll be a while. Especially if my tíos get in on it too. Long enough for me to make my way through my entire family and say my hellos and *thank you for coming*s.

"Mi'je," Mami says as I come in for a hug, kissing her cheek. "You're late."

"I think this is where you're actually supposed to say 'Happy birthday, my favorite child. I love you so much, Ander.'"

"You should be congratulating *me* today. You didn't do nothing. *I* pushed you out."

"Whatever. And we're not *that* late. It's not as if these things ever start on time anyways."

She rolls her eyes and goes back to her margarita. "What were you up to all day?"

"Hanging out."

"Hanging out *in your bedroom*?"

"*Jesus*, I—we went to the park."

"Cute," she replies in a half-invested tone. "He doing okay?"

"Mostly."

"Good. But don't think we're not talking about this later."

"*¿Por qué?* What is there to talk about?"

"Plenty, Ander."

I groan, craning my neck back. "I really don't get you. But, whatever. I'm gonna go see Tita."

In addition to frustrated Mami, I get some tempered happiness mixed with worry, especially with what happened yesterday, from Tita—who takes a break from owning my cousins at beer pong to hug Santi and me for entire minutes—and then the usual casualness from Pa that he uses to bury the stronger emotions that Mexican men refuse to show. For better or worse, they're all invested in not just Santi as their employee and me as their kid but both of us as a couple. And our well-being.

When I'm finally free from Pa and my own "I know I told you this when you started dating, but . . ." talk, I find Santi sitting in between an empty chair with a plate of tacos and a drink in front of it and Zeke. Both of them deep in conversation.

"What're y'all talking about?" I ask as I sit down, leaning toward Santi.

"You," they both answer in unison.

"Why'd you never do anything cute with me like you did with Santi, AJ?"

"*What?* I've painted you tons of times."

"Yeah, but you never did while we were on a date at the lake."

"You've come with me to, like, half of my Beautify projects."

"*That's not the same,*" Zeke whines, his mouth in a pout.

"Are you jealous?"

"*Slightly.* More, like, wow, I really swept in for sixteen-year-old Ander thinking that you were at the pinnacle of your game. Not so. Santi got that. I'll concede. It's cool."

"How long did you two date?" Santi asks, his eyes going to Zeke first and then me.

"Ten months," I answer.

"And it wasn't hard going back to friends after that?"

"Oh yeah. It was rough," Zeke says. "How long did we go without talking, AJ?"

"Probably, like, what? Five months?"

"We ended up hashing it out. This huge argument and then sobfest and then a couple blunts later, and we were . . . well, we definitely weren't where we'd been *before* we started dating, or where we were as a couple, obviously. It was the beginning of a new era, formed by all the good and bad and easy and hard times and was exactly where we needed to be. Some real mature, ending of a Netflix, indie, coming-of-age movie sort of shit, you know."

"Are you dating anyone right now?"

"Two people, actually."

Both Santi and I give him confused looks. Santi's mixed with impressed and mine with *How the fuck did you pull that off?*

"How's that?" Santi asks.

"Extremely tiring in every single way you can think of. But also really cool?" Zeke takes a couple chips and dunks them into queso, holding up a finger for us to wait on him to swallow. "Let's get back to talking about how it's been dating AJ so far."

"All almost forty-eight hours of it?" I ask.

"The best forty-eight hours," Santi says. "Not even la puta migra could ruin it."

"*They sure did try,*" I groan before taking a big swig of sweet tea.

"But, yeah," Santi continues, reaching his arms around me and giving me a quick kiss on the lips, "besides that, no complaints."

"*Yet,*" Zeke adds.

"I'm gonna need you to shut up."

"So, when you said your family, I thought you meant tus padres y jefa y Chachi. Not half the neighborhood," Santi starts while we hang out in Tita's living room, waiting for Chachi to get out of the restroom and take us home, me sitting on his lap while he tries not to fall asleep on a recliner. Most of the party's gone now, except for a few family members who'll be outside with Tita and my parents until the sun's up. "¿Todos son tu familia?"

"You're Mexican and you're surprised about someone having a big family?"

"Ah, sí. That's true. *Oh*, and you said you were bad at dancing when you aren't."

"*I never said that*. Ronnie said that. I said he was lying. And, see? He was. Except for that one song you were going way too fast with."

"That was the tempo of the song! You were going too slow. You got it, though. Next time you'll be ready for some spins."

"Nah, I don't need you throwing me over the bar."

"*Chinga'o*. I promise I won't throw you over the bar. I won't let you go."

"Better not," I reply, squeezing his hands in mine. Thinking about the many ways he meant those words. "I won't let you go either."

Santi is still for a moment before adjusting himself, wrapping his arms around me. He tilts his head back, a relaxed sigh coming out as he closes his eyes. Not saying a word.

Is he thinking the same thing as I am right now? That here is actual, physical proof that we mean it when we say we aren't letting each other go. That I've got him, no matter what, and no matter how terrible or desperate or scary things get. And that when I need a reminder, I can remember this moment and know that he's got me too.

"Are you okay with me calling you *cielo*?" Santi asks.

"What? Yeah. I like it," I tell him. And, I guess, no, we weren't thinking the same thing. "Why?"

"I started calling you that without thinking about how you're nonbinary. And I remembered how your family doesn't use the *o* ending for words they call you, so I wanted to make sure it doesn't bother you. I can call you something else."

"It doesn't bother me."

"You're not just saying that, right?"

"I would let you know if I found it problematic for me. Trust me. I am extremely fine with you calling me cielo. But don't ever say *el cielo*, okay? No *el*. Soy *tu* cielo."

"Eres *mi* cielo," Santi repeats. "I think you were always meant to be that for me. We were meant to cross paths right now. Find each other."

"You believe that?" I ask, leaning more on him to rest my head on his collarbone, looking to him for an answer.

"Sí. And there's a chance I'm only saying it out loud because Zeke gave me an edible—"

"When did Zeke give you an edible?"

"Don't worry about it. But I really do believe that everyone who comes into your life is meant for a specific purpose. Like how you and him were always meant to be best friends, even though it didn't seem so easy for a while. And then there's you and me. Maybe—I hope—who I am to you, you can feel me in your gut—"

I let out this awful, gross throaty laugh. *"Oh my god, sorry,"* I tell him. "I think that got lost in translation because when you say I can feel you in my guts, like, that, it—"

"Eres necio."

"You said it! And now I'm having flashbacks. Anyways, continue. Please."

"I—where was I?"

"I can feel you in my guts."

Santi takes a second. He bites down on his bottom lip,

fighting the urge to admit that now it's funny to him too. "'Te'l hocico. I was trying to say that, I felt something for you the moment I saw you. And there has to be purpose behind that. I believed that even more when I saw you again after nearly convincing myself I only imagined you, and then again after that, and again after that. Eres mi cielo. For however long we have."

"All the time in the world."

That's what I have to believe. That's what I have to speak into the universe. A part of me had been comfortable thinking that maybe this would be some short-lived fling. That we'd have a few months before I leave for Chicago, bang it out before I get on the plane, and never think much of each other after that. But yesterday changed a lot of things. Most of all, it made me realize I'm going to be a lot more invested in this boy than I thought I'd be.

And I'm very okay with that.

"All the time the world."

25

L et's talk."

"Okay. Let's talk."

Mami stares at me from the far end of my bed. Doing this thing where she tries to gauge how much of a fight I'm about to put up. Seeing what the odds are of her preemptively having the upper hand on this.

"I thought we had an understanding, Ander. Did we not? I said—I told you. Not him."

"We—things changed."

"And that was before or after he almost got taken away?"

"I—" I wish she hadn't brought that up. Or said it like that. Not after I spent last night haunted by a nightmare of some ICE agent dragging Santi out of Lupe's. I tried to stop it, but I was like a ghost. No matter how hard I tried to push the guy away, nothing I did would work. No matter how much I tried to scream, no sound came out of my mouth. Neither of them realized I was there until the very end, when Santi looked back and our eyes met, and the words "Help me" came out of his mouth. His voice hoarse and scared.

But I couldn't. Nothing I did mattered.

"It was before. Doesn't make a difference, though."

"How does it not make a difference?"

"Because why should it matter whether the guy I'm dating

is something as, as—*ugh*." I squeeze the top of my head while letting out a groan. "What do you have against me dating an undocumented person?"

"Don't word it like that," Mami scolds. "I worry that you aren't thinking about what could happen to you. The danger you're putting yourself in. For what? What is even going on between the two of you? Hm? ¿Son fuck buddies?"

"Why do you even know what f—Never mind. We're dating. He's my boyfriend."

"I really wish that wasn't the case. As much as I've never been the type to tell you someone is off-limits when it comes to dating. You've never needed that—"

"Do you think I need that now?"

"I think it doesn't matter to you what my opinion is. I can't tell you what to do. But I can tell you right now that the way this ends is either you're going to get hurt or you're going to give that boy a lot of hurt."

"Damn, thanks for the pep talk."

"*Language.*" Her eyes glare with the slightest tinge of anger now. More at the use of the word *damn* than anything else. "Is this going to be something serious between you two?"

"I don't know, Mami. Honestly, I have no idea. Maybe it won't be. Maybe by the time August comes around, we'll decide to end it. Maybe we won't even make it to then. Or this could be serious, and we figure out something long term and become those gays who wear matching pajamas every Christmas."

"What do you want it to be?"

"I—I really like him. Enough that I hope this could be something that won't end for a long time. I wanted the opportunity to try if Santi wanted that too. And he does. So, ya basta. That's it."

Mami sighs, unsure of where to go with this talk now. Hopefully nowhere. Figure out that there's no way she's going to change my mind or Santi's mind and get on with life.

"No more taking Zeke's shifts, all right? You weren't even supposed to be pinche working at all. We fired you—"

"I thought I was just 'let go'?"

"Pues, well, now you're really fired. I fire you. And, *actually*, ya, if you're even at the restaurant, it should only be because you're working on the job Tita is paying you for or if you're picking up food. I don't even want you eating there unless you're having a meal with Tita or me or Pa. Got it?"

"What? No. Why?"

"Because I said so."

"You just said you can't tell me what to do but you're gonna literally tell me what to do and then say 'because I said so'? No."

"Ander. Do as I say for once in your life, please? This one time."

"I need a reason."

Mami quickly stands up, her arms opening wide as the words start coming out of her mouth: "Because if ICE comes in and takes Santi, I want to do my best to make sure you don't have to see him get taken away." She turns around so her back's to me, but I can see her hand going up to her forehead. "I don't want either of you to have that be the last memory you have of each other. And I'm not saying that because I care about you two as a *thing*. I'm not. But he's my worker and we have to look out for him. And you're my child. I love you, and I want you to experience the least amount of hurt in your life as possible. If I can help that in whatever way, I'm going to. Y también, porque te conozco, mi'je. I don't want you putting yourself in the middle of that situation. That's going to make it worse for both of you and for everyone."

"I—" I have nothing to say to that. Nothing that would help my case, at least. Because, yeah, she does know me. She knows that I'd punch the shit out of any ICE agent who even thought about touching Santi. If they want to kick him out, they might as well kick me out too.

But those aren't words I'm going to tell Mami.

"Do you have a problem with me taking him to work and back to his house?"

"No. But, again, unless you're coming in with paint, I don't want to see you hanging around."

"Or him being here?"

"Santi can be here as much as he wants. But wait until no one is home if you two wanna have sexy time. These homes have thin walls."

"I can't stand you."

Mami gently pats at my cheeks about twelve more times than necessary. "The feeling is mutual, mi'je. I want you to know, though, I say and do all of this out of love for you and a want for Santi to live as safe of a life as he can."

"But is it worth it if he's never able to actually live his life?"

"That's a decision he gets to make. *Only* him. He *should* be able to. Entiendo. And, well, that's all I'm saying. That and watch out for him, okay? Como que, how do I put it? Help him keep an eye out for stray bullets, but don't put yourself in front of one for him."

"That's bleak."

"That's the world we live in, Ander. All we can do is try to make it a little less terrible. And you've always been very good at that. Mi linda y mi valiente. Pues, my little shit too."

"Wonder where I get that from."

"Oh, your papi," Mami replies with all the certainty in the world. "The original little shit."

⸻

"What's your take on predetermination?"

"I didn't even know you knew that word," Zeke replies after taking a hit of my bong. Smoke leaves his mouth as he speaks, mixing with the air while we sit on the roof. There are a few big gray clouds in the sky, and it's windier than usual. But until I start smelling the beginning of a rainstorm, I'm all right staying out here.

"Shut the fuck up. I'm serious. Like, do you think we were destined to be friends?"

"Well, if you think about groups of queer people of color with what it feels like to start high school or go into any brand-new environment, it's natural for people like us to gravitate toward each other. So, I mean, I'd argue that it's not destiny. It's more, like, sociology or anthropology."

"Cool, thanks for shitting on that question."

"This isn't me trying to change your mind if you believe in something, AJ. You asked a question and I gave you my best answer."

I light the bong, hearing the gurgling of the water, letting in, and then out a cloud of smoke. "I didn't say I—I was only bringing up an interesting concept. What if you were meant to be in that throuple? Or what if we and Mo were meant to be best friends, and what if the friends Mo is making up in Denton right now were meant to be in his life right now, in this exact time, and what if—"

"Well, the throuple is no more, so I wouldn't use that to build your argument."

"*You just told me about them two days ago.* What happened?"

"Didn't work out. It's whatever. Anyways, back to you and your whole 'What if there's some greater meaning to it all?' Because I think what you really want me to validate for you is that out of anyone who jefecita could've hired, it was Santi, someone who in every other time line you never would've ever known existed, who showed up that day for an interview."

"I mean, yeah."

"If you're convinced there is, then let there be. You're here. He's here. Let that have as much meaning as you want. But—"

"But what?" I ask when he's still silent after five and then ten seconds.

"What do you make of that meaning when August comes around and you're leaving?"

"Meaning that only lasts five months can still be meaningful," I answer. "I'm not saying that I want to break up with him when I head to Chicago, but—we'll see where we are when that day comes."

"I hope it lasts as long as you want it to. As your best friend and as your ex-boyfriend, I really and truly mean that. There's a lot out there that's trying to get a say in whether or not or for how long this works out for you and Santi, but even though it's only been—what? Three days?"

"Yep."

"Yeah. Wow, it feels like a lot longer. Y'all've been on each other for a while, though."

"Shut up."

He laughs, smoke coming out of his mouth and nose. "Anyways, even though it's only been three days, my bet's that you're gonna have three more days and three more days after that and way, way, way, *way* more three more days."

"I hope so."

26

A bar on the St. Mary's Strip is closing down and offered to give us these. Beautify doesn't need them, but if you want them, they're yours. I'll make sure we get them power washed first and all the straight people sweat cleaned off. Just let me know where to drop them off.

I stare at pictures Juni sent me after the text of these large, still blank, mask statues gathered inside an empty building. There's at least ten of them, and Juni's next message is talking about how they come up to about his chin, so basically my height. They're longer than they are wide. Less masquerade and more lucha libre.

Wait. Lucha libre. *Yes*.

Give me the day to find a place to store them, but yes, I need. For what? No idea yet. So, more of a want than a need. But I literally do *need* them.

"Pa!" I start yelling from my room. "*Pa!*"

Pa, Tía Mila—his older sister—and her wife, Tía Olena, stand on either side of me, all of us watching four guys unload the mask statues one at a time into one and then another storage garage. Well, I'm doing most of the watching. Men doing physical labor really does something for me. Pa and the lesbians? Not so much.

My tías and their storage business they've owned for decades immediately came to mind when I started thinking of a place to keep these big bitches. Tías Mila and Olena are *always* down to help their favorite brother and his gay, nonbinary kid. Especially since I painted their office building last summer. New coat of white on three of the exterior sides, and on the road-facing side, a giant lesbian flag covering the entire wall. Which, like, easy. Stripes are nothing. And if it gets me a couple free storage spaces twelve months later, I'll paint as many lesbian flags as they want.

We're able to fit sixteen masks between two storage garages next door to each other, the statues lined up in rows of four, all facing the front, which is super fucking scary and I need to remember to never be here alone with them at night. I don't need to be around when they all come alive.

"These are cool," Pa says, standing behind one of them. Bending down so I can see him through one of the eyes, winking at me before sticking his hand through the opening like he's expecting something magical to happen. "What are you using them for?"

"I—Figuring that out still. Ask me in a few weeks," I tell him while taking pictures of the statues so I can use them as references when I start working on designs later. "What if we put them around the patio?"

"I don't think we can fit sixteen giant sculptures in the patio. We still need, you know, to make sure there's tables."

"I don't know if I agree with that."

Pa lets out a snorty laugh and shakes his head. I can hear the *cabrone* coming out under his breath. "And you'll be painting them inside the garage? Seems like an easy way to have a heat-stroke."

"No, I was planning on taking them out one at a time."

Pa pushes on the statue he's been standing next to, his eyes and this scrunch with his lips giving me a lot of doubt and apprehension. "*You're* going to take these out?"

"I'll get help if I need to."

"You'll need to," he says while walking out of the storage unit. "I don't need Milagros calling me because you got squished by a giant mask."

"This is what you get for not being one of those dads who pushes football on their kid."

"Ander, my child, one thing your mami and I learned very quickly about you was that you were *never* going to be the football-playing type."

"I'm sure you were very disappointed."

"I was. Un poco." He starts pulling down the door to one of the units while I get the other. "Until I found out Chachi's got an arm on her. I knew *one* of my kids would turn out to be a future 49ers QB."

"Glad she could keep the dream alive for you."

"Me too. I was about to start convincing your mami to give me baby number three. Imagina. *Three of y'all?* Glad we dodged that bullet."

"Where are we go—*Oh.*" Santi's eyes widen when he sees that I'm not lost on the Eastside of San Antonio, and actually know exactly where I'm going.

Today I'm taking Santi to a couple of my favorite spots, starting with Essex Modern City, a building complex that stopped being constructed a quarter of the way through and then someone saw the concrete ground and open walls and said "lemme make this into an art gallery." So now it's covered in murals, including one by me.

I know that, even on a weekday, this place can get busy around lunchtime and in the evening. It's one of the most Instagram-able spots in all of San Antonio. So our best bet at having this place to ourselves is in the morning. I picked him up before the sun had risen, we got some breakfast tacos and iced coffees, and then drove to the other side of Downtown to, just as I thought, an empty EMC.

"Who is that?" he asks when I show him my mural of a shirt-less man, chest up, with a short beard, mustache, and Vinny Guadagnino of *Jersey Shore* haircut holding a large bundle of lilies. A blended background of reds and yellows behind him.

"One of my cousins. His name's Nate. Nataniel. He lives over on the Southside. He was at my birthday party. The one holding up Tita while she was doing a keg stand."

We sit side by side on top of the picnic table closest to my mural, admiring it and the ones nearby while eating our break-fast. "Yours is the best," Santi says while unwrapping his third chorizo, bean, and potato taco from its aluminum foil.

"You're *supposed* to say that."

"I'm being honest. Mi novie es le artiste más talentose en el universo."

"I don't know about that," I tell him before taking a sip of coffee. "At least, not yet. One day."

After we eat, I take his hand and we walk all the way around Essex, slowed down by both of us recording each other nonstop for our IG Stories, and then stopping when he wants to get a picture with one of the murals in his weirdly angled Instagram poses even though *I've told him* that's not how you take pictures with murals. And when we finally make it to the YOU BELONG HERE mural—the words in bold white in front of vertical stripes of greens, purples, pinks, blues, oranges, and yellows that start at the top of the wall, go all the way down, and then jut out onto the ground—other people are starting to arrive. Which is perfect timing for someone to take pictures of us in front of the mural and then mine before we're out.

"Where next, cielo?"

"As much as it pains me to even make this suggestion, I will take you to the River Walk if you've never been and want—"

"*Yes*," Santi replies excitedly before letting me finish. "Please, let's go."

And this is how we end up spending three hours Downtown walking on a crowded sidewalk, then a riverboat tour, *then* back on the sidewalk, buying a straw hat for Santi because he gave me a "Lo necesito, cielo" with the puppiest of eyes. More pictures and short videos. Getting lost somewhere around the Henry B. González Convention Center.

Definitely one of the better afternoons spent at the biggest tourist trap in the city.

And, as evening hits, we're back on the Eastside, stopping at my favorite fried chicken place before heading to the Hays Street Bridge. What was once for trains but is now used as a walking path, photo op for engagement photos, spot for great views of Downtown, and hanging out with boyfriends.

We sit down against one of the reddish-brown metal beams, grabbing at chicken pieces and french fries and going through all the pictures we took. Santi with his new hat, gray cotton shorts, and white tank with his trusty navy corduroy shirt in hand, and me, no hat (as much as Santi tried to convince me to try it), making an actual attempt at posing versus my boyfriend's more natural photogenic-ness, a cropped UNT shirt showing off my stomach, and black running shorts.

I stop at the pictures of us at the YOU BELONG HERE mural.

One of Santi holding on to me and both of us looking at each other. He must've said something funny just before because we're both laughing. Then the next one of us kissing, and the last one of my head leaning on his shoulder, both of us giving less of a smile and more of a smize.

If Santi ever believes anything other than what those words are saying, I hope he'll see these and know that he does. That this is his home as much as any white person or foolish-ass, brown-nosed Chicane. That I'll do whatever it takes for him to never think he doesn't belong anywhere else than here. With me.

And, *ugh*—

"What's wrong?" Santi asks.

"Nothing, querido," I tell him before grabbing a couple more fries.

I don't want him to know that I'm worried about what happens at the end of August. I'm worried that I told him we have all the time in the world but what happens if I can't keep that promise. I feel like the spark that Santi and I had from the first moment we saw each other, that's quickly become more like the most beautiful lightning storm, is going to . . . what? We take our chances with distance? We let it die out?

The perfect day that today has been makes me crave *here*. And what *here* is has never been better or more exciting or more meaningful since Santi came into my life.

27

I don't get it," Santi says as soon as he's out of Lupe's, seeing me leaning on my car. "Why do Americans get hard for Cinco de Mayo? It's not even that important."

"You know this country likes to act up in as many ways as possible."

"And then all the white people coming in, like, 'Oh my god,'" he starts, mimicking this whiny, fake-white-girl voice. "'Can you believe *Cinco de Drink-o* is on a Taco Tuesday this year? Can't wait to play *low-ter-ee-uh.*' I'm glad los jefes only have me working until seven today. I wouldn't be able to handle drunks tonight."

"Tell me how you really feel," I tease.

"¿Estoy exagerando? I'm not, right?"

"No, definitely not. You being annoyed at everyone here not giving a shit about Mexico except for when they can drink margaritas about it is valid. *But* let me know if you want me to pretend I've never referred to it as Cinco de Drink-o."

"*Verga.*" Santi draws out the word to show exactly how annoyed he is at me right now. "Qué gacho. You too?"

"I was a very different person at eighteen."

"You've only been nineteen a couple weeks."

"That's not important. What is, is that I've been standing here for whole minutes now and you haven't kissed me."

"We should fix that, then," he says with a smirk, holding my side with one hand and pulling me close to him. And just as our lips are about to meet, we're interrupted by a loud whistle.

"Who the—*ugh*—" I grunt when I look over Santi toward the restaurant's front door and see Zeke waving at us with a server I've never met before behind him. Mami really got rid of me and hired a ton of new people. Also, this girl *definitely* looks like she's trying to get at Little Zeke.

"AJ, didn't think I'd catch you. Was literally about to send you a text," he shouts as he runs over to us. "Sixty-Nine tonight?"

"*What?*" Santi asks in almost a yell.

"It's a club," I assure him. "Zeke wasn't—no."

"I mean, I'm not trying to tell y'all that you *can't* do that," Zeke continues. "But, yeah, I meant the club. They're having a Cinco de Mayo party. Part of it's in the club and part's outside. They're gonna have a bunch of inflatable pools, calling it Cinco Swim—"

"That's clever."

"I know, right?"

"Qué la—" Santi groans as his head goes back. "No. What does that even mean? Are they filling the pool with aquacate?"

"Jose Cuervo, actually," Zeke answers with a smile that says just how funny he thinks he is. "Anyways, you're both coming and we're gonna shake our ass to 'Cobarde' and dance like Scarlett Johansson when 'Fotos y Recuerdos' comes on."

"I—I, uh, have to work the breakfast shift tomorrow," Santi says. "But it sounds like fun."

"We can get someone to cover it," Zeke replies in a whine. "It's always the *best* night to be out. SA gays know how to Cinco. Like, remember last year, AJ? Our very first night out, freshly eighteen. That old couple buying us tequila shots who were definitely problematic, now that I'm looking back on it, but—"

Santi squeezes my hand, but not in the usual, playful way. There's a tension coming from him. Swear, if he hears the word *cinco* one more time, he might turn a table over, like—

No. Wait.

Clubs. Clubs require IDs. They're going to want to check ours at the door. There're cops all over the streets. And Santi—

"Zeke," I snap. Probably harsher than I was trying to be. Processing too many things at once. "It's cool. You—y'all—go. Invite your Incarnate Word friends. We'll catch you next time."

"*What?* Really, AJ? We can go inside right now and tell jefa to get someone to come in early. We haven't taken Santi out yet."

"Yes, really. We can—" I glance over at new girl who's trying her hardest to make sense of this entire situation, even though there's no way she's putting this together right now. "We'll take him out some other time, all right?"

"Damn, getting boring the second someone puts a ring on it."

"That's not what's happening, cabrón. You should—*ugh*." Zeke is so fucking useless sometimes. He knows. He has all the knowledge it would take to connect the dots about why Santi wouldn't want to go out and also, like, a hundred IQ points on me. But pendejo's wheels aren't going at normal speed for some reason today and he's refusing to think.

"We gotta go," I tell them. "I'll see y'all later."

———

"I'm sorry I'm boring," Santi says as his head rests on my chest, his arms wrapped around and under my body, probably numb, and his breathing calm as my fingers trail from the top of his head down to his neck.

"The hour that you put in tonight is proof that you are *definitely* not boring."

"But—you know you can go out, right? Without me."

"*Yes*. I'm choosing to be here. This is what I want. And Zeke honestly *way* oversold how fun it was. Going to a club on a weekday, especially when you're not twenty-one yet, is kind of sad. Except for those Latinx Nights I mentioned to you way back when. I'd rather spend a Tuesday night under my boyfriend."

"What happens when you're twenty-one and wanna go to clubs and bars?"

"I—Don't take this the wrong way, but thinking about things that are two years away might be getting too ahead of ourselves. As much as I like the thought of that. But if I'm putting together a hypothetical scene in my head, by that time I'll have made millions from my art because some white gay with connections loved, I don't know, my mural of a light-skin Latina with a flower crown, and I can use that money to open up my own club where you wouldn't have to worry about what happens if some random at the front door asks for an ID and you don't have one. They'd know to let you in."

"What would you call it? Your club."

"I used to think I'd name it Haus of Haring. In honor of the greatest artist to ever live. Or even Bar Haring. And the entire aesthetic would be modeled after him and his art and the whole club kid scene. Pop art, graffiti, aesthetic as fuck."

"How long have you been thinking about this?"

"Don't worry about it," I tell him, and then pause for a moment to concentrate on the hand on Santi's head and the other scratching the skin of his back between his shoulder blades and how he's become a little heavy after neither-of-us-knows-how-long most of his body has been lying on top of me, but there's something that's as equally comforting as it is uncomfortable. "Or maybe I'll call it Para Santi."

His stomach spasms from a laugh and he buries his face into my chest, kissing that space in the middle before picking his head back up. "I like that one best. Then I could just walk up to the front and be, like, 'Soy Santi. Perdóneme.'"

"Also, in case you show up to the Strip drunk and have trouble remembering which one is mine."

"Hm." Santi takes a deep inhale while squeezing me. "I mean it, though. If you want to do things I can't, don't worry about it. If you want to go to a Latinx Night or out on a Friday or Saturday or take a trip somewhere that would involve passing a checkpoint or going on a plane—"

Santi gets quiet. Like he's realizing how long this list is, now that he's putting thought into it, or that in just a few months I *will* be getting on a plane, or how it could all affect whatever we are and whatever we will be. That we only have a limited amount of time before we have to decide exactly that.

He's scared. I am too. Because I like picturing myself two years from now with Santi. Wherever that means. Location's not important. I like thinking of us as twenty-one-year-olds, still together, knowing so much more about one another.

"If I want to do those things, I'll know you'll be right here when I get back," I finish for him.

"I—Claro. Esperando estar contigo aquí."

I focus on the feeling of his body on me. On the warmth of his cheek and the comfort of his arms. On the sound of the lo-fi hip-hop that's been playing as background music ever since we transitioned from him plowing me to cuddling me. On him.

Conmigo.

28

S o *this* is the Santi that's been all over your Instagram Stories?" Juni asks as we walk toward him. He's brought us to an empty performance space off the Main Avenue Strip, a few blocks away from where most of the clubs and bars are. "Maybe this time paint won't end up everywhere *but* the wall?"

"Yes, definitely. We'll be on our best behavior."

"I don't believe that for a goddamn second," Juni replies while handing Santi a bag full of pan dulce from Rosie's. "But, really, no more of that. *Please.* The inside of a building is a lot harder to clean up."

The space is an abandoned warehouse with a stage. But in a few weeks, this same building is going to be full of high schoolers for the annual post-Pride Born This Güey Youth Ball. And the first thing they're going to see when they walk in, besides a huge crowd of teenagers, is a mural going along the entire length of one of the walls. By me.

"You got a plan for it?" Santi asks while digging through the bag, his eyes set on an empanada at the very bottom. A hungry smile covers his face as he takes it out and bites through a good third of it.

"So, I don't remember if it was the second or third year of this thing, but at some point, Youth Ball became this really alt, anti-capitalist, anti-cop sort of situation. Which is really cool, and the vibe of it all is, like, *Mad Max* meets Hot Topic meets a PG-13 version of Folsom."

"What's a Folsom?"

"Basically a lot of leather and penis," Juni answers for me. "Whatever you do, don't Google Image Search it."

"Yeah," I continue. "But insert the leather and take away the abrasive number of dicks out in the open, and that's the vibe."

"That's what you want?"

"I—I guess. I don't know. I know I want it to be really queer and the least cis or het."

"Which would be what, exactly?" Juni asks, the snark in his voice telling me he knows I have no ideas yet.

"You will find out . . . as soon as I figure it out."

The sound of my head hitting my desk and everything on it shaking from the impact gets Santi quickly sitting up from where he's lying on my bed and (was) deep into whatever book he's reading.

"¿Qué pasó?"

"Doing art is a scam," I say into the desk. "It's been days and I still don't know what I'm doing."

I can hear the bed as he gets up and then his quiet footsteps until he's standing behind me, making me sit back up. Feeling a small bit of comfort when his hands start massaging my shoulders and the bottom half of his face rests in my hair.

"You have any ideas?"

"Yeah, but they're all over the place, so, in the moments when they don't all seem shitty, picking one has been impossible. *And* it's gotta be a theme I can do across six different boards."

"Dime, porfa. Tell me what you have."

"I—*fine*. It's just that I don't know whether I want to go, like, really Mexican with this or if I want to do some very American mural or maybe go with something that everyone will recognize."

"What do those look like?"

"For the Mexican one, my thought process is what if Felix d'Eon did street art? Except, and I can't believe I'm saying this again, but without the abrasive number of dicks. Not that there's not a place for that, but this isn't it."

"I don't know who that is."

"*What?* He's Mexican."

"Do you know every American artist?"

I turn my head to give him some annoyed eyes. Annoyed because he's right. "Point made." I grab my phone and go to Instagram, finding Felix d'Eon's profile and handing it to Santi. "Imagine slutty mariachis and folkloricos and taqueros and vaqueros who are all super queer and kissing and alluding to things with where their hands are going."

Santi looks at the pictures for another minute before giving me my phone back and going back to the bed. "What makes you think this is a shitty idea?"

"Well, it's not the *Mad Max* aesthetic I thought I wanted. And it—Remember how you said you hoped no one would ever take away the love I have for my art?"

"Yes."

"Sometimes it's hard. Sometimes I don't know whether this idea is really a concept that comes from me or if it's me trying to say *fuck you* so hard to those people that I want to think of the most stereotypically Mexican idea possible. There are these moments where I can't tell the difference between authenticity and trying to make a point. I don't know if I see heart in this."

Santi stares at me with sad eyes and this small frown for a moment before holding his hand out. "Ven," he tells me.

I get up and sulk over to him, standing as he sits on the corner of my mattress and wraps his arms around me. "I'll figure it out. I—I don't know. It'll come to me. I just need to keep thinking."

"I think you need to *quit* thinking," Santi says. "For tonight. Let your head rest. Do anything else except for the Pride art. It can wait."

I let out a big sigh and hug him back. "But—"

"No buts, cielo. Except for yours. Pero, sin pensar. Relájate. Por favor."

I look into his eyes and know that there isn't a way out of this. He'll keep me trapped in a hug if it means getting his way right now. And that, for once, I'll listen.

"*Fine*. No more thinking today."

The "no thinking" helped.

Santi dragged me out of my room; we went for a walk, got mangonadas, found a park and swung on swings, and I didn't think about responsibilities at all. And then I woke up the next day and it was all there in my head, waiting for me to bring them to life. And that's been my whole existence. The next seven, eight, maybe ten days is me not leaving my room unless it's to pick up Santi or the one time Zeke makes me get out of the house and the couple of nights Mami makes me eat dinner with them. Otherwise, I'm at my desk or on my bed or lying on the floor, iPad open to the folder of reference photos for me to use that will, one by one, create this giant cohesive piece. I'm playing with paints and figuring out how to make specific shades of red and greens and all the colors of the rainbow. All of them individually take up enough time and effort to be their own project, and together, it's basically the work of a small gallery showing.

Yeah, I might be excited because the inspiration is flowing out of me, but this whole thing has been a pain in my ass.

"What are you doing on the floor?" Santi asks after tapping at my door and then coming into my room.

"When did you get here?"

"Just now. I came with your apá."

"I would've picked you up."

"You weren't answering your phone. We both tried to get a hold of you."

"What? That's not true, I—" I grab my phone that's been lying next to me all day, that I *know* hasn't chimed or rang or beeped or made any other sound lately. And when I tap it to show Santi that neither of them tried to reach me . . . nothing happens. Black screen. "Shit. My phone died. I'm sorry, it—"

"It's fine, cielo. I brought you a torta, in case you're hungry. And because your apá said you probably haven't eaten today."

"I was *about* to," I tell him while taking the Styrofoam container. "Split it with me."

We lean against my bed, quietly eating a milanesa torta and fries, sharing a Coke, and I show Santi the drawings that are now mostly finished.

"The one of this drag queen eating hot Cheetos and cheese is kind of hot, no?"

"I know, right?" I reply with a laugh. Juni was able to get me some photos of local alt drag performers. This hot Cheetos drag queen with a chola aesthetic. Another one of a queen giving grunge vibes coming out of a dumpster. A drag king as the devil with his top surgery scars painted black to contrast with his red body. And this one that's an agender performer that's wearing a corset that's about to break their body.

"What about the other two? What will those be?"

"There's an old picture of my tías Mia and Olena that I'm gonna make into a mural. And I was kinda thinking the last one could be the two of us wearing leather harnesses?"

Santi might've given himself whiplash with how fast his head pops up at that. His face is showing some obvious interest. "Really?"

"Honestly, I just wanted to see how you'd react. Which is a lot more excited than I thought you'd be."

"So you were lying?"

"*No*. Stop crying," I tease. "I didn't know if you'd say yes, so I had another idea, but it seems like we're going with us in leather."

He continues to go back and forth between the drawings on my iPad and the practice versions kept in a sketchbook, sometimes zooming in on or hovering a finger over the colors and detail, even though I keep telling him that they're only rough renditions of what's going on the wall, and sometimes asking me to go back to the photographs so he can compare them and tell me how cool my versions are.

"Was this, like, always you?" Santi asks. "Not the painting thing, I know that already. But the, I mean . . . were you ever not an Ander who could draw drag queens and two gay people in harnesses kissing and think nothing of it?"

"Are you asking me if I've always been this queer?"

"Basically."

"Yeah, pretty much. If you ask Mami, she'll tell you it's because she was going through a major Shakira obsession when she was pregnant with me. And Tita says it's because she'd bring me with her to all the JCPenney's sales and get my opinion on the outfits and shoes she liked. The first *probably* isn't true, but I would definitely give some blame to Tita. I've never been anything else other than this, and my family and friends and most of the people around the neighborhood that I've interacted with have either never had much of a problem with it or kept quiet about their opinions—otherwise, they'd catch my parents' and Tita's hands."

"That's cool. I mean, if things had been different, you might not have become someone who does art like this. I can't imagine you any other way."

"What about you? What was little gay Santi like?"

"Little gay Santi didn't exist," he says before taking the bottle of Coke in his hand and tilting it up into his mouth. "My dad and older brother were puro womanizers. Babosos. And that kinda shaped my way of thinking to, you know, girls are it. That's the only option."

"So there've been girls?"

"Yeah. Why, you jealous?"

"Of your pinche preteen girlfriend? No. Of course not."

"There was more than just one."

"Now you're trying to get a reaction out of me," I snap, bringing my knee down to hit his leg. "Did you like them? I mean, do you like girls? Like, was using *gay* the wrong word?"

"I—I don't know. I'm pretty sure it's the wrong word, but I don't know what would be. Is it weird that I don't know?"

"What? No, of course not." I lean into his side and lay my head on his shoulder. "Labels are complicated. And, more importantly, not mandatory. You can just be you. It's fine."

"It's not that I *didn't* like those girls. I did. But it's more complicated than that. Because, sure, I liked them. I liked holding their hands and kissing and all the other stuff we did. But I like guys too."

"Have there been guys?"

He's quiet for a couple seconds. His hand even goes still. Looking like he just got caught stealing piñata candy. "Crushes? Yeah. But nothing more than that."

Santi's arm goes around me, making sure I stay close to him. His hand gently goes up and down my side. Almost enough to be ticklish. "And now I'm dating a nonbinary person, and I really like you. More than I've liked anyone. I think . . . if I had to say what all of you have in common, it's probably that everyone I've liked has been pretty. I like pretty people."

"But, out of all of them, I'm the prettiest, right?"

ander & santi were here   195

"*What?*"

"You heard me."

"*¿Por qué eso importa?*"

"*Because*. Were your girlfriends pretty?"

Santi gives me some heavy side-eye, like we both have very different ideas of what *important* means. He's been working with Mami too long. "Then, sí, ellas eran bonitas."

"Prettier than me?"

"Why are you acting jealous?"

"I'm not," I whine, my head moving against his skin, and my mouth finding his neck, leaving a torta-flavored kiss there. "I'm only saying, you agree, I'm the prettiest person you've ever dated. Or had a crush on."

Santi laughs as he picks my chin up, giving himself access to my lips. "What if I told you were *second* prettiest?"

"I'd say give me their name and address," I start as I pick myself up. "I've got some hair to pull. See you later."

"Cállate, cabrone." He grabs at my waist and pulls me back down to the floor, sitting me down in between his legs, bringing my back to his chest.

"Does your mom know?"

"Yeah. And she knows about you too."

"Really?"

"Claro," Santi answers, and then starts pecking at my shoulder. "She approves."

"Well, of course she does. I'm a catch."

"Qué humilde," he says while moving to my neck.

"*Muy* humilde."

"Y más bonite," he adds in a whisper, his lips now at my ear and asking for things he should've requested *before* the torta. "Más linda. Más hermosa."

"So—yeah. So, um, so, so pretty."

here you are!" Juni yells when he sees me in line to get into Pride, between Zeke, Chachi, her friends, and Santi. "Took me forever to find you."

"I told you I was in line."

"*An-der,*" he says back, clapping with each syllable, "this line is longer than Saturdays at Fiesta Texas. Be more specific. Between point A and point B. 'I see this tent and that tent.' It is a thousand and three degrees out here and I'm just trying to sit in some shade. *Anyways,* stopping by very quickly, like, not even here, and then running because I had to let you know that someone is interested in purchasing the wall you did for Born This Güey. Not going into a lot of detail, but a new shop is opening up on the Main Strip, and the owner wants those pictures in his store."

"Wait, what? I—You're joking. The one that's up right now?"

"Yeah. They were always meant to be a temporary installment. And while we've never sold anything before, we also never had any plans for them after today. And it is *your* art. I had some preemptive conversations with the Beautify powers that be, and they decided that if you'd like to sell, we will ask for compensation for the boards, but the rest would be yours." Juni shows me the screen of his phone. "And by *the rest,* I mean *this* number."

"That—Wow. *Okay.*"

"You don't have to give an answer now. We'll handle all the technical stuff, but expect me to reach out to you within the next few days about this. Anyways, that's all I needed to tell you, so I'm going back in. Come by our table if you need to get out of the sun or want to rest your weary legs. Oh, and here." Juni pulls out a wad of tickets from every pocket. "Take these. Split them up with everyone. We don't need them. Okay. Gotta run."

"So how rich are you about to be?" Zeke asks, both him and my little sister staring at me with huge eyes.

"I'm not telling you. Also, I have to get my tías' permission for the one I did of them and—" I turn my head to see Santi at the corner of my vision, tapping on his hands clasped at my stomach. "What do you think?"

"Why does it matter?"

"Because you're in one of them too. I already got everyone else's permission to use their likeness in whatever way I want and whether I made money off it or not."

"I actually meant to ask you," Zeke interrupts. "Did you take pictures of y'all and then paint them or go from what you got up in your head?"

"We took pictures. Why? You want me to send them to you?"

"I mean, if you're offering—"

"*I'm not*, pendejo. I was kidding. Not about the pictures, but about them ever heading into your texts."

"I don't mind," Santi says. "About the mural. But if you want to send Zeke those photos, that's fine too. Mainly the mural, though."

"*He's not getting shit.*"

———

San Antonio's Pride is at Brooks City-Base on the southeast side of the city. This and the Barbacoa & Big Red Festival are the only reasons I'm ever out here, not because it isn't pretty but because it's so damn far from everything. The street is lined with flags on flags for every letter of the spectrums and the noise *has* to be carrying all the way up to Santos Vista. Inside, the park is filled with tents: some for banks and businesses handing out fans and koozies with rainbow print and YAS, QUEEN on top of a Wells Fargo logo, others for local queer and trans organizations, a couple political candidates, Etsy stores showing up with temporary tattoos and iPhone cases. Everything you could think of. And then there are the stages spread throughout the park. Drag kings and queens over there. Ballet folklorico over here. A dance team. Todo.

"What do you wanna do first?" I ask Santi when Zeke leaves to go find one of his cousins who's here for the weekend with a group of her friends and Chachi and her little pack all start sprinting toward this woman who probably thought it'd be a cute day painting four-year-olds' faces and is seeing that illusion shattered by a stampede of rowdy-ass teenagers.

"Uh . . . oh! Flower crowns?" He points over to a tent that looks like someone shat an entire craft store floral section. Or two or three.

Santi holds one and then another to his chest and the black mesh tee he's wearing, getting a feel for whatever aesthetic he's trying to go for. "¿Te gusta?" he asks, putting on a crown of maroon sunflowers that match his shorts.

"Sí, querido. Muy lindo."

I pick out a crown with pink roses and little white flowers that match my cropped tank and shorts and then Santi drags me around to a giant wood pallet standing against the side of the tent with AMOR ES AMOR written on it in big white letters. Como que Pinterest.

Usually that sort of stuff I leave for the white girl Instagram influencers playing ally. Zeke too, who is undeniably very queer in his own way, has never been the flower-crowns-and-kisses-for-the-Gram sort of person. But I'll buy into it for today. I could make a backdrop a billion times better than this, but it's cute. Santi's excitement about this makes it cute. And we're photogenic as fuck. Even when he starts doing those weird selfie angles that he's obsessed with and most of them are of half my face mid-yell because he never gets my good side and by this point, he knows this and is choosing to go for it anyways. *Híjole.*

There's nothing Santi doesn't want to do. I get pulled to the inflatable obstacle course (and beat him) and then the paletero and the food truck selling pizzas and the drag queen performing Gloria Trevi. Going back and forth between crowds of people, holding on to him so I don't lose him. I don't even want to imagine what he'd be like at a Six Flags. Or, maybe I do, because seeing him with this smile that has not faded since we stepped into the festival and when he gets annoyed at me for going at any less than a sprint and starts yelling, "¡Ándale! ¡Corre, cielo!" might actually be my favorite thing in the world.

I manage to get Santi over to the Beautify tent, only because he couldn't carry a box of pizza, eat the pizza, and drink his agua fresca all at the same time while walking. We sit back-to-back on a sarape blanket spread out on the grass, him eating like he's never tasted food before and me putting my weight on him, half-asleep, ready for a nap and to be somewhere quiet.

Until Chachi comes sprinting over to us, almost slipping when she tries to stop at the tent. "AJ! AJ! They have chicken on a stick! Gimme some of those tickets you've been hoarding like a gay dragon. The need is *immense.*"

"I'll go with her," Santi says, standing up without warning and letting me fall back. "I want a chicken too."

"*Ooh*, that'll give me a chance to haze my sibling's boyfriend."

"Don't say *haze*," I snap while digging in my pocket and then holding a handful of tickets up in the air while I lie on the blanket. "Get me one too."

"Me four!" Zeke adds as he comes in out of nowhere and sits down cross-legged next to me, handing me his bottle of water.

"How was hanging out with your cousins?" I ask after Chachi and Santi leave.

"She brought, like, five of her friends and her boyfriend. They're trying to go to every single Pride in Texas or something. Last week they were in Houston and Dallas a couple before then. Three of the five guys with her said they're straight, but I'm not buying it. One, max. So I'm staying in the back and waiting to see if they need to do some exploring, because call me Dora. And the other girl besides her is pan, and I can tell she has a wild side."

"No gays?"

"The other two guys, but they're dating and don't seem interested in a third."

"Did you do anything *besides* see which of her friends you could hook up with this weekend?"

"*Yes*. She also happens to be one of my favorite cousins. Hot friends or not. And—Oh, hey! AJ"—Zeke points to a tent across from Beautify's—"Campaign for Justice for the Undocumented. They should really workshop that name. I'm using a lot of tongue muscle and not in a fun way. But maybe they have some stuff to help Santi. Let's go over."

He's picking himself back up before I have a chance to process what's happening. "Zeke, no, it—Oh my shit. *Wait*."

My least favorite part about the human experience is those moments when I'm happy and content and having a day that is free from drama and worry only to have it all suddenly come crashing down on me from every side and the only thing I can do is watch it happen. Like when I was little, Mami would take me to the park. I'd rush to the swings, always working my way higher and higher with every up, down, and back up, getting as high as I could before jumping. Feeling the sun and breeze all around me as, for a few seconds, I flew before my feet would hit the ground. A universally great experience.

Except for this one time. It's always just *one time* that scars a person for forever.

Park, great. Swings, not a creak or squeak in them. The excitement of being on top of the world as the ground gets smaller and smaller, surreal.

But then, right as I was throwing myself off, my shirt got caught on the chain. I'd been betrayed by the swing set. All I could do was watch as the ground got closer, knowing I wasn't going to land on my feet. Wishing I could be a time traveler and go back three seconds.

That same exact fuckery is unfolding right now. By the time I catch up to Zeke, he's telling these people about me and my undocumented boyfriend. And, right at this exact moment, Santi and Chachi appear, each holding five or six chickens on a stick per hand. And I can only watch as my best friend turns this up-to-now great day into a spectacular shit show.

"That's him, right there. Santi! Santi! AJ, go grab him."

"*Zeke. Shut up.*" I'm grabbing at *him*, trying to pull him away. He doesn't even pay attention until he's stumbling back with me.

"What the hell, AJ? I was just—"

"Qué tal?" Santi asks, holding out a chicken for me.

"I'm trying to tell Zeke—"

"They help undocumented people," Zeke interrupts. "So *I* was telling *you*, AJ, that we should tell them about you. You as in Santi."

"Which is—you're being careless," I shout, getting in between my best friend and boyfriend, turning to face Zeke. "It's incredibly fucking careless of you."

"How? I was just trying to help him."

"But you're not! You're literally telling everyone here—which, sure, includes some well-meaning people but also includes all the cops wandering around and people we don't know—something that *you* have no right to be saying out loud. You're putting him in danger. You—for someone so smart, why didn't you let yourself think about this for a minute?"

"No one's going to do anything here."

"*You don't know that.*" Jesus Christ, I kind of want to punch him. And the only reason I don't is because these Campaign for the Undocumented people or whatever they're called are watching, and, more importantly, Juni and the Beautify people are watching, and this kid with a non-binary flag standing close by with their friends is watching and I don't want to look bad in front of one of us.

But I will yell. "*Ugh*, Mo would've known how to responsibly do this without actually pointing out my boyfriend in front of God and everyone. Don't assume shit about a thing that doesn't affect you. That you could be wrong or right about but it's whatever because it's not *your* life that would get turned upside down because of it. Shut. Up."

I'm able to calm myself just enough and for just enough time to take the food from Santi's right hand, give it to Zeke without using the sticks to stab him, take my boyfriend's hand, and walk away. Passing whatever their nonprofit was called, and Beautify, and the people at the tents next to us who all got a front row seat to me blowing up. I'm probably going to hear it from Juni and how I represent Beautify and need to not scream in public.

And while I realize I didn't overreact, the volume at which

I appropriately reacted didn't make the situation better. So now I'm juggling the anger I have for my best friend with the anger I have for a world that could take Santi away from me the second we slip up with the anger I have for myself for not being the wiser, better person and letting my emotions out in an incredibly unchecked way that wasn't helpful to Santi.

"I'm sorry," I tell him. "Do you mind if we go?"

He shakes his head, his eyes big with concern. "Vámonos."

30

T he only time I let go of Santi's hand on the way home
is when we have to separate to get into the car and then
again to get out. Other than that, I only need one hand to unlock the front door and to lead him upstairs into my room and
out onto the garage roof. Even though we were already outside,
being here *specifically* makes it easier to breathe and to think or
to not think. As if I'd had a pillow held over my face for the last
half hour and now it's finally gone.

"You don't have to protect me," Santi says in almost a whisper. There's a really bothered force behind it too. I look up from
where my head's resting on his shoulder to see him staring out
into the distance. "You don't need—I don't want—*Chingada
madre*. I can handle things getting out of hand. I'm not your
responsibility."

"I know that. I know you can fight your own battles. But—"
I inhale and then let out a long sigh, tightening my grip on his
hand. Adjusting my body and lifting my head so we're eye to
eye. "When it comes to my friends, I'm going to check them
when they need checking. Zeke would've done the same thing
if it was the other way around. I hate that it had to involve you,
and—*ugh*. Can we not talk about this?"

"What do you want to talk about?"

"I don't know."

I bend my legs up so I can lean into my knees, folding my free arm to make a nest for my face to hide. Trying so hard to not concentrate on the feeling of Santi watching me, sending frustrated energy at me that's like a finger poking at my side, telling me we aren't done with this conversation yet.

"I wish you wouldn't worry about me."

"I can't help it," I say. Not caring whether my voice is too muffled to hear.

"That's why I didn't tell you not to." His hand leaves mine and goes under the back of my shirt to lightly rub my skin. Going from just under my shoulders to right above the waist-band of my shorts. "I *wish* you wouldn't, but I know that's not something I can wish away for us. So I don't tell you not to. Even though I want to. I don't like you being in the middle of my shit."

"We're in this together, though. From the moment you kissed me at Lupe's. Before that even."

"I—ugh." Santi's hand stops for a second, like his body and mind together need a moment to think about what's happening next. "But we're not. You get to live with a different set of rules and I know you know that, but, cielo, that doesn't mean I want you fighting my battles for me. You being in the middle means you're in front of me, and I don't want that. Side by side, I can live with. Me in front of you, having a chance to keep you from some of it, that'd be better."

"I don't think I'm the stand-in-the-back type of person."

"Yo sé." He lets out a loud sigh and, barely under a face that's heavy with frustration and stress, there's the tiniest smile. "I like that about you. But it makes me worry about you *and* me. About those times when it becomes less helpful."

I don't think I can do what he's asking me to. There's this feeling that squeezes all my organs, puts this pressure on me like I'm in a room where the walls are quickly closing in, and it's constantly telling me the moment I let my guard down is when I'm going to look up and he won't be with me anymore.

"I—I'll try. But—" I turn my head to rest a cheek on my arm. "How are you not always scared?"

"Who said I wasn't? *I am*. I'm terrified. Every day I wake up not on a bus heading toward México, I'm both grateful because I have the morning and so, so scared because that means there's still the uncertainty of the afternoon and evening and night and tomorrow. But I can only focus on either being grateful or scared, and the moment I walk outside my house every day, I tell myself it has to be the gratitude. I have a lot more to be thankful for than I have to fear."

"I wish you didn't have to be afraid."

"You're a good distraction."

"That's cheesy as fuck."

"'Te'l hocico, coñito.'" Santi grips a hand at my side and pulls me with him as he lies down. His eyes haven't left the sky.

"What're you thinking about?"

"I reread this book recently. These two boys get phone calls telling them they're gonna die in the next twenty-four hours."

"That's depressing. Do they legit die or is there some happy ending?"

"They die. The first time I read it, I threw it across my room. Then went to pick it up and threw it again. But now—now I see myself in them. I get dressed and see you waiting for me in the driveway and go to work and hang out with you, and I think, if this is my last day, the last day of life as I know it, the last few hours of happiness and having things and people who can take my mind away from the worries and mierda out there, then at least I know I've made the best out of it. Which I want to believe is how the characters also ended up feeling. They made the best out of the time they got, they had someone there to remind them that good exists in this world and to take as much of it as they can, and they helped someone else find their best at the same time. That's what I mean by you're a good distraction."

"We're not dying at the end of this, though, right?"

"No. We got a lot of life left. Te lo prometo."

"Are they always like this?" Santi asks before biting into a jalapeño pepper and then his third chicken on a stick. Chachi brought entire bags full of them home with her from Pride, and after giving one bag to Santi and me and another to Mami, she and her friends sat in a circle on the floor and are now in the middle of a very competitive contest of who can fit the most chicken in their mouth without choking.

"No, it's usually so much more chaotic. Like this one time—"

"¡Bebite! ¡Santi!" Tita yells as she pushes the front door open, three or four large plastic bags hanging from her arm. Pa behind her with even more. "I brought—Wait. You went and got la Popeye? Chinga' su—I have all these tacos for us."

"We'll eat them," Santi tells her with half a chicken in his mouth. I'm still figuring out where the hell it all goes.

In a matter of minutes, everyone's got plates stacked with tacos and fried chicken, a Jarritos at their feet or beside them, Gansitos at that perfect been-in-the-freezer-for-a-couple-days temperature, and talking at a volume that people in a white neighborhood would probably mistake for an underground wrestling club, but in Santos Vista, this is at about an "inside three."

Tita somehow gets herself involved in the chicken-in-mouth competition with a couple of Chachi's friends while my sister and the rest of her friends are reenacting the "Yo Perreo Sola" music video and Mami is showing pictures of Bad Bunny in drag to Pa and I'm only *mostly* certain Pa isn't ready to end it all for a chance at Bad Bunny in a wig and fake boobs.

"¡Escúchame! ¡Google!" Tita shouts at the small speaker under our television. "Pinche pendejo robot. Play 'Ven Conmigo,' porfa."

The beginning accordion instrumentals start playing at the highest volume the speaker can go, and Tita pulls Chachi's friend Raúl to the center of the living room with one hand, the other resting over his shoulder, holding on to a bottle of tequila as they start dancing.

"Dance with me?" I ask Santi, holding out a hand for him.

"Are you leading this time?"

"Fuck that. I'm not trying to trip over your feet. You lead."

I follow Santi's movements, a little scared when he starts going more freely this time, but I stay with him, both of us singing at each other, letting myself go with it.

"You've gotten better."

"I practice in the mirror in my room."

"*¿Verdad?*"

"*No*, not really."

You make it easy. That's what I think while resting my head on his shoulder as we dance across the living room.

Easy to dance with. In these small moments, easy to not think about whether I'll wake up and he'll still be here or, best-case scenario, whether we'll still exist months from now as the number of days until I get on a plane and go to a place he can't come with me to gets smaller and smaller. Easy to convince myself that, even then, during that semester-long trip up to Chicago when I'll be telling myself over and over again that Santi will be here, waiting for me, it'll be true. He will be.

Even when my friends act up, as well meaning as it was.

I have to believe in hope and knowing that I could text him or FaceTime him and he'd be on break at Lupe's and Tita would steal the phone from him because I hadn't called in seven hours and she was worried I'd died. Or maybe he'd be hanging out here in my room because Mami and Pa are totally fine with him being around the house when his seems too claustrophobic. I want to believe that when I text him good morning, he'd text me back and tell me that he's safe and fine and happy and counting down the minutes until I'm home.

And I can believe that. Here, dancing with Santi, it's impossible not to.

"Can we not break up?"

I'd been holding in the words for a few minutes, instead just staring at Santi in the passenger seat of my car. At him resting the side of his face against the headrest, his eyes closed, his reddened lips and a little dark mark on his throat that is totally my fault, I shouldn't have gotten that excited. But now that we're not making out in the driveway of his house anymore, it's not like there's anything else keeping me from saying what I knew I needed to say before he left tonight. I need to make sure we're on the same page.

"I mean, if that's okay with you."

"I wasn't planning on breaking up with you," he says in a low, sleepy voice without opening his eyes. His hand on my leg grips into my skin, adding emphasis. *I'm yours.*

"Even when I leave?"

Santi's chest fills with air, and I listen to it leave through his nostrils before he opens his eyes and looks into mine. His hand comes up to my cheek, and a small smile forms as he slowly strokes my skin with his thumb.

"I wasn't planning on breaking up with you," he repeats.

"I'm scared of leaving you."

"You have me. Being a few miles away won't change that."

"A little more than 'a few.'"

The sound of the air conditioner blowing through my car's vents is so loud in the silence. Such a drastic change from the noise that's been a constant through today.

"We're going to be okay. Don't think of any other possibilities. And don't think of staying here for me."

"I wasn't," I whine. "I—There are lots of reasons I've thought about not leaving home."

"I'm one of them."

"You—"

"*No mientas*, cielo."

I burrow my face into his palm, hiding any reaction that might say guilt. "You aren't the *main reason*. Even after what happened today or at Lupe's the day after we got together. I just—*ugh*. I'm starting to feel this new sense of confidence about what I do and what my art is. But what if I get there and that goes away? What if I'm back into this headspace of, what, being unsure or scared to do what I want to do because of how people will react to me or if they'll take me seriously? Or what if I'm actually not that good?"

"There are two things I've learned since I met you," Santi starts. His hand goes back down and his middle finger traces the strawberry candy tattoo. "One is that you are irresistible. De muchas maneras." His eyes stare at where his finger is, and the lip bite happening is telling me that so many of those things that make me irresistible are not anything he could say in front of my parents. Until he catches himself daydreaming and clears his throat, looking back up at my eyes. "And, uh—y dos, you are more talented than anyone I've ever met in my entire life. And you are the only one who does what you do. As much as they try to make it seem so simple, you are you and not Diego or Frida or anyone who did the Chicano Park stuff you showed me or anyone else. And this world needs you doing exactly what you want and what makes you feel good. Sometimes it can be hard to remember, I know that. So, whenever you need me to remind you, whether you're here or in Chicago, I will. All right? You stand side by side with me, but I stand side by side with you too. I'm not letting anyone make you hate or doubt what you do."

I sniffle, trying hard not to cry as I nod. Unable to hold back a couple tears when Santi leans toward me and plants a kiss into my hair. "Okay."

"So, you're going to Chicago? For sure?"

I nod again. "I am."

"Bueno. And we'll figure us out. For as long as we're meant to be together, we'll figure us out. I believe in that con todo mi corazón."

"Me too."

31

Y ou're gonna want to talk to your parents about taxes and all that stuff next year, so remember that," Juni says as he watches his printer slowly spit out a small stack of papers. "And try not to spend it all in one place. If I find out you blew this much money on a night out in Boystown when you're up there living your best gay-in-Chicago life, I'll go up there and kill you myself."

"I won't."

"I don't believe you," he replies with a teasing smirk. "You excited?"

"For what?"

"*Chicago*. Heading off to a sickening-ass art school. Showing those lake people the talent that comes from Texas. And, generally speaking, attaining greatness."

"Oh. Yeah, definitely. Hard to believe I'll be gone in a couple months."

"Figured out what you and the boyfriend are doing?"

"We don't plan on breaking up. I'll be back in November and then we'll have all of Christmas break, spring break, Easter, summers. And phones exist, there're millions of ways to talk on video. It's not something I'm worried about."

"Good for you. And he has a lot of people here watching out

for him. Remember that. Try not to worry. He'd want you to concentrate on you and your career."

"I know, I know," I tell him in almost a groan. Since we decided we're going to try to make this work past August, I've basically heard this same set of lines from Pa, Mami, Tita, and Ronnie. "We'll be fine."

"You will." Juni sets all the paperwork and receipts from the sale of my murals—all neatly stapled and organized inside a bright orange folder—on the desk between us. "He loves you, you know."

I choke on my iced coffee, nearly dropping it because Juni had to go and say something wild like that. "Shut up," I say after clearing my throat.

What I don't say is *No, he doesn't.* Because I know Juni's right. I know that we've been in that place for a while now. At least, I've been. There's no denying I love Santi. But we haven't gotten to a place where we could say it. Where it felt right. A couple times it's been close. Heavy in my throat and I could tell it was right there in his too. But not yet.

Either way, Juni's getting a laugh out of seeing me fully break any cool I had coming into his office. Because he knows he's right too. He saw how we were together at Pride. At least, the good parts before Zeke went and ruined everything.

"So, you're all set. That's all handled."

He sits up straight in his chair, hands together, watching as I take the folder and set it behind me in my own chair. He's got this weird, almost creepy smile. And not saying anything. Just . . . sitting there.

"*Are we done?*" I ask slowly, unsure if I should start getting up and leaving now. Usually, he tells me to go away, so this is very different.

"No, I actually have incredibly exciting news to tell you, but I want you to ask me about it. So go on. Ask me what the incredibly exciting news I have for you is."

I let out an annoyed sigh. "*Why can't you just*—Whatever. What's the incredibly exciting news you have for me?"

"The guy who bought your Pride pieces looked into the rest of your work."

"Okay? What, is he gonna buy the Selena mural off of H-E-B's wall?"

"*No, you troll*. He probably would if he could, but that's not my business. What *is* my business—well, sort of . . . I'm more of a messenger here—is that he knows some people who know some people and he's told me there's some space at the Blue Star Contemporary opening up and they're considering offering it to you, but—"

"*What the*—" I nearly fall out of my chair throwing myself forward onto Juni's desk. "Yes. Yes. Absolutely yes."

"*How-eh-ver*," Juni adds, stressing each syllable, "like I was trying to say, it wouldn't be until the beginning of August for an almost-four-month exhibit. With you going to Chicago later that month, I'm not sure—"

"I could have someone take over it while I was at school. And then I'll come down for Labor Day and then when it closes in, what? That'd be around Thanksgiving?"

His eyes squint and mouth makes little movements as he calculates in his head. "Yeah. Around then. How feasible is this actually, though? Do you have things ready? Is this something you'd be prepared for by August? That's not a lot of time."

"*I can do it*. I promise. I—I have the mask statues that I can use. They'd be perfect. And give me the day and I can come up with a theme if they need one, or I can use my free time to just create."

Juni's eyes squint even harder and he gets into thinking-face mode. One of his fingers taps on his desk and he lets out a long, quiet groan. "Okay. I will talk to them. And vouch for you. Consider it done and yours. Let me just say right now, though, you're gonna have to show up, all right? This is big. Bigger than what anyone your age gets. I'm doing this because you're talented and you've done some fan-fucking-tastic work the past year. More importantly than the person who bought your work, *I* will be attached to whatever you put out whether I want to or not, so make me want."

"I will. I promise. You're the actual best, Juni. Have I told you that?"

"Not nearly enough."

I don't know who decided that me working on the statues was also an invite to some live, artist-in-their-natural-environment sort of situation. I told Santi about the Blue Star exhibit and how now I need to work double time on these statues and I'd pick him up so he could help me move them in and out of the garages, but I distinctly remember not inviting Ronnie, Chachi, and Pa, the last of whom comes with a small grill and starts cooking burgers and hot dogs like we're at the park or something while Ronnie brings out a cooler of beer and Cokes and turns his car radio all the way up, blaring some classic reggaeton through the whole neighborhood. These people are not normal. Supportive? Sure. But not in the normal way.

I could use the noise, though. After talking with Juni, I'd emailed my SAIC advisor and told him about this super cool thing I get to do expecting, like, *Wow, oh my god, this is incredible, you are an icon of the artistic experience* or something like that. All I got was a reply this morning about "I saw these Mexican saint candles while at the Farmer's Market. That could be a really great experience to do an exhibit on. Catholicism and Mexicans and how you love the candles and Mary."

I immediately closed my laptop and have refused to think about it since.

Zeke's absence is unusual, even though I haven't spoken to him much since Pride. I miss him and wish he was here fucking around with everyone else, but I'm waiting for him to acknowledge that he made a wrong decision and he's sorry. But one thing about Zeke: he's going to be the most stubborn person ever. It'll be a few more days before he comes around to apologize. Which is whatever. I'm not losing any sleep over him being a child.

"How many of these have you got done so far, AJ?" Chachi asks from her foldout chair in between bites of hot dog.

"About a third of them," I answer while brushing a light purple up and down a statue. "Keeping things pretty simple, sticking to a basic lucha libre mask, but going for soft, pastel colors like this lavender. Might go back and do some pattern work if I have the time. And then Doña Ymelda is gonna order a shit ton of different flowers to match them. Like, something very masculine heavy and traditionally cis meets the feminine and queer. Picture the *Gentefied* mural episode, but going even gayer."

"Which you've repeatedly called the greatest half hour of television in the history of TV shows," Ronnie adds.

"*It is* and Netflix is racist for cancelling it, and, as usual, if you think differently, you're wrong," I tell him, holding out my brush like an extended finger for emphasis.

"And what about the actual exhibit?" he asks. "Do you bring in your own walls or what?"

"I have to bring my own work, since they technically can be purchased. I texted my old high school art teacher. She knows someone who can get me some ten-by-ten canvases on the cheap and, like, tomorrow. I'll have to figure out getting out the best shit I've ever done while also doing the Lupe's murals and, at the same time, making sure I've got everything ready to go for Chicago."

"Get ready to stay that busy, kid. You're gonna be a household name one day. Trust me on that."

They stay until about eight o'clock, leaving Santi, me, and a couple of Tía Mila's work lights to help with visibility while the sun starts heading out until tomorrow. I eventually let Santi help me paint the statues, showing him exactly how the strokes of the brush should go, and then how to cover them in the clear gloss. Every once in a while, I'll spend a minute glancing over, observing and making sure he's doing it all properly. Not because, as he claims when he catches me, I like seeing him all sweaty and shirtless singing and dancing along to "Gasolina" because he hasn't been able to get it out of his head since Ronnie played it earlier. No. Definitely not that.

"Ellas dan miedo," Santi says, looking into a garage of completed masks, all of them facing forward, directly at us.

"Don't worry, querido. If they come alive and try to fight us, I'll protect you from them."

"I don't like our odds."

"You haven't seen me in a fight. I'll kick some stone mask ass. Bet."

"Como un chihuahua," he says through a laugh, getting a glare from me in return.

"I know you don't think *you* could take them all."

"Probably not, but if I'm getting jumped by giant lucha masks, at least I'll go down with you."

"Through happiness and destruction. Even made-up destruction." I laugh as I push myself onto his side, and then yell when his arm comes around my back and hooks around me. His other arm reaches around too, holding our gross, sweaty torsos to-gether.

"What are you doing?"

"Protecting you, cielo," he answers before starting to peck at my cheek. "This is the best way to guard you from devil mask statues."

"That's not true," I groan while trying to wriggle free. "*Ugh*, you're all stinky."

"*No*, ¡eres maliolente!"

"Swear to God, I'll let those masks eat you, Santiago!"

n the nineteen years I've been alive, I've never seen Lupe's closed for more than a day.

But here we are, four days into an entire week of restaurant renovations. The first couple Tita dedicated to replacing the floors. I'm not sure what color they were *supposed* to be originally, back when this place first opened in the 1800s, but I'm glad to see those yellow-tinted squares going straight into the dumpster. And the rectangular white marble tiles Tita ordered that create a chevron pattern all over the restaurant are so pretty. Big fan of this decision.

Tomorrow the new tables and chairs come in, which means we have about twenty-four hours to get all the walls stripped, reprimed, and painted. Not a lot of time, but I'm confident in all of us. My family, Ronnie, Santi, we got this.

Once we strip the walls of their paint and clean them off, I have everyone start priming. While they're busy with that, I mix gallons and gallons of drywall mud with some water until it's like waffle batter. Using a sponge, I dip and then put some pressure on the wall over and over again until—*bam!*—I've created texture on the wall that, once dry, we can paint over.

This is the most tedious part of the job. Pressing sponges onto walls for hours, trying to make sure that no part is too textured or not textured enough. An hour into it, and I'm regretting ever having this idea. But once it's finished and dried, I know it's going to be exactly what I'm wanting.

A light pink goes onto the walls, creating the exact—in my opinion—vibe that Tita was asking for.

She puts on some Natalia Lafourcade, which gets glares from every single one of us. Nothing against Natalia, but she's not music for staying up late and painting. She's more of a getting-high-in-a-flower-field type of musician. Pa changes it to Los Ángeles Azules, and, if I had to pick parent-friendly music to listen to while spending all night painting walls in their taquería, they'd probably be it, so good choice, Pa.

"Up and down," I tell everyone spread around the large dining room and again to Pa at the front. Glancing out the window, I realize that we've been at this for at least sixteen hours; we started before the sun was up and we're now at sunset and I just want to go home. Not that I don't love this, but we're getting past "nice Ander" hours. "None of that side-to-side or diagonal mess. ¿Entienden? We won't have time to go back over it if you mess up and we have to wait for it to dry first."

"*We got it, mi' je,*" Mami replies with a lot of annoyance. I'll be sure to remember that when she messes up and they're stuck with her fucked-up paint job on the walls for forever. Especially because there's too much to do still for me to be only supervising.

Santi helps me build a wall of square tiles. After lots of practice and then actually doing them for real, I managed to paint a few hundred of them, all by hand with small flowers and designs, that we carefully start gluing. Getting them onto the wall is a simple thing to do, just requires a lot of attention and focus. And using Santi as a ladder, since Mami didn't want us ruining her new floors already, trying to keep steady sitting on his shoulders when we get to the higher parts.

"Qué hermoso," Tita says over a yawn as the walls start

looking like they're supposed to. "It's going to be so nice when it's done, no?"

"When it's done and after I sleep for twenty hours," Mami tells her.

To our credit, it's already pretty good pre-catching up on sleep. As we all sit in the center of the dining room—Mami leaning on Pa, Tita lying on Chachi's leg, Santi sitting in between mine, leaning into me, losing consciousness after taking an after-painting Whataburger meal break and eating three honey butter chicken biscuits, and Ronnie lying on his stomach in the middle of all of us, too tired to get up yet even though we know we can't sleep here—I think, *This ain't half bad.* Mami didn't manage to mess it up, Chachi or Tita didn't get distracted, Pa listened to me. This is what happens when everyone believes I know what I'm doing. Even when it's a simple wall.

All they have to do now is bring over the paintings I did for this Fiesta-themed showcase my senior year that Tita's kept in a spare bedroom, and it'll look like a brand-new restaurant.

"Tu novio está durmiendo," Tita says, looking at Santi with his eyes now closed, her words tired. "Time to go home."

"Finally."

———————

We get back home around four o'clock in the morning on Thursday. I first wake up at noon, and then again six hours later, never staying awake for longer than a few minutes. The third time, I only open my eyes because I feel a finger softly poking my cheek, bottom lip, forehead, and nose.

"What're you doing?" I groan.

"I got bored of waiting for you to wake up," Santi replies. "And I'm hungry."

"There's food in the kitchen," I tell him while turning around to face away from him.

"I want to eat *with* you. Despierta, cielo. Let's go find food."

It takes about ten minutes for me to get up. Lots of internal and out-loud debating over the fact that food will still be there, but this specific spot on my bed and how comfy I am right now? That could be lost for forever. It's a big risk.

Santi was super over it very quickly.

Downstairs is silent. Chachi's asleep, my parents and Tita are probably at the restaurant with some of the staff putting together tables and chairs. Would be a perfect time for *other things*, but now that the kitchen's in sight, my stomach is growling and food is the only priority.

"How long has the masa de maíz been in here?" Santi asks as he sticks his whole head into the fridge. "¿Y los frijoles?"

"Someone must have brought them over today. They weren't there yesterday, and I doubt Mami spent any time since this morning cooking. What're you thinking?"

"Huaraches?"

"I don't know what that is."

I've never seen Santi so ashamed. His mouth goes open, his eyes squint, and his head tilts at me like he can't believe what he's hearing. "We're fixing that right now."

While we set aside some shredded chicken to reheat over the stove, Santi shows me how to make huaraches. He gets a ball of masa, making a hole in the middle but careful not to go all the way through "como un doughnut." In the hole goes a big spoon of refried beans before he squishes it together and makes an oval shape out of it, keeping the beans inside.

"Now what?"

"We cook it, of course."

We make six, and I get the responsibility of watching them cook on the stovetop, making sure they don't burn, while Santi digs through the fridge again, pulling out pickled onions, nopalitos, salsas, and queso fresco, and checks on the chicken, trying it with the guisada he made. Starting his training back in the kitchen a few weeks ago got him looking like a proper taquero.

He comes next to me, picking up one of the huaraches and carefully inspecting it.

"I think we're done. I'm gonna construct these for you and you have to tell me how your life is forever changed now."

"We'll see about that. But if you put salsa roja on mine—"

"*Cálmate*, mi chingone. I know what you like."

Santi sits next to me at the dining table, watching me with the impatience of a four-year-old who was told they'd get a dipped cone from Dairy Queen if they were good during Mass. His face getting even more intense when I take that first bite. I can almost feel the way he's screaming in his head.

And that bite—*fuck*, that bite. How does doughed corn and beans taste this good?

"¡Lo veo!" Santi yells, jumping in his seat. "¡Tu sonrisa! ¡Te gusta!"

"Yes, *okay*," I yell back with a mouth full of huarache. "It's amazing and I hate my entire family for never introducing these to me. Now, stop talking to me, quiero comer."

"¡Ya! Come, cielo," he says with the smirk of someone who's won and I wish I could be salty about it, but he deserves that smirk. And as much as I am truly in A Mood about being forced away from my bed and also having gone this far in life without knowing these exist, the fact that Santi is the one who gets to introduce me to them makes the wait worth it. And I really want a lot more late nights eating things we cooked together. I don't think I could ever get tired of this.

33

Okay, see! This is what I was talking about," my advisor says, getting his iPad screen in view so I'm seeing the mural idea I had for the front of Lupe's. "This is fantastic."

I'd sent him the Pride projects and a couple ideas I had for the Blue Star exhibit: one of Chachi holding a beheaded piñata and another of Santi holding two chicken on a sticks with fat jalapeños skewered on top of each. It was looking like we wouldn't even have time to talk about my work; most of it was spent on making sure I knew exactly what classes I'd be taking and all the housekeeping things we needed to cover, now that we're firmly in July and only about a month and a half out from the start of the semester. But he was eager to spend an extra ten minutes having this conversation, so here we are.

"This piece with the chola and the one of your aunts, these are where you shine, An—*Ander*. Really, whenever you get here, you'll have to find yourself in Little Village and the South Lawndale area and Pilsen. It's very Mexican, very . . . very you."

I don't know why that breaks me. Maybe because it's at least the fifth time he's mentioned this or because I've started really holding on to the love I feel for the art I'm doing and specifically for the art he's looking at right now. Or maybe because the limit that exists of me letting his passive racism fly does exist and it's reached that ceiling.

"Why do you always mention those neighborhoods?"

"What? Well, because——"

"You realize you've never once brought up a museum that I might like to see. The school is on a fucking museum's campus and you've never once at least said them or any specific exhibit that could interest me. You only ever bring up the Mexican neighborhoods. Even for museum-y things, you're always *only* going on about Mexican muralism."

"You do murals, Ander. I'd think places like that would be where you'd want to get inspired from."

"A mural is just a surface. It's not a subject. Anything can be on a mural. Andy Warhol's *Marilyn Diptych* could be a mural. The whole-ass *Mona Lisa* could be a mural. And murals exist outside of those couple of neighborhoods. I'm also nonbinary and gay. Are there not places in Chicago that I'd think would be cool to see because of those parts of me? Are there not just generally great places to see street art that *anyone* would be impressed with?"

"But these specifically would feel familiar to you, no?"

"Why go all the way to Chicago to be motivated by the familiar? Why can't I be introduced to subjects that bring me out of my comfort zone and figure out how to make them my own with everything I'm learning here? Why can't I have both Pilsen, which I already know about and have been to and love, with other parts of Chicago that could be inspiring? This residency has been my comfort zone; why go all the way there for something I'm doing already? If anything, at least here I don't feel so boxed in as when I'm talking to you and listening to you mention the same three or four brown artists. Why do you—We wouldn't be having this conversation if I was white. Or if I wasn't so good at the art you expect me to be doing. Hell, I'm good, *period*."

"Ander, listen——"

"No, I don't think I will. And, actually, I have somewhere to be right now. So, yeah, thanks for this hour and a half or whatever."

It's never felt so good to hang up on someone before.

It's only ten in the morning and I'm having my second art-related meeting of the day. Tita and I have been sitting at the patio bar for half an hour now. She's quieter than maybe I've ever seen her in my entire life. Her attention at nothing except my iPad and the mural idea for the wall out here. I want to keep the front-of-the-building piece a secret from her, so she (reluctantly) allowed Pa and Mami to have final say over that one. I watch her zoom in on some parts and then hold her hand up to her mouth, which is usually a good sign. She's at least having a reaction.

"This is, and I don't mean it in a bad way, bebite, pero—es un poquito simple."

"Do you not like it? The wall isn't huge, and I don't want to make it too busy or crowded."

"No, no. I like it. The papeles picados on top are nice and this circle—"

"It's supposed to be a sun."

"Sí, your sun. And where did you get this from? The words? This Mexican Heaven?"

"'Mexican Heaven' is a poem. Well, like, it's a bunch of poems. I don't know how to explain it. Mo was reading a collection by this guy, José Olivarez, for one of his summer classes and sent me this part. And, I don't know, it made me happy. I think a lot of people around here see this place as their own little slice of Mexican Heaven."

"Ay, qué precioso. I hope they're all going to church, so they get into real Heaven too. There are no tamales or tortas in Hell."

"Or there are, but they're only made by white women with food blogs who say *tor-til-uh* instead of tortilla and put peas in their guacamole."

"*Qué feo.*" Tita takes one last look at the patio mural before handing it back to me. "If you can make it a *little more* busy, I wouldn't be mad."

"Understood."

"And you don't want to show me the other one?" Tita gives her big, abuela eyes and clasps her hands as she asks.

"It's supposed to be a surprise."

She sighs and rolls her eyes before digging into her purse for her credit card. "Well, if you want to come back with a few shirts and some of those putita shorts and a new iPad with your paint supplies for the murals, you know my email to send your idea for the front."

"You're bribing me? All for—Wait. Did you really just call me a putita?"

"No, I called your shorts putita."

"Is there a difference?"

Tita turns away from me, gets up, and speed-walks away without answering.

Hateful-ass family.

"Why is elote not on this list?" Santi asks, going from my iPad to me, acting like he's helping me while on his break. We'd been doing exactly this but while sitting at a table with a couple aguas frescas, literally for not even thirty seconds, before Mami sends me a text, all **I told you if you're not here to work or pick up food I don't want you here.**

Giving her the biggest eye roll of my life, I type back, **CAN I NOT TAKE FIVE MINUTES?**

Apparently not. So we fake it. I can take a pencil to this wall, doing absolutely nothing, and claim it's part of the process. She can't prove me wrong.

"I don't know. I didn't write it."

"Elote is the most important food in México."

"Okay, we get it. You love corn. But if you think about it, elote is also in basically every single one of these. I mean, until you get to the last row. There's masa in tamales. Corn tortillas for tacos and tostadas. Tortas . . . well, okay, not tortas."

"So it doesn't deserve its own word?"

"I didn't say that or decide that," I reply defensively. Any amount of insulted he's feeling because of this poem should not be taken up with me, a person who has no power over that. "But I'm not going to add it. This isn't my poem."

"I might," Santi says back with a lot of snark in his voice. "I mean, corn is *from* México. Y sin maíz, no hay país, ¿tú sabes?"

"Did you make that up?"

"No. It's a saying."

"Huh. I should've went with that instead. I like how it rhymes. This poem doesn't even rhyme."

"You could change it? You haven't written anything yet."

"Yeah, but I'm already sort of sold on this idea. Keeping that corn thing for something else, though."

"Good." He hands me my iPad and kisses me before adjusting his bandana. "Okay, gotta go back to work now."

"Same."

I start with a light brown at the bottom of the wall and then use different greens to create desert plants and a large cactus at the edge. Then there's the big, deep orange circle on the opposite side of the cactus going into the middle of the wall, and, finally, papeles picados along the top in burgundy, burnt orange, gold, and brown. All of it together creates a simple scene of

Abuelo Willie's ranch out in Marfa that we'd spend a lot of time at growing up before he died. Besides the taquería, it was his favorite place to be. Puro hijo de la tierra. Could never be me.

Next is the script, which I'm a little out of practice on. When I was in middle school, I got into sign painting, mainly because the taquería needed something for the (at the time) new bar on the patio and my parents thought it'd be easier for me to learn a new skill than pay someone else to do it. But it's been a few years since I last did a sign and, while it left me with the confidence to just put paint on something and do the strokes boldly and accurately with my murals, I don't want to mess this specific piece up.

I take it slow. An *M* and then *E*, *X*, *I*, *C*, *A*, and *N*. Drawing out each letter with a white charcoal pencil at first, making sure they're all equal from the beginning, otherwise it won't come out right. And then, after a deep breath, I take the brush to the outlined letters. It's just like riding a bike; my hand going without needing any instruction. And, not to eat my own ass, but the white of the paint contrasts beautifully with the dark gray of the concrete wall and the orange and brown earth tones. Good decision, Ander.

By the time I'm finishing HEAVEN, my mind is in the zone. No concept of time or existence or the heat of the July afternoon. Just me, this wall, and my paintbrush.

"There," I say through a deep exhale, picking myself up from squatting. Turning around and jumping when I see Santi sitting at the table next to me. *"How long have you been there?"*

"About half an hour. You said hi back to me when I sat down."

"I don't remember that." My attention goes back to the wall. Might need to go over the papeles picados once more to really get them popping. And the white of the print too. But that'll have to wait until tomorrow because, seeing the time on my phone, I've been here eight hours already. It doesn't seem like a lot, but the amount of time it takes to go over cacti again and again and again so that the green stands out and isn't muddled by the dark wall is *work*.

Anyways, enough complaining. I chose this life.

"*Querido*, can you get a container of barbacoa while I put my stuff up?" I ask Santi, giving him the widest smile I can before adding a long, drawn-out "*¿Por favoooorrr?* I'm done for today. Let's go make out while Netflix plays in the background."

"*Qué romántico.*"

I finish the mural only hours before July's Second Friday employee kickback. Perfect for an ego boost—all the cooks and waiters taking turns getting pictures in front of it, telling me how much they like the colors, and lots of "When are you gonna come paint the side of my house, AJ?!"

"Pues, lemme know. What was it you wanted? A lowrider on the side of your garage?"

"Sí, I want it to be—¿cómo se dice?—like driving in *Grand Theft Auto.*"

"Get at me sometime before the end of August or it's gonna have to wait until December."

It takes almost half an hour of getting through everyone giving me compliments and waiting for a photo with the artist before I'm finally able to go find Santi, Chachi, and Mami sitting at a table, going through a pile of flautas while Pa and Tita run around.

"Did you say hi to Zeke?" Santi asks as I start reaching for the fried taquitos.

"No."

"You going to?"

I let my eyes barely glance over at Zeke, sitting with Ronnie and a couple waiters. And, because God has the biggest sense of humor, his eyes are on me too. Both of us jump back to our own tables, acting like we aren't being super weird right now.

"Wasn't planning on it."

"Don't you think you're overreacting at this point?"

"*I'm not overreacting.* I'm not reacting at all. I'm waiting for the person who was in the wrong to gird his motherfucking loins and admit it."

"I'm going to talk to him if you aren't."

"*Okay.* Well, I'm not. So, by all means. Have fun."

"I will."

"Then do it."

"Okay."

"*Está bien.*"

Santi stares at me with the most annoyed face I've ever seen from him. As if I actually give a shit. I'm annoyed at *him* for bringing this up. For bringing it up constantly over the last week. It's Zeke's fault it's gone this long. If he wants to not talk for a week, whatever. Two? Bueno. And if he wants to not talk for a month because he refuses to say he's sorry, his choice.

My boyfriend lets out a huff as he stands up, shaking his head while walking away and toward Zeke, sitting with a few of the waitstaff. I keep the corner of my eye on them. Enough to be aware that they're probably talking about me but not enough to actually seem like I'm trying to pry myself into it.

"You two never change," Ronnie says as he takes Santi's chair.

"Shut up."

"I'm just saying, it's funny. Because y'all care about each other. Even if you don't like him very much right now. Pero, gotta forgive eventually, kid. Like always."

"*I know.* I can be petty, though."

"*También yo sé.* Again, you never change."

"*And we're happy.*"

I prefer sunny days to cold ones or rainy days. Even when it tops a hundred, that's fine with me. I'd rather spend any of those days outside than painting in forty-degree weather. Fuck that entirely.

Guess that's why I made the smart decision on moving all the way to Chicago. Because the one word everyone thinks of when they hear Chicago is *hot*.

I mix a rose quartz paint with the lightest gray Home Depot sells and some white. No idea what I was going for at first but ending up with this light but muted pink that I'm incredibly happy with. Taking my painting roll, I dip it into my creation and start covering the wall of the new BiblioTech building opening right here in Santos Vista. They wanted something pretty, mentioned "plants or something" to Juni, and that was the beginning and end of their instructions.

I've been wanting to do a piece with monstera plants, so this is perfect. Say less.

The wall is a weird, skinny, long rectangle on the side of a not-rectangle-but-not-a-trapezoid-shaped building. Ideal for the long stems and big green leaves I'm imagining. Simple but effective, and pretty. Exactly what they asked for.

Where are you? I text to Chachi. She said Pa was going to bring her over to help since she doesn't have summer football training on the weekends and Santi's working. The moment I mentioned Juni was getting me a basket crane to use for this, she was immediately screaming at me, begging to let her help. And, against my better judgment or because I don't value my life enough, I said sure.

But now she's half an hour late, so she's about to get left behind if she—

"Hey."

"What are you doing here?" I ask as Zeke walks up to me, one hand in his pocket, the other holding a drink container with two cups of iced coffee, looking like he half expects me to blow up on him again if he says one more word.

"I—Your sister asked if I could help you out today. Something came up."

"Bet." My eye roll can't be contained. Both of them are being punk-ass bitches right now. "So, what? You wanna help?"

"Yeah. If you want me to."

I groan, fighting another eye roll because I'm not about to have my face get stuck like this. "If *you* want to. It doesn't matter to me."

"Pues, güey, it doesn't matter to me either. I'm just trying to help."

"Yeah, well, you can imagine why I'm not rushing to accept."

"You don't have to. But you also don't have to be a dick when I'm being nice."

"Being nice and being helpful can be two different things, Zeke. You—"

"*I'm sorry*, okay?" he says while setting the coffees down next to the paint supplies. "I told Santi I was sorry. We talked it out. Can we move past this now?"

"Do you understand all the ways in which you were being a pendejo?"

"Yes. I do," Zeke answers, taking the other long paint roller and fiddling with it like always until I reach out a hand to adjust it for him. "And I feel horrible about it, all right? I was trying to be helpful, but I—You were right. I was being careless."

"Yeah you were," I snap.

"But you reacted kinda carelessly too."

"I acted that way as it pertains to Santi, which doesn't concern you. *You*, though, you're lucky I didn't punch you in the mouth."

"Do you want to punch me in the mouth?"

"No," I reply. A loud, frustrated breath follows. "It wouldn't help now."

We don't say anything more for a while. Silently painting the bottom portion of the wall. Zeke watches me mix more when we go through the tray, looking like a scientist making sure my chemicals don't blow up as I work on getting as close to the exact shade I've been doing; holding up a notecard with a streak of the exact color it should look like close to the paint and watching as they both start looking like the same shade. Both of us in this dip, paint, dip, paint pattern. Every once in a while, we'll catch the other's eyes, at first pretending to be annoyed, but eventually small smiles start coming and then little chuckles.

I can hear Ronnie's voice in the back of my head. *You two never change.* Chingón.

"You scared?" I ask him when one of his hands reaches for my arm and the other goes for the metal railing, gripping tightly as the crane starts lifting us higher. Knowing for a fact that the only time he's been okay with heights is when he's on the roof, and even then, he can get a little shaky at times.

"No. *Bitch*," he replies. His voice a little trembly. "Just don't move."

Zeke spends a minute working up the courage to get back

to painting, taking his sweet-ass time at first before getting the hang of it and realizing that, no, he's not going to die today. As long as he doesn't look down, he'll be fine.

"I want you to feel like Santi will be okay without you here."

I keep painting. I'm not going to do anything else until I know what I want to say to that. Because I've had that conversation with Santi. I've had it with myself plenty more. But telling someone else that I trust them, I don't know if I can honestly say it.

"He can take care of himself."

"Well, yeah. But I don't want you to think he's *only* gonna have himself. Or that—I don't know—that I'm not here for him. I did what I did genuinely wanting to help, as unhelpful as I ended up being."

"*Entirely* is the word you're looking for."

"¿Y tú?

"This isn't about me, right?"

"Whatever." Zeke sets his rollers against the railing and carefully squats down to get his coffee that's just melted ice now. "Real talk, you're my best friend, AJ. And Santi is *a* friend who's also a coworker and who's also dating my best friend. And I know you've spent every single day since you found out he's undocumented worried about what happens when you go to Chicago. We got it, though. I'm invested in this. You got a smart boyfriend, a smart best friend, smart family. No sweat."

"You can't guarantee that."

"Yeah, but I can be optimistic. I can see all the evidence that points to Santi living the American Dream in all its mediocrity for as long as he wants."

"Sure. Okay. Can we move on now? I'm not in the mood to keep talking about this."

"What do you want to talk about?"

"I don't know. Tell me what classes you're taking this semester. Or what Mo's up to while interning for whoever-the-fuck. Some Dallas state rep, ¿verdad? It's been a while since I've talked to him for longer than a couple texts once a month. Catch me up."

"How much time we got?"

"All day."

I take a seat on the sidewalk, my back leaning against the now completed wall. A pretty gray-pink background, some more white added to give a sort of cloudy effect, with giant green leaves that can be noticed from all the way down the block. I'm so sweaty on literally *every* part of my body, and it's only continuing as the sun points its heat directly at me like a warm hug browning my skin. Exhaustion and tiredness but also a lot of pride covers me along with it. I got another mural done, didn't kill myself using that crane or damage any property, and over the couple of days that Zeke was around, we both fell back into normalcy. Life is all right again.

Not too much left to do here.

I was good at ignoring it up to now, but the number of days I have until I'm at SAIC is getting smaller and smaller. In only a few weeks, I won't have Tita or Mami or Pa, Chachi, Zeke. No Santi.

Fuck. I'm not ready.

Why didn't I think of staying in San Antonio? Going to UTSA. Or just *somewhere* in-state. Why'd I have to listen to my high school art teacher? Why'd I let her convince me and my family that I should aim big? Why was I "RISD or The New School or SAIC or Seattle are the only options for me"? Bien tonte.

Everyone will be okay. Tita and Mami will survive. Pa will have Chachi. Zeke's got his college friends. Santi's got all of them.

But those thoughts don't keep the tears from falling.

"¿Por qué estás siendo un chillone?" Pa asks from his pickup, stopping right on the street.

"*I'm not*. It's sweat."

"You're sweaty. But you're also crying." He holds up a large cup from the restaurant, shaking it a little. "Brought you an horchata. You want?"

"Claro," I reply, wiping my eyes and standing up. I lean into the opening created with the window down and grab the drink.

"Need to talk?" Pa asks as I start taking long sips.

"No."

"You sure?"

I give Pa an annoyed glare while continuing to drink my vanilla-and-cinnamon rice concoction from Heaven. "Yeah. I'm sure."

He gives me a look right back. One of those that tells me if he finds out I'm feeling worse later when he tried to help, he'll beat my ass.

"*Ugh*, fine." I hand Pa my cup, offering him the rest of it. "When . . . how do I know I'm ready?"

"Ready for what?"

"For *anything*."

"Preparation. Doing everything you can to make sure you have all the tools you need to—"

"I don't mean that," I interrupt. "What if I know I'm techni-cally ready for something, but I don't *feel* like I'm ready, or that I'm heading for something right but not ready for what it means for the rest of my life?"

"Embrace it," he answers. "Do you think the baby bird feels ready to fly when their mami pushes it off the tree? You have the instinct and wisdom to do many things you'd think are impos-sible, Ander. If you wait around for some *feeling*, you're going to miss out on experiencing life. You of all people should know that. You're good at jumping into situations and coming out better than anyone would expect. You've made plenty of choices that could've sounded right and ended up very wrong."

"That was shade, wasn't it?"

"If the shoe fits."

Pa's eyes meet mine for only a moment. Like a mirror that ages a cis-male version of me by thirty years and adds some height and tortilla weight. I want to ask him if there's anything he would change. Any moments in his life that he let go by because he was scared of failure or loss.

"Everything is going to be okay, right?"

"No. But that's okay too."

35

Santi smiles and waves at me through one of the large taquería windows, finally noticing my car in the parking lot. Then a hand goes into his pocket, coming out with his phone.

Sorry I was learning some of the kitchen stuff and we lost track of time. Be out in five, he texts, and then **Also your amá wants to know if you want bacon and egg tacos.**

Porkchop pls. And it's fine. I love late morning naps in my car.

Is that sarcasm?

Can't answer rn. Asleep.

I actually do fall asleep right after sending that text. Stirred awake by Santi tapping on the passenger-side window and the aroma of food all over him as he settles next to me.

"Have fun learning how to be a taquero?" I ask through a yawn.

"Sí. It's a lot, but it's fun. I—Are you okay to drive?"

"Yeah." Another yawn coming out makes the word sound like just weird noise. "I can stay awake for a few minutes. And then we can nap in my bed."

"Sí, porfa. You were up way too late working on your exhibit. I was up way too early for work. I'm gonna cuddle your culo so hard and knock out until the weekend."

"Don't you have a shift tomorrow?"

"No es importante, cielo."

One hand goes for the steering wheel and the other reaches for Santi's hand. I don't even have to think about it anymore. As if my hand is a flower and his, the sun that I grow toward. Might have to paint that later.

I get a few quick moments to glance over at him. Trying his best to keep his eyes open, using the headrest as a pillow. Letting out quiet laughs whenever I shake his hand when I catch him falling asleep.

"We're almost there, querido."

"Yeah," Santi says before taking a deep breath in through his nose as he stretches. His head turns to the side window and, very suddenly, his hold on my hand tightens as he looks closer into the small mirror attached to my door. "Hey, have—How long has this van been behind us?"

"No sé. Haven't been paying attention. Why?"

"Turn."

"What?"

"*Turn,*" he pleads, more aggressively. "You need to turn. *Now.*"

"Are you going to tell me what's going on?"

"If you turn, yes."

I switch my blinker on for only a second before taking a quick left, my tires letting out a short squeak.

"Santa mierda," I hear Santi mumble.

"What's going on?"

"That van is following us. I—it's ICE."

A pressure squeezes my chest and everything in there. There's a weight on my throat. Everything feels heavy. And the world seems to have slowed down but is also moving way too fast for me to decide what I need to do next.

"Call Mami." I don't know why this seems like the best first decision. Maybe hoping for someone who's smarter than me to tell me how or what to do or that everything's going to be okay. Or, even better, to tell me that this isn't real.

Santi starts talking in rapid Spanish. Way too fast for me to follow along. I can only catch a few words: "Following us." "Where do we go?" "They're okay, I promise."

"She says get to your house."

"Should I try to lose them?"

"No. Don't be reckless. Just do what she says."

Every second we're in this car, my mind heads further and further from reality. Scenes of Santi being dragged away. Never seeing him again. And then more ideal scenarios because I don't want to think of that option. Of us somewhere in the middle of nowhere together. Far into the desert while it rains.

I don't think there's enough oxygen in here. My hand on the steering wheel feels like it's going to bruise with how hard I'm squeezing it. Each light we hit is like a little purgatory. Us and that van right on our ass. The couple of people walking stop so abruptly I'd almost think time has stopped completely if it wasn't for how their faces go from disinterested to fearful and worried when they see the IMMIGRATION AND CUSTOMS ENFORCEMENT on the side of the vehicle behind us. And then they look straight into our souls, sending telepathic prayers.

God's never been a thing I've been *into*. I grew up on it, but then Mo started talking about how Christianity is a tool of colonialist oppression, and honestly, he has a point. But fuck it if I'm not holding on to the rosary Tita hung on my rearview mirror when I first got this car a couple years ago.

Get me through this, I pray as I continue to weave left and right, no longer paying attention to where I'm going and letting my subconscious take us where we need to be. *That's all I need.*

"Cielo." Santi's voice sounds planets away from me. "Cielo. Cielo. *Ander.*"

"Huh? What?"

"You passed your home."

I think it was purposeful. A lot of me doesn't want to stop at my house. I don't want them to know where I live. Where Santi goes to feel safest. Where we escape the world. They don't deserve to know that space.

But if this is what Mami says to do, I've got to trust her.

I start making slow lefts around our block. There's no way out of this, and that makes me want to cry. It makes me want to scream. To be reckless because they don't deserve my cooperation. But I've got to trust someone is going to get us through this. And I need to get my shit together, otherwise . . .

I pull into the driveway. Something as simple as that takes a whole lot of fighting against myself. *Don't park. Don't turn off your car. Go somewhere safe. Somewhere away from here.*

I can't. This is it. I'm not letting Santi go.

A tear starts heading down his face. He turns to me when my thumb wipes it off his cheek. His mouth starts to open like he's about to say something, and—

Both of us jump when a knuckle taps the passenger-side window. The voice of some man hiding his eyes behind large sunglasses asks if one of us is Santiago López Alvarado. Those glasses don't hide his brown skin. His barrio accent he probably tries to bury when he's around white ICE agents. They don't cover his betrayal, and I really want to yell that at him.

"Mírame. Querido, mírame," I say instead. My hands go to Santi's face, physically turning him to me. Speaking in a whisper only between the two of us. "Keep your eyes here, yeah?"

"Estoy asustado," he says. I can feel each shake of his voice in my palms. The fear in how tightly he's gripping my wrists.

See how he fights keeping his eyes closed, somewhere in the back of his mind telling him to hide there. "No quiero que me lleven."

The pain that happens in my heart hearing those words feels like someone's squeezing it until it bursts. Like a hammer smashing into it, right at its center. So much of me wants to come to terms with how helpless we are. How hopeless this all seems.

"It's okay if you're scared. I'm scared too." The words come out shaky as I start crying with him. I rest my forehead against Santi's and move my hands to the back of his head, slowly rubbing back and forth, trying to calm down his trembling. "And they aren't going to take you. Te protegeré. Siempre. I know you said you don't need me to, but—"

Santi grabs on to my wrists and he shakes his head back and forth, rubbing against mine. "No. It's okay."

"We're gonna be okay." I repeat the words like a chant over and over again. Trying to convince myself as much as him. "Te prome—"

"*Back the* fuck *away from my child!*"

Santi's head moves the slightest bit to the side. "Is that your apá?"

"I—I think it is." I turn away from Santi just enough to see out the window at Pa getting right up in the ICE agent's chest. "Don't pay attention, though. Okay? Solamente tú y yo."

If only that was so easily done. I hear a third, unrecognizable voice. Probably another ICE agent. I bury the urge to go help Pa. He's fine. Santi needs me. Although, I wish I could separate myself in two and do both.

"I did a painting of you while you were at work yesterday," I tell him. "I kept thinking of the Easter thing at Lupe's. Of you with two little Snickers in your mouth and smiling, already opening another one. All the bright colors that were around you:

the baskets and the fake grass and the eggs. Trying to get that specific really light pink of the tank you were wearing that day. And I kept thinking of how happy you looked there. How much fun I had that day because I got to spend it with you."

"I had fun that day too. I think that might be one of my favorite days of my whole life."

"Me too. When we get inside, I'll show you—" The voices of a lot more people have me going quiet. There's got to be four, five, seven at least. I turn around and—

"What the—Mami? Tita? *Zeke?*"

He runs over to my side of the car, leaning into the mirror. "We're gonna get y'all out," he says over the shouting of one of the ICE agents. "Hold on, all right? Hold on."

Zeke comes back with one of the ladies I remember from RAICES and at least twenty others behind them. She starts directing everyone, "Make two lines from the car to the front door. You remember Red Rover, yeah? Like that, but backs to them."

"Can you both come out the driver's side?" Zeke asks.

"Yeah."

"Okay, whenever you're ready."

It's felt like hours that we've been in this car, and now time seems to be moving so quickly. Too quickly to process anything more than Zeke's words and Santi next to me. "¿Listo?"

"Mhm," Santi answers with a small, shaky nod. I grab his hand, making sure every finger is locked with mine, and take the shortest second to kiss his lips.

"No looking back, right?"

"No looking back."

I jump out of my car and as soon as I see Santi on the ground with me, we're off. Moving so fast, so focused on getting to the front door, on making sure the hand squeezing mine doesn't let go, everything else around us is a muted blur of noise and color.

In moments that happen and end almost too quickly to process, I get little bits of what's happening and who's around me.

Zeke yelling "*¡Corre!*"

The RAICES lady and Mami yelling at the ICE agents.

Them yelling back.

This whole neighborhood showing up for us. Fighting for us. For someone who's always called this place home and another who deserves a place to call home.

The closer I get to the front door, all the emotion that's been building up inside me and filling my throat, begging to be released is getting harder and harder to keep down. The fear, sadness, hopelessness, and gratitude. The tears that started coming out as soon as I stepped out of my car.

Almost there. Almost there. Almost there.

I've never been so relieved as I am when I hear the slam of the door closing behind us, muffling the voices from outside. The abrupt, sharp silence that rings in my ear for I couldn't even say how long. Silence is good. Silence means the people who tried to take my boyfriend away can't do that anymore.

At least, not for right now.

Santi and I end up on the floor. Which one of us started falling, I don't know, but our arms wrap around each other and refuse to let go, standing, sitting, kneeling, however. That silence turns into the sounds of crying and sniffling and my heartbeat drumming in my ear.

Of Santi, his face buried in my neck, breaking down. Of me crying with him, trying to stay strong for him, needing him to know that everything will be all right.

"It's okay. You're still here."

"I know. But I almost wasn't."

"But you are. You are."

almost lost him.

My heart and lungs and stomach are all trying to break out of my body, bouncing around like I'm a human pinball machine. Every time I close my eyes, I see that ICE agent standing outside my car, waiting for Santi. I see how robotic he was. How he didn't recognize the humanity in either of us. How he refused to.

And I see Santi's eyes. Hear myself tell him over and over to concentrate on me. "Don't look anywhere else."

My phone rings, **Mami** displayed on the screen.

"Are you okay?" she yells in almost a cry.

"Yeah." My answer is quiet. Breathy. Like I'm still trying to hide us from the world and don't want anyone to hear me except for her. But also like I have something lodged in my throat.

"Do you need us to stay? We can stay. We can close the restaurant for the day and—"

"No, Mami, don't. It's fine. Don't worry about it. Santi's taking a shower. I'm—I don't know, I'll make us something to eat. We're good. We're safe now."

I know neither of us really believes that.

The sound of her sigh carries through the phone. "You know what to do if they start knocking on the door?"

"Yes. I know."

"Don't open it for anyone."

"I won't."

"Okay. I—we'll be back later. Te quiero, mi'je."

"Te quiero, Mami."

The world has never felt so silent as it does when she hangs up. There isn't even that annoying ringing that happens in my ears when it's quiet. Like some sort of vacuum has sucked up all the sound in the universe and left.

I walk into the garage where the washer and dryer are. Where the huge canvases for my Blue Star exhibit are being set up. That Santi helped me set up, asking so many excited questions about what I'm doing with them and telling me how he knows they're going to look so good.

I couldn't be doing any of this without you.

I almost had to.

I hate that thought. I hate it so much. I can't hold in how much I hate it.

So I scream. To let it all out. To make sure that sound still exists. To let out everything that's been holding itself in. To remind myself that I'm still here. Until my throat hurts to remind myself that I can still feel.

My hand trembles as I grab a towel from the dryer and my feet feel heavy while I walk upstairs, as much as I also want to run. Wishing I could teleport to Santi. Remind myself that he's still here too.

"I'm coming in real quick," I shout after knocking on the bathroom door. Opening it, I'm overwhelmed by the change from air-conditioned hallway to humidity trapped in this small space. My eyes go to the brown smudge that is Santi's body behind the iced shower door. I can tell his arms are stretched out, hands resting on the walls, standing still under the shower head. Unmoving. Letting the water run over him.

"I got you a towel. It'll be on the counter."

I wait for some sort of response. An *okay*. A little movement. Something.

And then, after the longest seven seconds of my life, his hands come off that wall. I can make out him shaking water off his head, him turning around and over to the sliding door, and pulling it open enough for his face and half of his torso to pop out. We don't say anything. Both of us only stare into red, tired eyes.

"Do you," he starts. Quietly but then begins again more loudly, "Do you want to come in?"

"I—yeah. Really? You sure?"

Santi nods and then reaches out a wet left hand. "*Please*. I don't want to be alone."

I hastily start taking off my clothes. In a rush not necessarily because being naked with Santi is usually a very ideal situation, but because ever since he let go of me to walk into the bathroom and take a shower, I've felt scared and powerless and alone. I need to remember that neither I nor he are any of those things. And I'm now incredibly certain he's feeling the same way at least a little bit.

The moment his hand is holding mine, pulling me into the shower, is healing and reaffirming. No more tears. We let our eyes take in each other and we kiss and wash each other and I wrap my arms around him and let my face rest against the back of his neck, smelling my shampoo on him, listening to the sound of water hitting skin and tile. And I tell myself once, twice, and then once more that we are not alone.

We have to take turns with the towel because I only brought one with me, and I sit on the counter while Santi dries off and we kiss some more, and I can see and then feel him smile against my lips and nearly start crying from that smile.

I lead him into my bedroom. And with every touch, I am

reminded that we are powerful. That our existence is powerful. That we can be both protector and protected. That what we're doing right now is undoubtedly a way for us each to cope with trauma, but it's also him reminding me and me reminding him that we exist. Together. Right here and now, with each other. And no man or government or racist ideology can ruin this.

At least, not right now.

Not while I lie down with Santi holding himself up above me. Not while I hear him hum and his breath catch from what my hand's doing to him. Not while he looks right into my soul through my eyes after his hands have had their turn with me and asks if it's okay if he keeps going. Not as he starts kissing my ear, neck, chest, stomach, then my ankles, calves, left thigh, and finally the right, first hovering over my tattoo before letting the tip of his tongue glide along the outline of the strawberry candy. Not when his hands go down to my hips and up the back of my thighs, feeling both soft and strong as he grips my skin and holds me steady. Or while he kisses me through the quick second of discomfort that turns into pleasure and then through moans escaping out of my mouth and filling his.

He is here. We are here. And I want us and who we are in this moment and who he is to me to be memorialized in this space. In honor of Santi, and his bravery when things are difficult, who chose to let me into his life as complicated and terrifying as it can be. Who is love and hope and decency and—Jesus Christ, is really fucking good at this.

We don't leave my bed. Arms wrapped around each other, legs tangled together, lips pressing softly against skin, Santi's head under my chin, buried into my chest. My only focus is on the slow and steady pattern of his torso inflating with breath and then exhaling out. On my fingers gliding over the top of his back and neck and head and arms. On how he does this weird thing where he stretches his toes when his mind goes empty. On the light coming into my room getting brighter and then dimmer as the sun makes its way west.

I focus on Santi. On the weight of him asleep on me. On those moments where he unconsciously tightens his hold on me and I put so much hope that whatever's going on in his mind right now is only good things.

And in my own head I repeat *he's here; he's okay; he's with me* over and over until I fall asleep.

37

S anti?" I whisper as I reach for him but only grab pillows and comforter, my eyes still closed, not ready to wake up from what feels like the most amount of sleep all day. "Santi?"

"Estoy aquí," he answers, tapping my ankle with his toes. I pick up my head to see him sitting at the foot of my bed, leaning against the wall.

"¿Qué estás haciendo?"

"I was watching you sleep. But, not creepy."

"How long have you been watching me?"

"Mm, I don't know. Half an hour."

Okay. Any more than that might've been kind of creepy. But I won't think nothing of it right now. I'd be doing the same thing if this had been reversed.

"What time is it?"

"About eleven."

"In the morning?"

"Night. Sun's gone."

"Oh. Yeah." I hold my hand out, waiting for Santi to take it and lie back down with me. "I was kind of hoping I'd fallen asleep until tomorrow."

"Nope," he says, and then pecks at my cheek. His fingers move hair out of my eyes. "Still stuck in today."

He doesn't hide his resentment in those words. How much I

can tell he wishes it was any other day but today. Even waiting an hour seems like too much to ask for. The frustration in his face says so.

"I don't like being stuck."

"I know," I tell him. Mad that I don't have anything more meaningful to say right now.

"All of this shit, it—it makes me want to go somewhere. It makes me feel trapped and needing to break out."

"Where do you want to go?"

Santi shrugs and turns so he's facing the ceiling. Pulling my hand onto his chest. "I've always wanted to see the ocean."

"Wait. You've never been to the beach?"

"No."

I lift myself up a little, so I can see his whole face. "Okay, so I'm not saying whether you should or not or if it's at all a good or smart idea, because that's not—it's something *you* tell *me*. I'll go along with whatever you want. But if what you want is to take a drive, just say the word."

"Now? Really? You would? *Right now?*"

Do I think this is a good idea? No. Not at all. There's this fear that all of Homeland Security is out on our front yard, waiting for the moment we're too relaxed. The moment to rip Santi and me apart.

But I can tell he needs this. He needs a chance to breathe. And if I can give him that, I will. No more convincing needed.

"If it's something you want and feel safe doing. Again, up to you. But, yes, I would."

Santi's face lights up with a smile that's reaching for excited. A smile I haven't seen in too long and I'm glad that the world hasn't taken away.

"Vámonos."

We carefully tiptoe downstairs. I can hear Mami and Pa talking in the kitchen, and slow, calm music playing from Mami's laptop on the dining table. If we're extra cautious, we could get out without them seeing us.

Squeak.

"Fucking old-ass stairs," I mutter through my teeth. My parents' heads poke out into the living area, catching us.

"You're awake?" Mami asks.

"We, uh. We—"

"Tengo hambre," Santi says. "Ander me va a llevar a Whataburger."

"We have food here, Santi. I can make you something, mi'jo."

"Yo sé. Pero quiero un Honey Butter Chicken Biscuit."

"Are you sure? You're okay leaving the house right now? For a chicken?"

"Sí, jefacita. Más bien."

I can see it in her eyes. She doesn't believe a word of what he's telling her. No one has ever gotten their pendejismo past her. We aren't even trying to not be obvious. She sees the backpack strap over one of my shoulders.

"Be careful," she says like a warning. "Look out for each other, yeah?"

"Yes," I answer for us. "Thank you. Love you. Bye."

I drag Santi with me, rushing out the door and to my car. Half of me is expecting Mami to change her mind and come sprinting after us. I give it five seconds of my head going back and forth from Santi to my house.

No Mami. We're good.

"You realize she's gonna wonder where we're actually going when we aren't back home in twenty minutes."

"Yeah. I can text her if you want. *And* if we go to Whataburger on the way, it's not like we lied."

"Good luck getting her to believe that. And wait until we're out of the city before letting her know. We'll need a big head start."

On the road, it's almost complete darkness. Driving into a new day, we're free.

It takes a few minutes for Santi to get fully comfortable. To stop looking to the sides and behind us. But we get there. Once we're out of the city, we find freedom.

Going through chicken strips and fries, sipping on milkshakes, singing "What's Up" by 4 Non Blondes with our entire chest, so it comes out as more of a yell. Santi's eyes are closed, his fists clenched, like this is the last song he's ever going to sing.

And, shit. I love him so much.

I love him so much and I almost didn't get to tell him.

"*Wait!*" Santi screams, his hand going to my stereo and turning down the volume. "Is that water? Is that the ocean? Are we here? Where are we?"

"Port A," I answer through a laugh while letting our windows go down and the salty, humid Gulf air into the car. He immediately puts his head out the window like a puppy, taking it all in. "Eh, I mean, we're in Aransas Pass still. But, yeah, a few more minutes. Hold on."

When we get to the causeway, leaving San Patricio County and, with it, the mainland, into Nueces County and the islands, Santi's hand flies to mine, squeezing me.

"Don't be nervous, querido. The bridges are stable."

"*I know that*. I'm not nervous."

The first bridge, he's fine. It's over in a blink. The second, though, as we head into a black late-night, early-morning abyss, the only light coming from the plants around here, his grip gets even tighter. But I can tell there's excitement in there too. The way he keeps turning in his seat every direction and his free hand makes waves in the wind tells me that. So I let him adjust. I don't ask him if he needs me to turn around.

Stepping out of my car and onto the beach parking lot, we're welcomed to the coast by a cloudy sky. It's not that humid, though. At least, not any more than usual for the Gulf. And I don't smell rain. Only a little breeze carrying the scent of salt water. As ideal as I could've hoped for.

Santi is immediately taking off his shoes and running toward the sand. "Come on, cielo!"

I sprint after him as we take off our shorts and shirts, throwing our clothes onto the beach before diving into the water. Both of us laugh and scream and grab for each other and make out while we float in the Gulf. The beat of his heart pounds into my skin and mine, his.

"Te quiero," he says after his lips let go of mine. The words go right into my mouth as if he wants to plant them into my soul.

"Te quiero," I tell him back. It's like a relief, finally saying those words. Knowing how long and all those times I've wanted to say them but didn't. Sitting in that car hours ago wondering if I'd never have the chance to say them. I hold on to his face and go back for more kisses. Tasting the salt of the seawater and the sugary strawberry of his milkshake. Feeling his hands grip on to my thighs as I wrap my legs around his waist. "Te quiero. Through happiness and destruction."

"Por siempre."

We amble down the concrete pier jutting into the water. Shorts back on, a beach towel draped over Santi's shoulder, his hand in one of mine and both of our shirts in the other. We're silent as we walk, staring at the seemingly endless body of water surrounding us.

When we get to the end, he leans on the wooden railing and I wrap my arms around him, putting my weight onto his side. I lightly kiss my way up his biceps while he continues to look out toward nothingness.

"Have I ever told you why I call you *cielo*?"

"No. Dime. Si tú quieres."

Santi kisses the top of my head and then rests his on mine. Staying quiet for a couple seconds. "Because I'd started believing that my life was going to be hell. It's been struggle after struggle for a long time and I was almost convinced that's just how it was going to be until I died. And sometimes wondering if existing is even worth it. Trying so hard to get nowhere. Until I met you. Until you came, almost crashing into my life."

"You're not funny," I groan while he laughs at his own joke.

"That was a little funny. Don't lie."

"Keep going and I'll really run you over."

I squeeze him when I feel his body convulsing from laughter. "Until I met you," Santi repeats. "And you became my Heaven. You are the person who takes me to a place where, maybe the bad things still exist—obviously. But—but you also make me feel like I can overcome them. And you're the person who helps me leave all the bad behind for a while. It's so easy to leave reality with you. To go with you to a place that's our own. Nuestro cielo. Y eres *mi* cielo."

"I—" I don't know the words to follow that. How to tell him how much he means to me. How so much of my happiness, of my self is tied to him. How I don't want to leave that place with him. Except—

"Come with me."

"What?"

"To Chicago. Come with me to Chicago."

"I—but, how? Are you serious?"

"What do you mean 'Am I serious?' Of course I'm serious. I could, I don't know, cancel my flight. We can take my car up. As long as you're okay staying in a studio apartment I got for the year. I have the money from the murals at the restaurant and from Pride, I'll hopefully sell my work being shown at Blue Star, and if we need more, I can think of something. And you can do whatever you wanna do. If you wanna work at a restaurant up there, my tita will vouch for you, but if you're into something else, then do that."

"You really, *really* mean this?"

"Yes. I'm not kidding. I—soy tuyo. And I want to stay in this Heaven with you. I want to make a Heaven up there with you."

Santi leans away far enough so that he can see all of me. Into my eyes and think about whether he's going to do this with me. And when I see that little smile and hear that breathy chuckle, I know what's coming.

"Okay. I'll go with you. Yo y tú."

"Tú y yo."

38

Santi and I ended up staying in Port A for the weekend, napping in my car those first hours and getting woken up by the sun before finding an Airbnb only steps from the beach and acting all domestic for a while.

We weren't ready to go back. "Just a few days," we said. Away from the fear and hopelessness we'd felt. Instead in a place where no one knows us. Where we could spend from sunup to sundown with our feet in the sand, pretending worries don't exist, that life beyond tomorrow can be put on hold.

And, especially when Mami found out what we really did that night, it was best to give her some time to cool off.

But back home, the reality of what happened has been impossible to ignore. As much as we try to hold on to the future we've set for ourselves and can count down the days until we're leaving together, the anxiety is louder. That time ICE was at Lupe's was scary, but this was so much more. It was targeted. It was meant to stay with us like a recurring nightmare that we can't escape from.

"What if you don't go in to work today?" I ask Santi while leaning on the hood of my car as he comes out of his house. Actually, *ask* might be short selling it. I came prepared to beg. We just got back to San Antonio. I'm not ready for this yet. "It—no one would be mad about you not feeling up to it."

He kisses me before moving toward the passenger-side door. "I do feel up to it."

"Okay, but no one would blame you for not wanting to put yourself in danger."

Santi's head tilts a little. His face telling me he doesn't want to start this today. "Then what would we do instead, cielo?"

"I don't know. We could hang out here."

"We're not hanging out here."

"Fine. Then my house."

He closes his eyes and lets out a loud breath, whispering words in Spanish too softly and quickly for me to pick up on. "So we just stay inside for forever?"

"Not forever. Just until we leave for Chicago."

His glare is heavy. He shakes his head as he starts, "Cielo, no. I—"

"You just wanna act like everything is normal?" I didn't mean to be so snappy, but I thought this would be easier. That he'd actually have come out here all, *Yeah, fuck work for today.* That he wouldn't be so casual about this. "You want me to drive you to Lupe's and spend the whole day wondering if right now is the last time I'm gonna see you?"

"*Eventually.* I know it's scary, Ander. I told you that. I know more than you ever will. But I—sooner than later I'm going to need you to let me have a little normal in my life. To go to work and do something that I really like with people I feel safe around. *Your family.* I don't want you to be worried, but I also don't want to have to keep myself locked up inside a house. The world doesn't stop going just because we want it to."

"I know. And I was so ready to let you live the best life you could. I want that for you. But then they were right there and—" I didn't realize how much my voice was trembling, how on the verge of crying I was, until Santi's hugging me and my hands are grabbing at his back. "I need—can you give me the day? I won't force you to stay at home; I promise. We can go to, I don't know, Target or IKEA. Look for new bedding and some plates and bowls and shit for our move. Just for today."

He looks at me for a moment before letting out another sigh. His head falls onto my shoulder, and I feel him nod into my skin. "Fine. But just for today. And only because that sounds like fun. Tomorrow we have to go back to as close to normal as possible. Please."

They know who he is. Where he goes. And nothing I do or want is going to change that. But I *can* support him. I can trust him. I *do* trust him. And the one thing I don't want to do is keep him from happiness. To keep him from living.

"Sí. Claro, querido. Te lo prometo."

⸻

"I need to tell y'all something."

"Okay," Mami and Pa say in unison from the other side of the couch. Pa puts down his newspaper and Mami mutes the television before they both turn to me.

I'm scared to say the words. Maybe I could get away with not telling them and then wait until the end of August when they see me leaving in my car with Santi.

No. I told him I'd tell them. He wanted to be here too, but I thought it'd be better if it's just me. He'll be at Lupe's with both of them tomorrow, and it's less likely they'll act up at the taquería.

"Santi's coming with me to Chicago."

"*Huh*," Mami lets out in a single, gross laugh. "That's funny. And I'm gonna leave your pa for that actress who plays the mom on *One Day at a Time*."

"Not to defend AJ, but she is on your hall pass list, so I don't know if that's as exaggerated as you're hoping you'd be."

"And if you don't be quiet right now, I'll walk out that door and go find her," Mami snaps at Pa.

"*Y'all*. I'm serious."

The way her face goes from *Wow, my child is a comedian* to *I think the fuck not* is terrifying.

"What do you mean Santi's going with you to Chicago?"

"He's gonna stay with me in my apartment and find a job there while I go to school. It's safer than staying here."

"When did you two decide on that arguably untrue idea?"

"Uh, this past weekend." The words come out in a mumble. Saying it out loud makes it hard to not think about how it sounds like a decision we made on the fly. In a time when maybe we weren't thinking as clearly as usual. Even though I meant it when I asked, and Santi meant it when he said yes.

"What—how? How is he getting on a plane without any ID?"

"We're driving. Tita's already refunded the plane ticket she bought me, and she's giving me the money for gas."

"*Tita knows?*"

"I just got done telling her." That was a much easier conversation to have, and one I was okay with Santi being there for. Tita is reasonable. Mami? Not so much.

Her fingers press against her forehead. "It might take him a while to find a job, and we aren't giving you enough money to feed two people."

"I still have some money in savings from when I was still at Lupe's. Santi does too. And what Tita's giving me for the mural plus the ones I sold at Pride and whatever sells at my Blue Star exhibit will be more than enough to get us through a few months. And Tita said she'll get on the phone and talk him up to anyone if he wants to go to a restaurant up there. That he's got a really good handle on how a kitchen works now, and she'd vouch for him."

Mami huffs and throws herself back on the sofa. "You don't have anything to say about this?" she asks, glaring at Pa. "How your mother went and figured this all out with them without telling us?"

"You should've came to us first, Ander," he says, leaning forward and resting his arms on his crossed leg.

"I'm sorry."

And then he breathes in a long inhale before letting it out in an even lengthier exhale. "When we call, you answer. Understood? You'll let us know your class schedule, so we know when you're busy, but otherwise, no excuses. Even if you're in a library or some gallery, I expect you to find somewhere you can talk and run there."

"I understand."

"And when we ask you how y'all are, you answer honestly. Good, bad, boring, all of it."

"Okay."

"Because it's a new place. You two are only nineteen. It was already not going to be easy. And it won't be perfect. This is . . . this is a very drastic decision you two are making and you'll have your bad days. Bad weeks. So I need you both to let us know *especially* when things are difficult."

"We will."

"And I'm going to tell Santi the same. The minute he gets a job, I expect to know his schedule because I'll be calling him too, and if he's not working, he better answer."

"That's . . . reasonable."

"Okay. Then I have nothing else to say."

"*Really?*" Mami asks.

"Sí. Did you ever actually think this wasn't going to happen?"

"I was hoping we'd avoid it, yes."

"When has our child ever been reasonable, amorcita?"

"*I'm right here.*"

39

How long until we get our garage back?" Mami asks, coming through the front door and walking right past the television while Santi, Zeke, Chachi, and her friends are in the middle of their scary movie binge night that I was dragged into against my will. "It's a mess in there with your giant paintings."

"Only a couple more weeks," I shout at her, assuming she hears me from the kitchen. Not that she's actually needing an answer. She found a reason to complain at me for a second and is running with it.

"You're gonna end up painting for, like, forty-eight hours straight, huh?" Zeke asks.

"*You're gonna paint for forty-eight hours, huh?*" I repeat back to him in this low, mocking voice. "I'm on schedule to finish these on time with the least amount of stress. I know what I'm doing."

Santi scooches closer to me, using his arm to pull at my waist. He waits until everyone's attention is back to the movie and the noise is loud enough to not be overheard by Zeke and Chachi before putting his lips near my ear. "You're not on schedule, are you?"

"Don't worry about it."

I get about three hours of sleep in between finishing the second movie, telling Santi, "I need help finding something in my room," during the third movie, never making it back down, and then being up at 4:00 a.m., grabbing a pair of old cotton shorts and not even worrying about a shirt that'll only get paint stains on it. My feet have never been quieter going downstairs to the kitchen and then to the garage. I turn on the couple of fans we keep in here to help with the stuffiness, since opening the door is going to be the loudest, clunkiest wake-up call my family and Santi never asked for. After setting down the gallon water jug and bottled Frappuccino I grabbed from the fridge, I carefully maneuver one of the taller-than-I-am canvases against the wall. Then I pull up Procreate, where I've already drawn what I'm going to do, get my productivity playlist going, and start working.

The photo I'm working on re-creating right now is from a Film at the Field at Centro Quiroga. It used to be a drive-in theater and even did a few outdoor plays way back when, and is still used to show movies and does some cool things once in a while, but no cars allowed on the grass anymore. This was specifically on *Coco* night. A mariachi group from this local performing arts high school came to play some songs from the soundtrack before the movie started. And what got the crowd screaming was when one of their vocalists-slash-vihuela players came out dressed as Miguel, letting out a grito and acting the part as he went into "Un Poco Loco." I was lucky enough to get a good picture of him mid-grito, and knew I had to do something inspired by him eventually, especially when I found out he's from the neighborhood.

Every time I finish one of these squares, I feel so accomplished. Knowing I've never created anything as good. But then I move on to the next one and reality sets in and reminds me of how there's still so much left to do.

"Zeke got to you?" Santi's voice says from behind me, making me jump and almost mess up my lines.

"*Pinche madre*, don't scare me like that." I flick my hands a few times, getting out any leftover shakes. "What are you doing up? It's barely six."

"Realized I was cuddling a pillow and it wasn't as nice," he answers through a yawn while taking a seat on the concrete. "You didn't answer my question."

"No, Zeke didn't get to me. I was already planning on being up early and working."

"No te creo."

"That's something you're gonna have to make peace with then, querido. No sé qué decirte."

Santi watches as I continue painting, silently observing and taking in every dip and stroke of my brush like he's committing them to memory. And I glance at him with the corner of my eye every once in a while, seeing him, unmoving, trying to remember this for later. Him in a pair of his sleep boxers, the little smile on his face, his tired but so deeply interested eyes that go between my painting and my ass every time I bend over. I might have to save one canvas for this image.

"What do you think of while you paint?"

I stare at the exact spot my brush was about to touch, it only an inch from the canvas, paused in midair. But it's also as if I'm not looking anywhere in particular. Thinking harder than I'm seeing. Wondering because, well, "I've never thought about that question before."

"So, nothing?"

"I mean, sometimes, kind of, yeah. It's like I let my hand do what it knows to do, and my brain clocks out. But other times it's different. I guess it depends on where in the process I am. At the beginning, I'm putting a lot of thought into making sure I know exactly what I have planned and what the end result is supposed to be. And then when I'm able to relax a little, I start vibing to the music, letting that get any remaining stiffness out of me. Then it becomes thinking about whatever it is I'm painting. Like, this. I was thinking about hearing the mariachi and watching the movie and how nice it felt outside that night. But eventually, I just start going. I'll come back in when I need to put some thought into getting a color right or something, but other than that, there's not a whole lot going on up here."

"Why doesn't that surprise me?" Santi asks with a smirk and gets a middle finger in return.

I finish adding a little more red before turning back to him and walking over, taking a seat beside him. His hand immediately goes to my leg; his thumb going back and forth over my tattoo. I look at his face, never going anywhere else except to all the work I've done so far, giving himself a minute to silently take it all in.

"Right now, though, with this whole gallery thing, a lot of my thoughts have been about you."

"What about me?"

"How, like—how you've helped me. With my family and Zeke, whenever I'd talk to them about shaky confidence or when the uncertainty comes around, they'd just say keep going. That it'll fade eventually. 'Walk it off.' But you? You tried to understand from the beginning. You didn't come at me with 'Just feel a different way, then.' And you gave me a kind of encouragement no one's ever given me before. I know they all think I'm great and they tell me that, but you . . . when you told me how my art feels like home to you, and then when I realized how much that actually means, it felt, I don't know, important. And not that I need everything I do to be important, but that let me start allowing myself to fight this thought that because some white guy says I'm supposed to be doing this, it automatically cheapens in value. You helped me start really loving and standing up for the art I wanna do. And this exhibit is gonna show the whole world that."

Santi turns his head to look right at me. "Te dije, the world's a better place because of your art. And I'll always be around to tell you that."

"Te quiero," I tell him before going in for a kiss. "And thank you. For everything. Okay, I need to get back to work. Stop distracting me."

"*You were the one who sat down and started talking.*" How his voice sounds, mixed with tiredness and the tiniest dash of annoyance, has me holding in a laugh.

"Can't hear you." I answer, turning my back to him and taking a brush to the canvas. "I'm working."

There's a solid three minutes of silence before Santi's asking, "Can I ask one more question?"

I turn my head to him for a second, trying to guess whether this is going to be a real question or another about how I'm empty in the head.

"I'll allow it."

"Have you ever thought about how one day you'll have your own huge studio to do this in and what you'll think of when you're thinking back on today and painting in your parents' garage?"

A soft smile forms on my face. Of course, I've thought about those days. About a future in some nice, hipster apartment with cement floors or exposed brick walls and an entire room for me to work that's air-conditioned and doesn't smell like gasoline. Having the newest iPads and even the biggest Apple TV so I could mirror my screen onto that and see my designs on something bigger than ten and a half inches.

But here, with Santi, hanging out together while I do what I love more than anything in the world, considering the potential of taking a break after I finish painting Miguelito and pulling my boyfriend up to my room for about twenty minutes and then ordering some breakfast tacos before spending most of the day on finishing this painting, knowing that I could do this all over again tomorrow. How there are going to be so many more days like this with him. That's what I really want. I know *where* I paint isn't what's important. I mean, my preferred location is outside on a building. It's never been about where.

But I also know that someday will be the last day I ever paint here. And as happy as all the other thoughts make me, that one brings a real heaviness to my heart. As excited as I am about what the future will look like for me—

"I think," I start to answer, drawing out each letter as I speak, "I think I'll miss this."

40

O kay," I huff to myself after throwing my body back into my seat and letting out an annoyed groan. "What's taking him so long?"

I texted Santi at exactly one o'clock that I'm outside. And then again ten minutes later, when he hadn't come out yet. Even though, looking through the window into Lupe's, it doesn't seem like a busy day. Is Tita trying to keep him longer? Do I need to go pull him out? Five minutes ago, I sent a third text, still, with no reply: **Are you pooping or something?**

I step out, even more bothered now by the difference a hundred and something degrees of heat feels hitting my air-conditioned body. I wasn't even planning on getting out, leaving my house in a pair of slides, nalgas shorts, an old UIW shirt I'd stolen from Zeke last year, and my arms covered in specks of paint because I'd been spending the entire time since I dropped him off this morning trying to finish the last of my Blue Star murals. I'm so close but I can't get it done if I'm spending the whole afternoon sitting out here.

"Hey, where's my boyfriend?" I ask Ronnie as soon as I step inside, seeing him busy behind the counter instead of his usual spot at the patio bar.

"La jefa took him home."

"*What?* No one told me this was happening."

"Seemed like an emergency."

"*The fuck? Again*, why did no one tell me this? Is he okay? Is everything all right? Did—"

"I don't know the details, chamaque. I'm sure Santi will tell you. Calm down."

"That's not an easy thing to do."

"I realize. Figure it out. You're not doing anyone any favors getting all feral. Go put in your earphones, play music way too loud for your little ears, keep prepping for that big exhibit you got in a couple weeks, and let your boyfriend take care of things he can do on his own. When he needs you, he'll let you know."

"I—"

"What'd I say?"

"But—"

"What. Did. I. Say?"

I huff and spin around, turning toward the door. "*Fine*. I'm gonna go paint."

"Oh. Wait," Ronnie shouts as I take my first step. "You eaten lunch yet?"

"No, but I'm not hungry."

"I didn't ask if you were hungry. I know all you had for breakfast is some iced coffee, and I'm not about to be murdered by la jefa because when she comes back and asks, 'Did you make sure mi bebite preciose ate?' I have to say no. So stay right there. I'll be right back with a couple tacos. As long as I see you leave with them, my conscience is clear. What you do after, not my business."

"Aren't you a fucking angel."

I stop painting when I hear the quiet sound of someone carefully and slowly opening the garage door behind me. When Mami or Pa's voice doesn't follow, I quickly turn around and there Santi is, standing still, hands in his pockets. His eyes are a worrying shade of red, and just the way he says hey is all I need to know something is wrong.

I walk over to him. My hands take their time going up and down from elbow to shoulder once and then again before resting in his hands. Every part of him is trembling.

"I'm sorry I didn't let you know I left early."

"That—don't worry about it. What happened?"

Santi's silence feels like it goes on for forever. He closes his eyes and presses his forehead against mine. His hands squeeze mine and I squeeze back. *I'm here. It's okay.*

"Can we not talk about it yet?"

"I—" It puts me in actual physical discomfort to keep from saying what I really want to say. But, "Yeah. That's fine, querido."

Santi lets go of my hands and tightly wraps his arms around me. His head falls into my shoulder and everything that he'd been trying to hold in starts coming out in painful cries. My arms go around him, and I stay quiet, letting him get it all out.

I cry with him. Tears because I hate seeing him hurt this much. Because I don't know how to make it better.

"Te quiero, cielo," he says softly, his voice a little rough. "Prometo."

"Yo sé," I reply, squeezing him in my arms and resting my forehead against his. "Nos—"

"Ander," Santi interrupts. "De verdad. *Te quiero.* Por favor, recuérdalo."

"Okay. I will."

He starts crying again, not that he really stopped. It's quieter this time. And he feels so exhausted. Like whatever happened has been weighing on him all day.

"Do you wanna sit down for a while?"

His head nods into my neck. I grab a hand and we don't say a word as we take a seat on the concrete. On the exact spot he usually sits and watches me. But today he hides his face in my neck while I wrap my arms around him and try my best to comfort him as my hands rub his back and scratch his neck and head.

Ronnie's words replay in my head. When Santi needs to tell me something, he will. Right now, he needs me to just be here. To not ask questions.

I'm okay with that.

I mean, not really. But we can pretend for a while.

––––––––––

"We need to talk," Santi says as he sits up. He stares at me for a moment before standing up and walking into the house. I follow him upstairs, into my room, and out onto the garage roof.

He's already gotten comfortable, legs up to his chest, eyes toward the setting sun like usual, by the time I'm climbing out the window. I sit down next to him, a couple inches apart, watching and waiting for him to start.

"I don't know how to say what I need to say. Where to begin."

"Take your time." I say those words for him. Inside, I'm holding on to all my restraint wondering what's going to happen and what has Santi so shaken to his core.

He lets a hand fall between us, and I grab it. I concentrate on how rough the skin feels, what his hands have been through. But, also, how gentle and reassuring they are. How well they tell his entire story.

"My amá disappeared last night."

Santi's grip tightens when he says the words. His eyes trying to hold back more tears.

"I—Does anyone know what happened?"

"They think it was a gang. At least eight women are gone from the camp she and 'manita were staying at."

"Oh my god, your sister—"

"She's alone right now. She called me this morning when I was at work. That's why I had to leave. We were on the phone for hours, trying to figure out what we could do, what we need to do."

"Which is? Are the police doing anything?"

Santi gives me a face like we both know the answer to that question.

"Querido, I'm—I'm so, so sorry." I don't know what else to say besides that. To put hope into anyone finding her or her being alive is like putting faith in what you know isn't true. As much as I am putting all of mine into that chance. We both know how these things work living in a world where lives are taken so easily.

"I—I have to go, cielo."

"What?" No. I had to have heard that wrong. There's no way he said—

"We're having trouble getting in contact with family in México or anyone that could take care of my sister. And, even then, she's *my* sister. I have a responsibility. I have to go back."

Just a week and a half ago we were processing ICE agents standing outside my car. We were going through so many emotions and carrying each other through real-life nightmares. And we'd made it. We were figuring out how to shape this life for us, and we saw a future that was promising and hopeful.

And now it's gone.

"I'm sorry," Santi says. His free hand goes to my cheek and wipes a couple tears making their way down. "Cielo, I—"

"You have nothing to be sorry for," I say, my voice cracking through it. "I'm—This is just a reaction. Don't be sorry, okay?"

I grab his hand that's stayed at my cheek, wanting to impress his palm into my skin. I'm trying to be selfless. To remind myself that, as much as this hurts likes knives going into my heart, lungs, guts, and brains, the pain is this intense because we love each other. That what we have is *so good*. And I want to hold on to it for just a little longer.

But I can't. It's too much right now. "I can't."

"Cielo," Santi begs when I stand up, forcing my hand from him. "Ander, por favor."

"I can't do this right now. I—fuck." I'm actually crying now. On the top of the roof like some over-the-top scene in a gay telenovela. "I promise I'm not angry. Not at you. I'm so, so sorry, Santi. I—I need to be somewhere else. I love you. Okay? I love you."

I rush back into my room, out the door, and then into the bathroom, locking myself in before falling to the floor.

I'm selfish.

I couldn't be there for Santi in what is probably one of the scariest moments of his life. After he's had to make one of the most difficult decisions of his life. Convincing himself to go back to the place he never planned on returning to.

I'm so selfish.

I couldn't help but make it about me. About us. I took a conversation that should've been about his sister and her safety and started crying because of how this is going to affect me.

I'm so, so fucking selfish.

I left him. I told him that I'm not strong enough for this. That I refuse to hear the words *our time's up* even if it's because of a totally valid reason and something neither of us could've seen coming. I told Santi I'd stick with him through it all, and I lied.

I told Santi through happiness and destruction, and I lied.

All I can do is stay here in the fetal position, the cold of the hard tile screaming into my skin as I cry. I feel abandoned and like the worst person in the world because I'm also abandoning him, but this entire world can fuck itself if it can't give Santi just one time in his life to be happy and not only exist but thrive. Fuck a world that would separate him from his mother. That would take her from him.

And fuck a world that would take him from me.

I'm angry. Not at him. At this entire situation. At all the ingredients that have come together to shit on Santi, on his family, on me. On us. I'm so angry I can feel it in my stomach. Building and intensifying like the inside of a volcano, more and more until I'm sitting over the toilet and throw-up is coming out of me while I continue crying.

We were supposed to make it.

Please don't leave me.

41

A week.

In seven days, Santi will be heading back to México. I know he wishes he could leave now. That every minute he's not talking to his little sister, he's worrying about where she is and fighting to keep his mind from going to dark places. But sneaking into this country takes planning, and sneaking out of a country he was *never allowed to be in* takes just as much caution.

Not that I'm hearing any of this from him. When he started knocking on my bathroom door yesterday, begging me to let him in, I wouldn't. I couldn't. My heart couldn't take seeing a face that would no longer be a part of my life soon.

"Go. Please, go. I'll call you a Lyft."

I could feel him on the other side of the door. Hear his body lowering and his knees hitting the floor. The quiet thumps of his head and hands knocking against wood.

And I leaned against it, crying more and more, searching for the strength to keep telling him to leave while also wishing I could ask him to stay. Wishing that I could be there for him like he needed me to be.

Why am I so weak?

Why was it easier for me to try to push him away rather than spend whatever remaining hours we have together? Why was it easier for me to give up? And is that what's happening? Am I giving up?

Yeah. I think I am.

⁓⁓⁓⁓⁓⁓⁓

"Jefa is gonna love this, AJ," Zeke says while handing me a large cup of water, standing with me, focused on the front of the taquería, now almost completely outlined and about ready for paint. "Might be the best thing you've ever done, TBH."

"Thanks," I reply in between gulps. "Hope she agrees when she's finally allowed to see it."

I want to keep going. Even though I've been at this the entire day now without any breaks besides drinking water. The chorizo-and-egg tacos Mami brought out for me this morning and the torta Pa left for me a while ago are still wrapped in their foil, sitting on the ground next to my supplies.

I can't stop. Stopping means there's nowhere else for my mind to go to besides thinking of Santi. Of every single thing about him that makes me happy: his cute little laugh, that time I got him high while we hung out on the roof and how he vibed out to La Garfield, the comfort of falling asleep next to him. And of the things about him that annoy the shit out of me: how he *always* steals my fries, how he likes to see how high his hand can go up my leg while we're eating dinner with my family before getting a reaction from me, and the way he continues to post pictures of half my face in the weirdest fucking angles.

How we were just getting started. I wish we could go back to when our biggest worries were about how we'd survive our first Chicago winter and trying to figure out how their trains work. When we were so excited about the future we were supposed to have together.

Stopping means I'd think about how we looked each other in the eye as he was leaving Lupe's today with Pa. How that sad smile he gave me nearly broke me into a million pieces. Maybe someone can find all these shards of who I once was and make a mosaic and dedicate it to that saying: Better to have loved and lost than never to have loved at all.

Bullshit.

I mean, it's not. I wouldn't trade the past nearly eight months for anything. I wouldn't erase what Santi and I have or had for all the money in the world. I don't ever want to forget the first time I saw him that cold January day and all the love he's brought into my life since then. But still, whoever wrote that probably never felt this pain. This invisible, never-healing scar that goes from throat to heart to gut and reopens and bleeds every time he comes to mind.

He's not even gone yet, but it feels like it already. And I know that that's my fault. His texts last night asking if I was okay and the ones this morning pleading for me to not let us end things like this prove that whatever I'm feeling is the consequence of my own actions.

It's the end of the world, and I had the chance to live it up or lie down and wait for it to come for me. And I chose the latter.

"You're crying."

"Wha—*fuck*. Sorry. I—"

Before I can finish, Zeke is hugging me, squeezing me in his arms. "It's cool, AJ. You can cry."

"I don't want to."

"Do you *need to*, though?"

"Not in front of the entire neighborhood, no."

"Then do you want me to let go of you?"

I think about it for all of three seconds before letting my body relax in Zeke's hold and my head fall into the crook of his neck. "No. Keep hugging me, please."

"Why are you sitting on the floor when there is plenty of furniture all around this house?" Mami asks while pushing my bedroom door open. "Acting like I don't give you a bed."

I only shrug, not bothering to give her my attention. I've been holding on to the picture Santi painted during our first date, staring at it since I got home. Continuing to stare even as I feel Mami walk closer and hear her taking a seat on the floor next to me, her back against my bed. Involuntarily leaning into her hand as she drags her fingers through my hair.

"You haven't eaten all day."

"Is that a question or a statement?"

"Don't be smart with me. I made caldo de pollo."

"It's a hundred and three degrees outside."

"Good thing you're eating it in a house your pa keeps way too cold."

"I'm not hungry."

"No, you are. You're just sadder and angrier and a lot of other things more than you are hungry. It's either you eat something or you let all of those feelings eat at you, and as your mami, it's my job to make sure you're fed. I don't care if you sip on spoons of chicken broth. You need to get something inside your stomach."

"And then what?" I ask as she starts standing back up. "What do I do after that? When I'm actually not hungry anymore but I'm still sad and angry?"

"You make the best of it."

"Tita?" I mumble, still half asleep, unsure if I'm imagining her through squinted eyes.

"Try to sleep, bebite," she says, barely paying me any attention. She's fiddling with something on the small table next to my bed. The last thing I see before falling back asleep—or maybe this is all a dream, I don't know—is a small flame at her finger-tips. And the last words I hear are her quietly reciting some prayer or Bible verse.

"We also glory in our sufferings, because we know that suf-fering produces perseverance; perseverance, character; and char-acter, hope. And hope does not put us to shame, because God's love has been poured out into our hearts through the Holy Spirit, who has been given to us."

I wake up to an unlit, but definitely once lit, Saint Jude candle. Under his name and picture, PATRON SAINT OF LOST AND DES-PERATE CAUSES. Next to the candle is a statue of La Virgen, a rosary, and photos Tita's taken with her Fujifilm instant camera we got her for Christmas, of Santi and me: the very first night we worked together that I remember Ronnie taking, at Easter, my birthday, and a couple others I can't place.

I was going to give you these the day you leave for Chicago, but I think you need them now, she's written in her tight cursive on a piece of paper. *We don't choose to not take a journey because we know the ending, bebita. We endure. We find the beauty in every step. And you still have a few more steps to go. Don't wake up in a few days wishing you could change how you left him.*

"I'm not strong enough," I say to the empty space where she was hours ago. "I can't. Isn't that just delaying the inevitable?"

"Isn't waking up in the morning instead of letting ourselves die also delaying an inevitable?"

"*Jesus, fuck!*" I scream, unaware that Pa has been watching me for at least the past ten seconds. "Can you knock?"

"Can you not offend Jesus with his mom right next to you?" he answers while walking in, picking up a couple shirts off the floor and draping them over my chair. "Your door was open. I won't be long. I'm going to McDonald's and taking Santi some pancakes. *Or* I could pick up Santi and bring him and pancakes for both of you back here."

"Pa, I—"

"He doesn't stop talking about you. About how he feels like he betrayed you."

"He didn't."

"And how happy you make him. *Make. Still.* Not past tense. He wanted to stay and watch you work on the mural yesterday, but I told him it'd be better to give you some space right now. Santi wants to spend the time he has left here with the person who's made this place feel like home, Ander. I'm not going to tell you what to do, but even if throwing something away might hurt a little less than having it taken from you, at least with the latter, holding on to it for as long as you can, fighting for it with everything you've got, you'll know you gave it your all." Pa turns around and starts walking for the door. "You have five minutes to text me, letting me know to bring him over. If not, okay. Your choice."

42

Six days left.

Santi and I eat pancakes in bed. We cry and say sorries and tell each other how we'd do anything if it meant everything would magically work itself out. We kiss and taste maple syrup on our lips and tongues.

Five days left.

I take Santi to New Braunfels and we spend the day floating the Comal River. Then we go to Buc-ee's and run around through the Walmart-size gas station, buying brisket sandwiches and more snacks than we can carry before heading to the drive-in theater out here. And when we're back home, after Mami and Pa have already fallen asleep, we go to the roof and get high and go through the bags of chips and dark chocolate almonds and beaver nuggets we didn't finish, trying to stay quiet enough to not wake up the entire street with our laughs and screams and music.

Four days left.

We go to H-E-B for exactly two things: lube and Powerades. The girl checking us out tries her best to keep her lips sucked in so she won't laugh when I tell her that we have a long day planned and Santi closes his eyes with an embarrassed pain, looking away from both of us as if that will make him invisible. And then, just like I told her, we spend the entire day using up the entire bottle and maintaining our electrolytes. Hoping that my parents will choose to leave all correct assumptions in their heads and stay quiet about the hickeys and their child's wobbly legs and why I'd prefer not to sit on my ass tomorrow.

Three days left.

A lot of crying. Not a lot of talking. "It's getting too real," I tell Santi before asking if I can get a moment by myself on the roof. That moment turns into an hour. When I come back into my room, I grab a folder sitting on my desk filled with papers and show him the portrait I drew of him the first day we met and give him all the paintings and drawings I did when I've thought of him over all the months that have passed by. Things that I was hoping he could find a place for in our apartment in Chicago. We manage to laugh at how weird I am for drawing a portrait of someone I saw a couple of times for only a few minutes. And I draw us in my bed. Our bodies tangled together. In a moment where no one can separate us.

Two days left.

Santi brings over a book of short stories. *Something, something, something Kentucky Club.* He reads them aloud to me. The first story makes us both cry. It reminds us of his amá. He shows me a couple pictures of her that he's saved to his phone.

"Ella era hermosa."

"Sí. Más hermosa."

"Would it be okay if I painted her?"

"I would like that a lot."

We talk a little more about his amá before he gets back to his book. A few more of the stories make me cry. Him reading makes me cry. How much I want to listen to every word he speaks makes me cry because I'm putting so much hope that this will help me remember what his voice sounds like for forever. I don't know what I'd do if I ever forget the sound of his voice. How he says *cielo* and *te quiero*. Or what he looks like. I'd draw him every day for the rest of my life if I need to.

One day left.

Sex. Crying. A lot of emotions that can't be placed.

We drive around and walk around even more, taking Santi to see my murals. The ones that mean the most to me. Yeah, the anime and the monstera plant were cool, and I liked getting to do them, but these—the cacti and *Como la Flor* and *Sylvia Rivera* and *La Chalupa* and the Pride murals of Chicane drag icons and the two of us that are now displayed inside a *very interesting* store on the Main Avenue Strip—these have my heart. And it's Santi who helped me get to this point where I allow myself to love them. Wholeheartedly and passionately and unworried about what anyone else thinks. And I'm going to keep loving them for both of us.

The car ride back to his house is silent and tense. I try to give him his Virgen de Guadalupe pendant back, but he tells me to keep it.

"Te pertenece. It should stay where my heart is."

We kiss slowly, neither of us eager to end it. But eventually, I pull away. We wipe away tears. And this is it. This is what making the best of our situation brought us to.

"I'm sorry."

"I know."

I hate this.

I don't think I can be there tomorrow, I start to type while lying in bed. Occasionally I'll turn my head, hoping that if I blink enough times, Santi will appear next to me. **I can't watch you leave. I hope that's okay. And that you don't think I blame you or your family for this. Or that I'm angry. I am angry, but not at you. I'm angry at the world that for some reason can't stand us being together. You're so beautiful and wonderful.**

You're fucking art, Santiago. And right now I can't imagine a life where I'm not in your presence. I won't. I refuse to.

Te quiero, querido, I continue. Please remember that. Just like you asked me. Feel it whenever I speak those words into the universe and know that they're meant for you and only you.

Te quiero.

Te quiero.

Te quiero.

turned off my phone as soon as I sent those texts to Santi.

I don't want to see his responses or listen to any voice mails he leaves me. Not yet. Not while he's still here but might as well be on the other side of the border already.

Jesus. Fuck borders. Fuck some arbitrary lines that colonizers made up on land that doesn't even belong to them. And fuck how those lines have become a way to make people hate each other and fear each other and want to keep each other out and have no guilt about any of it.

Fuck anyone who is responsible for deciding that Santi's mom didn't deserve to live. That his little sister doesn't deserve some sense of safety. That he doesn't deserve the right to happiness and the life he wants. A life that makes this whole world better.

"Your pa's leaving to see Santi off," Mami tells me, her body bent down to talk through the space of open window at me on the roof like she's working the Whataburger drive-through. "Not too late to go with him."

"I'm not going."

"You don't want to say goodbye?"

"Do you *think* I want to say bye?"

"*Don't be sassy.* You both deserve some closure, mi'je."

"I don't want closure!" I snap at her, as much as I was trying to not be rude and take out my anger on her. But any chance of being calm or reasonable has left the building. "I want to hurt because the first memories that come to mind of him are all good. They're of him with me. Here. If that changes . . . if all my mind pictures when I hear his name is him leaving me—no. I don't want that."

Mami lets out a loud, sad sigh. "All right. Chachi and I will be at Lupe's for a while. When we get home, I'll have your papi barbecue some chicken. And maybe even make some margaritas? Sound good?"

"Mhmm," I breathe out. A minimally better response than what I wanted to say: *I don't know why you'd think I'd be hungry at all today.* I'll still probably get a smack on the back of the head for it later.

I watch her and Chachi drive away. Give a small wave when Mami taps on the horn a couple times. And another one when Pa backs out onto the street, his serious eyes and small nod visible even from up here.

I wonder what he thinks of me. Especially after our talk last week. If he thinks I did give this my all, or if I stopped just short of that by not going with him. If he's disappointed in me and will never say it out loud.

He told me not everything is going to work out. But that in the end, it'd be fine.

It's not fine. Nothing about this is fine.

"Fuck," I groan as I fall back onto the roof, clasping my hands behind my head, feeling the heat of the sun already putting in work and it's not even ten in the morning yet. Whatever. Fry me, bitch. I'm not moving.

Santi and I watched the sunset up here yesterday. And right before it disappeared completely, I grabbed Santi's face and kissed him. I thought, if we stay like this, eyes closed, mouths pressed together, we won't ever have to see the sun leave us. We could keep tomorrow from reaching us. We can stay in this moment in time forever. Together. Nothing else is real.

I can remember so vividly the way his muscles went from being tight from surprise to relaxed. Giving. How his lips and tongue became as invested as mine. As desperate. How, with closed eyes, I let him pull me onto his lap, straddling him. Feeling his hands go underneath my shirt and to my waist.

"Don't open your eyes yet," I told him as we caught our breaths.

"I won't," he replied.

But we did. We had to. Because time continues to exist whether we acknowledge it or not. Shitty things continue to wait for us.

I don't bother to pick myself up when I hear the familiar sound of Pa's truck coming back and the garage door opening under me announcing in the loudest possible way that Santi's not here anymore. He was only gone for, what? Maybe half an hour. That makes sense. Santi and whoever was taking him to point A of however many letters are involved in getting him back into Mexico were probably on a strict schedule. Quick goodbyes and *vámonos*.

That would've hurt even more. To only have a few minutes with him. To be pulled away. Yeah, I'm glad I didn't go. I wouldn't have been able to handle it. I—

"Hola linde. ¿Tienes novio?"

My neck pops from how quickly I turn my head. And—*no fucking way.*

"You—you're here?" I ask the boy standing in my room in his usual white tank, today with an open forest-green button-up. The boy who I thought I'd never see again.

"I'm here."

"The heat's not making me hallucinate?"

"No. It's me. But if you've been out here that long, maybe you should come in?"

"I—" I force myself up and rush into my bedroom, flying through the open space of my window and then get my footing long enough to tackle Santi onto the floor.

"You're hot. Like, actually hot. *How long were you outside?*"

"I don't know. An hour and a half? Maybe two. But—wait." I move off of Santi, enough so that I can sit on the floor with him but leave my legs over his, his hands immediately going for them. "You shouldn't be the one asking questions. What are you doing here?"

"I've been texting and trying to call you all morning."

"Oh. Yeah, my phone's off."

"Pinche Ander." He stays quiet and watches his fingers slowly graze my smooth skin. "A tío reached out. He's in Reynosa with his wife and three kids. Heard about Amá and 'manita and said he'd go get her. He should be there . . . actually, he's probably already there."

"Then what?"

"He'll take her back to Reynosa, make sure she's okay. But eventually we'll try to get her to our older sister and tía in Arizona. That's what Amá would want. She left everything she knew *for us*."

"And you?"

"What about me?"

"Is this just y'all refiguring everything out and you're still leaving at some point, or are you staying?"

His eyes look so deeply into mine as he says, "I'm not going anywhere, cielo. I'm here. With you."

And I want to smile and cry out all the happiness, but—

"Where are you? Like, mentally. Emotionally. Especially with your amá."

When Santi goes silent, I lean toward him and wrap my arms around him. His body feels loose, but not because he's relaxed. I know what relaxed Santi feels like. This is from fatigue. From trying to juggle us the last week with everything going on with himself and his family.

"A part of me knew I'd never see her again when I crossed. That when I told them bye, it would be for good. I mean, I still talked to her on the phone as much as I could, but that's different from being able to see her and hug her. And if I had known our last call would be the last time I'd ever hear her voice—"

I tighten my hug and he hugs me back. As annoying as Mami is, I don't think I'd be able to exist if we were in Santi's shoes. Just thinking about not being able to yell at her face when we head to Chicago makes me depressed. To entirely lose a mom? No one deserves that.

"I don't think I've come to terms with her being gone yet," he continues. "Not that I'm holding on to the chance that she's still alive. I just—I can't acknowledge it yet."

My head rests on his shoulder, and we sit here on my floor for I don't know how long. Long enough for Santi to get some tears out. For him to tell me more about his amá. How she made the best tamales and loved sunflowers and sitting next to a window on rainy days. Allowing him some sort of memorialization of the woman who brought him into this world. And by the end of it, we're lying quietly on the floor, one of his arms flung around me and his head at my chest.

I'm really happy to have him with me still. Obviously. That goes without saying.

And I acknowledge that we'll have that time to be happy about it. But right now isn't for that. It's for him and whatever he needs me to be. I was already selfish when he first told me she was gone. I'm not doing that anymore.

"I have an idea. If you feel like staying in bed all day after this, no one would blame you, but if you wanted to do something—something for her—I know a place."

He picks his head up and moves enough to kiss me. Our noses brush against each other's as he nods. "Take me."

At the southeastern-est part of San Antonio is the Traders Village, this huge-ass pulga where you can find literally anything. They got clothes, raspas, toys, all of it. Goodwill has nothing on this place.

That's not really important. What is important is, just past that, there's a giant sunflower field in the summer. And when Santi mentioned that sunflowers were his amá's favorite flower, I felt like this is a place he'd like to be.

It's as if we were meant to be here right now. We're basically the only ones besides the people that work here. It's sunny but beautiful out. The flowers are huge now, nearly as tall as Santi is. Green stalks and leaves lead up to gorgeous, giant, bright yellow petals. The kind of vibes that make me feel like she's here too, with him.

He takes my hand and starts down a path into the field, taking slow steps, letting himself notice every single sunflower. I squeeze his hand and kiss his shoulder when I see him smiling but with a couple tears making their way down to his jaw.

"She would've loved this place," Santi says. "She'd love that I'm here right now. That you brought me here."

"Anytime, querido."

We walk some more, mostly in silence. Sometimes taking a second to appreciate a particularly perfect sunflower. Sometimes stopping so Santi can get a picture of one of them. Sometimes looking forward and then behind us before getting in a kiss.

"She always said one of the reasons she liked these so much

is because they're Mexican," he tells me. "That's where they're from. I mean, we've got a few flowers native to there, but those especially she really loved. Her abuela had a whole field, probably like this, behind her house when Amá was growing up. She always said that being in a sunflower field felt like being in church. Like being surrounded by her ancestors. Como si estuviera con Teotl. I get that now. That feeling of her with me."

When the late afternoon hits and it starts getting actually hot, we head out with a bouquet of sunflowers and a vase Santi found at the pulga next door. We drive to his house and I go inside with him for the first time. It feels like Tita's house. Smells like chiles and coffee and masa. Like I just know that older mexicanas run this place. In the room he shares with three other guys, we stand at his little dresser, setting up the flowers with a picture of his mom and a candle. He whispers in Spanish about how much he misses her. How he's okay. How his little sister is going to be okay. How he wishes she could've met me. How he's going to make her proud and that he loves her.

And, in the darkness of his room, he sends her off to whatever heaven she believed in.

44

There's a character in *Gentefied*, Ana, who I've always resonated with from the moment I first saw her. A queer, brown street artist? It's like they based her off me.

She's at the front of my mind this morning, as we cross I-10, leaving Santos Vista and everything our barrio is with its the-most-Westside flavor and enter Southtown. Here, the effects of gentrification can be seen in real time, with microbreweries, new apartment complexes that no one who's born and raised here could ever afford, sushi restaurants, and, of course, the Blue Star galleries, all within walking distance from the old, modest, wooden homes of abuelas that have been here way longer than some twentysomething Spin Cycle instructor using space that was once a local restaurant or panadería.

Am I grateful for this opportunity? Sure as shit, I am. And do I think that there should probably be a different set of standards when it's a brown person taking up space built by and primarily for gentrifiers? Yeah. I do.

Will a small part of me always feel like a sellout in spaces like these, seeing the horrifying differences between the haves and the have-nots all within two city blocks? Yep. Definitely.

When I've talked to Zeke and Mo about it, Zeke's always said I'm thinking way too much. "It's like that episode of *Avatar: The Last Airbender* when Aang finds those refugees living in the

Air Temple and, even though they kind of fucked up the whole place, realizes that there can be some good from that."

"You were really watching a completely different show, huh?" Mo asked him with a devastatingly judgmental face.

Needless to say, Zeke wasn't of much help.

Mo did tell me that, as long as I have this mentality of being cognizant of the ways I'm benefiting from the mistreatment of communities of color and always try to find ways to uplift those communities and then actually put in the work to do that, then I'm doing more than most. So, that was pretty useful advice.

"Be careful," I groan at Ronnie as he drives one of the two U-Hauls it's taking to get all my lucha libre statues and crates on crates of flowers to the gallery over the bumpiest train tracks in the world.

"I am, kid, calm your pits."

Hearing the slightest movement coming from the back has me so tense, closing my eyes and taking deep breaths, telling myself that it's fine, they'll be fine, nothing will break. We bought all the bubble wrap four different Walmarts had. They're good.

But then another bump and a little more racket and I'm screaming through closed lips and squeezing Santi's hand until he's wincing.

Getting them out is even more stressful. Pa and Chachi, Ronnie and Zeke, and Santi and I all pair up with the three dollies we have, slowly getting a statue onto one, leaning the dolly back, and then carefully taking it down the ramp onto the parking lot of the Blue Star Complex. Juni is running over to us from the long, orange and white bricked renovated warehouse buildings and starts leading Chachi and Pa to the space I'll be at, with Zeke and Ronnie not far behind.

I'm eager to see Santi's reaction when we get inside. While he was at work yesterday evening, Mami, Tita, Chachi, and I got all the canvases up, between the two rooms of the gallery, and I did the last-minute painting on the walls to bring it all together. I've only ever seen Mami cry twice in my entire life, and one of those times was last night. So, I'm hoping my boyfriend will be some kind of over the moon about it.

"Ay, qué—*guau* . . ." is all he says, standing awestruck at the entrance and looking around, still holding on to the dolly.

"Let me get that," Pa tells him, taking the statue from Santi and searching for the taped X labeled for that specific mask. "Show him around, Ander."

I wait for Santi, who still hasn't moved from the door, until he's ready, reaching out his hand for me to hold it. "Show me."

The first room is titled FROM THE OUTSIDE . . . with the words painted in red comic book font (or, at least, as close as I could get to copying the lettering) on the wall connecting the two spaces. I wanted this wall to be what inspires me about San Antonio and the Westside and Santos Vista. *Coco* Night, Guadalupe Theater, Rosie's Panadería, Santos Vista High School, Lupe's pre-new paint job, Pride, the La Michoacana I grew up going to with Mami and Tita, San Carlos Park during the city's annual Tejano Music Festival, Juan Diego Creek Park, a couple guys playing soccer at the Guadalupe Fields, and two canvases put together of Santi and me on a painting date at Elmendorf Lake. So much color and vibrancy—fitting for the place that raised me.

We walk around the room, going to each painting one at a time. Santi pauses at each, his mouth staying open, letting out little gasps and *ooh*s and silent awe that turn into smiles. I stand behind him, tiptoed the tiniest bit so my chin can sit comfortably on his shoulder while my arms hold him. Letting go whenever he says, "Okay, next one." And then right back to where I was.

His hands linger just above the last canvases, middle finger nearly touching painting-me, eyes toward painting-Santi, who's busy, face down at his work, creating his masterpiece. Maybe thinking back on that first date that seems like a lifetime ago but also like it was only yesterday.

"You can touch it," I tell him. "It's all right."

Santi does so, so lightly. Like he's scared he might wipe the paint right off. "You're amazing, cielo," he says, his fingers and eyes stuck on my image in the mural as if he's talking to that version of me.

"We're only halfway done," I reply before kissing his cheek. "Come on, there's still another room."

Stepping into the other half of my exhibit, the first thing we're met with are the words . . . LOOKING IN. The murals here are like the ingredients that make up my soul. There's a painting of Zeke, Mo, and me from Mo's going-away pool party, Chachi on the rafters from when we painted *La Chalupa*, one of Pa throwing two-year-old me into the air, of Mami reading to six-year-old me at the table at the entrance of Lupe's, of Tita and Abuelo Willie and me at my First Communion (with nails that Tita painted for me as a compromise for not being allowed to wear a veil). An audible gasp comes out of Santi when he sees the two of him— one of when he was sitting in the garage while I painted and another of him on the roof, face forward and a little up, toward the sky. Then another gasp when he sees a wall dedicated to his amá and Abuelo Willie, with murals of both of them. On Abuelo's side, I've added marigolds and on Santi's amá's side, sunflowers and monarch butterflies are painted on the wall.

"I—Can we go see her real quick?"

"Of course," I reply. "I'll follow you."

I stand beside Santi, but with a little more space than before, for right now. I don't want to come in between any feeling or moment he needs to have. His lips move, but no words come out.

At least, none that are loud enough for me to hear. They aren't for me anyways.

He doesn't really resemble his mom. They both have the same deep brown skin, and maybe Santi's hair would be straight like hers if he actually grew it out, but her face is a little wider and her eyebrows aren't as visible as his. But he does have her eyes. Dark and strong and comforting.

"Okay," Santi starts as he turns to me, closing his eyes and taking a deep breath in and out.

"Good?"

"Sí. Vamos a verme." He points to the pictures of himself and pulls me over to them. His smile returning as he starts walking. "I look good."

"Are you complimenting me or yourself?"

"Two things can be true, cielo." His attention is on the one of him in the garage, staring at something not pictured with a small, dimpled smile tilted to the right and the eyes showing as much interest and adoration as I could get even though nothing compares to the real thing, and in those same pair of sleep boxers he was wearing. "This was a good morning."

"It was."

"I want lots of mornings like that with you. Like this one and the one of us painting on your birthday. Everything."

"Good," I reply, taking his hand and bringing it to my lips, kissing it. "I do too."

"¿Listos?" Pa asks, coming up from behind us. "We got all the statues up. Juni says he's taking care of the flowers?"

"Yeah. He's doing that for me."

"Bueno. Then let's hit the road. We've got a long day ahead of us still. This isn't your only showing today, remember?"

45

Y ou're not peeking, are you?"

"No, bebite. La blindfold is still on."

Pa and I take careful steps helping lead Tita to the middle of the parking lot, where our family and Lupe's entire staff are already gathered. And even on a day that makes me feel like my body is going to dissolve into a puddle because of the heat, everyone's anxiously waiting for her to see the finished front-of-store mural. At this point, she's the only person in Santos Vista who hasn't yet.

"Ready?"

"*¡Sí, sí, sí!*"

"Take off the bandana when I count to three."

"Okay."

"Uno," I start, and everyone else jumps into the countdown with me. "Dos. *¡Tres!*"

I watch as she pulls the bandana covering her eyes down to her neck and immediately does this squeal-ish gasp. One of her hands reaches for mine, shaking as she continues to take in the wall. Her other hand goes to her mouth, stifling the sounds of happy sobs.

Next to the front door at the far left of the building are the words LUPE'S TACOS written one over the other, one in bright red and the other in deep green on an off-white wall. And to the right of that is a painting of Abuelo Willie and Tita from the waist up. A replica of a picture I stole from her house. Abuelo is holding Tita's hand to his mouth, and his lips are forever touching her skin. His eyes are closed while hers look at him with all the love I could translate onto a wall.

"Ander," she starts while wiping her face. "Bebite. You did this?"

"I did."

"And—wait, I thought I lost that picture. You took it?"

"I can give it back. I borrowed it for reference. I'm so—"

"Keep it. I think your abuelo would want you to have it. And I get to come to this every day now. It's even better."

"So, te gusta?"

"Claro, lo amo. Es perfecto. Muy perfecto." Tita pulls me into a hug, rocking our bodies back and forth while pecking at my cheek, covering my face in her red lipstick. "I—No tengo palabras."

Tita, Pa, and Mami all walk up to the wall together, letting her point out different things to them and touch different parts of the mural together. Her arms open wide, like she's trying to embrace younger Tita and Abuelo busy being in love with each other. And when they're done, the waiters and cooks start lining up for their turn, getting pictures in front of the LUPE'S TACOS part of the wall while I just kind of stand here taking it all in.

"This is it," I tell Santi when he pulls me to his side, watching with me. "This and the exhibit opening tomorrow are the last things I have to do before leaving."

"You feel ready now?"

"Ask me tomorrow. After tonight's kickback and I sneak a few glasses of champagne on the gallery's dime. No, the morning after tomorrow. When I have to start packing after all that."

"When *we* have to start packing," he corrects. "Vamos, I want a picture with the words!"

———————

"Is this the first *normal* picture you've ever posted on IG?" I ask Santi while looking at the post of us in front of the restaurant. He's only half-listening, too into the new work shirts he got today, now with LUPE'S TACOS on the front, and taking sips from the frozen sangria Ronnie pushed toward me. My attention goes from his phone over to the table next to us, making sure that Mami doesn't notice. Although, I think she's had about three too many micheladas to even care anymore.

"I know a drag king up in Chi-Town if y'all ever want to get into the clubs up there," Ronnie says in between bites of flauta. "They got some wild places, I know you'll be living the life, A.J."

"Yeah, but is the food as good as it is here?"

"The pizza's either a hit or a miss. Personally, more of a thin crust person myself. And if you're craving comida that compares to what las jefas y tu pa and those cooks do, nah. Although, I've seen Santi back there too; he's picked it up pretty quickly. That 'something special.' Made to make sure you always come back. Con alma y corazón. You just gotta look at your mural out front to know that."

"And no one's making drinks like you in Chicago either."

"You know that's right," he replies with a laugh, lifting his beer in recognition of the praise. "Those white twinks up there behind the bar are good for a cherry vodka sour, maybe. But—in my humblest of opinions, and three years of winning San Antonio Current's Best Bartender under my belt—I'd show them up with my eyes closed and one handed."

"Yeah, *super humble*."

After we eat and share two more margaritas, Santi holds a hand out for me. "¿Bailas?"

"Claro, querido," I answer, grabbing his hand and following him to the empty space of the patio like we have for months now, letting him lead in the back-and-forth, right-then-left steps to the music. Swear to God, I've never really been into those blue jeans, ranchero, beer-drinking mexicanos that get into this kind of music. At least, not before Santi. But the first time he showed up to one of these in tight-fitting Levi's and a white cowboy hat, I could barely make it through the whole song while thinking about leading him behind the bar and getting those jeans around his ankles. And the hat? That *stays on* during sex.

I've already been considering whether I could take him to the bathroom with me right now. If anyone would notice we were gone for ten minutes.

My family lets us get through exactly two songs before they're lining up. Tita dances with me first, then Mami, Pa, Chachi, Zeke, Ronnie, and a couple waiters who've been working here for years. All of them, in their own way, taking a minute to remind me of how proud they are of me, how talented I am, and that I better come back around the minute I'm back in the state.

"What am I supposed to do without *either* of my best friends?" Zeke asks as he clumsily leads us around the patio. *How much has he had to drink?*

"You'll be fine, Zeke. I promise. And isn't your cousin gonna be in Austin? Drive up there on the weekends and work your way through some Longhorns."

"Okay, but that'll only keep me occupied through, like, October."

"You need to *calm down*."

"But seriously. I know we weren't supposed to talk about

this, but now we're almost here and I'm gonna miss you, AJ. You fucking mess."

"*You fucking mess,*" I yell back, restrained enough for my family to not hear me over the music.

Damn. It's here. A year ago, I was in my head about taking a gap year while my best friends were getting ready to start college, and now it's my turn.

I remember praying that this wouldn't be the worst decision I'd ever made. Hoping that I'd figure out exactly the kind of artist I am. And that whoever that is, I'd also find confidence in it.

In the last year, I've covered Santos Vista and so much of San Antonio in my work. I've had days where I felt like giving up and days where I'd never been so happy to be doing what I do. I've learned how to defend what I love doing. That the art I do is a part of my soul I can't help but want to share with everyone, and no one can fit that into a box. No one can simplify that if I don't let them. And I won't. Not anymore.

I found the meaning I was searching for. In San Antonio. In Santos Vista. In my family and friends. So much so in Santi.

But in me too.

I did it. And I'm ready to go.

"You sure you can't stay with me tonight?" I ask Santi as we sit in the back seat of my car, catching our breaths, parked in his driveway. I pull on his denim button-up shirt, leaving it open while he wipes his sweaty face and then his chest with my tee shirt.

"I need to do some things around the house in the morning," he replies. But I can see it in his eyes. All the things he'd rather be doing if I give him a good fifteen-minute break than leaving this car and going into that house right now. "I'll let you know as soon as I'm done, though. And we'll spend the rest of the day together being lazy until your gallery opening tomorrow night."

"Promise?"

"Promise." Santi leans toward me and kisses me. And then I kiss him back, hooked on the feeling of his lips and tongue on mine.

"Thank you," I tell him when I finally force myself away from his mouth.

"For what?"

"For . . . everything. All the past months. Today. All the months we're gonna have. I—You make me really happy. And I'm thankful that you ended up in my life."

"I am too." He follows his words with more kissing. His hands going to places on my body that are tired right now but are not above requiring a lot more attention if he doesn't stop acting up *immediately*. "*Qué la*—Eres irresistible. Okay. Ya voy. Before I bail for another round and have la señora throwing all her chanclas at me. I'll see you tomorrow, cielo."

"Te quiero, you fucking tease."

"I don't think it can be a tease if we already did it?"

"Wanna bet?"

"Nope." He kisses me one last time, and I can feel the evil grin forming on his mouth. "Te quiero más."

I stay in the driveway awhile longer after he's inside. Maybe I could wait here until tomorrow. *Nah*, I need a shower and my bed.

As I drive home, at every red light I look up into the sky and thank the universe for the boy who didn't know how to take pictures at murals (and still refuses to do it right) and walked up to Ronnie and me on that cold January day. For all the days— good, bad, beautiful, and terrifying—that have led to us here now, ready to get on with an exciting, but also still terrifying, future. Whoever's up there and decided they were going to cultivate some fates has all my gratitude.

———————

"Ander. Mi'je," Mami says. She's forceful, assertive, and rushed with her voice and the way she shakes my arm. *"Ander."*

"What?"

"Get up. *Now.* Something's happened."

"Tita?" My head turns to her, and I pick up my torso, holding myself up with my arms.

"No, it—it's Santi."

My heart starts thumping a thousand miles an hour. I can feel every heavy breath going in and out of my lungs. My throat swelling up because I don't want to let that breath out. I'd rather suffocate than be able to ask the inevitable.

No. No. *No, no, no.* Anything but this. Anything but the words I know are about to come out of Mami's mouth.

"Santi, he—he was taken."

46

A couple lawyers from RAICES are already sitting with Tita by the time Mami, Pa, and I get to Lupe's. They're all deep in conversation, files and laptops spread on the table along with mugs of coffee. None of their faces are optimistic. But dealing with this on a Saturday instead of enjoying their weekend, I wouldn't be able to think happy thoughts either yet.

Do they ever go into this knowing they're going to help keep someone's life intact? Or do they realize they're set up for failure? That everything about this country has been made for it to be easier to kick out brown people than it is to embrace us, and now it's about to do that to my boyfriend. Mi querido.

"Lo siento, bebite," Tita says softly into my ear when I bend down to hug her. "I'm so, so sorry."

She pulls out the chair to her right for me to sit and calls the closest waiter, asking for an horchata for me. Mami sits on her other side and Pa across from her with the attorneys.

"Tanya Muñoz," one of the lawyers says, holding her hand out for me to shake. *Wait*, she was at my house that day ICE followed Santi and me home. "Ander, right?"

"Yeah."

"I remember. You did our mural. Hopefully we can have a chance to pay you back now."

I want to tell her that she's already done so much. That this might've happened a lot sooner if it wasn't for her. But all my mind can focus on is right now.

"You think you can really get Santi out?"

"We can certainly make a case. La señora in charge of the migrant house Santiago was staying at said that he'd only been out for less than ten minutes. Was going to the corner store for some chips and teas. A cop stopped him right in front of the store, something about getting a call regarding a guy walking around with a knife. Wouldn't let him leave and kept him there until Immigration showed up."

"That—*that's bullshit.*"

"*Ander,*" Mami snaps. "Bring your voice down to a two, mi'je."

"I haven't been able to talk to Santiago yet," Tanya continues. "But I'm pushing to get in within the next couple of hours. Until then, what I know thus far about him has come from tu abuela, Señora Martínez here. With it being his second apprehension—and his first one is still on file—"

"That was fifteen years ago," I interrupt. "None of that he had any control over."

"I know. But this is the reality of the situation. DACA didn't exist back then. And, because of his age at reentry, he wouldn't be eligible for any of those protections now. Anything we might be able to do to create a case for Santiago to legally be allowed to stay here is incredibly loose at best. Even if it were an option, most judges wouldn't allow us to claim any qualifications. He's only been here a little more than a year and a half, didn't finish school in Mexico. The law is great for immigrants when they can tie humanity to their ability to better the economy, which, one, is horrible, and two, isn't on our side. And there are very clear, albeit grossly amoral, guidelines that state what happens when someone is deported for the second time. However, with his mother's . . . disappearance, it—if we can get the right judge, an argument for special circumstances might be successful. Asylum is definitely within the realm of possibilities. Also, I think we can safely assume that Santiago was committing no crime when ICE took him into custody. Not that that isn't the norm, but, again, if it's someone on our side hearing us out, we could get him back."

"So, we're leaving it up to chance?"

"We know the rules as well as they do. Better, even. It's our job to know these laws better than ICE and police and—let me stop myself before I say something divisive but honest. But, yes. Chance is really all we have. *Oh*," she continues, bringing a laptop closer to her, quickly typing and then turning the screen toward me, showing me a Twitter post about an upcoming rally. "Your friend Ezekiel and your sister are also working with our organizing and outreach people. They've already started spreading word planning protests at the detention center Downtown, where Santiago is currently being held. The first one will be tomorrow afternoon. So maybe chance isn't all we have. We also have our voice. And your voice is powerful, Ander. Never forget that."

Okay. Maybe a *little* idealism helps.

———————

"Are you sure you've got this?" Juni asks as he follows me up to the front door of the Blue Star gallery hosting my exhibit. He already knows everything that's going on. I had to tell him, in case I break down in the middle of this place because my boyfriend got taken this morning.

"No," I say bluntly and quietly as I stare at the door. "But I need to follow through with this. I can't go home knowing there's nothing I can do for Santi *and* I bailed on my very first exhibit."

"No one would blame you."

"No one knows, though, Juni." The words come out in almost

a frustrated laugh as I tilt my head up and tighten the muscles around my eyes to keep in the tears. "All they'd see is some un-professional kid. They don't get to see what I'm going through. The pain I'm feeling. I've let them in on my happiness already, it's inside there on those walls for everyone to see. But this—no. I need to do this, and I'm gonna do my best. For Santi."

"Then, in that case—" Juni steps in front of me, his eyes do-ing a quick take on my outfit, straightening out the lapels of my skinny-fit pink sports coat sitting over a white granddad collar shirt. "Nails, fierce. Hair, fierce. And this ensemble? She is fierce as well. No llores, hermana, ¿sí?"

I let out my one and only laugh for the day. "Sí. I can wait until after this is over."

I enter the gallery to applause from a huge crowd of people filling the room, standing by my lucha libre masks, all painted in light yellow, pink, green, blue, and purple pastels with similar-colored flowers at their base, my murals on the wall, and tables of champagne and conchas. And I wish I knew I'd remember this all clearly later, but my mind and sight are hazy as soon as their clapping fills my ears. I'm here physically but clocked out in every other way. Escaped. My soul fluttering, lost up in the sky.

No. Locked up in some room a few miles from here.

I know that Juni, in a full professional godmother role, leads me around the first room, introducing me to important people he's invited and told all about me. I hear his voice tell me that he's overheard a couple talk about purchasing one or two of the murals. And I feel a weight in my hands when he sets a plate with two concha quarters in my palms and my fin-gers clutching on to the edges.

"Mi'je," Mami says when she takes me from Juni in the sec-ond room. "You okay still being here?"

No. I'm not. I know they're barely hanging on too. I told them they didn't have to come. That I wouldn't even be here if I actually had a choice. *We're in this together*, Pa told me, and—maybe for the first time in my whole life—I didn't try to argue with them.

I catch myself reaching a hand out into empty space, forgetting that Santi isn't here. Isn't next to me. When someone accidentally leans into my back, I, for a second, think it's him, about to hug me. About to congratulate me and kiss my cheek and tell me about how successful this all is and remind me of his favorite murals and what he likes best about all them. But it's not him.

I was going to talk about him here, in front of all these people. About how grateful I am to have met this person who showed me I could love the art that fills this place. Art that is solely me and everything about me. That maybe has little bits of inspiration from David Alfaro Siqueiros and Frida but also maybe even a little bit of Andy Warhol and for sure Kehinde Wiley, all shaped into something my own about things that bring me joy and make my heart and soul feel so full. That, as grateful as I am to everyone in my life who has pushed me, I'm so glad that Santi could be part of my life too, as someone who allowed me to sit and breathe and figure myself out and consider the good I bring in every present moment instead of focusing solely on what I'll be doing five, ten years from now or trying to impress people who don't matter.

I was going to give that speech and hold his hand and try not to look at him, otherwise I'd start crying.

Now I just want to scream. I'm going to scream. My body is shaking from holding the scream in. People keep coming up to me and saying words but mentally I'm not here; I don't think I ever really was. They're all too close.

I tried my best, but I can't do this.

"I need to leave," I tell Mami, not bothering to wait for her to answer before I'm walking out. And right as my feet step onto the concrete stairs at the entrance of the gallery, I'm crying for the exact opposite reason I planned on crying about. And I'm screaming. And I wish these people wouldn't get to see my hurt, but some things I can't help. Some hurt hurts too much to hold in.

I told myself I could get through this. I could go a couple hours and put on a smile and act like this is the best day of my life. That's what it was supposed to be. Instead, it's the worst.

Pa hugs me and I continue to cry into his shoulder as he pets my head with one hand and my back with the other. Mami's quiet voice tells him she's going to get the car, and I can feel Tita's presence behind me, not wanting to leave me but not knowing what there is she can do.

If she manages to figure that out, I'd sure love to know.

47

You and Chachi work fast."

"Thank Mo," Zeke says as he follows me into my room with a bag of breakfast tacos. "Called him and two minutes later, I had a list of people to reach out to."

We sit on my bed, backs up against the wall. I look at the pillow next to me. The one Santi uses. That he should've been using right now as we stayed in bed and ignored alarms. And he'd be half-heartedly trying to convince me to get up because I said I'd start packing for Chicago this morning.

Packing is the last thing on my mind right now. Being anywhere that he's not is the last place I want to be.

"If you aren't in a place to go to the rally, you don't have to, AJ. We'd understand."

"No. I'm going." I grab my iPad and go straight to Procreate. "We've handled ICE twice already. *Together.* This isn't gonna be any different."

And the times I didn't show up for Santi are still heavy on my mind. Times when he really needed me. I told myself I wasn't doing that anymore. Through happiness and destruction, I'm with him. I'm not letting how weak I feel right now keep me from fighting for him.

"But—that office supply store over on Libertad can print posters, right?"

"Yeah. That's where Mo got all his StuCo President campaign stuff done," Zeke replies.

"Okay. I need to do one more thing, and then we can head over."

A few adjustments, some text, make sure the quality is high enough, done. Quick drive to La Vista Office Supplies, get a two-foot-by-three-foot poster printed, and then ten more when the manager realizes what it's for.

"How many do you need, joven? Don't worry. It's on us. Consider it a contribution."

When we get to the Bexar County Courthouse, the front of the building and into the street is covered with people. Some I recognize from the neighborhood: from school or at Lupe's or in passing at H-E-B or la panadería. Most of them mine and Santi's age and in groups of four or five or at tables getting people information on different local organizations and passing out crackers and bottles of water. One group's even brought a couple guitars and an accordion and are singing corridos. There are poster boards with ABOLISH ICE and NO ONE IS ILLEGAL ON STOLEN LAND held high up over the crowd. I can't believe Zeke and Chachi did this. I can't believe people actually showed up.

Zeke takes my hand and leads me into the sea of people. "Come on. The organizer's somewhere around here."

We squeeze our way up to the front, where five people are talking next to two large speakers, all dressed in a range from carefully thought out athleisurewear to brown caps and lighter brown shirts to loose tank, a bandana around the neck, and baggy black cargo pants. One of the athleisurewear people has a mic in their hand, held away from everyone. Another immediately starts waving at Zeke and me when they notice us.

"This must be Ander? Le artiste, right? Mo's friend."

"Yep," I reply with all the awkwardness of someone who has no idea what they're doing. "Hi."

"Took a look at your Insta. Good shit. And, sorry, I'm Marcos. Mucho gusto. I'm with Jóvenes por la Justicia, one of the groups Zeke here and Mo reached out to. I'm extremely sorry for what you've gone through and what this country is continuing to put you and especially Santi through." He motions us forward with his hand, leading us over to everyone else. "We have folks from the Brown Berets, some orgs from a few universities, RAICES, of course, and Les Guerres. We're keeping an eye on them, though. They like to get kinda 'hands on' with their protests, if you know what I mean.

"Anyways, we'll be starting in a few minutes. I'll say some words, pass the mic to the lawyers if they got something to add. And the walk will be up to Commerce, take a left, then another left on Santa Rosa, making a square that will end at the detention center on Laredo. When we get there, if you'd like to, I think we'd be all ears for anything you have to say."

"You want me to speak?"

"I'd love it if you would, yes."

"I didn't prepare anything."

"Say what feels right. Again, only if you feel called to do so. If not, one of us will take it from there. But personally speaking, I think you could really move some people. If you can talk anywhere as good as you paint, it's gonna be a powerful moment. And—Oh, shit. Speaking of, did you do that poster?" Marcos points to the posters in my hand that say FREE SANTI in bold black lettering on the bottom with his face—the one I drew before we were anything more than two people who kept running into each other, fully colored in now, with a pale red background.

"Oh yeah. This was me."

"Damn. You're a talent."

"I actually have more, if there's anyone who wants one."

"Oh, for real? Yeah, we'll get those passed out." I hand him the extra posters, and they're handed off to someone else who starts passing them out. "Grab a water bottle, some trail mix or chips if you need something to snack on before we start walking, and, yeah. Feel free to stay up here at the front with us too."

I've been to plenty of marches with Mo. But being front and center, hearing how the voices of this mass of people roar like a wave starting from the beginning and carrying down to the back with chants of "No justice, no peace!" and "¡El pueblo unido jamás será vencido!" is so different. How I came here not knowing how my presence would matter, but now feel so powerful surrounded and supported by all these people. Marcos yells into the mic, and added to the crowd, it creates a sound that vibrates off buildings and rings in my ears even after. It's a surreal experience.

We have our voice. And our voice is powerful. Our voice can change this world and free people. We can free Santi.

The detention center is this six-, maybe seven-story building on the other side of I-35 from Santos Vista. I honestly don't think I've ever realized it was here, watching one of the brownest communities in San Antonio (which is saying *a lot*) like it's that tower with the eye from *The Lord of the Rings*, always observing and waiting for the right moment to fuck up our entire lives. And it did.

"¿Listos?" one of the Brown Berets asks me, motioning over to the microphone in Marcos's hand with his chin.

"I—yeah. I'm ready."

The mic feels heavy in my hands. Like every possible outcome of this moment depends on the words I speak into it. And—maybe I'm not ready. Maybe I don't have the words—

"You got this, AJ," Zeke says, putting a hand on my shoulder. And then Chachi is hugging me on my other side and all her friends are standing next to me shouting, "We love you, AJ!" and "We're here for you!"

And then I see my parents and Tita moving up to the front. Mami's eyes are tired and sad, and Pa's this strong, proud energy. He nods and I can read his lips saying, "Go on; you can do this."

I can do this. I have to. For Santi.

"I can put you on my shoulders," Zeke suggests.

"Uh, yeah. Sure."

Chachi and her friends help keep me stable while Zeke lifts me, giving me a view of the endless number of heads and signs and flags, all here for us. For Santi.

"I—uh, hi," I start. My voice cracks a little, but people are quick to encourage me to keep going. To say what I need to say. "My name is Ander Martínez. Or AJ. Pronouns are *they*, *them*, *elle*. And I—*I'm fucking angry*."

That gets a loud roar from the crowd.

"I was born here, in San Antonio. I live just a few blocks down on the other side of that freeway, actually."

"*Westside!*" someone yells, making me laugh. That helped.

"But my boyfriend, Santi, he wasn't. He was born in a small town in México. He is someone who doesn't break rules. He's careful, considerate, and kind. He's one of the few people on this planet that makes this world a better place. And he's been trying to survive his entire life. He's gone through more than what anyone should have to. But because of where he's from, people don't see that. They don't see *him*.

"I wish they could see him. I wish every person who fears us because of the color of our skin or our accent or where we were born could get some clarity. Some empathy. If only for a moment. Then they might realize what their hate is doing.

Who it's hurting. *I* am fucking hurting. And if they could only see the humanity of the boy I love, maybe they'd stop. I don't know. Maybe.

"Regardless, we're going to free him. And then we're going to tear this building down and free all the brown and Black lives this place and places like it have ruined. Because Santi and all of them don't deserve to just *survive*. They deserve to live. To thrive. They deserve the opportunity for happiness in whatever way that comes. They deserve it because they're human. Fuck any other label. They're human, and they deserve humanity. And I won't stop until they get that. I won't stop until I get to see Santi's smile again and wake up next to him and get to say all the way too corny pickup lines I can think of to him. I won't stop until I get him back. Puro desmadre. Bien desmadre. Juntos."

And when the crowd starts shouting and chanting and raising their posters as high as they can, I know we're going to. I know it.

Mi Querido,
It's empty without you here. Here, like, my bed, my car, the roof, the house, Lupe's, the neighborhood. The world. Me.

Tanya told me that I can write you notes and at first I was so excited about it because at least that's something it's better than being cut off from you completely but this hurts. I want to talk to you. I want to rest my head on your shoulder and tell you things. I want to go numb from you lying on top of me and falling asleep. I want you to tell me everything that's on your mind in between your seventh and eighth flauta. I want to hear your voice. I want to look into your eyes. I want to hold your hand.

But until I get to do that again, this'll do. So I want you to imagine me screaming the words "te quiero" to you over and over again. No, not even te quiero. Te amo. Te amo, te amo, te amo. Hear those words, please. Because I'm yelling them. I'm yelling them so loud and I really hope you can hear them.

Te amo, Querido. Con toda mi alma.
Tu Cielo

Hola Cielo,
I miss your bed. And you too. I don't think I've ever told you but sleep and I haven't been friends for a long time. Or the night. Bad things happened at night. My parents fighting. The sound of cars slowly passing by our house. My amá crying when my apá and brother didn't come home. What each night could bring when we went north. At la casita too, it was never very comfortable sleeping on a bunk bed

and sharing a room with three other guys. They snore too loud.

The first time I really had a good night's sleep since maybe in forever was the first night I slept over with you. And I'm sure all the things we did that tired me out was part of it, but so was lying next to you. My face in your chest. My arms around you. Your hand brushing my head y cuando me hacías cosquillitas, which is probably my favorite thing in the world. I'd never felt so relaxed before. You do a lot of things to me, cielo, but I think most importantly, you make me feel safe.

I only feel rested when I rest with you. I wish I could rest with you right now. I wish you would kiss me and give me cosquillitas until I fall asleep and I'd wake up and we'll still be holding onto each other. I wish I could kiss your skin until you wake up complaining and whining that it's still too early. That's what I want more than anything.

Te amo, Cielo. Te amo mucho y mucho más.

Tu Querido

Mi Querido,
There's a photograph (by an actual photographer) I've been thinking about lately. I won't tell you his name or describe it to you like how you always do with the books you read. I'll spare you. Although I'd give the world for you to tell me about your favorite books right now.

I want to dance with you again. I miss that. The specific happiness you have dancing. How your face looks smiling and singing and concentrating all at the same time. And then when we wear ourselves out, you can rest your head on me and you can have all the peace y besitos y cosquillitas I can possibly give.

Just take the lead. I'll follow you anywhere.

Te amo, Querido
Tu Cielo

Mi Cielo,
Can you tell la jefa that I miss her gorditas? I think, behind you, they might be the best thing your family's ever given this world. Actually, I don't know, I could really go for a gordita right now. Might be a tie.

Te amo, Cielo. Y también las amo gorditas.
Tu Querido

Santiago,
You're not funny. And whether or not that made me laugh doesn't matter because you're not funny. It's a good thing you got me to fall in love with you before I realized how not funny you are.

Te amo, mi Pinche Pendejo Querido Más Baboso
Tu Cielo

Mi Cielito Linde
Maybe I'll tell you about how much I miss your body instead then? I'd give up eating gorditas for the rest of my life if it meant I could have you right now. I close my eyes and you're here with me, and my mouth so badly wants to go to every inch of your skin that I'm hungering for. I could tell you

about it, but I don't know if I have enough paper for that. I can try.

Te amo, mi Cielo Linde
Tu Querido

Querido,
I did my best to come up with anything else to say to that. Something cute or happy or meaningful. But all I can think of is that Tanya better get you out of there right the fuck now so you can absolutely wreck me into next week. And then do it again.

Also, I fucking miss you. I miss you so much. And I can't wait to hold you again. I need to hold you again. I don't know how much longer I can take it.

Te amo, mi Querido
Tu Cielo

Mi Cielo,
All I can think about today is how much I miss you too. It makes me angry and sad and lots of other things that I know the touch of your skin and the sound of your voice and the way your laugh makes my heart beat so fast would make all go away. Please stay hopeful, Cielo. Por favor. For me. Can you? Because I'm finding it hard to be hopeful. But I'll try my best if you will too. We have all the time in the world, ¿Recuerdas?

Te amo te amo te amo te amo te amo te amo te amo, Cielo
Tu Querido. Por siempre.

48

How much time has to pass before something—someone—can be nostalgic?

Can I be nostalgic for ten days ago, when I could go pick Santi up from his house? When I could throw a paint marker at him after catching him staring at me while I worked? When he'd sit behind me and lean his body on me and watch as I got lost in whatever new idea I had to get out on my iPad? When I could kiss him on the roof of the garage? When I could wake up to him in my bed? When we were just two people in love, fogging up my car's windows?

When I thought we had all the time in the world? When he told me he wasn't going anywhere?

Even if we're so close it hurts, at least he's not *gone* gone yet. But it still hurts. It really fucking hurts.

Every day comes with some sort of update. The things Tanya is trying to do, words and legalese that make no sense to me. All the things she's *tried* to do but didn't work out. Asylum. Bail. And then the things that she only gives me. The words he leaves her with and then I give her back for him like those friends in school that would help pass notes between crushes but if those crushes were actually experiencing the end of their world.

Each afternoon we go back to the detention center. We chant

more, march more, scream our righteous anger about an organization that shouldn't exist. We stay there until after the sun sets, leaving only when the cops start getting a little too aggressive about us being out here.

And at night, I sit in front of the small altar Tita made and pray to Mary and Saint Jude and Jesus and a god I'm not sure I even believe in. I beg them to come through for us. I ask God what would it take to have Santi back with me? To create a present where our future isn't torn apart by soulless men in ICE jackets. Because I'll give it. Nothing is off the table. Whatever they want. I'll start going to church. I'll say the rosary and pray every night. I'll make Pope Francis my phone's wallpaper.

But today I woke up with a feeling that God had forsaken me. I woke up with it heavy in my stomach and empty in my heart. And a pillow already stained with tears.

"I don't have good news."

I want to walk back upstairs and hide under my comforter. I want to close my eyes and whisper Santi's name and then see him when they open and realize that none of this was real. I want to find the darkest space in the universe and let it swallow me whole.

"We didn't get the judge we wanted," Tanya continues. "It was barely two minutes, the entire thing. All he saw was what was on paper. There's nothing more we could've done."

"How much time does he have?" Pa asks.

"Three days. Maybe five. I'm going to bother the shit out of Immigration until they tell me exactly where he's headed. Could be Reynosa. Or they might drop him off in Nuevo Laredo or Matamoros. And the time—"

"So, we're giving up?"

"Ander," Pa chides.

"No. I'm serious. Are you asking me to give up? What do you

expect me to do? Out of all the times that this has almost happened, or he's almost had to go back, this is what does it? Pinche going to get an AriZona tea and some Doritos? If he'd—" I'm struggling to breathe or form thought or control any reaction wanting to come out of me. My fists slam onto the table and I let out a frustrated scream. "If he'd just stayed with me, this wouldn't have happened! If I'd stayed with him. Why didn't I stay with him? I could've gone to the store. And then he wouldn't be in there right now. He wouldn't be leaving me. He'd be here. I—"

Pa's arms wrap around me like they have so many times over the past week and a half when I've broken down. When the emotions are too big and loud for me to handle. And he lets me sob and scream and my hands claw at his shoulders and back.

"Don't," he whispers. Little *shh, shh, shhh* sounds come out of his mouth like he used to do when I was a kid and would hurt myself falling from monkey bars or something. "Don't blame yourself, Ander. It's not your fault. I need you to believe that."

"I could've done more."

"You did your best. You showed up for him. You looked out for him the best you could. Santi wouldn't want you to carry the blame, mi'je."

"We were so close. We almost made it. We *should've* made it."

"I know. I know."

Gasping for air and crying, I wish that Santi was here beside me so he could hold me and tell me that none of this is real and he's here and we're here and nothing bad can come for us as long as we're together. So I could tell him that I love him too.

More than anything right now, I wish I could tell him how much I love him.

"I need to talk to him first," Tanya says as we walk into the waiting room that leads into one of the visitation areas of the detention center. "It'll be quick, and then you'll have a good twenty-five or so minutes with Santiago. I'll still be there to make sure none of the agents or guards tries to separate you."

You mean, separate us again, I almost say.

"Wait here, watch the TV, and I'll come get you when we're ready."

I take a seat on one of the uncomfortable plastic navy chairs lined up in rows under the harsh fluorescent lights. The television's set to Fox News, and I'd rather bash my head into the brick wall that was once white but's now an almost yellow? *How does that happen?*

I think this room does everything they want it to. It feels like hopelessness. Like I'm in my own little prison forced to think about all the times Santi and I made it.

And the one time we didn't.

The sound of the door opening gets my attention, and I breathe a sigh of relief when Tanya's head pops into the room. "Come on. It's time."

I walk into a large gray room. There're bars covering Plexiglas windows, circular tables in three rows from one end to the other, and—

"*Santi.*" I run to him, then hold him tightly in my arms.

"Hola, mi cielo," he says. The words fill my entire soul with a warmth that I thought I'd never feel again.

But then I look at him—at his tired eyes, the bits of facial hair growing in that he usually only lets get to a shadow before shaving. How he seems paler. And reality sets back in. "Querido, I—I'm sorry."

He holds my face in his hands, keeping me still while coming in for a kiss. Hoping it will somehow take away all the shit that we've gone through and will change what the future has in store for him. For us.

"Don't open your eyes yet," Santi says when he pulls away.

"I won't."

"Think about when we painted that white wall. And the first time we kissed. And our first date. And our first time together. And all the times after that. And us on your roof. And that trip to the Gulf, and all the car rides. All the good times."

"I will."

"About the first time I saw you, and how I'd never wanted a job more if it meant I could be around someone so beautiful. The first time I got to see you paint a mural, and how I'd never been more impressed by anyone in my entire life. How I *knew* that I was going to fall in love with you. Before then, even, at Easter, when at some point that night, I knew I already had."

It's not until I feel his forehead pressing against mine and I hear him sniffle that my eyes open. I wipe a thumb across his cheek and kiss him once more and then again.

I don't want to tell him goodbye. I don't know how. I'd like to tell him how he's given me hope and belief and happiness, but that would mean also telling him how I don't know what I'm going to do without him. That not a day will go by when I'm not thinking of him.

So maybe these kisses will be enough. Maybe our hands and fingers having a little more time to memorize the feeling of each other's skin will be enough. Maybe we'll keep saying "Te amo," and "Te amo más," until we know we won't forget what it sounds like to hear each other say those words.

Or maybe we can let ourselves believe that they will be enough, while deep down knowing that nothing will ever be enough.

"You changed my life, Santiago López Alvarado. You made it colorful and meaningful. And my biggest wish is that you could've stayed in it longer. That we could've had one more day at the park and painting and eating chicken nuggets with you on the floor of my bedroom. One more evening on my roof. One more night in my bed."

"Sounds like Heaven," Santi replies. "Actually, yeah. That 'Mexican Heaven' poem you like got it wrong. That's not Heaven. Heaven is chicken nuggets and lots of barbecue sauce and *your* french fries because stealing yours tastes better. And paletas and raspas and tacos, pero only from Lupe's and only when I'm sharing a table with you. And dancing to norteño music. And seeing the ocean with you. And drinking as much margarita as possible before your amá catches us. And the sound of your laugh whenever I kiss your stomach."

"I told you I'm ticklish there," I whine.

"It's a cute laugh. Oh, and the sound of your breath when I kiss your tattoo."

"*Shh,*" I snap, glancing over at the guards.

He laughs and we both turn to Tanya, who lifts a hand with her fingers raised and thumb bent inward.

Four minutes.

"We were supposed to have all the time in the world."

"Yo sé, cielo."

I kiss him and stare into his eyes, trying to make sure I'll always remember the exact dark, almost black of his irises.

"I believed we would. I believed in us. And I've never loved anyone like I love you. You're my Heaven."

"No, soy tu querido," he jokes. "*Tú* eres *mi* cielo."

"*Oh*, sí. Eres mi querido. Por siempre."

"Through happiness and destruction?"

"Through happiness and destruction."

49

I didn't want to go home after I left Santi. I didn't want to go anywhere, really. All I knew is that I wanted to cry. That I almost broke down when our time was up and two men grabbed Santi's wrists way too tightly and walked him out of the room. That nothing had ever felt so empty as that room did when the door closed behind him.

"I'm not gonna let them see me cry," I said under my breath over and over again until we were out of the building. Even in my car, while in the parking lot, I didn't allow myself that. They don't get to hold that over me.

I can't even say I was fully conscious of my decision to take a left onto Santa Rosa instead of staying on Buena Vista and heading back to Santos Vista. To Lupe's, where my family and Zeke were waiting for me. Or that I remember driving at all or how I got to the Blue Star Complex. All I know is that suddenly it's an hour and a half later and I'm parked in front of my exhibit building. My throat hurting and my eyes red and my face wet from tears and my entire body won't stop shaking.

I open my glove compartment and reach for any bandana in the pile. My heart goes heavier when I look at my hand and the pink bandana held tightly in my grip. The same one from the night Santi and I first worked together. Wiping my face dry with it, memories of me almost crashing and tying the bandana for him and the way he bit and then licked his lip and his eyes telling some explicit stories (and all the times after then that he'd do that because he knew *the look* was the quickest way to get my clothes off) and how he saved me from falling face-first onto the concrete floor of the patio. How quickly he became such a huge part of my life.

And how quickly he was taken away from it.

I step out of my car and take a deep breath. Wait for the shakes to go away. Wait for the heavy emotions crashing into me like waves to calm down as much as they can. And then I open the door into the gallery and feel cold air hit my body.

At least it's quiet. And no one's here except for the gallery manager. I'm thankful for that. If I start crying, it'll only be awkward for the two of us.

I'm careful not to look at the giant mural of Santi and me on our paint date yet. I need to get calmer, cooler, and more collected before that happens. Not that I believe I will. Just delaying the inevitable.

A few of them have little stickers by the title plaque, noting that someone's bought it. The gallery manager pointed it out to me when I told them who I was. Which would have been a lot more exciting if I'd had Santi with me and we'd start talking about the extra money we'd have for Chicago and how maybe we wouldn't have to live off of ramen and hot dogs.

I try my best to focus on happy thoughts while looking at the mural of us. Of that date and taking him to my birthday party that night. Of all the other dates we've had and nights turned into mornings turned into entire days spent together.

It's harder to keep up the happiness in the next room, standing in front of the two murals of just him. I kind of regret sharing these with the world. Moments that were just between the two of us. Of a Santi only I got to see. But I'm also kind of incredibly happy I have these made permanent, up on a wall for me to see. Memories that are connected to them that, still, are kept only between the two of us. And no matter how separated they keep us, no one can take those away.

"Hey," the gallery manager calls from the first room. Lisa, I think her name was? Or Julissa? Either way, she's getting closer, and hopefully she won't ask me if I remember her name or why it looks like I've been crying. "I forgot to mention, but a lot of people coming in have been bringing up wanting to buy prints. You don't by chance sell them, do you? Like, digital or physical?"

"I, uh—I haven't, no."

"Oh." Her reaction sounds surprised. "I guess I'm behind on this one. "Well, for those of us who can't afford the original, or don't have the space for a ten-by-ten, we'd gladly splurge on a three-by-three. And I heard you're leaving to Chicago? Could be an easy way to make some money while in school. I bet you'd make a ton off these or if you have other work too. Consider an Etsy, at least, yeah? And let me know if you do, so I can pass along the shop info."

"Uh, yeah. I will. Thanks."

And it hits me. As I turn back to face the murals of Santi, a bunch of thoughts and scenarios and alternate realities start playing out in my head, becoming the single most wild idea I've ever had. The least-thought-out, incredibly rash, "no plan B"–ass idea ever conceived.

But it's doable.

My hand presses on the mural of him sitting in the garage. A couple tears start falling, but I let them travel all the way down to my chin. Standing here, not moving, for what feels like hours.

"I'm not ready for this to end," I tell painting Santi. "I'm with you, anywhere. Always."

"What are you doing here?" Juni asks, staring at me from the other side of his desk. His hands held out as if he needs an actual, physical reason for me being in his office and is waiting for me to reach in my pocket and give him one. But I had to rush over first thing in the morning. Before I start acting rational.

"Hi to you too."

"Aren't there things you should be doing? A whole semester you should be getting ready for? Emotions you should be processing? A step on the grief cycle to be leaning in to? Actually"—he sets his elbows on the table, leaning so his head is resting on his fists—"not trying to be your therapist, but where are you with everything? And don't say you're fine, because we know that's not true. You look like you haven't slept in days."

"Don't worry about it. *Please*. I have a question."

Juni rolls his eyes at me and lets out a sigh. "What is it?"

"Can I sell prints of my murals?"

"Like, what you did on Procreate or you want to take pictures of your murals and sell prints of the photographs?"

"Uh—" I hadn't thought about the difference, but, "I came here thinking mainly the first one. Selling prints of the concepts I made. But, also, I guess since I'm here, the second one too."

"Yeah, that's fine," he replies. "It's your work."

"I know, but that contract you had me sign had lots of pages and I didn't want to do something and have to apologize for it later."

"God knows some white girl has probably already done it and is marketing it as *authentic*. Again, your work, do with it what you will. I'll even say the things you did for my friends—the animes and the cacti and whatever else I signed you up for—is fair game too. Why?"

"I need money."

He tilts his head and squints his eyes. "I have an assumption in my head, but I'm not going to ask anything, because I don't need to be putting that out into the universe, especially if I'm correct and then become part of allowing this whole assumption that I am not going to put any truth to, to become reality."

"What?"

"Don't tell me anything more about this."

"Oh. Yeah. It's probably best that I don't."

"Okay. Well, away with you, then."

I start to turn around to leave when a thought light-bulbs in my brain. "Actually," I continue, spinning all the way around, "I need a favor. Something you might not be able to do, but I wanted to ask either way."

"Which would be?"

"That wall on the building next to Lupe's. The one I covered a few months back."

"Give me a time and a list of supplies you'll need," Juni says. "I'll have it all out there for you."

"Are you sure? Like, that's something you can do?"

"Yeah. It's taken care of. They're a friend."

"How many friends do—Never mind. You're the best." I turn back to the door, already taking a hurried step forward. "Thank you, Ju—"

"*Hold it*," he snaps, and I almost trip spinning back around. Juni gets out of his chair, walks around his desk, and comes up to me. And, in what might be the first physical sign of affection he's ever shown me, he hugs me.

I hug him back. My arms tight around him and my face in his shoulder. "Thank you for everything, Juni. The only reason I can do this is because you believed in me."

"As much as I'd like to take credit, and I will take some, *you* got yourself here, Ander. And if you could do that, you can do anything you put your mind to. Especially with the support

I know you're gonna have, as reluctant as I'm sure they'll be at first." He lets me go, but leaves his hands on my shoulders, squeezing them. "Be good. Okay? And *do good*. And cultivate goodness. You're gonna go far, kid. Keep in touch and tell me about it."

"I will."

"You're what?"

"I'm not going to SAIC."

My advisor looks more aggravated than I've ever seen him. And confused. Like he wants to call me some words but also ask what the hell I'm thinking.

Which is a question I might not know the whole answer to. But I got him on Zoom right after leaving Juni's office, still parked in the lot. If I picked my head up, I'd see the big Beautify logo on their window in front of me. I didn't want to waste any time with this.

"*What the*—" I can tell how much it took not to continue that. I think his head might explode. He puts his hands in prayer formation and over his mouth, probably thinking about how to say those same words more professionally. "Do you realize what you're saying? The opportunity you're giving up. My time you've now wasted doing these correspondences over the past year. You're supposed to be here in a week, Ander. What could have possibly compelled you to make this decision? It better be something good."

"It is."

That's all he gets to know. I've had enough of him tokenizing my life. I'm not trying to give him any more.

Honestly, telling him that I'm doing everything I need to do to withdraw from SAIC feels . . . good. Give my spot to someone who wants it. To someone who would benefit from it.

Hopefully someone not white, and even more hopefully someone not straight and cis. Someone who will come into that school and fuck up this guy's world and the worlds of everyone who treats us and our art like they do our food and our music and our humor: as something they can take in and consume without seeing our humanity.

I was never going to be the person to do that. But I've become the person who maybe will inspire some little queer brown kid to express themself loudly and brightly. And I don't need SAIC for that. Maybe I don't need college at all. I just need people who will love me and who I can love back and create in honor of that love.

And when our Zoom session ends, I feel relieved. I feel ready for what's next.

50

When I get home, I rush upstairs and slam the door behind me, grab my iPad, and throw myself onto my desk chair. There's a lot I need to do and very little time to do it all. Including figuring out how to tell Mami, Pa, and Tita. My stomach hurts just thinking about that. If they weren't happy about my gap year, they really aren't about to love what I'm doing.

I get on Procreate and start perfecting all my projects that've become murals. Before this, they've all been good, but basically just a guide for when I put it up on a wall. Now's the time to make sure they're frameworthy. *La Chalupa*, the pan dulce wall, the RAICES mural, the monstera plant, about half the pieces from my Blue Star exhibit. Compiling a portfolio that encompasses an entire year of work.

And maybe even more than that. Art that is going to keep me here even after I'm gone. Each with a little part of my soul. All of them together telling my story.

Then I go onto Etsy and, in a process that is much easier than I thought it'd be, create a store. *Boom*. For right now, they're only digital purchases. Anyone with ten dollars can get an entire folder of any one of my works and fit it to any size frame they could think of. Once I'm settled, I'll add more of my work and an option for personal commissions for a lot more money, but this is good enough to get me going. To get *us* going. Crossing my fingers that it is.

I open my phone, go to FaceTime, and—

"Long time no talk," says this lanky guy with a faint line of mustache hairs, hair tied back into a bun—*since when has that been a thing?*—and a UNT RESIDENCE LIFE shirt on, walking through what looks like his college campus. But that big smile's still there. The same Mo that I've always known.

"Yeah. I'm sorry. Thanks, though, for everything you did with the rallies. Zeke told me how you really came through."

"I wish I could've done more."

"I know. Me too." I look up, out my window, at the roof. Thinking about Mo and me hanging out on there. Santi and me on there. The times when it was just me. How empty it's going to be soon. "I wanted to ask you, I made an Etsy store to sell prints of my mural concepts. Would you mind sharing it on your socials?"

"Sí, 'mane. You know I will."

"I—yeah. Thanks." I get comfortable in my chair, sitting up straight, taking a deep breath. "And can I tell you something real quick? Before I tell everyone else."

"I'm all ears."

"I decided . . . I—" One more deep breath. "I'm going to Mexico. Like, I'm leaving."

Mo walks into a building at the same time I say it, and I'm not entirely sure he heard me. I hope he did because that took a lot out of me and it's going to be weird to have to tell him again.

"You're gonna want to pronounce it *México* when you get there. Otherwise, you're just making it easier for them to clock you as American."

"That's all you have to say about it?"

He laughs as he steps into an elevator. "Also, I'm glad. Out of the three of us, someone's gotta be the one to make the questionable big life decisions. Not to shit on Zeke staying in San Antonio or me sticking meticulously to my life plan, but—live some life for us, AJ. We got your back always, even if we're quiet about it."

"I know. Love you, Mo."

"Love you too, 'mane."

An hour later, the link to my shop I posted on Twitter has gone viral with retweets and quote-retweets and comments and shares, thanks to Mo and Zeke and Lisa/Julissa and all the gays who follow me. I'm already getting notifications about sales, messages about special commissions and when to expect more work. This is good. Promising.

I can't let it distract me, though. Next is the big stuff. Like, *no going back after this* big stuff. But under the fear and anxiety of this decision, there's also excitement and knowing that I'm making the right choice. I believe that.

I keep that belief at the front of my mind as I email my admissions counselor at the School of the Art Institute of Chicago. Time to make it *official* official. I click on Send and, in that tiny action, change the entire trajectory of the path I thought my life would be going in.

It's okay. I'll be okay. Get the heart to stop beating so fast. Get the breathing back to normal. There are a million ways to get to where I want to be. This one feels like the right way. The way things are meant to work out. I've jumped off higher cliffs.

At least, that's what I'm telling myself.

Now it's time to really jump. Fuck. I'm doing it.

I buy a plane ticket. And then another. I go to Lupe's, act as inconspicuous as possible as I head to the office and print out all the confirmation stuff for one of those tickets. Tell Pa I'm really busy when he asks if I want to eat something as I'm running out. Then I go to the bank, withdraw enough cash from my savings for a taxi and a couple meals, and break a handful of traffic laws getting to my last destination. But I'm smiling through it all. I'm happy and optimistic and hopeful for the first time in weeks.

"I need to talk to you!" I yell when I get to Tanya's office in the RAICES building. A little out of breath from running to make sure I got here before she left.

"Okay. Let's talk. Close the door."

––––––––––––

"You sure this is what you want to do?"

"I already made that choice. Yes. This is what I'm doing."

Tanya huffs as she locks the building's front door. "You told your parents?"

"I—I'm still figuring out how to tell them. *I will, though.*"

She shakes her head and starts walking around to the back of the building, where their parking lot is at. I follow at her side, keeping up with her pace, which is faster than most straight people I know. Maybe she's one of us.

"You can do this, though, right?" I ask.

"Yeah. It's simple. You're the one that's got a lot of planning to do in a very short amount of time and then figure out how to stay alive after that."

"Do you think this might be too wild? Some flying-too-close-to-the-sun type of shit?"

"Yes," she says bluntly while opening the door to her car. "But you've already decided that, so what's my opinion matter? And if it happens to matter at all, what you're doing is also brave. And it shows a lot of love. Those are both excellent qualities to carry through life. Knowing what's worth taking risks for, even when it's terrifying. Stick with that, Ander. And don't ever get to the end of anything wishing you'd done more. Felt more."

"Thanks, Tanya."

"Claro. I'll text you when it's done."

51

I've never been so nervous in my entire life. Also, *why did this specific patio table become the serious-conversations table?*

I don't know. But at this point, I'm just trying to keep myself distracted. And I know that Mami, Pa, and Tita can tell I'm doing it too.

"Don't be mad."

That was the absolute worst way to start this. Because now Mami is already preparing her mad face, Pa looks like he's getting ready to keep his wife from killing me before I say anything, and Tita looks worried.

"I'm leaving in four days," I start. My eyes glance at all three of them and then to anywhere but them. "But not to Chicago. I—I'm going to Mexico. *México*. To be with Santi."

"Ander—"

"Hold on," I quickly let out before Mami can start chewing me out. "Please. Look, I found a decently priced apartment in a good neighborhood in Me—Ciudad México. At least, from what I learned about the neighborhood on Google and asking people on Twitter. And it's fully furnished. One of those long-term-stay Airbnbs. It'd mean I wouldn't be in school still, but I'm okay with that because I need more time to figure that out. If it's something I really want. And if I do, there's UNAM. It's no top-ten-in-the-world art school, but it's still a great one, and the best in the country. Also, when you think about it, Ciudad México is closer to San Antonio than Chicago is. I—"

"*Stop*," Mami snaps. She sits back in her chair, arms crossed, staring at me. A whole minute goes by and she hasn't said anything. No one has. All of us too scared to before she says whatever it is on her mind.

And then she turns to Tita. "You said if anything happens, it'd be on you. *Well?*"

"Mami—"

"*Cállate!*" She stands up and looks at me, then at Tita again. "*See what happened?* No. No. We're not doing this."

Me calling out "Mami!" mixes with Pa's "Amorcita!" and Tita's "Nuera!" none of them doing anything to stop her from walking off and back into the restaurant. And then they call after me too when I get up and rush to follow her. Their voices go quiet when the door closes behind me.

"Me hablas," I say, stepping into the office and closing that door, looking at Mami on the couch, leaning her arms on her legs.

"What did you expect? You're only nineteen, Ander. And this isn't the same as moving away to college or when you and Zeke and Moisés wanted to move in together after y'all graduated. What am I supposed to do? You're going to be all alone."

"No I won't. I'll have Santi."

"So two kids, barely nineteen years old, in Mexico City by themselves. Bueno, that makes me feel better. Do you even know what you're doing? Or are you going to end up getting kicked out of Mexico?"

"I'm not gonna get kicked out. Getting a temporary visa is complicated. But if I can sell some digital prints, even take some commissions, and keep my income at a good place for the next few months, it could work. I'll have to come back too; make sure that I don't mess up any little part of their requirements, but that basically still lines up with when my exhibit ends, which kind of works perfectly, even though I wouldn't be able to bring Santi with me. I—yes, I know what I'm doing."

I walk over to Mami and take a seat on the couch next to her. I lean on her, my arms going around to hug her. Waiting to see if she'll yell at me or tell me to go away. And grateful when she doesn't.

"I didn't expect y'all to understand, but I hoped y'all would try. And, I don't know, maybe be a little proud of me. I—Mami, this will always be my home. Wherever you are is home for me. But my heart isn't here anymore. My soul isn't here anymore. And I need to go to that place. To where they are. Where *he* is. To see if home can also be somewhere else. With someone else. I know you're scared. *I'm scared*. This isn't gonna be easy. But I can't just not do something because it's big and scary. Not when it's for someone I love. And maybe it won't work out. Maybe *we* won't work out. But maybe we will. Maybe *I* will. And maybe we'll be great."

I tighten my hug on her, thinking of all the times we've sat here. When I tripped and busted my knee and she tried to keep me from screaming as she wiped alcohol over the cut. When Zeke and I got into a huge fight during one of our shifts right after we broke up and she sat with me and let me cry for the rest of my shift. When I had to decide between different art schools and only wanted to know where she'd choose.

"I'm not asking for permission, but I am asking if you would root for us. Pray for us. Tell me that you think we could do this."

Mami turns her head to me, her eyes watery. Seeing a tear go down her face is going to make me start crying too. And then she kisses my cheek.

"Mi'je. If there's anyone I'd lose my voice for cheering on

any day of the year, it's you. And if there's anyone who can do this, it's you."

"So you're okay with me going?"

"No. But that's not important. So I'll be mad, but I'm not going to stand in your way." She kisses me again. "Te quiero, Ander Justino."

"Te quiero más, Mami."

"Sometimes I wish I was La Chalupita."

"Sometimes I wish I was dating her," Zeke adds.

"Same," Chachi says back.

All of us have been sitting on the other side of the creek, me in the middle of both of them, staring at my mural, lit up by solar lights lining the wall. Satisfying some post-weed munchies with gas station hot dogs and bags of hot Cheetos filled with processed cheese.

"She seems like she really enjoys life, you know? She ain't got no problems. Everything figured out," he continues.

"It's because every answer to every question in the universe is in her boat," my sister tells him.

"*Fuck*. That's deep."

It could be the weed—actually, no, it's definitely the weed—but I swear she's really actually on the water. No longer attached to some wall. Ready to venture wherever life takes her.

"I'm leaving. To be with Santi."

"I figured as much," Zeke says, leaning onto me.

I look at my sister, her head down, watching as she slowly keeps flicking the pull tab of her Coke can. "Are you scared?"

"Yeah, of course I am. Not enough to change my mind, though."

"Have you ever changed your mind about anything in your life after you've decided you're going for it?" Zeke asks.

I laugh, thinking back on it. "No, I don't think I have, actually."

Chachi scoots closer to me, our arms touching and her head falling onto my shoulder. "I'm glad you're my sibling."

"I'm glad you're my sibling too. And take care of everyone, okay? Make sure to bother Mami at least once a day. Let Pa cheer as loud as he wants at your football games. And dance with Tita at every kickback. You're in charge now."

She brings her hand up to her forehead like a salute. "Mrs. Obama, it's been an honor."

"So motherfucking weird," I mumble before grabbing her Coke and taking a couple gulps.

Zeke's curls tickle my face as he leans in further to stretch an arm out and pat Chachi's head a couple times before resting on the middle of my back. "We're not done being best friends, all right? That predetermination stuff, I'm gonna believe in it all of two times: once for you and Santi, and once for you and me. We got a lot more future ahead."

I believe him. Even as Mo's become less and less a part of my life and I've learned how to not be salty about him spending time with a group that isn't Zeke and me, it's because he's been one of the best friends I could've ever asked to be a part of my life and other people deserve to have that kind of person in their lives. And I know that we've got each other no matter how far. But Zeke? Nah, we aren't done yet.

"Also, I'm taking your room when you leave."

"You have a dorm room and your actual room at your house."

"Now I'll have three rooms."

I hate him.

"Better not do anything nasty on my bed," I say back, and tap my cheek to the top of his head before starting to stand up.

"Come on. I've sobered up. Time to get us home. I need to pack up my last bag real quick."

"Don't you still have a few more days?"

"Yeah. I just have something I need to take care of before I go. One last project."

52

Let's get started," I whisper to myself, walking up to the back of the apartment building next door to Lupe's with a case of Red Bull in hand, setting it down next to all the paint, supplies, lights, and everything else Juni left for me.

At first it's as if my body's going on autopilot. My muscles telling my mind, *It's cool, we got this*, as I outline building-size bodies. All of it ready for color by the time the sun's come up.

As the wall gets covered in the browns of my and Santi's skin, my mind goes back to the specific night this piece is partially inspired by. Of both of us out of breath. Of me straddling his lap as he sat on my bed. My fingers tracing his skin: his arms, the scars on his left arm that I'd later learn were from deep cuts made by a fence, his shoulders, his neck. Of his head resting on my shoulder.

Especially of his head resting on my shoulder. My hand lingers over the black of his hair, careful to not mess up the paint but eager to feel him again. To kiss his head and let my fingers absentmindedly rub from front to back over and over again.

The form of his back takes shape, and I think about how when we didn't fall asleep face-to-face or with him knocking out on top of me, he liked being little spoon. And I liked holding him. I liked kissing his back and neck and tracing the muscles and crevices with my finger.

The forms of his arm, going up and eventually ending with our hands clasped together takes shape, and I think about how much I miss him holding me. How, as much as he might say I was his safety, he was the same for me. He was support and love, and damn it if I wasn't immediately turned on every time he wore a tank and showed off those arms.

Mami or Pa come get me when it starts to get dark, knowing that I'd spend every minute between now and when I leave right here otherwise. And then I'm up in the morning and the morning after that, continuing right where I left off, fresh off dreams of the two of us, the white of the wall turning into skin and shadowing and then more colors and more shadowing. Knowing how long I've been without him and how tired I've been since he was taken, but also that I'm almost there. *We're* almost there.

Knowing even more so when my phone rings from a text. It's Tanya, letting me know Santi's got the backpack I asked her to give him. Which means it's all real. We're almost out of here.

And Santi's leaving. That's what that text really means. That right now there's a bus of people—mainly men; teenage boys, fathers—leaving the detention center only a few blocks from here. Santi's on that bus. Heading back to the place that he's fought to survive in for so much of his life.

There's a crowd of protesters there too. I know this because Marcos, from the first protest, and Zeke both text me about it right after Tanya's message, letting me know that they're there to support me if I want to show up. A part of me does want to. But I can't. I need to finish this.

Still, those images come. Of him leaving. Of this part of our story coming to an end. Of every memory—good, bad, beautiful, and terrifying—that led to this moment. And I cry. Right here, out in the open, I let myself cry. I wish that this wasn't the world we're forced to live in. And I try to hold on to all the memories that make me so thankful I got to experience life here with Santi.

I picture his loving eyes. Listen to the sound of his laugh playing in my head. Remember what it felt like to scratch his scalp while his face was planted in my chest or his cheek in my palm. How his hand felt when I gripped it tightly, and think about how, this time, I'm never letting go.

And thinking of all this, I go back to work. I finish what I need to finish. Standing in the sun that touches both Santi and me, that has gone from waking up to sitting high in the sky and beginning its way back down, I create one more lasting piece of evidence that he did exist. That we existed.

I drop everything from my hands, take a deep breath, and step back from what used to be, three days ago, a blank wall on the back of an old apartment building next door to Lupe's. Along with that specific night, I also took inspiration from Robert Mapplethorpe's *Two Men Dancing*. Decided against the grayscale, going with our actual skin tones. And then I added crowns of small green cacti and pink- and coral-colored blossoms instead of actual crowns like in the original picture. Engulfed us in an off-white with the extra cans that weren't used for the restaurant. Santi's resting on me, his eyes closed as we hold hands, an arm outstretched, like we're dancing.

Like he's finally being allowed to be at peace.

And the words ANDER & SANTI WERE HERE are written along the top. Big and bright and bold. Wanting the world to know that we gave it our best and that that has meaning. That we loved here, and no one and no amount of hate can ever erase that.

I fall to the ground, sitting and staring at my final piece of art that I will give to San Antonio. Well, maybe not *final*. But it'll definitely be a while.

My phone starts ringing again, and this time it's a number I've been waiting all day for.

"Hey, querido."

"Hola, cielo." His voice is soft, calming. Enough to know just from hearing it that he's all right.

"You got your surprise."

"I did."

"Everything's in there? The money? All the plane stuff you'll need?"

"Everything's here. I'm on my way to the airport right now."

"Okay. Good. My family should be walking over soon, and then I'll be out and on my way."

"I—you're sure about this?"

"*Yes, I'm sure*," I shout. "The whole point was to not give myself enough time to think rationally about my decision."

"Chingada madre. Okay. No pienses."

"Exactly. Head on empty."

Santi chuckles and then goes quiet for a moment. I almost think I lost connection with him or something before hearing rustling on his end. "I can't wait to fall asleep on top of you again."

"Well, if you get to the apartment before I do, you better not knock out. Wait for me!"

"I will," he says through a laugh. "No more falling asleep unless you're the last sight I see. We'll have all the time in the world, right?"

"All the time in the world."

"Bueno. It's a date. Te quiero, cielo."

"It's a date," I say with a huge smile covering half my face. "Te quiero más, querido. Oh, and I'll send you the code to get inside the place right now before I forget. Okay. I love you. Again."

I hear Mami, Pa, Tita, Chachi, and Zeke coming over right on time, just after I've hung up with Santi. See their waves and their arms and hands going up to the mural. Behind them, Lupe's and the mural of Tita and Abuelo Willie on the place that's been my upbringing and life and gave me the person who's worth all the happiness and destruction the world can throw at us.

I know they're still feeling a type of way about this. That they're scared. That tomorrow they'll wake up and I won't be there, in my room, and I won't be there the next day or the day after that and none of us are ready for that pain. But neither Mami nor Pa nor Tita taught me to be the type of person who gives up. Who lets the good in our lives go too soon. And I know they know this is something I have to do. That I have to go. That I have to try. And that I can only do this because of them.

Te amo, Santi. Y te veré pronto.

Epilogue

My Mexican Heaven.

Waking up to Santi's lips going from my forehead down to my nose and then to my own lips. The feeling of his mouth forming a wide smile when he realizes I'm not asleep anymore. Of his hand at the small of my back, pulling me closer to him. Of our bodies pressing together.

The smell of fresh pan from a Ciudad bakery. Café con leche. The best mango I've ever tasted in my life.

The walks around the city, discovering more murals than I'd ever be able to appreciate. Coming back to our apartment, to the extra room we've turned into a studio space, and creating; imagining all the neighborhoods I'm familiarizing myself with that one day I'll get to paint on.

The smell of maíz and spices Santi carries with him when he comes back from work at this incredible neighborhood taquería. How excited he is to cook for me and show me everything he's learning there.

And I have to say, his gorditas might be better than Tita's.

Falling asleep with Santi resting on me. A small pool of drool forming on my chest. My hand slowly rubbing his head. A bedroom made even more stuffy from everything we've spent the past hour doing. Knowing that tomorrow we get to do this all over again.

Having all the time in the world. And peace. And happiness. And rest. And knowing that we are here, we have each other, and no one can take that from us now.

No one can take him from me now.

Mi querido.

Mi Santiago.

acknowledgments

As of this book's launch date, it's been three and a half years since Claire Draper became my agent. And since then, they've been second to none when it comes to championing my incredibly queer, incredibly Mexican book ideas and making sure that there's at least a dash of plot in the vibes. They saw the potential for this book, pushed for nothing less than what it was worth, and, for that, I am so very grateful and appreciative. And, even more, I can't wait to scream about many more book ideas in the years to come.

To my editors, Sylvan Creekmore, who so passionately took on this story and helped make it into something so incredible, and Tiffany Shelton, for all of your work and care and dedication that was put into this book and its launch into the world.

To Max Reed and Kerri Resnick for creating and designing *the most perfect* cover ever in the history of book covers. I think I can safely speak for everyone—like, literally, all the people—when I say we will forever be in awe.

To Wednesday Books and all the teams and individuals who had a hand in making *Ander & Santi Were Here* far better than I ever could have on my own and those who so passionately marketed this story: Eric Meyer, Alexis Neuville, Brant Janeway, Diane Dilluvio, Mary Moates, Eliani Torres, Devan Norman, Carla Benton, Jen Simington, and Hercilia Mendizabal. And so much gratitude to my audio team: Emma Paige West, Ally Demeter, Amber Cortes, and Avi Roque, whom I've now been blessed twice to have as the narrator of one of my books.

To my family, for all their encouragement and support and love.

To a certain very famous Mexican author who, multiple times, praised *American Dirt* and books like that, written by authors who don't know us or our lives, as resources for audiences who might not want to read a book by someone with a last name like hers or like mine. You keep doing you. I, for one, will keep writing for my community and supporting fellow Mexicans writing for our young people. Thanks for saying some truly wild shit and, as a result, lighting a fire under my ass to write this book, write it as well as I could, and offer it as something that shows just how beautiful and powerful and worthy our comunidad is.

To my nonwriter friends. I listed all of y'all last time. You know who you are. Chances are, I am probably drinking right next to you at this very moment. So we'll call it a day here.

To my writer and bookish friends. I'm very blessed to have my circles of support made up of such incredible and incredibly talented people who make this life and career far less lonely than it could be. Soni and Enemy—I mean, Emery. Tori. Amparo and Adri. Aiden. Aaron. Anna. My fellow Musas: Laekan, Crystal, Olivia, Mia, Angela, and so many others whom I'm thankful beyond words to know.

To e.E. Charlton-Trujillo, Cam Montgomery, Dustin Thao, and Becky Albertalli, for letting me share this book with y'all early and saying such kind things about it. I'm still overcome with emotion over some of my favorite people, who've written some of my favorite books—including a couple aforementioned in the previous paragraph—expressing such love for Ander and Santi.

To my readers and supporters. To Latine readers. To Mexican readers. To queer readers. To QTBIPOC readers. To high school teachers and to librarians for giving my book space in your classrooms and on your shelves. All my thanks to you. I hope you've enjoyed this story. And I hope you'll allow me to tell many more in the years to come. I cannot wait to meet you all and talk books and characters and favorite tacos and Selena songs.